FLEUR BRONKE

Whispers of Water

Book one

First published by Boekengilde 2024

First edition

ISBN: 9789464913545

This book was professionally typeset on Reedsy.
Find out more at reedsy.com

Acknowledgement

Thanks to everyone for being so supportive on this crazy journey. Thank you to the people who would listen to my non-stop rambling about my book. And to my husband who had to endure the most of it. A special shout out to my friend who read it religiously and made the writing even more fun.

A special thanks to my amazing help Deborah June (all the way in Oz) for being an amazing beta reader.

I hope you have as much fun reading it as I have writing it.

Prologue

Eros ran to the hidden room at breakneck speed, the only thing on his mind was a name: Hera. A poster was the only thing that looked down on him as he ran through the empty street. On it, grotesque caricatures of a man and woman stared at him. *Beware of the Tainted* it warned, followed by a text that encouraged people to turn in their neighbors if they suspected them.

His hurried footsteps echoed loudly in the empty street. He clenched his fist, and the muddy road behind him froze, making it difficult for any pursuers to keep up with him. Little ice particles floated through the air. He flung open the door to the safe house, slamming it shut behind him before taking a nearby bucket of water and flinging the contents back at the door, freezing it shut with a flick of his wrist. People looked up in alarm, but he ignored them, panting for breath as he ran for Hera's room.

The burning fireplace struggled against the cold for a place in the room. Hera barely heard the crackling of the wood or the gusting wind outside as she hunched over the desk, working on the false identity documents. Once she was done, another family would be transported out tonight. She looked at the names, the mother had a little spiral next to hers. *Another elementalist.* With stinging, tired eyes caused by a lack of sleep, Hera went through the documents of the refugees. She copied the Leader Suprema's signature with the utmost care. With every loop of the pen, she prayed that the family would get out safely.

The corners of her mouth lifted as she thought of her own little daughter, Elara. She would turn six in a few months, and though she was biased, she thought that Elara was the smartest and prettiest six-year-old to ever walk around in the Capitol. The thought of her only daughter made butterflies fly through her.

The door flew open, hitting the wal with a wood-shattering bang and Hera's eyes shot up in alarm. Her gaze met Eros's deep green eyes. Eyes that were wild with fear, his face was so pale it reminded her of her daughter's white crochet blanket.

"We need to go," Eros blurted, his voice high and frantic. Hera sat frozen in her seat, her muscles locked in place. "Why?" she managed. But she knew why. Her rational mind was already telling her to run as her body remained seated. A loud noise from somewhere in the building reconnected her brain to her body and she jumped up, taking Eros's outstretched hand.

Together they made their way through the cramped concrete corridors. A woman with a pile of reports in her hands looked confused as they scrambled past her, but others joined them rushing toward the exit. Hera squeezed her husband's hand, afraid of being left behind.

Outside, bombs went off and shook the building, throwing them to the ground. Hera landed painfully on her right knee, her hand nearly torn from Eros'. Above her, the building moaned once as a part of the roof collapsed. Blinding pain shot up her leg and she cried out. "Eros!"

Her hand lost his.

Her bone had splintered and the sharp edges dug into her muscles. Tears of pain streamed down her cheek.

Eros looked on in utter panic. A block of concrete lay on his wife's leg, crushing it. It would be difficult to heal, but not impossible, not for him, but he needed time. People ran past, in a hurry to save their own skin as Eros hooked his fingers under the concrete and pulled as hard as he could. Hera screamed as the concrete shifted.

Ice formed in the hall as Eros redoubled his efforts, using all the strength he could muster. The concrete finally gave way, and Hera scrambled away. The sight sent pain shooting through his heart, the gore enough to turn his stomach. Still, no one stopped to help.

Eros crouched down next to his wife. Her blond hair was tangled and her eyes clenched in pain.

He took a deep breath and took a white stone out of his pocket. With the other hand, he turned his wrist in circles as if tugging on an invisible rope. Water formed around it and it glowed as he made a stroking motion just above the injured leg. The bleeding ceased, and Hera's breathing evened out.

"You need to run," she whimpered as she looked into his eyes.

"Never without you." Eros lifted her up into his arms and she wrapped hers around his neck, holding on weakly.

Click

The sound of a gun being cocked from behind made him freeze. "I'm unarmed," Eros said.

"I can see that. Turn around slowly," a man rumbled.

He turned, Hera trembling in his arms. "Please. She's hurt… and… and we have a daughter. Please." His voice shook as he beheld the biggest man he had ever seen.

The man holding the gun was shaven bald, with a large mustache dangling over his upper lip. In his enormous hands, the gun looked laughably small, though still deadly.

"You are with the resistance," he said simply.

"I'm just a doctor."

"Tainted."

Eros nodded slowly. He could have taken this man, no matter his size, he could have frozen his eyes, frozen his muscles into place, or simply made his brain boil. But not faster than this man could pull the trigger, and not while holding Hera.

The man's piercing blue eyes scanned him, then looked at Hera. The gun remained steady, still aimed right at Eros' left eye. Hera whimpered softly, her grip on his neck loosening.

"Please..."

Chapter 1

Dies Saturni

I lie on my back in the park in the early morning, grateful for the shadows cast by the trees and the breeze coming off the lake. The smell of hot earth and dried grass tingle my nose. On a day like this, it's easy to forget that our country is fighting a war—not that anybody talks about it. The last time newspapers were distributed was weeks ago, so we depend on people with the Wireless. Gran won't have one in the house, so the only way I hear anything is if someone tells me. The inhabitants of Eden don't talk about the war because they have no interest in it. War's no good to simple folk. It hinders the routine. And what a routine it is. Most people already ignore things that are unpleasant or far away and *especially* things that are unpleasant and far away, and the war is both.

Dry grass pokes at me through my striped summer dress, and I try to ignore it. It's absurdly hot, even for midsummer and the pace of the town has slowed down. The children have grown silent with all the others. The pond in the center of the park, usually full of children, is empty, the water no longer a refreshing temperature. From under my straw sun hat, I peek upward at the tree. Even the leaves seem unhappy, hanging there listlessly with a yellow tinge. But I still appreciate the respite the leaves give from the relentless sun.

A disgruntled voice asks the oppressive air, "Is there ever gonna be an end to this summer?"

I wipe sweat off my nose. Eden has never seen such a scorching summer. Lucky for us, Eden hasn't mingled in the nation's affairs for decades. Gran says we'll be alright, although the look in her eyes when she says it worries me.

The war has been going for roughly two months now. Still, it's weird. Tensions are reported to be at an all-time high, but nothing of note has happened here, aside from the occasional refugee. People are fleeing the cities and coming over the mountains. Just thinking about it causes nervous butterflies to stir in my stomach. Gran and I have fled from war before and I have no desire to be on the run again. *But we're safe here.* For years we have been building a life and working on a future here in Eden.

"Have you noticed the new people around here?" I ask as I shift to get comfortable.

The owner of the disgruntled, soprano voice comes into view as she sits up, pieces of dry grass sticking to her soft pink dress. Darya's blonde hair is meticulously styled into a fashionable bun, and with her button nose and the dark blue eyes of the sea goddess, she's the most desired bachelorette of Eden. The white lace compliments her bronze skin, and the effect is dazzling whilst remaining conservative. "There are some newcomers that want to buy Mom's fruit. They disappear right after, though."

"Where would they go?"

Darya unfolds a big pink fan and fans herself, wafting the smell of Jasmine toward me in the breeze. "Maybe they work on the farms, or something. You should ask Lilly."

"I haven't spoken to her since she brought our order for the apple pies," I say. "I'll ask her in class."

"Do you think soldiers take a break from fighting in this heat?

Maybe they do… Call a ceasefire or something." Darya giggles as she closes her eyes. "Imagine all those hot, shirtless soldiers bathing in the sun!"

My heart speeds up, but not for the same reason as Darya's. I turn to look at the Town Hall. White stairs lead to intricately decorated wooden doors that are easily twice my height. The elaborately painted face of Goddess Quatahna watches us from above the door, her dark blue eyes overlooking the park.

"May Goddess Quatahna drown them," I say, avoiding the painted stare of Eden's most celebrated deities. Darya hands me her water bottle. "Elara, drink and you won't get angry. The water will carry the white bile from your body," she says, regurgitating the old texts.

I wipe the sweat off my forehead and take a sip, feeling my heart rate return to normal. "You thinking of the Boyle brothers?"

"Ew! No!" Darya giggles and smacks me on the head with her fan. "I don't like redheads. Though I'll forgive Zale for being one." She continues to flutter the fan like a butterfly's wings, and now and again, a small breath of air finds me.

I feel guilty for taking Quatahna's name in vain, though Darya has already moved on. That's one thing I love about her -she isn't one to hold a grudge.

She grins at me. "We should go out again! We haven't had a party in, like, forever! We could see if Raph is working tonight and…"

I let her talk while I fidget with the hem of my dress. The summer heat finally gets to me, and I drift off.

I was playing on all fours on the carpet with my stuffed toys, which were sitting in a circle and drinking tea. Mr. Bear was complaining about loud noises at night, and his wife was saying he shouldn't be in such a foul mood. The fireplace's crackling heat was pleasant, and the sweet, aromatic smell of smoke drifted through the air.

Gran, Mom, and Dad were sitting behind me at the dinner table, their faces tense. The stress had been etched on their faces for a long time. That's why Mr. Bear was so grumpy. Gran started to cry, hunched over the table, her body wracked with sobs as Mom held her from behind. Dad was pale, even in the orange glow of the fire, his eyes trained on his tea mug.

His voice was hoarse when he spoke. "Those people are Dogs! Dogs of the military. They don't question what orders they get"

I walked up to Gran and gave her a hug, trying to comfort her. "Don't cry, Gran. The nasty dogs won't get in. We locked the door..."

"... and Alphonse is getting hot now after he's courting Lilly... Lucky Lilly," Darya says and groans, letting her head fall back in exasperation.

I raise my eyebrows. "You were courted by Alphonse. You thought he was too needy."

Much to her parent's dismay, and despite her popularity, Darya shows no interest in settling down. Mr. and Mrs. Ballard are very vocal about it being time for her to find a respectable husband—after all, she has been of the marrying age for at least two years now.

In my opinion, there aren't a lot of eligible bachelors here in Eden; even so, I would think she would have found one by now.

Gran says I should count myself lucky to worry about such things as college and men, but the latter subject always makes me a little agitated. "Have you finished Mrs. Storms's essay yet?" I ask, my voice slightly high.

* * *

Gran runs a petite bakery on Main Road, so tiny that six customers inside feels cramped. It smells like sweet pastries in the afternoons, the big ancient oven usually burning. The sounds of wood crackling and Gran humming fill the small store. She hums most of the time unless she's excited—then she'll sing. Above the bakery are our bedrooms and the bathroom. My room is small but with a large window to let in the sunlight. Most of the time, it looks like a hurricane went through it, but today it's relatively tidy.

Papers cover every inch of my wobbly little wooden desk which sits below the window, with a view of the street and the trees welting underneath the glare of the sun. The bed takes up nearly half the room, and currently has all my laundry dumped on top of it.

Monster lies on the carpet that I got secondhand from Darya's mother. Covered with hair, it's more black than green now. Shelves along the walls are overloaded with stuff. Front and center is the jewelry box I got from Gran the first year we moved here, full of beaded necklaces, twine bracelets, beautiful stones, and shells from the beach. Books are crammed onto every other available surface.

My room is my haven, a tranquil place that smells of wood and baked bread. It's never completely quiet. The house is full of sounds, wood creaking, sounds of the street, or sometimes rain ticking against the roof and window.

When it rains the fresh smell of mud and wet leaves floods the small space. An enormous mirror fills most of the wall behind the bed. It was already here when we moved in, which is the only reason it's still here—Gran doesn't like mirrors, because they 'remind her of how worn out she is.' Still, she usually says it with a smile.

Everything important to me is here in this tiny space and it's where I get ready for my night out with Darya. Usually the mirror reflects the sun, filling my room with golden light—right now, it only reflects my depression. My dirty blond hair won't hold the finger curls I'm trying to weave in and there are bags under my eyes.

"Why am I doing this?" I ask Monster. His doleful brown eyes watch me full of expectation and he thumps his tail on the rug in answer, sending up dust. I question my wardrobe choices, examining my reflection wearing a tiny black dress. It used to look good on me, but now the hem barely falls past my knees. I strip it off and put on a long gray skirt and a red blouse.

Darya parades into my tiny bedroom, the smell of Jasmine following her like a shadow. She looks stunning and does not share my dark mood. Her blond hair sits in a perfect updo, and she's wearing a short blue dress that shows her knees—her parents would not approve, which is why we're getting ready here.

"All the girls will envy you," I say, feeling inadequate. Darya lets the compliment slip over her as she twirls around and trips over Monster. Monster flees out of my room and makes his way down the stairs, away from the chaos as we laugh.

Chapter 2

A squat, elderly man with gray sideburns- named Mr. Sosa, owns the village's only bar. He has decided it's too hot to be inside, so the band, a makeshift bar, and tables are now arranged outside in the town square.

It's a raging success. The band plays beneath the enormous tree opposite the bar, creating a dance floor in the middle. Lanterns hang in the tree casting a soft light over the band, while torches mark the perimeter of the dance floor. Their light reflects in the dark windows surrounding the square, giving everything an orange hue. The sweet smell of smoke hangs in the air, masking the sweat of dozens of dancing bodies. Everyone from my class is here, the girls flaunting their knee-length dresses and the men wearing dress shirts and slacks. It's an undulating crowd of color and movement and even the music can't drown out the laughter and buzz of conversation.

A few wallflowers are firmly planted near the bar. Raphaël is running around, assuming the role of bartender for his father. He's sweating, trying to remember what everyone has ordered. He attends nursing classes with Darya and me, as well as helping his dad on the side.

I'm clapping my hands to the rhythm of the band. My heart is pounding as I stomp my feet to the beat. *By Quatahna I'm having fun!* The singer's deep, rasping voice sings, *"The ocean is as deep as my love for you."*

Darya dances in front of me, her eyes are closed and a wide smile on her face glistens with sweat.

"This was a really good idea!" I shout over the music.

Darya's eyes flutter open. "What?"

"I need a drink!" I shout into her ear as the trumpet player starts a solo.

"Me too!" she says with a grin, closing her eyes again and losing herself in the music.

I dodge waving arms and turning torsos as I make my way to the bar. Stepping off the sweaty dance floor is quite refreshing, the fresh air cooling my skin.

Raphaël is alone behind the bar, his mane of shaggy brown hair stuck to the back of his neck like a wet rag. I find the bar top is sticky only after leaning on it. The smell of spilled beer has settled so deep into the timber no amount of scrubbing could ever remove it. Raphaël doesn't see me wave, as he's entertaining a few older men. He lets out a hearty laugh, running his hand back through his hair. I look back to the dance floor and find Darya being entertained by a tall blond gentleman several years her senior. *Alphonse?* I'm so distracted I miss the man trying to get my attention—I only notice as when he squeezes in next to me, his arm brushing mine.

"I don't think this side is any good," he says, struggling to be heard over the enthusiastic trumpet player.

He must be one of the newcomers because I've never seen him before and I know most everyone in Eden. His clothes are very modern. A green dress shirt peeks from beneath a coal-gray, pinstriped jacket.

The fact he must be a refugee makes me uncomfortable, but I know what it's like, so I decide to make an effort for his sake. He gives me a flash of a smile and for the first time, my eyes find his face. He has

Onyx-black eyes and matching black hair peeks out from under a fedora. His strong jawline, high cheekbones, and straight nose make him look like the Gods chiseled him out of a block of marble.

Just as a flutter stirs in my stomach, Raphaël pops up behind the bar and stops me mid-gawk. I order two strawberry ciders with extra ice. Raphaël makes the drinks, vigorously shaking the container while making sure everyone around can see him flexing his muscles. Even at the bar, the music is loud, so I have an excuse to move closer to Onyx Eyes. My lips are near his ear when I speak.

"I don't know you."

I try to channel my inner Darya, putting my hand on the bar as I lean in—and quickly regret it. *Oh, right -sticky.*

The man sighs as people brush by him, and he leans into me. "I'm new, got sent here for work." His cologne is fresh and floral and entirely incongruous to the sweaty evening. It's intoxicating.

"I'm sorry," I say, wiping my sticky hand on my skirt. Even if you aren't a refugee, coming to Eden as a stranger isn't easy. It took Grand and me years to be accepted as one of them -until then you're basically half a citizen.

He leans in close to speak into my ear, his breath tickling the hairs on my neck."I'm not." I hear the smile in his voice and a warm glow glides over my face that has nothing to do with the temperature.

He winks at me. "It's not every day I see women order strawberry ciders with such confidence."

"What's wrong with strawberry ciders?" I ask, playfully, placing my hand on my hip.

"Everything!" His eyes twinkle and little creases appear at the corners of his eyes.

I can't help myself, and lean closer to him. "What kind of drink would you suggest?"

"For a lady like yourself?" He looks me up and down. "I would

recommend a 'Blue Angel's Kiss'. It would get your taste buds tingling."
He winks, a boyish gleam in his eyes.

My face blooms red again and I look away, catching sight of Raphaël, who is waiting for me to pay up. I do so, grab my strawberry ciders and walk away from the bar, with a straight spine and my chin up-not looking back. I wish my hips wouldn't sway like they do.

The smell of sweat and smoke clouds the air of the dance floor. I find Darya dancing in the middle of it all with Alphonse, Eden's heart breaker. He smiles when I greet him. His wavy blond hair and perfect teeth open all the doors and turn a lot of heads too. It doesn't hurt that his parents are some of the richest people in town. He might look like the perfect catch, but he's about as sharp as a spoon, with just as little personality.

Darya takes her drink from my hand, finishes it in one go, hands the glass to a passing barman, and asks, "Who is Mr. Sexy over there?"

"Dunno, some new guy." I try to look anywhere else, but he's become magnetic to my eyes.

Darya grins, eyes twinkling with mischief. "Let me just welcome him to Eden!" She swaggers off, a woman with a target and I let out a I sigh.

"Isn't Darya the sweetest?" Alphonse says. If I were sitting on a chair, I would have fallen off it. The poor doofus is kind, yet he has the perceptiveness of a rock.

After another song, which gets a big round of applause, Darya returns with a face as red as beetroot. She avoids my gaze and focuses on Alphonse, shaking off whatever troubled her.

I spot Onyx Eyes talking animatedly to an older-looking man in a gray shirt and green waistcoat. They laugh loudly and the older man claps Onyx Eyes on the back.

Looking around I realize how many more unfamiliar faces there are in the crowd, and it makes me uneasy. One of them catches my gaze, his cold blue eyes piercing. He lifts his drink in a mock toast and smirks, making my skin crawl. I look away, ignoring him.

Darya's older sister, Delphine, is standing by the bar, and I decide to join her. She beams when she sees me. Delphine has always been voluptuous, and tonight she chose to wear something that shows off her 'top half' that Gran would never approve of.

"Elara, darling, it's great to see you have a night out on the town. How are you doing?" She gives me a warm, squishy hug. "Keeping my little sis out of trouble?"

"As much as I can. It's like trying to control a dolphin," I say with a smile and a shrug. When she orders a drink Raphaël stares at her breasts for half a second too long and I shoot him an incredulous look. He shrugs.

"Can I have a Blue Angel's Kiss?" I ask and he nods, combining a dizzying array of ingredients before handing it over—the resulting cocktail is very, very blue.

When I take the first sip, the alcohol hits me like a small electric current through my brain. It tastes amazing. People continue to dance, but the band has turned shrill and the number of unknown people here is still bothering me. I want to ask Delphine what she thinks about it, but her attention is elsewhere, her lips pursed in disapproval as she watches Darya practically dry-humping Alphonse. A feeling of shame fills my gut and I try to distract her by changing the subject to the upcoming Solemnitatum. Delphine expects her boyfriend will propose. With a jolt, I realize I don't have a caller yet and my throat turns dry. *If I don't get an invitation for Solemnitatum, I don't think I want to go.* But Gran has been hoping for me to find someone to settle down with.

"Have you seen the strangers in town lately?" I ask, trying to change the subject before my self-pity overwhelms me.

Darya and Delphine live in a huge townhouse on the outskirts of Eden, so it would be one of the first houses any refugee would come across. Even with their mother's garden struggling with the dry summer, it's yielding extra cash for them. Not all of their visitors are friendly though- Mr. Ballard has become uneasy about it and has acquired a gun "just in case".

Delphine continues to be distracted by her little sister's behavior, glancing over with a disapproving look. My cocktail continues to get tastier with every sip, so when it's finished, I order another.

"Are y-y-you sure?" Raphaël asks, raising his eyebrows at me.

Nodding enthusiastically, I push strands of sweat-damp hair out of my face. The band finishes their song, I excuse myself and return to Darya with my drink. The moving limbs have become harder to avoid, and the ground has grown more uneven. Alphonse maintains Darya's full attention, and I miss the enthusiasm I had before.

"Darya! I'm going home!" I shout, but she can't hear me. The rhythm picks up and people are moving faster. Somebody bumps into me as I turn around and Darya's hand grabs my elbow. She's finally extracted herself from Alphonse but he tries to pull her back.

"Not now Alphonse," Darya says sweetly. She wrestles out of his grip and pushes him away. "Later."

His shoulders droop and his brow furrows. "Doll, what's the matter?"

I almost feel sorry for the poor soul.

"I need to talk to Elara. Why don't you get us another drink?" Darya winks at him and makes a shooing gesture. Alphonse sighs and turns around, blending into the crowd as he makes his way to the bar.

It's the two of us again and elation hits me as we dance to another song. Darya swings her arm over my shoulder as we sing along, getting half the words wrong but neither of us cares. *I don't know who you think I am. But you have never seen a wave like this one!"* We are horribly out of tune.

A bushy head appears through the crowd.

"Lilly!" I give our classmate an enormous hug, back on my original high. I have to bend over, as she's quite a bit shorter than me. The smell of juicy fruit is embedded in her aura and I breathe it in. Lilly gives me a smile that lights up her entire freckled face and I pray she hasn't seen the scene that Darya and Alphonse have been making.

"Having a good night?" she chirps as she pushes a few curly locks of hair out of her face.

"Yeah, it's been amazing!" I say with a smile, "There are these things called blue angles- no, Blue *Angels* Kisses and they are fantastic." To prove my point I take a big gulp and hold out the bright blue liquid for her to see.

Lilly smiles politely and shoots a quick look at Darya. "Shall I go get us these 'blue angel kisses'?"

"Yes!!" I give Lilly another big hug. *This is the best idea I've ever heard!*

She takes some time to navigate her way back to us with fresh drinks. She hands one to me and one to Darya.

"Thanks, Lilly," I say and take a big sip from my drink."Who are you with?"

"I came here with Tennin but he went home already." She makes a face. "But I'm glad I ran into you!" She gives me another one of those bright smiles.

"What a shame!"

"Yeah, he didn't like that so many strangers were walking around tonight." My eyes return to the man at the bar, his back turned towards me. The band announces the new song and we dance to the new rhythm. Lilly is the shortest person in the crowd, yet her energy might be twice as high, and before long, she's drawing lingering stares.

During the next song I bump into Zale, sloshing most of my drink over him, the smell of sugar and alcohol burst into the air like a bomb.

"I'm so sorry!" I gasp.

"Ah no! My clean shirt!" Zale looks at his waistcoat which has just turned blue. His red hair is messy under his flat cap and clashes with his now blue shirt. My cheeks burn and I rush off to grab some napkins from the bar. With an unsteady hand, I try to pat him down, but he refuses.

"No, no, it's alright Elara. It's a good way to cool down." He grabs my hand, his skin cool against mine and smiles—for the first time, I notice he gets dimples. "You have been having fun I see," he says. I nod, smiling, and offer him a drink.

"That would be nice." He takes a dignified sip out of my now half-empty glass and his face crumples. "It's… really gross. Could you get me a whiskey?"

"Shure, mishter fancy pants," I say in an attempt to sound sophisticated and failing miserably. Raphaël waits for me behind the bar and, with a sigh, waits for the question he knows is coming. "Could you get me another couple of the Angel's Kisses and a whiskey?" Raphaël shakes his head but goes to work.

Zale grins at me when I give him his drink. "Did you finally give up on strawberry ciders?" I give him a little shove in response. His blue-stained dress shirt mocks me."How is college going?"

"Yeah fine," I say, "We just have half a year to go and then we're done. What about you?" The buzz of the crowd is fading as people start to leave. This means we can finally speak without shouting.

"Good, good. I'm already working with Delphine's dad in the shop. So maybe I can take over his business after he retires. You know, with none of the sisters being especially into carpentry." He shrugs and I laugh.

"How are your brothers doing?"

"We haven't heard from Wade and Seger for a while. I'm sure they'll come back soon though. Especially with Solemnitatum around the corner."

The mention of Solemnitatum puts my hands to work, my fingers make tears in the damp napkin. "I'm sure you'll hear from them soon."

We talk about the letters his brothers sent him from the Capitol. I push my own opinions of the military aside when I see the pride on his face. He smiles as he talks about how much it means to his mother that she receives some extra cash from her oldest sons. She's saving up for a proper costume for Solemnitatum this year and she hounds him about finding a proper candidate. He laughs it off awkwardly, and to my dismay, asks me if I have an invitation yet.

I am forced to offhandedly say not having an invitation doesn't worry me and I have enough time to find one. His smile is polite, but I'm not sure he believes me. Before he finishes his drink, I leave a hand of white confetti, that was once a napkin, on the bar and slink back to the ladies.

I press a drink into Darya's waiting hand. At a small distance, Onyx Eyes is walking away from the bar talking with the same man as before.

"Who is he?" Lilly wonders, following my gaze.

"I don't know..."

"He is cute though... with those muscled arms and dark hair- if you like that sort of thing," she chirps. I wave the thought away, but warmth still creeps into my cheeks. She nudges me playfully, not buying it.

"I'm off ladies, the sun will come up in a few hours and those apples won't pick themselves," Lilly says.

"I just need to use the ladies' room for a minute," I say. The world tilts left and right and I choose my steps carefully, but my body can't seem to move in a straight line.

The bar stands deserted, and I steady myself against the door frame before proceeding to the lady's room through the empty, dimly lit space. It's warm in here and my skin starts to tingle.

A puddle in front of the basin has turned the floor slippery and I skid over it. With a giggle, I hold on to the door handle until I get my balance. Fresh water fills the basin, and I splash myself, finally finding some relief from the heat. The fresh water on my skin is wonderful, and the room seems to steady. I lean on the basin as I inspect my makeup. *It looks fine. I look fine.* A wave of nausea hits, and I take a deep breath. I plunge my hands into the cool water and the water flutters against my skin and I giggle. My fingers play with the foreign feeling and the water spills over the rim. I scrutinize my hand, narrowing my eyes. *Did I make enough movement to make the water slosh this much? I must be really drunk.*

Outside I hear voices and I try block out the sounds. In my right hand, there is a pulse, soft and fluttering fast like a mouse's heartbeat, and I am so excited it nearly slips away.

"Ha!" I exclaim, a broad smile on my face. Once more I breathe in and hold on to that fast, pulsing feeling. My fingers move through the water. *Maybe I can make it move,* my drunken brain thinks boldly. *Like the First Men did.*

"My, my, my."

The temperature in the room seems to drop. In the mirror, I see it's the blonde man who caught my eye in the crowd. His reflection comes into focus as he slowly steps into the room with the precision of a cat stalking his prey. *He's not supposed to be in here, it's the lady's room.*

He wears an expensive striped jacket, his blond hair tucked meticulously under a bowler hat, his eyes narrowing as he studies me.

I feel exposed. My heart pounds in my chest and I want to excuse myself, run away, but I'm frozen in place. My thoughts scramble over each other, but none stay long enough to be coherent. I turn around to face him without thinking, like I'm a puppet on his string. My scalp tingles as inhale sharply and finally stare straight into his dead eyes. My heart turns cold with dread.

One.. two... breathe. My head is trying to keep me from having a panic attack even as every fiber of my being screams at me to get out. The temperature drops ever lower as he steps closer, too close for comfort. I want to move away from him, but I'm no longer in control of my body. *Someone, anyone, please help me!*

The smells of cigars and spice fill my nose as he smiles like a shark and the blood rushes from my face. "How pleasant it is to meet someone as—" He takes a strand of my hair between his fingers and sniffs it. "-undeniably green as yourself, hmm?"

One, two... Please! Breathe, *no, please, please.*

His cheek nearly touches mine and my breath comes out in tiny puffs of white, the hairs on my neck standing up. He pauses, and I can feel his body heat through my clothes. *Someone! Help me!*

"Come on, I know what you were doing," he whispers. I can feel the warmth of his breath on my skin and it turns my stomach. "Show me, hmm?"

I stop breathing, my body trembles. *No!*

Unfamiliar brittle fracturing noises come from behind me, as the man grins.

"I could do things to you.." He traces my clavicle with his finger. It's cold, so cold it burns, and I feel a tear rolling down my face.

"You are impressive. A little cold for my taste, I must say. But I can remedy that." He smiles at something behind me. It grows even wider when a crystalline snap echoes through the room, accompanied by the sound of porcelain breaking. *What is he doing?*

"Baël, Hawkeye requests your presence," a man says from outside the bathroom.

The spell breaks. Baël turns around to face him but blocks my view of my savior. My legs give out as I gasp for air and my knees crash to the frozen ground.

Baël grunts. "Let's see what he wants from me then." His words go up in clouds. With one last backwards glance, he oozes out of the ladies room, his black polished shoes crunching on the frozen floor. *This should be impossible, these gifts are just old wives' tales.*

The sound of footsteps fade and I'm all alone. Microscopic shards of ice float through the air and twinkle in the light of the lanterns. I look behind me. The water in the sink is frozen solid and has broken the porcelain. A crack splits the mirror, dividing my face into two halves.

Dies Solis

The creeping sun sneaks into the house. I hate the heat, especially after those damn Blue Kisses.

"Mmm… Godshot, aruwake?" I ask Darya when I wake up.

"Mmm… Pff, tomudriink"

"Ufilikbreakfast?" I ask, kicking the bed sheets off.

Darya groans

"Park?" I croak.

"Innamin."

We slump back to sleep.

Oppressive heat fills my room, hot as an oven, but it's not just the heat that's uncomfortable. Breathing is difficult and the crack in the curtain is letting in a beam of fire- then the taste in my mouth catches my attention. Mothballs taste better than this. Darya's head rests on my belly and she is still dead to the world. It's impossible to move without waking her. *We're getting too old for this.*

My mind replays the unnerving events of last night and I shiver despite the heat. In a crash of sound and energy, Gran enters my room, her head inches from the door handle. "Darling, it's well past eleven. You best skedaddle before you melt into a puddle!" She coughs in her hand- the smell in here must be horrible. With her broom in hand, she opens the window, letting in a disappointing amount of fresh air.

"Shoo now, shoo!"

Darya is awake now and moans loudly. "Youuu oold womaan, I sleeep!"

"Old!? *Old!?* Out! Out! Out!" She waves her broom threateningly and we scramble out of bed, stumbling over the pile of clothes we left before we fell asleep. We quickly throw on the first thing we can find before she chases us down the stairs with the broom.

Darya runs out of the front door, bumping into a customer on her way out. Monster runs after her, barking playfully and I want to follow, but Gran stops me before I can escape. "Dear, take the bottle of water from the stack." I turn around and she smiles while she straightens her glasses. "Old. Ha! Oh, don't forget to take your keys. My meeting with The Foxes is in an hour." She turns away to help the customers.

Gran has this weekly 'discussion group' with a few ladies who call themselves The Foxes- it's actually a front for her weekly poker game. Her partners in crime are Lilly's mother, Mrs. Hydris, Raphaël's mother Mrs. Sosa, Mrs. Storm, and a few ladies she knows from the market. She's the oldest one there, though her mind is still razor sharp.

Orange dust covers the road, swirling up with every step we take. I'm thankful I'm not drunk anymore, but my head is throbbing from the relentless heat and alcohol. The air smells like dust and sun. Darya fixes her hair while we walk and I am too embarrassed to tell her about yesterday. *I must have given off some unintended signal...*

Beside us, Monster pants heavily, his huge tongue lolling out and little foam bubbles forming in the corner of his mouth. Even his usual preppy demeanor subdued by the beating sun, his black fur doing him no favors in this heat.

The Main Road leads us to the park, though 'Road' is an overstatement. The paving stones put here decades ago have all become crooked. The dust muffles the sound of our footsteps and hides the stains on our shoes.

A group of cyclists rides by, avoiding potholes. On either side of the road stand rows of light brown, wooden houses. Some people have plastered the front-facing side so they are more of a yellow. Slanted roofs throw shade on the road and in the nook of the roofs, large shells are displayed behind glass, to show devotion to Quatahna.

The newest houses were built 16 years ago, at the end of the civil war. Some refugees had enough money to build new homes, though as a single woman Gran wasn't allowed to buy a home, which is why we moved in above the bakery. Apart from the sign above the door now declaring it to be 'Gran's bakery', nothing has changed on this road since.

At the end of Main Road lies an extensive park covered in yellow grass and a small lake where people like to walk, and beside it, the ruins of the old temple where some children are playing hide and seek. Monster runs up to the kids and one of them climbs on his back and rides him like a pony—I swear I can see him smile.

Many years ago, when I was on one of my nighttime strolls through the fields, I found Monster. He was just a puppy, with a broken leg and I couldn't leave him to die out in the wild. Initially, I called him Ink because of his jet-black fur, but he didn't stop growing. I had never seen a dog as big or as monstrous as him, so the name Monster just stuck.

It's a difficult climb to our own private beach, but that's why it's remained our secret spot for many years. Monster flies over the rocks and patiently waits for us to arrive, wiping the sweat off our brows. The smell of salt and fish fills the air.

My skin tingles with pleasure looking at this beautiful place as we lean against the cool black rocks in the shade of a tree. The rocks are twice the size of me and form a natural barrier between the beach and the rest of the world. Their color contrasts sharply with the soft white sand and lush green trees. Water laps lazily on the shore and woven baskets of flowers and trinkets decorate the water's edge—these are the returned offerings the fishers made to Quatahna this morning.

Quatahna's worship is an integral part of the town's routine. Before dawn, the fishers make their offerings, then sail before first light. On their return, a crowd waits for them in the market. Mrs. Hydris, Lilly's mother, stands there with her fruit and other farmers sell their wares. Gran is always one of the first ones there because she has to buy ingredients for the bakery. Gran is already making dough before any of the other shops are even open for business. The townsfolk come to buy bread in droves and after high noon, calm besets the bakery, before the whole thing begins again the next day. This is how it goes, every day, year-round, except for Solemnitatum. That day is dedicated to a ceremony and night market.

Refreshing water tickles our feet and entices me to go deeper into the soft, cooling waves, and as each washes over me, I feel a little cleaner of that horrid encounter. Eventually, my heart unclenches. "That gentleman…" I start.

Darya is finally over her hangover and she will want to hear all about the stranger at the bar. Monster plays with the ebb and flow of the waves, barking at the foam as it recedes and running away when it tries to catch him.

Darya leans back on her elbows and nods. "I know." She smiles mischievously. "Why didn't you go back and make a move?"

I sigh as an ample wave washes over my calves, wetting the hem of my dress. The pull of the water sucks my feet into the soft, white sand. Darya stands up and Monster trots back to us, his tail wagging. Darya takes off her hat and pulls off her dress. Her undergarments are the same blue shade as her dress yesterday.

"He wasn't that interesting," I say and fidget with a loose string on my neckline. "and we said all that needed to be said." Again the bad feeling tries to come to the surface, but I push it away.

Darya looks down at me with disbelief. "He shot you down that fast?"

"No!" I say, feeling hurt. "I mean, we talked and then I got my drinks and it was over." A comforting wave strokes my toes.

Darya wades into knee-deep water as Monster follows, walking in circles around her. She looks back at me, the question clear.

"That's it," I insist. "He said it would take some time before Raphaël would serve us." My face turns red and I look pointedly to the horizon. Monster wades over and rubs against my leg, his tail smacking the water.

"And then what?" Darya asks, splashing me.

The cold water on my chest makes me yelp. "Alright, alright! I said he was right and asked him if he was new." I pull my dress over my head so Darya can't see my face flush as I remember my pathetic attempt at flirting. We wade deeper until our feet don't touch the ground anymore. The fresh seawater is a welcome sensation. "You went over to talk to him. What did he tell you?"

Darya shrugs and looks away. "He wasn't interesting to me either."

We enjoy the water in silence for a time.

"Do you think I made the wrong decision?" I ask.

"About those panties and brassier?" she smirks, splashing water at my face. "Absolutely!"

Monster barks at a few seagulls flying overhead.

Chapter 3

Dies Lunae

Monster whines at my bedroom door, and it wakes me up from an uneasy dream about a blond-haired man. His nose presses against the bottom of the door and he inhales heavily. The sky outside remains dark. "Momo, you idiot," I chide. "I'm allowed to sleep in today."

My pillow is soft but I still consider throwing it at him to shut him up. Instead, I open the door to let him out and he bounds down the stairs, not remorseful in the slightest about robbing his owner's precious sleep. The smell of bread wafts up the stairs.

I lie back on my warm bed and stare at the wooden ceiling for one more moment before getting up. My cotton work shirt is a shapeless, sand-brown thing and I slip it on before making my way downstairs, toward the sound of excited voices.

"-too, and I am telling you!" a deep voice says. "The war is getting out of hand. I think it won't take long before they're here. We have to protect ourselves."

My mouth dries up and a tempest churns my stomach.

"I wouldn't be surprised if the military is already infiltrating the town before the next moon," another voice rasps.

I inhale sharply.

"Next moon? It's only a matter of days. We need to be ready!" The sound of a fist hitting wood punctuates their point.

"You are a couple of saps," Gran says as if she's talking to naughty children. "The military doesn't infiltrate they just arrive. Nevertheless, this is far too conspicuous. Do you want to get yourself killed?"

"Nuriël, we will be fine. Don't worry, there's good people in Eden," the raspy voice says.

I shudder despite the warm air and make a lot of noise to announce my arrival. The voices stop as I open the door to the bakery, and two hooded figures quickly leave the store with a paper bag.

"Early customers today," I say, feigning ignorance.

Gran coughs. "Sometimes people forget to get ready... for the day." She brushes some imaginary dust off her belly and throws me some dough. My heart pirouettes in my chest as I spot a piece of paper on the counter, which is easy to read, even upside down.

Support the resistance!

Gran follows my gaze and snatches the paper from the counter, before wadding it into a ball, and throwing it in the oven. The message is clear- *not under my roof*.

Gran's face is as lost in thought as my own as a torrent of questions and memories stream through my mind. Faces of the brave and kind people who risked their safety to smuggle us appear before my eyes like ghosts—an old man with a toothless grin who gave me an apple when we hadn't eaten in days, a fat lady who hid us in the back of her ox cart while it lumbered over the mountains, the young father who pretended I was his daughter to get through the city gates.

The bakery and all its memories sigh with despair. My eyes form a mist that my mind forces down again. *Going through all that again... I couldn't bear it.* I don't tell Gran about my encounter in the lady's room and push the memory away.

* * *

Dies Lovis

The class is stifling hot and rowdy, but still Mrs. Storm drones on. Her gray bun bobs up and down as she writes a few phrases on the blackboard. Wet patches have formed under her arms, but she either doesn't notice or doesn't care. The whole class smells like stale sweat and the open windows provide no relief. In front of me, Darya leans her head into her hand -it looks like she's dozing.

My attention falters as I doodle in the book we're learning from. The pencil scratches softly on the paper and I pause. Between all the squiggly lines, I have drawn a droplet and a gun. The sound of my surroundings freezing lives vividly in my mind along with the blond-haired stranger and I shiver. *Was it him or me though?*

In the weeks, since the party, a subtle tension has been stirring the air, a kind of electricity, as if a big thunderstorm is on its way.

A bang on the door startles the class. Without waiting for an answer, it opens and Mrs. Storm pauses mid-sentence with her mouth hanging open. My breath catches in my throat and my eyes go wide as the biggest man I've ever seen fills the doorway, his blue-gray uniform unmistakably military. The Dog strides in, his bald head inches away from the ceiling.

A memory floods into my brain.

Gran is pressing my head into her side. Through her fingers, I can see a man in a blue-gray uniform with brown hair and black boots. They are holding a big rifle in their hands. They are aiming at something, and Gran is blocking my view. Someone shouts. Guns fire. A woman lets out a heartbreaking wail.

The Dog stares at the class with electric blue eyes, shocking us into a vigilant silence, mesmerized. Everyone sits up straighter as he comes to a standstill at the front of the class. He has a rumbling, deep voice that reminds me of the growl of thunder over the mountains. Mrs. Storm fidgets with the chalk as he says, "Did you receive our announcement? Good. I expect everything is in order?"

Even from the back of the class, it's clear that Mrs. Storm is trembling. Her gray hair falls in front of her eyes as she nods.

The Dog turns around and looks at the class. When his eyes fall on me, my heart pounds and I shift my gaze to my desk. He makes me feel like a tiny mouse under the gaze of a hawk. "Attention graduates!" He pauses, draws a breath, and continues. "I am First Lieutenant Klippa. My team and I are here at the behest of the Leader Suprema to inspect and evaluate your healing capabilities." My jaw clenches. "As per the law of 32.5b, you are obligated to fully cooperate. All your grades will be analyzed and recorded. In the near future, we will administer physical and cognitive tests."

Darya takes a a sharp intake of breath.

"Rest assured, your privacy will be respected and your records returned to you. If you meet the Army's rigorous standards, you will have the opportunity to serve as a healer in the military."

I want to disappear into my chair. I've worked hard to maintain good grades and now it's going to work against me.

"This is not just a job, it's a career opportunity of a lifetime. In Unity and Reverence!" He salutes.

No response comes from the class, as everyone is trying to process what's just been said. I hadn't expected this. If they are recruiting students, the war is worse than I imagined.

* * *

I wander home, distracted, and don't notice a big black shape bound towards me until he leaps up and puts his paws on my shoulders. I stagger, but keep my balance he wags his tail and licks my face in greeting.

"Hello Momo," I say with a smile, trying and failing to push him off. "How are you?"

He barks once in answer, face joyful. I scratch the sweet spot on his head and his back leg pounds the ground in enjoyment. Needing comfort, I give him a big hug. His hair tickles my nose and the familiar scent of him fills my lungs. He guides me to the bakery, looking up a few times to see if I'm doing okay, and I smile at him.

Gran has thrown the doors and windows wide open in a feeble attempt to catch a breeze, sending smells of fresh pastries drifting my way. A bell goes off in the back as I walk through the door. No one is in the front.

"Momo, sit!" I command as I peek into the kitchen. Gran is sleeping in her chair, gently snoring.

In my bedroom, I peel off my damp clothes with difficulty and throw them straight in the laundry pile next to the door. My work outfit smells like soap and it's a treat to put on. There's no time for an extensive rinse, so I splash some water on my face as I hear the bell ring.

"Coming!" Freshening up before I run down the stairs. Gran is still asleep in her chair. *She's losing her hearing.*

At first glance, it looks like nobody's there, but then I hear the happy thump of Monster's tail hitting the wooden floor.

Behind the counter, someone in an emerald shirt rubs his belly. Monster's tongue lolls out of his mouth as he smiles up at the man. When the customer sees me, he straightens -it's Onyx Eyes.

"Oh," I say, surprised.

He stands in front of the counter, tall, and confident. My hands are damp and I'm not sure if it's the heat or if it's the sight of him. He is just as gorgeous as I remember, and his eyes flash with recognition. "Hey there." His top two buttons of his shirt are undone, giving me a glimpse of some well-defined muscles beneath.

"Good afternoon. How is your day?" I tuck a strand of hair behind my ear and look up at him. His smile fades and he sighs.

"Not fun."

"Same here." I lean against a shelf and cross my arms. "I thought you would have… gone by now."

"There is too much to do here. We can't all just get up and leave, right?" He winks at me and my face grows hot.

"That was actually terrible advice you gave me," I say. He raises his eyebrows in surprise. "Those blue angels are deadly!"

Just thinking of them already gives me a headache. He laughs heartily, throwing his head back in amusement. The sound fills the air, and for a moment, the tension between us seems to dissipate.

"How many did you have?"

"I… I don't actually remember," I admit with a groan.

"This lady can't hold her liquor!" he teases. "Let me make it up to you. Would you like to show me how to have fun here, Eden style?"

Like a rendezvous? Now when the army is infiltrating? I take a deep breath to allow the tension to flow out of my body.

He smiles and before I can answer he says, "May I have three cinnamon rolls, please? And… your name."

His tone doesn't change. It is not a question, it is a command. I look into his Onyx Eyes. My stomach feels like a shoal of jittery silversides have decided they want to break free all at once.

"My name is Elara. What about you?"

"My friends call me Cas."

I tingle all over as I get his cinnamon rolls, his eyes never leaving me.

"Well, here you go… Cas."

He smiles when I say his name. "Then I will see you later... Elara".

My face flushes, but he is already gone with his cinnamon rolls, leaving me alone, feeling conflicted. As a solution, I stuff a cinnamon roll in my face. It helps slightly.

When rush hour starts, I wake up Gran to help. She refuses to admit she was actually sleeping. "I wasn't napping, my dear. I was resting my eyes for a spell."

The rest of the day, my mind is not where it's supposed to be. When Gran catches me floundering, she sends me upstairs.

* * *

The sound of my door creaking open wakes me. Sunlight has disappeared and Gran walks into my room holding a lantern, which bathes my room in orange light. Our house moans as the wind whistles along the beams.

"Hello, sweetheart." She chooses her footing carefully. "This laundry pile will be the death of me. I'll break my neck over it one of these days," she mutters as she scoots it over with her foot. My lips stay shut, but I roll my eyes. She can't see my face, otherwise I'd be reprimanded.

She sits down at the foot of my bed, her weight shifting the mattress. It's not cold in the bedroom, but Gran shivers. The light throws unsettling shadows on her lined face, making her look much older. "I must attend an emergency meeting at the Town Hall, my dear." The words rasp in her throat. "I wanted to let you know I'll be away for a spell."

"Can I come?" I ask. *It must have something to do with the Dogs arriving in Eden today.* I long to do something, anything to help get rid of them.

She puts her hand on my leg, gives it a squeeze, and looks at me somberly. "Please stay put, it will comfort me to know you are safe in bed." She gets up and walks to the door, pausing for a second. "We will discuss this in the morning."

I flee the house when I'm sure she's gone, leaving Monster looking accusingly at me. Over the abandoned street, in the darkness, I am a shadow and the dust mutes my footsteps. A few windows cast a faint light, but I dodge them and I give the Town Hall a wide berth -it's not my wish to listen in, but I need to think.

Gusts of wind blow salt spray in my face, tug on my hair, and ruffle my dress. Meanwhile, rays of the waning moon play with the waves as they roll on the beach with significant force - the sound the crash thunders through my entire being. I enjoy the unbridled nature.

Cool water tickles my feet and strokes my calves, it pulses as if it's alive. The sand is soft and warm in between my toes.

During the night, life seems normal. It's all far away, the war, the Dogs in the town, the sorrow.

I sigh and wonder what I can do. Should I wait it out until it is all over and done? Or do I sit here on my little patch, letting the world do its worst? An Onyx stone sparkles. I bend down, let my fingers travel over its smooth surface, and pick it up. It's light in my hand.

What if I flunk nursing school and take care of the bakery?

The thought of not becoming a nurse stings, though I'm unsure what my alternatives are.

I'm on the floor, playing on all fours with my stuffed toys that sit in a circle. Mr Bear is complaining and Mrs. Bear accuses him of having a foul mood and disrupting tea time. Meanwhile, the heat of the fireplace is pleasant on my skin. Outside, there is the sound of shattering windows. Daddy says I should pay no attention to the sounds and in the morning, shiny, multicolored pieces cover the street. We always stop to look at the sun reflecting off the pretty glass. Inside, the air is filled with the aromatic scent of smoke. Fire crackles happily as it emits a warm orange glow. Gran, Mommy, and Daddy are sitting at the dinner table behind me. Gran's sobs fill the room.

With tears in my eyes, I stand up and, with a yell; I toss the stone as far as possible into the sea. We can't lose everything again.

Gran understands if I drop out of college.

Dies Lovis

Gran's raspy voice disturbs a dream I am having and it puts me to a halt as I am chasing Monster through an unknown yet familiar landscape. There are seas of colorful flowers and snowy mountain peaks before me.

"Elara dear!" Monster vanishes and a wrinkled face full of flour smudges takes his place. "It's time to rise and shine. We've got work to do!" I moan in agreement, and the face dissapears, leaving me to get dressed while the sun is down. Fruity scents drift up the stairs and it tells me Gran has lit the fire in the oven.

During the days leading up to Solemnitatum we are swamped - many muffins and pies are to made. As I hobble downstairs and steal an apple from the fruit basket on the counter.

Flour covers Gran's apron. It's almost as if she has been rolling around in it instead of making pies. The result of her labor stands on the table, a few dozen pie bases that need filling and decorating. "My dear, would you be so kind as to whip up the Cherry Orange one first?" She points at the fruit basket on the floor. I didn't notice before now. "I made a change to the recipe. So be sure to read it through carefully before you mix it together."

"Gran, you promised we'd talk," I say, attempting to not come across accusing. There is a slight halt in her movement. The sound of the fire sizzling and popping fills the room. She meets my gaze with difficulty.

"I did say that, didn't I?" Bags show under her eyes. Clearly, she came home much later than I did -I'm not sure she got any sleep. Her face is pale. A small nudge could send her over the edge. I walk towards her and give her a big hug. She holds me tight and I smell eucalyptus. We hug until my back protests.

We break free and she wipes away tears, the last time I've seen her cry was years ago. My heart breaks and my resolve falters.

"It's okay Gran."

On the counter, the recipe for the orange filling lies there in anticipation. "When is Darya expected to be here?"

Gran gathers herself, gives a cough, and says, "She said she'd be there at eight."

The clock strikes six, but Darya is late, no matter what appointment she has. I learned to accept it, so I am not expecting her for another three hours.

I gather the ingredients and take a deep breath. "Gran, are they trying to recruit you for the resistance?"

She is vigorously attacking the dough with a rolling pin. "Don't be silly, dear. At my age, these things are out of the question." She gives me a sideways glance from under her bushy gray eyebrows.

"Gran..." I plead.

She sighs and lays the utensil aside. "You shouldn't fret about such things. You ought to be more concerned with boys and college, take an example of your friend Darya."

"Gran, I'm worried," I say.

Gran resumes her work with the dough, her eyes tired. "I can't change that, dear. You're far too young to get caught up in such matters."

"I'm 21! I'm not a child anymore. The Dogs are on our doorstep, but you only worry about bread." My hands hit the counter and Gran glares at me.

"Elara Ariël Waywater, I won't have this discussion with you, and that's final!" She moves a pie in the oven as she says this.

"No! Don't treat me like a child!" I say childishly. I gather the fruit and stone the berries. Our working hands, Monster's panting and the sizzling in the fire are the only sounds -until Gran breaks the silence.

"I can't bear to lose you as well," her voice trembles. My heart drops and I fight back tears. She walks over to me and gives me a big hug. "You're right, you're an adult now and I must treat you as such. If it pleases you, have a bag packed, just in case."

Both of us are misty-eyed, I breathe in deep to calm myself. *Is it possible to miss what is still there?*

* * *

Darya and I hurry to the last class before Solemnitatum. An excited buzz fills the room as the girls talk about their dresses. Mrs. Storm has bags under her eyes and her usually tight bun is sloppy. When we sit down, she starts by reading us the wrong chapter. Lilly points out her flaw before she finds the place we left off. She writes on the blackboard, glances out of the window frequently, and misspells words. I get the feeling she hasn't prepared for today's lesson, and not because of the upcoming festivities.

"Please, class! Try to focus, we only have an hour left. Darya SIT DOWN!" With her last outburst, more strands come loose from her bun.

"Yes. So as I was saying…"

But no one except Lilly pays attention.

The sweet scent of fruit fills the bakery and makes my mouth water as I walk in. Gran says goodbye to a few regulars, covered head to toe in flour, and red stripes in her updo. As soon as she bakes anything other than bread, it's as if she rolls in the ingredients, rather than mixing them in a bowl. Behind her tiny frame, two enormous pans are rising steam as the insides simmer. New bases for the pies are already baking in the stone oven. A half-full pan of new stuffing stands near Gran.

***

She smiles her broad smile that she only reserves for special occasions.

"Oh my, it's wonderful to have you here, my darling. I can hardly keep up with myself." She stirs and peeks into the oven while more customers walk in.

"I'll be right with you," I say and sprint up the stairs, don my working outfit, and run down again.

Later, Darya walks in, dressed in her old clothing, and skips to her pace.

"So, what can I do for you?"

Gran puts her to work, and Darya takes her place next to me. Her pace is slow, however every pair of hands is welcome. The air is thick with the perfume of oranges, cherries, and vanilla -it makes my stomach rumble. We work side by side in silence until Gran breaks it by humming her song. Her raspy voice, the fire, and the pot lids clattering in the background fill the small space.

What will we be doing next year? Will we still be here?

I take a steadying breath as I regard my best friend, my grandmother, and the bakery.

"Do you have an invitation to Solemnitatum?" Darya asks, to my alarm.

I shoot a look at Gran, who shakes her head.

"No, not yet.." I confess. It would be a lot of fun to go on a date, but I'm fine either way. Gran wants me to find a special man, so

I'm in safe hands should she one day pass away. It is customary for all unmarried girls to be escorted by a bachelor during the actual celebration. The bachelor sendd a letter to his interest, asking them to accompany them. If the receiving party is interested, he comes over to her house to meet the parents. It's also the festivity with the highest number of marriage proposals and thus a pretty big deal.

Does it still matter?

I double-check the recipe as I mix the cherries, oranges, and vanilla extract before I put the heavy pan on the fire to let it thicken for a while. Time passes and the sun creeps through the street as we continue on the second filling; figs and grapes. "What about you?"

The happiness radiates from Darya's face. "Zale wrote me a letter... And Alphonse too!"

"Ooh! I would definitely go with Zale," I squeak. He is a better match for her than Alphonse. Darya needs a husband who is grounded not one who is as fickle as a kite.

The first mixture has to cool down before we continue with this batch -we focus on making lemon loafs.

We mix the lemon - from Lilly's Orchard-, butter, eggs, sugar, flour, and baking powder. It forms a sticky, zesty-smelling batter. This is my favorite and I sneak a finger full of it, only when I'm certain Gran doesn't see it. Gran hums along, undisturbed.

"So.. what are you going to do?"

"Well...Zale's great and everything... Alphonse is a better match."

Gran coughs, but Darya doesn't seem to notice or care. The Ballards are pretty well off. However, the old-fashioned notion of marrying into a wealthy family is still very important to Mr. Ballard. Although I'm not sure if it matters much to Darya; she only wants to make her father proud.

She pauses for a bit and looks at the oranges thoughtfully. Sometimes I wonder what goes on in her mind.

"I believe he would be a wonderful husband," I say. He's not from a rich family, but he works hard and on top of that, he's good with kids. Darya nods, her mind made up.

* * *

Dies Lovis

CLANK!

An ear-splitting noise wakes me up with a start. With a crumpled face and Monster's stinky, warm breath, I push myself up. The sun hasn't come up, yet Gran scuttles around downstairs already. I attempt to push his massive body off the bed, to no avail. He refuses to wake up and I am not strong enough to move him. In the end, I climb over his peaceful sleeping body.

Dog breath lingers on my skin and I decide to take a quick shower. It's still dark, so I have to feel my way to the water closet. The rope I pull releases the water, and I gasp as the cold cascades down my back. Water renders me wide awake. With some lavender-scented soap, I scrub myself down in record time. Smelling and feeling a lot better, I grab a fluffy towel off the rack. Outside, sunlight is already sneaking into the house.

Gran has a big pink streak over her forehead, which tells me she is working on the cherry filling. "Good morning dear, I do hope you slept well?"

"Like a whale," I say while trying to rub off the pink stripe off with my thumb. "How about you?"

Her face is clean-ish. "I had a dream last night that I was busy making these pies. Believe it or not, I tweaked the vanilla peach recipe a bit!" Gran does this on the day when we're supposed to sell the cakes. During my childhood, she would start all over. Now I am just glad we didn't begin with that recipe already.

"If we add thick cream to the center, I think it would taste devine."

A sense of comfort creeps into me as I watch her. The scent of fresh pastries and the warmth of the oven make me feel safe. Gran effortlessly navigates the kitchen, her years of experience evident in every move.

I start with the peaches, one by one, they splash into the big pot that is already filled with vanilla -sending drops of the essence flying.

"How has college been treating you, my dear?" Gran inquires while her hands fly over her work.

"Fine, I guess -Gran, we need to talk about something. I know you've worked hard so that I could follow nursing classes… And you know that I have always…"

I fidget with the hem of my brown shirt. An anchor of apprehension scrapes against the bottom of my gut. Gran furrows her brow and stays silent.

"With everything going on… Perhaps I could be of a different use…" A thread comes loose. This conversation was a lot easier in my head.

"I have decided to quit college."

"No," Gran says simply and turns around.

"Gran, listen. They are recruiting healers. I need to get out before they force me to join!" My heart beats fast.

"They'll be on to you if you drop out now. We have to pretend life goes on as usual until the last second. Besides-" She gazes at me with affection in her eyes. "-your father would want you to learn as much as possible about healing. Even if it came from them. You can help people with your skills, Elara."

Caught off guard by the mention of my father I look down. "No one is going to hire me without a proper diploma."

"Healing is something that people will always pay for, official or not." Gran's face is serious. "Besides, we don't have enough money to go anywhere yet."

My fingers do their magic to decorate the pastries with tiny shells, my thoughts go to Cas and my stomach fills with butterflies. I got it bad. Staying a little longer isn't the worst.

The four of us are ready when Gran opens the bakery and excited customers spill in like a tidal wave forming a line in our tiny shop. Darya puts the cakes in a box and Lilly packs them neatly and I manage the cash register. This morning the cranberry loaves are doing better than last year.

Mrs. Hydris hands me a crisp banknote and Darya gets the muffins for her. Lilly finishes her elaborate packing and gives the package over to her mother.

"Keep the change." The coins clink as she lets them fall into my sweaty hand.

"Thank you, Mrs. Hydris!" I put our tip in a small cup. She waves at her daughter as she leaves. An out-of-townee has a big order next -the gentleman is bent over and smells of old age.

"Your Gran's baked goods are truly unmatched in their excellence, wouldn't you agree?" He gives me a smile that shows a few missing teeth.

An enormous man stands at the end of the line, wearing a blue-gray uniform. On his shoulder, there are three gold stripes and a single star. *He murdered people in the last war.*

My heart flutters and I try to control my breathing. I mess up Mrs. Boyle's order because I barely hear what she is saying. Darya saves it and we continue. With every leaving customer, he moves closer -as inescapable as a tsunami. A heavy-looking gun is slung over his shoulder and shines in the sunlight. My jaw clenches. When the last human shield leaves, he makes his way forward. *Were you at the Assault of Brudahr?*

My mouth is dry, but I attempt a smile while my fists clench. His towering physique dwarfs everything in sight. "It all smells exquisite," his mustache rumbles. He smacks his hands together with a force that would throw over a cart. I flinch. "What would you recommend?"

How many people did you kill to become First Lieutenant? My breathing speeds up.

Darya sees my distress and jumps in for me, she gives him her brightest smile."Well, lavender cakes are very popular this year. My favorite is the cherry-orange pie."

His eyes scan over the pastries. "Hmmm… Give me six of every treat you have!" His laugh resembles thunder and makes me jump.

"Of every-" Lilly and Darya look startled.

"The boys at the base are hungry. We need them to eat well." He beams at her as he opens his hands as if it's obvious. *The base? You mean the building you commandeered, you vulture.*

Darya and Lilly are a whirlwind of action while I stand, listening to the sound of my erratic heartbeat. *If I join the resistance... How could I ever take on someone so intimidating?* With icy palms, I accept the paper notes. Never have I held so much money.

He smiles politely at me and mutters, "Thanks, doll," from under his mustache. After such a big order, the shelves are depleted. Gran springs into action to restock. The Mountain accepts the bag of pastries from Lilly and with one step, he's out of the bakery. Lilly squeezes my hand and I shiver as I unclench my fists.

The row of people moves on and I regain my composure. The line shortens. Work becomes less hectic, and Gran takes over from Darya. As we say goodbye, she steals a cupcake without Gran seeing it.

One of the last customers is Zale. His red hair and friendly freckles are a welcome sight. He greets me with a smile.

"My mom asked me to get ten rose muffins."

Gran hears the order and scuttles off. Busy and rushed, I initially miss the implication. "That's a lot!" I beam at him when I realize what it means. "Are your brothers back?"

"Yes!" His smile reminds me of the sun breaking through the clouds. "We just got the letter telling us they are on their way." Lilly hands over the decorated parcel, and he nods in thanks. "I was wondering… Elara…"

Please hurry, there is a line behind you.

"Would you accompany me to the Solemnitatum?" he blurts. His face is as red as his freckles. He smiles awkwardly. I stare at him for a second before I blink, the line forgotten. Gran pretends to be occupied, while Lilly goes to make tea.

I don't want to be alone on Solemnitatum.

He has asked Darya before, but I expel that from my thoughts. Zale smiles at me as I accept his official letter. Gran gives the muffins to him as I turn my attention to the next customer, while smiling like a dimwit. *I have a date!*

We close early because Gran will stand at the market with her stall tonight.

"I laid out a dress for you on the bed," she says, and I fly up the stairs. On my bed lies a beautiful ocean blue dress with white lace sleeves. Gran walks upstairs and looks at me from the doorpost as I put it on. The velvety fabric of the dress feels water-like. Her eyes become misty when she sees me.

"This dress was your mother's." In her mind's eye, she sees her daughter. I swallow hard. "She wore this to the last dance with your dad."

The blue dress fits me well and I try to imagine how my mother felt when she wore this. *Did she enjoy the dance? Maybe she was nervous?* There is a faint perfume of lilac and berries on the dress. *Could it be the perfume she wore?*

The high lace neckline screams modesty, but when Gran zips up the dress, a significant part of my back and shoulders stay bare.

Gran gives me her prized pearl earrings to wear and braids my hair intricately. Cherishing every second, her fingers go through my updo. My eyes mist up when I see Gran watching me with pride. We chat about topics that don't matter as we do each other's make-up. She howls with laughter when she looks in the mirror.

"Ha! I'm an old fart!"

Chapter 4

A knock signals Zale's arrival, and after waiting for this moment for weeks, I have to restrain myself from skipping down the stairs. Through the glass of the door of the bakery, he appears confident.

"Good evening," he says in a deep voice when I open the door. He must have been practicing his pose in the mirror at home and in my mind, I see his brothers coaching him while doing so. His eyes go over my dress and he smiles. There is a warmth in his smile that makes me feel comfortable. Then he looks me up and down. "You're stunning, I wasn't aware you cleaned up so nicely," he says the last part with a teasing tone.

"Thanks, so do you."

Zale cleans up very well -his evening wear must come from the Capital. His red hair is tidy underneath his hat, and his green jacket compliments his eyes. All in all, he resembles a true gentleman.

With a little awkward bow and a tap on the brim of his hat, he greets Gran and I have to give her credit for not bursting out laughing. Although it costs her significant effort.

I save him by taking his arm and he leads me outside into the warm evening air. His woolen jacket scratches my bare arm.

Sunset bathes the entire street in glorious gold as we walk towards the festivities and Zale excitedly tells me about his brother's return to Eden. I find it endearing. After a short walk, we reach the town center where a lot of folk walk around amidst the smells of exotic food, incense, and smoke. The square is ablaze with a huge bonfire, its warmth reaching far and wide.

The night is full of sounds; jazz from a wireless that someone has put in the doorway, the crackling flames, shouting men, laughing women, and out-of-townees trying to sell their wares. Stalls are overloaded with jewelry, books, food, carpets, chandeliers, and much more, with some very eccentric clothed sellers. While we stroll around the little stalls, comparing tastes in decoration and literature, their voices call out to try a sample from their unique stall. Zale admits it has been a while since he actually picked up a book. I playfully scold him for it when he says, "I don't have the time!"

Darya isn't here, but I spot her sister, she is mesmerized by her caller, who is buying a fried fish on a stick for her. It is obvious she doesn't want to be disturbed. To my disappointment, Cas is absent, but instead, my gaze falls on the unwelcome colors of the military uniforms. They move like stains in the crowd and my jaw clenches. *They're already strutting around as if they own the place. Where did they all come from?*

"So.. what keeps you so busy?" I ask, in an effort to distract myself.

"I'm training for the autumn swim and it's been lovely to jump into the ocean every day with this heat." Zale bulges his biceps to show off his brand-new physique and I poke in them, seeing if they'll deflate, and we laugh awkwardly.

We wander, waving at familiar faces and greeting a few of his friends. Zale seems unfazed by all these soldiers around. In order to draw some of his courage, I lock my arm in his and he smiles.

Just behind him, Gran gives me two thumbs up from behind her stall. My cheeks flush. Bells ring and we all move toward the temple located behind the square. As we stroll towards the center of the festivities, I spot Raphaël in a dark alleyway with what Gran could only describe as 'uncouth youth'. He appears to be buying or selling something. We turn away and my grip tightens on Zale's. *At least I have a perfect gentleman.*

The old priest wears the ceremonial cloak of different shades that resemble rippling water, making his gray hair look like a spume. He flows onto the steps of the temple while the fabric trickles behind him. As he reaches the top he turns around to great applause. With a rise of his hands the noise dies down and his gaze wanders through his audience. His eyes, like a stormy sea, peer into my very soul so I cast my eyes down uncomfortably, afraid of what he might see in them.

"Countless years ago-" His voice crashes over us and the chatter ceases. "-the First Men were pursued by their cruel Gods. They left their homeland in search of shelter, food, and warmth. Only to die of earthquakes, starvation, and cold. Frightened and desperate, with only a sliver of hope, they sailed off venturing to these shores, trying to flee from their Gods' random acts of viciousness. For three moons, they journeyed before arriving here. They spotted a woman dressed in naught but the sea. Her hair was seaweed and her eyes were deep pools."

His arms are in the air, painting the picture he sees clearly in his mind's eye. "This woman was man nor God, she was the First Priest and taught them about the new Gods. Occasionally, they were righteous, sometimes they were violent and cruel. She showed how to appease them and how they could understand the signs they would send them. They named this place Eden after their First Priestess. She showed them how to extract the power from the water." I hear the crystalline cracks and feel the frozen floor of the lady's room. *Was that man an elementalist?*

It brings light to darkness, warmth to cold, protection during trouble, and healing for hurt. For generations, they lived in peace with these Gods and they prospered because the water God favored the First Men above all others. Until the day-" he raises his voice. "-the two brothers Llyr and Eitri fell in love. Believing they both had her favor, they fought each other on the shore. The dark claimed Eitri's life as Llyr drowned him."

He lowers his tone for dramatic effect.

"She was torn between despair and anger. For neither of them had understood her message. The sea belongs to no man and bows to none. She strode into the surf, her clothes dissolving and her body dissolved and it stormed for 40 days and 40 nights!" he yells.

"Furious that they had taken her gift and used it for murder, her punishment was great and fierce! She claimed all men who possessed the gift, embracing them in her watery hold to prevent selfish use."

He lets this sink in as we stare at him and he catches his breath. "Some chosen were saved to spread her warning. Eden's isolation ended when people emerged from the sea to share their knowledge. Tonight I tell you of her warning and her love, as we make our SACRIFICE."

He bows deep and then raises his hands up to the sky, his performance getting a whooping response.

The second part of the ceremony is already going on behind him. A big white horse, cleaned and dressed up in blue ribbons, has been led to the altar. They lead the mare to her final destination, and the chant begins.

Water is poured over the animal with wooden buckets, cleansing it. The mare whinnies as it cascades down her back, and she shakes it off. As the water falls over her head, she nods, thus giving her blessing for the sacrifice.

The Priest pulls out his ceremonial makhaira, this blade passed down among Priests for centuries. Bronze still shines sharply. With a single swift movement, he slits the animal's throat, and she whinnies.

Her eyes widen in shock and she tries to tug away, but the rope doesn't budge. She falls to her knees, whimpering as we watch. Feeling sick, I avert my gaze. After they gut her, they serve her meat to the people. Waste naught and share all; it is the way of Quatahna.

The mare shudders violently as her life flows down the steps. Her final breath leaves her. The priest kneels beside the now lifeless body. He strokes it before he buries the blade deep into her stomach. More blood gushes out, and also some of her entrails. Entrails, especially the liver, are important -they are to be extracted and examined to see whether the Gods accepted our sacrifice. If so, the ritual will proceed. That part is done in a closed circle, and I am grateful. Despite liking anatomy and the idea I could cure people, blood and entrails make me nauseous.

"Fancy another stroll?" Zale asks, pale beneath his freckles.

At least I am not the only one getting queasy.

Relieved, I nod, and we slink away into the fresher air.

"I never enjoy the last part." Zale admits to his shoelaces and he scratches his head.

I take his arm. "You're not alone, a lot of people get uneasy around blood."

"Don't tell anyone… It's not…" He scratches the back of his neck, probably thinking about his older, cooler siblings who happen to be soldiers.

I look around at the cheerful people, the blue-gray uniforms still stain the crowd, and I pull him closer. "Forget about it. Shall we get something to eat?"

He shoots me a grateful smile. "Yeah, anything not bloody would be nice."

We make our way to a little stall manned by an elderly lady selling all kinds of savory treats. She squints at us through thick glasses. "Ha! Youth! What can I do you for?"

"A bag of roasted nuts, please," Zale asks.

"And for the miss?" I order the same thing and she hands me the warm aromatic smelling food as Zale pays.

We run into a bouncy Lilly accompanied by Tennin. "Hey darling! How are you? You're looking divine tonight!"

By the blush on her cheeks and her jubilant way, it's obvious she already had some drinks. I struggle to stay upright as she tightly embraces me. She shrieks with laughter in my ear, splitting my eardrum. "I am great, thanks. It appears you're enjoying yourself."

"Yeaah! I am peachy!" Her beautiful orange and teal dress compliments her brown hair. "And you have an escort!"

Zale nods politely, unsuccessful in hiding his fear of a big bear hug.

"You've met Zale," I say and try to tell her telepathically that this is THE Zale. "Zale, you've met Lilly before?"

He nods at her in greeting. "You're the orchard's owner's daughter. Then you must be Tennin!"

"Yeaah! That's right!" She beams at him. "Have you seen Darya yet? She looked so 'ocupado' with her suitor when I saw her. Didn't want to disturb… you know…" She wiggles her eyebrows and giggles again.

As we gossip, the fellows have found common ground and are talking about sports. Sports here include, surprise, water. Townspeople learn how to swim before they can walk. Tennin is great at sailing and is a celebrity in our town. He's been doing a good job for some years, winning many games. After a while, we break apart and I walk alone with Zale again. He's delighted.

"Wow, Tennin is such an outstanding chap!" He gushes.

"He is charming," I say, eyeing the blue-gray uniforms. One of them is buying from Gran.

"Oh yeah, that too. But he is an outstanding sailor!"

I grin at his enthusiasm.

"Did you see the game when…" He recaps last year's race with big hand motions. Listening to Zale recapping it makes it sound much more exciting than when I was actually there. Our conversation shifts to my studies, the market, and other unimportant things.

A loud bell signals the next part of the ceremony and from a distance, I watch Raphaël leading our classmate Miriam towards the festivities. Her dark red hair glows in the light of the fire. Surprised by either of their choices, I raise my eyebrows. *They never got along particularly well…*

We follow a narrow street to the fire on the beach and remove our shoes to let our feet sink into the cold sand. Tiny shells and twigs tickle between my toes and massage my soles. I instantly relax. The salty sea breeze drifts towards us. A thin layer of sea mist covers the area. The sea calls my name and I have half a mind to kick my shoes off, run to the shoreline and jump in.

It would not be very ladylike…

The sacrificial mare has been skinned and cleaned, her meat has been placed over the open flames and she is sizzling. It makes my mouth water.

Two elderly volunteers are spinning the spit above the flames with a proud look on their face, due to their role in this ceremony. The Priest is already busy cutting thin slices of the meat. He hands it out to the eager people and after they have gotten their portion, they move along to get wine.

When we're up, he offers three slices on a wooden plate and brushes our forehead with the blood of the animal, signifying the blessing that has been given to us.

Zale's face is pale once more. As we walk to the wine stall, Zale gives me his portion. I look at him in mock disapproval, and he presses his lips together. We chuckle as we accept the wine and I give mine to him.

"No more drinking for you?" He asks me as he finishes his first cup.

"I think I'll abstain from alcohol from now on," I say while taking a bite of meat. The meat is tender, gamy, and sweet with a heavy, smokey tone to it.

We wander, searching for a private spot, and discover a fallen tree away from the crowd. It's high enough to keep my dress dry and low enough that the water plays with my toes. We sit down and watch the ocean, the starry sky, and a bright moon illuminate its waves. Zale smiles and I smile back while chewing a mouthful.

"Thank you for asking me out," I tell the ocean, avoiding Zale's eyes. "I'm enjoying myself." The waves lap lazily on the shore, orange in the fire's glow.

"Thank *you* for coming with me." Zale scoots a little closer to me and we gaze out at the stars. "Darya must have told you I asked her too."

Yes, if you would have kept your mouth shut, I would have forgotten.

The romantic tension deflates.

The waves sparkle in the moonlight. "Yes, it's a pity she didn't accept your invitation."

"Err-" He laughs awkwardly. "-she accepted."

My heart does a somersault. "What?"

"I was advised not to accompany with her. Because of... um... she's known for... you know..."

I wait for him to finish his sentence with raised eyebrows.

"Uh... Oh, come on... you know.." He sputters and holding his hands out in defence. "She is.. a bit.. well.. promiscuous," he ends. The confidence he has carried all night washes away. A familiar couple waves before Zale continues, "They told me it would give the wrong impression to people."

I can't say Darya isn't a bit.. bold, but she is my friend. My friend who I stole her suitor from, what a nightmare.

Have I been a horrible friend for presuming she would choose for money and status?

The waves lap the shoreline beneath my feet while the stars sparkle up ahead. *This would've been a romantic night if I were with someone else. If only Cas would have asked me, he's able to woo a lady.*

"You are more decent," Zale says in a way of a compliment. "that made me think of you."

More decent? Not prettier, not cleverer, not even more hardworking. He chose me because I'm decent. That's a story to tell our kids. Your Mother was the most decent girl of the village.

My appetite lost, I put the plate down next to me. People say hello, but being 'decent', I let Zale do the talking. I pray to Quatahna, Darya won't see us together before I have a chance to check if she isn't hurt about my suitor. When I hear her voice a short distance from us, Zale's panicked face mirrors mine and we bolt. With him on my heels, we spurt through the soft sand towards the pebbled road and the cover of houses.

"That… was…" I pant, holding on to a beam of the porch fence. Zale looks at me and we both burst out laughing. Out of breath, out of sight, and out of our minds. The buildings on this street are all dark, their white fences stark against the shadows of the front doors.

"That was probably the silliest thing I've done since kindergarten." Zale's hair's disarranged, and he pushes it out of his face, smiling.

"Spur of the moment," I admit, fanning myself with my hand. We both giggle while we try to catch our breaths. The wall behind me is warm and smooth against my bare shoulders. It's actually nice to be here in silence with Zale. Noises of the celebrations are muted behind us.

"Do you want to return to the beach?" he asks, gazing at me, leaning his elbows on his knees.

"Of course." Instead of getting up, he shimmies back to lean against the wall next to me. He traces his fingers along a line of my arm, trying to ignite the romantic feeling we had before. We let the silence grow. I wish I had butterflies when he touches me.

"I was wondering…" He looks at me sideways with those big green eyes. "Do you remember anything from your childhood in the Capital?"

"No." I withdraw from his touch, drawing my legs up close.

"Nothing? You were what… six when you settled here?"

"Nothing."

Walls painted red, broken glass on the floor, riots, and fear. So much fear, you could nearly taste it.

"And now there is another war." At this point, I am unsure what Zale wants from me.

If this is his strategy to woo the ladies, he'll surely die alone.

Despite the warm breeze, I shiver. Zale opens his mouth to speak, but a passerby stops right in front of us. My heart skips a beat when I hear a familiar voice.

"Good evening," Cas says. He looks down with a grimace as if he heard a bad joke. My heart thumps and I am very uncomfortable on the cold ground, looking up at him. He has swapped his fedora for a classic top hat and a cane.

"Happy Solemnitatum!" Zale greets him as I jump up, cleaning the dirt from my mother's dress.

Why do I feel like a turtle caught in a net?

"You are one of the Boyle brothers, aren't you?" He offers Zale his hand and pulls him onto his feet.

"Yes, sir?" Zale's confused at how this stranger knows him. Zale is tall, yet not as tall as Cas.

"I am Captain Castiël Hawkeye."

I step backward, feeling as if I have been plunged into ice. *A*

Captain!?

"Your brothers have recently been assigned to my platoon. They told me they had a younger brother living in Eden. Who was incidentally taking out my dear friend Elara here." He winks and I blush despite myself. *He's almost human.*

"The party seems to have relocated, do you know where it went?" He asks politely.

"It's down there. We can accompany you," Zale says.

Zale, you moron!

"Much obliged, Mr. Boyle, but I think I can find it from here." He shakes his hand. Then Captain Hawkeye takes my hand in his firm grasp, bends down, and kisses the top of it. As his lips brush my skin, an electric current runs all the way to my core. *Really Quatahna, this is my choice? Zale or the Dog?*

"Miss Waywater,-" He says as he smiles with those wonderful Onyx Eyes, something in my lower belly stirs. "Will you be joining the festivities?"

"No, Sir. I'm heading home," I say, rubbing the kiss away.

"Shall I escort you to your house?" Zale and Captain Hawkeye offer in unison.

"I'm sure I can find my own way, thanks." I turn on my heel and leave them there, escaping the net, but the kiss burns on my skin.

* * *

Dies Donars

Another sunny day announces itself through my bedroom window. I don't have to get out of bed, but soon it will be scorching hot, so I get dressed and walk downstairs. Gran sings an old melody to herself while sweeping the floor.

"Good morning El, did you have a restful sleep last night?" Her face expectant. "How was Solemnitatum with Zale?"

"Pleasant..."

"Oh my, that terrible? Darling, I know you are an educated lady, but with the war, you need someone to support you. Keep in mind I won't always be around."

"Not always-" A tinge of unease settles in my chest. My hand hovers over the cinnamon rolls. "-long enough to at least find someone suitable." I grab a piece of leftover lemon loaf instead, give her a kiss on the cheek, and inquire about last night's sales.

"Well enough. Dear, could you swing by the market for me? This dame's feeling slightly under the weather." She coughs and then returns to sweeping.

My mouth is filled with a big bite as I sputter, "No problem!" The baskets are under the counter and I grab them while I whistle for Monster.

"Ask Darya to join you. Two pairs of hands are always better than one, and it would be lovely for you to gossip about Solemnitatum, hm?" She winks at me and smiles.

I swallow the last piece of the lemon cake that has suddenly gone stale. "Of course..." And leave the bakery with Monster for Darya's house.

* * *

"Oh Elara, the market, really? We could be doing so many other, more FUN, things!" Darya fans herself with her pink fan and her hair floats in the breeze and the scent of Jasmine finds me.

"We could have been done by now if you hurried up," I say curtly. The nerves of the last few days have made me short-tempered.

"You could have gone without me, you know."

"And miss your sunny attitude?" She shoots me a death glare while I smile widely at her and give her a playful shove. Trying to push the persistent *I am a bad friend* from my mind. "Let's go to the beach after dropping off the groceries at the bakery."

"Yes! Let's do that! I have this bathing suit I'm eager to try out, 'cause…" We saunter to the market, all chats and giggles.

Chapter 5

We take a shortcut through an alley and bump into Alphonse who's surprised to see us, but smiles, well.. he smiles at Darya. Who nods at him, but he pushes onward like a ship without a rudder. "Good morning gorgeous girls, what are we up to today?"

"On our way to the market, just us two!" she says, throwing her arm around my shoulder. Also, Monster lays down between us and Alphonse, he pants while looking up at him. *My hero.*

"Shopping for new clothes are we?" he teases.

"No," I tell him and his eyes shift toward me I raise my basket like a fool, as if this is the undeniable alibi. "We are getting some supplies for the bakery!"

He kisses Darya on the cheek, she looks away as he does. "Don't let me hold you up then."

"How was your Solemnitatum with Alphonse..?" I ask as he walks off.

She averts her eyes. "Yeah, it was alright. We were having a grand time, then he wanted to go home.. and I really didn't want to, you know..." She makes herself small. Suddenly she's very fragile and very unlike herself.

Suddenly I feel protective over her. "So what did you do?"

"I kind of ran away when he wasn't looking." She looks tormented for a second before we both burst out laughing.

The market is unusually quiet today as I walk past the stalls with nervous butterflies. *It's the time of day... Most of the people have gone home by now.* Meanwhile, Monster walks protectively at my side, his head low and his tail still. The same smells hang on the square as always, a combination of salt, fish, and pastries, but it smells different. And although the salesmen shout out the prices of their wares like always, it sounds shrill as the voices bounce along the walls of the surrounding houses. My eyes dart around and eventually I spot the reason, Dogs patrol the marketplace and their guns glint in the sunlight. A nervous tinge sits in my heart as a couple of them walk by and a salesperson shoots them a nasty look.

Darya, though, seems oblivious to the tension and takes her time to stop at a jewelry stand and admires a necklace while a woman entices her to buy it. My eyes are drawn to a big pro-army poster plastered behind a window of one of the houses.

It shows the Nation's flag with their disgusting slogan: In Unity and Reverence.

I feel light headed. Monster coaxes me onward exactly where I need to be, the milk stand is very near the flour store and thankfully we only have to do a quick run.

"Ah, Elara! Excellent to see you again, I've got your supplies right here!" The bald man behind the stall says. "Will you be able to manage it all alone?" His enormous hands gesture at the bags of flour while his eyes follow the Dog moving past.

"No problem, I've brought back-up," I say and wave at my team, only one of them looks happy about it. With two big bags we move on to the milk stand, where an elderly lady sells her wares. The square is so quiet we can hear seagulls squawking overhead. My skin tingles from the nerves.

A smile appears on the lady's wrinkled face when she sees me. "Elara! Good to see you! How is your Gran?"

"She is fine ma'am, just a bit under the weather, I think the excitement for Solemnitatum had a strong impact on her," I say.

"Can I talk to you for a moment, dear?" Her cheery tone changes as she takes me aside behind the stall. Her fragile frame bends towards me and says, "Nuriel owes some money here, and with the war and all… it's devastating for business. I'm sure you understand, she needs to pay before Dies Martis."

"Oh!" For a second I am speechless. *I didn't know Gran had an open tab…*

"Yes, of course! I'll tell her when I get home, but can you still put the milk on the tab for now?" I ask with big innocent eyes, afraid she will refuse.

The old woman nods after giving me a long look. "Fine, but only because I like you. I would feel guilty sending you home empty-handed." She hands over 6 bottles of the white liquid.

I strap the bottles tight so they won't fall out. He wags his tail and with his massive tongue, he tries to lick my face, but I dodge it and rub him between the ears instead.

"Do I also get a scratch?" Darya asks playfully.

I pat her on her head. "Good girl!"

We return, all sweaty, while Monster did most of the hard work. He parades through the tiny store with his bags still on, it makes him proud to be of service and doesn't let me take the thing off.

"Alright, this is about all the tanning time I can miss, let's escape this stuffy old place!" Darya states. She stalks out of the bakery and I wave at Gran, kiss Monster goodbye, and follow suit. *I'll bring up the tab later…*

* * *

Seagulls squawk overhead in their choir as they search for food as we navigate through the crowded beach towards our private spot. Darya gets a few looks from boys here and there, one even whistles. She is dressed in a baby blue skirt that flutters in the wind.

"Why aren't you wearing a bathing costume?" she asks.

"Oh, I forgot. It's not *that* warm." I groan as we start our climb. She blinks and probably thinks I'm mad but leaves the topic alone. The thought of those skimpy costumes makes me fidget, they are too small and don't cover up enough.

"How are your sisters?"

Darya has five sisters total, all older than she is, married, and moved out, except for Darya and Delphine. Being the youngest of six girls makes her a bit rough around the edges, but is sweet when you get to know her.

"Delphine is getting very serious with her suitor." She pulls herself up over the edge with a groan. "We haven't heard from her since Solemnitatem so I'm suspecting he proposed. So it won't be long before she moves out, and then I will be an only child." She flashes me a smile. "Like you."

"I wish I had sisters," I say as I jump off the last stone. "Then I wouldn't have to support Gran and the bakery on my own." The idea of Gran having an unpaid tab worries me, she has never been one for spending frivolously, especially in these times. Worry leaves my mind when my soles hit the sand, it's empty except for a few birds picking through the washed-up offerings.

"I love to help out," Darya says as she puts her towel down in the shade. "When you're shorthanded, give me a heads up". I nod absentmindedly as I walk toward the clear blue water. A wave cascades over my feet as the wind strokes my face. *Bliss.*

"El… About Alphonse… He's fun when we are together in a group, but… he gets… pushy." She sighs and gazes at the horizon. "And I have to report to him everything I do. He doesn't like me spending time with Raphaël," she complains. I give a non-comment full shrug. Darya hanging with him does not sit well with me either, not because I'm jealous but because Raphaël is a bounder and just a little too intelligent for his own good.

"He got so angry last night, he said I would have to decide between them." She lies down with a thud. The sea is trying to draw me in and I wade into the refreshing water.

"What will you do?"

"Well… I guess that if he forces an ultimatum… I would choose him," Her muted voice says from under her sunhat.

An unexpected massive wave almost topples me over. "What!?"

"Yeah, I mean. I can lose Raphaël as a friend if need be…" The sun hat tells me, she pushes it up and looks straight into my eyes. "What would you do?"

My feet find the shallow part of the shoreline and I walk closer to her while I mull it over.

"If someone would dictate who I could see, I would stop seeing the person that would give me an ultimatum."

Waves crash while she thinks over my answer. "El, you don't understand," she concludes. "Gran gives you all the freedom you need. Father needs me to have a suitable gentleman." *She's right. What do I know? I just had a horrible night with the only man who asked me out and I have the luxury to stop things.*

"Darya..?" I say while sitting down on the soft sand next to her.

"Hmm?" The sunhat says.

"I had a date too." I wait for an accusation, an angry stare, or even a hurt one. She sits up. "I knew it!" and punches the air and her voice goes up an octave or two. "Telll meeeee!!!"

"It was with Zale." I have the decency to blush.

"I heard…" Of course, she would have, how could anything in this little town remain a secret? She exhales. "How was it?"

The only sound is the crash of the waves and the cry of seagulls for a couple of seconds. I confess it was not a great success.

"Okay, I figured. Otherwise, you would have told me sooner, right? Will you keep seeing him?" She watches me with her big eyes.

"He'll come by the bakery to get bread."

Darya snorts. "I mean will you be *seeing* him?"

"No," I say disappointed, my fingers find the place where Captain Castiël Hawkeye brushed his lips. Darya misinterprets my facial expression.

"You're allowed to have my hand-me-downs, right? It's no biggie!" She winks at me as her words sting.

I deserved that.

* * *

I walk into the bakery, Gran is cleaning up but turns to me as the bell goes of in the back of the store. "Oh my, you got a sunburn!" I let her fuss over me, and she sits me down next to the counter and rubs her self-made lotion on my neck.

"Darling, do tell," she says and as she applies the cream over my burnt skin. "Is Darya still keeping company with that Alphonse fella?"

I confirm her suspicion.

"And.. are there any other interesting gentlemen for you?" She asks, her voice conspiratorial. "Is Raphaël not your type? You would have a wonderful influence on him."

"What? No! He's the last one on my mind."

I change to the subject that has been bothering me all day. "Gran, Sophie from the market said we have an open tab… You have to pay up before Dies Martis."

Gran averts her eyes, exhales, and scrapes her throat.

"Gran, are we in financial trouble?"

"Now dear, don't you worry about it."

That means yes.

My stomach drops and I push on."How come?"

She tells me supplies have been getting more expensive in the last few months, but she refuses to raise our prices, afraid our customers will buy bread elsewhere. An uneasy feeling creeps up on me as I recall the deserted market, but I keep quiet.

"We had a great turnout on Solemnitatum, so don't think we're going to run out of funds anytime soon!" she says.

"Can we talk about the resistance now?" I ask and I turn around to face her.

Gran shudders and something dark flashes behind her eyes before she nods, and walks to the kitchen. The kettle clatters on the stove, louder than it should. The sun emits an orange glow outside while I wait for her to return. It gives me the time to think about what I want from them, or how I could be of worth to them.

Gran comes back and sits her slight frame down on the wooden chair. She fidgets with her skirt, a habit I'm familiar with. "This is not something you should take lightly, Elara. There's a thing or two you ought to know. Darling, the military, they recruit folks with… Unique talents. That must be why they're interested in Eden because Eden itself doesn't have anything to offer on its own."

She clears her throat. "These special militants are the most dangerous. You see, there are some Dogs out there who will extract all the details they need out of you, even if you don't intend to give it."

She holds her hand up when I open my mouth to interject. "It's crucial to possess as few facts as possible. The more scattered the information, the harder it'll be for them to piece together what we know and what we're up to. That means if we want to be ready to run, we should have a minimal amount of about it." Gran sighs deeply.

She's small, with her hands on her lap and her wrinkled face turned up at me.

"So you have to trust me that I'll share what you need to know, though I can never tell you everything."

"A few years back, Carpathia had a change of heart nobody saw coming. Perhaps it was fear, or foresight, or perhaps it was greed. Who can say? Anyhow, she decided the Tainted shouldn't be persecuted anymore, at first it looked like it was a victory from the resistance. However, she wants to recruit them for her army to fight at the front. Cost of a war is always high, especially for those who begin with little. Carpathia is selecting people who could help her with her new plan, stretching of the love of her state, she calls it."

Gran chooses her next words with great care. "This ambition is not… embraced by everyone wholeheartedly. The factions are coming back to life and not all of them… align with our values, Elara. One as green as yourself might not see the difference between what is good and what is right."

Chapter 6

Dies Veneris

The sky is a navy blue and I give my usual grumpy grunts as I pull my working clothes over my head and trudge downstairs. Gran kneads the dough and has put some aside for me. With my morning temper, I soften the dough. Gran has stronger fingers than I do, and she makes the best bread -all I can do is try to keep up. She sings, my alto hums add to her soprano and I sing with a smile on my face. My heart bursts with contentment.

I throw some sunflower seeds in the mix because that's a personal favorite of mine. My mind goes over what is going to happen and Gran hugs me when I leave. "Be as truthful as you can today. They'll know when you're lying," she whispers in my ear.

* * *

In the old college building, we line up in an orderly fashion as instructed to wait for our teacher, Mrs. Storm, but she fails to show up.

A Dog in a blue-gray uniform tells us to stand in alphabetical order of our last name in front of the classroom. Darya and I exchange nervous glances and my mouth is dry. She put herself through some trouble to take the tests after me. Otherwise refusing to participate at all and, in the end. They allowed it. So now I'm clutching onto her clammy hand. *Please don't let go*.

Dogs in uniform patrol the building. Students have different attitudes toward them; some are as uncomfortable as I am, others approach them and start a conversation. I make myself as small as I can while waiting my turn for the tests -we're called in one by one. Even Darya is not her usual blabbering self.

"I heard Tamarah burst out in tears during her cognitive exam!" Miriam whispers while she twirls a lock of red hair through her fingers.

"They hurt you in order to see your reaction to pain," Lilly murmurs. Her freckles are awfully bright on her pale face.

"You have t-t-to look at p-pictures taken of mutilated people while they check your p-pulse," Raphaël says, while his thumb traces his suspenders.

Despite the heat, I get the chills. *They can't do that! Can they?*

"Being a d-d-direct descendant provides certain skills, D-D-Darya will know all about that, don't you DayDay?" His voice makes my hair stand on end. He gives her a wink and I try to block him out. Lilly has caught his interest. "So Lilly, you are one L-Lovely Lilly Lady."

"Go away Raphaël!" I snap, which is a mistake because now his attention has turned to me.

"Ela, Ela, Ela, you really d-d-don't have a sense of humor, do you? Is it b-because your grandma raised you?"

The sound of my heart pounds in my ears. My hand flies out to his nose. He loses his balance and falls over with a heavy thud with a shocked expression on his face. *What am I doing?* "I… I'm… I'm sorry. I didn't mean to…"

Raphaël gets up, dusting himself off. Instead of anger, loathing, or even a hint of fear, I see a look of respect. It takes me off guard.

"I'm so excited about what they will change in our curriculum!" Darya whispers and she peeks at me from the corners of her eyes defensively. "The military does have the latest technologies and research."

"Yes, in exchange they want you to sell your soul," I say and focus on a thread on the hem of my sleeve. Darya sighs and rubs her temples.

"They can be our highway to success." She looks at me as if she's trying to bore this message through my skull.

"Or suicide," I mumble into my hands. A tinge of fear sits in my chest. *Will I lose her over this?*

After two stressful hours, which on my behalf could have lasted days, it's my turn. My body trembles and I try to swallow.

"You have to let me go now," Darya says. "I'll be right here."

I take a deep breath before I release her hand and reach for the door handle.

It opens before I touch it and a Dog with a notepad and glasses appears -dressed in his uniform with an insignia which shows off his rank. His black hair is graying around the temples and wrinkles line his forehead and eyes. My scalp itches as if there are a million electric currents tickling it.

"Come in… yes, come in, Ms. Elara Waywater," he says from the other side of his notepad. He closes the door behind me. My heart jumps at the sound. The Dog strides over to his chair and scrutinizes me. "Oh my, you look absolutely dreadful… Are you feeling under the weather?"

His face is sincere and without waiting for an answer, he says, "Let me get you something to drink!"

He walks to a corner where some pitchers and cups are stored. My eyes follow his every move like a duck eyeing a wolf.

"I'm afraid it's warm water. The military doesn't even send ice cubes this way." He laughs and winks at me as if I'm in on a joke as he gives me the cup. "Come on, drink."

I stare at him as I drink, unaware of the liquid entering my mouth. A tingling sensation starts on my scalp. Distracted, I scratch behind my ear.

"My name is Second Lieutenant Michael Winchester. Let me tell you what we have planned for today. There are three parts to this evaluation. Don't take it too seriously, we don't." My eyes flutter to his insignia. My scalp continues to itch, but I don't want to scratch my head. *So that's what it stands for. How did this idiot make the Second Lieutenant?* Something flickers in his friendly gaze, but it fades so fast I decide that I imagined it. I blink at him.

"It's all standard procedure. Part one is I ask you a few questions and you answer as honestly as possible. Part two is with Mrs. Applegarth. She'll guide you through the practical part, if you get that far, anyway. Corporal Baël conducts part three, he will asses your stomach… but you will get to that when you get to that."

My ears ring at the name as my heart sinks. I take a sharp breath and swallow with difficulty.

"First part one, he?"

Remembering Baël's shark-like smile makes my body tense, and I have to ease my grip on the cup before it breaks. I clench my jaw and give him a nod.

"Ms. Waywater, sweety, this won't do," he says fatherly. My scalp continues to itch. "I can loosen you up with a clever technique." He grabs something from inside his uniform. For a moment, I panic. Ready for anything. What he draws out is a picture, and he hands it to me. The black-and-white photograph shows a little girl in a spotted dress, and dark ribbons in her hair hugging a huge stuffed toy horse. I glance at Winchester, who is positively glowing. "Isn't she a darling? She is going to turn four this winter. Isn't she the most gorgeous creature you've encountered in your life? I know she's the prettiest thing I've ever seen. Do you see that horse? I bought it for her last birthday and she loves it so much! My prettiest little girl, my little Terra!"

What's happening? "She is very pretty, mister… Winchester… Sir," I say, forced. *What does he want from me?*

He doesn't deflate by my subdued response and beams at the picture, mumbling sweet words under his breath. If I wasn't so tense, I would have found this hysterical. Nevertheless, I loosen up a bit.

The Dog places the photograph back into a pocket in his uniform and watches me, not unkindly. "So, let's proceed, shall we?" He smiles at me before he puts on a serious face. He conjures up a stack of documents from under his desk and drops it on the surface with a thud. "Cause this will require some time." I am surprised by the enormous pile of paperwork, but he already skips ahead muttering to himself.

"Yeah… 21… hm… great. Alright, listen up, I'm gonna ask you a series of questions, and I expect honest answers. No need to worry, there ain't no right or wrong response. I want you to give me a number from 0 to 5 for each question. Zero means you disagree, while five means you can relate. Clear? Now let's get started."

"You have an insatiable thirst for knowledge and an unwavering desire to enhance your skills. "

"Uh… four," I say.

"You possess the stamina to handle multiple tasks simultaneously," he says and keeps his eyes on the documents.

"Three." *What do these answers mean to him?*

"You carry out your duties with utmost seriousness."

"0," I say.

The Second Lieutenant looks up sharply. "We are going downhill, aren't we? Didn't I say you have to be honest? Try again." He repeats the question.

I sit in silence for a while, listening to the crows outside. My fingers clench. "Four."

"Very good. Be warned, I know when you are lying!" He winks at me. I believe him.

"You require stringent regulations."

"Two." *I hate when people tell me what to do.*

"The military presents a favorable career prospect for you."

"Zero."

"You would make a valuable contribution to the army,"

"One…Two." *I could help the wounded as a nurse.*

The Dog lets his pen hover over the paper for a second before he writes it down. "You excel in a collaborative setting."

"Four."

"You possess the ability to coach a team of your own."

"Two." *There is no way I'm getting a positive score on this test.*

And the questions go on and on, page after page… Am I a leader? Am I honest? Can I work under less-than-desirable conditions? I slip into a dull state. The tickling on my scalp continues. It's actually relaxing. I'm not thinking anymore, just droning up the numbers.

"Have you encountered any traumatic experiences in your life?"

Dad is sitting on the couch. He's reading a book as the fire in the hearth has died down to a pleasant glow. He has put his arm around me as I try to keep up with the speed he is reading. It's a story about a man on a boat, traveling somewhere cold. Mom is in the kitchen and you can hear the noises of pots and pans. The room smells like dinner and my tummy rumbles. Suddenly, people outside scream and Dad lets me go. He walks to the window to see what is going on outside. Then the window shatters as something comes flying into the room.

"Zero," I say firmly.

Is that so? The whisper in my head makes me jump and peek up at the Dog, but he looks at his forms. Unaware of any strange voices, my overwhelmed mind has conjured up. *It must be my own conscience.* My heartbeat searches for its normal rhythm.

"You refer to the military personnel as…"

"Dogs," I say without thinking. *Shit!*

My eyes snap wide open, and my face tingles with fear. The Dog leans back in his chair and massages his temples while he studies me with no trace of emotion. My heart thuds so hard in my chest, I think it wants to make a run for it and leave me behind. I don't blame it. My fingernails dig into my palms. *No way I can stare him down so I won't even try.* Nothing happens. I'm afraid to move, not wanting to give him a reason to lunge at me or hit me. *Will he punish me for this?*

He stays silent while the temperature of the room falls and I get goosebumps on my bare arms. Outside, there are noises of people leaving. Tension builds and silence lasts about as long as I can bear. He sighs. "Congratulations, you have completed the first part," he states. With wide eyes, I stand up, but his face is not unkind. He stands up to open a door that I haven't noticed before. It strikes me how tall and tough he looks. My legs are as heavy as lead, and my eyes are on the floor.

Mrs. Applegarth looks up when I walk in. A breeze of cold air catches me by surprise. Her garment, stitched with red, distinguishes her from the Second Lieutenant's uniform. Others are already in the sunlit room and I walk to an empty desk. I recognize Trent and Raphaël, but there is a girl with a short blond bob who I don't know.

"Elara," I say to the new girl. Barely audible.

"Thalassa," she says with a weak smile.

I sit down, cross my ankles, and put my clammy hands in my lap. Raphaël catches my gaze. His face is solemn.

"There will be no frivolity in this session. You need to assimilate what I am about to teach you. Moreover, discussions concerning the contents of this course to anyone outside of this class is forbidden until you receive your scores." Her tone is strict, but the way her mouth rounds the words reminds me of Gran. "If you do, rest assured there will be repercussions." She looks at Raphaël as she says this, who looks impressed.

"Thalassa is a third-year student but has exhibited tremendous proficiency in her studies. However, you are all beginners in this art, so I don't expect it to be a problem," Mrs. Applegarth says with a slight smile. She clears her throat. "We shall commence with a overview of history, a subject with which you are likely already acquainted."

Mrs. Applegarth walks up and down the room as she speaks, "When Goddess Quatahna left this world, she took the gift of Aquakinesis with her. However, some people today still have this gift." *Are these the tainted Gran told me about?*

"Now I will share something very controversial." She pauses and I don't know if it's for dramatic effect. It works either way. "The Leader Suprema has been in pursuit of recruits with such a talent for some time. Today we shall determine if you possess the gift as your forebears did. This skill is most valuable to a healer, granting you the power to alleviate pain, mend wounds, cure the ill, and even extract poison." My eyes grow big as she walks to the blackboard with her hands on the small of her back. *Is this a joke?*

"Anyone here already attempted this?" The only sound in response is the humming of electric light. She folds her arms while looking at us, eyebrows raised. After two seconds, she goes on. "Kindly fetch a container from the table behind me, and form pairs."

Thalassa is the first to collect her bowl. Raphaël and Trent follow her lead and I bring up the rear with little enthusiasm -it's filled to the brim with water. Thalassa and I team up and we huddle together at a desk. Thalassa's eyes shine with excitement. She leans in and whispers, "I've read about this in the First Men's texts!"

On the blackboard, Mrs. Applegarth writes.

The Cork

"Officer Winchester has identified your aptitude for mastering this skill. The following exercise aims to teach you the fundamentals of the Aquakinesis technique."

I feel adrift at sea and want to ask how, but I swallow away my questions.

"Perceive the water as an extension of yourself and not as a separate substance. It has its own spirit and reacts to yours. To discern any movement, a cork is put into each of your bowls. Once it has stilled, close your eyes and attune to the water in front of you."

My curiosity gets the better of me as I look around. Raphaël leans away from his bowl with folded arms. His narrowed eyes are fixed on Mrs. Applegarth, who smiles at him. "I can understand your reluctance, Mr. Sosa, but rest assured that the gift is not Tainted in any way," Mrs. Applegarth says. Raphaël inhales while he studies her -he must decide he believes her because his shoulders relax. Then he does as he is told. He closes his eyes and his brow furrows in concentration.

Mrs. Applegarth nods at me and looks pointedly at my bowl. I close my eyes and do as I'm told. "Clear your mind, sense its energy, and merge it with yours. Envision it in your mind's eye. There is a link between you and the liquid. Feel its smoothness, its cool healing properties. Now try to replicate those sensations within yourself. As you have authorities over your own energies, so do you control water."

Something clicks in my brain and my eyes shoot open. *The Tainted. They stole something from the Gods. They want to know if we are Tainted.* I could burst into song. As long as I don't show any signs of the Gift I'm safe.

"Induce a gentle current in the bowl. Use your mind's eye. If it helps, motion your hand the way in your desired direction. Sense it's increasing strength, always accelerating. Grasp onto this sensation, open your eyes, and remain in control." My cork floats exactly where it was before.

Next to me, Thalassa gasps and I glance at her unmoved cork and wonder why she's so excited. Her eyes focus on Raphaël. Raphaël, who has not only moved the cork, but commands a miniature water spout. He stares at his own work with raised eyebrows. The spout is beautiful as it glides over the surface. It's mesmerizing. "Impressive, b-b-but what's the p-practical use of this? Can we summon water spouts in the heat of b-battle?" He asks his gaze curious.

"An excellent question. The Laws of Nature come into play when working with Aquakinesis." She writes the first three words on the blackboard. "Nothing arises from nothing. Floating a cork for a minute may only demand a limited amount of energy, but manipulating large amounts of water or healing a person from a serious injury requires a substantially larger effort."

Raphaël nods in understanding and mutters. "So, this m-means we can't go around using these abilities r-recklessly without conse-quences."

"Correct." The door opens and a tall man with immaculate blond hair and an impeccable uniform steps inside. My insides freeze as I recognize him.

"Ah! Hello! What a wonderful day this is, hmmm?" I see a glimmer of recognition in his eyes when he sees me. He smiles broadly and sits down on Mrs. Applegarth's chair. "Don't mind me, I'll be sitting here." It's like the floor gives way from underneath me. My fingers flex and extend smoothly as I check if I still control my own body.

Mrs. Applegarth continues, but the corners of her mouth are strained. "Thank you for your assistance, Corporal Baël. Class, remember what I taught you and you can commence."

My hand hovers over the water and instantly the fluttering sensation takes hold. I peek up and meet the intense blue eyes of Baël. His gaze makes my breath catch in my throat.

Thalassa conjures a storm in her bowl and the water sloshes angrily over the sides. Proudly, she smiles at Mrs. Applegarth, who nods at her with a smile. "Well done."

Trent's water is as still as the surface of a mirror, while his brow furrowing in concentration, yet nothing happens. He drops his hand and sighs. With a disappointed look on his face, he shrugs his shoulders.

"I guess I just don't have the right lineage."

Mrs. Applegarth puts her hand on his shoulder and says, "It's alright Trent, this doesn't make you any less of an asset. There are other ways you can contribute."

Trent nods with that same disappointment. Corporal Baël hasn't let his eyes stray from me and goosebumps crawl over my body and the hair on my neck stand on end. But the water doesn't move and I thank Quatahna. *Breathe, one, two, three, breathe*, and I make a fist. The water is just as still as Trent's and I smile. The sun shines a brighter and the birds sing a little louder. My gaze is fixed on the door.

"Thank you both for t-" Mrs. Applegarth starts.

"I think Missy has a case of *cold* feet," Corporal Baël's interrupts her. "I've seen her work the water and quiet impressively at that."

"Wha- n-no I haven't," I stutter.

"I'm very sure you did," he purrs, and his eyes glint dangerously. All I want to do is wipe the disgusting smile off his face. "You gave me such a beautiful taste of it. Don't tell me you've forgotten about our wonderful meeting."

It wasn't him who made the room freeze.

"Mr. Hunter, you are excused from further testing. Miss Waywater, kindly remain here," Mrs. Applegarth says. I would give anything to switch places with Trent, who leaves with his head bowed. My hand still hovers over the bowl while I stare at it in violent desperation. *Don't work, let it be a fluke.* Steam starts to swirl up and angry tears sting my eyes. Little bubbles rise to the surface until the water boils fiercely. I grind my teeth to hold back a wail. *I'm Tainted.*

Corporal Baël leads me to the last evaluation. The room smells strongly of bleach... It's as if I swallowed a clamor of nervous crabs, all scuttling about in the pit of my stomach. Being alone with him in a closed space is the last thing I want. But there's no escape. He orders me to sit down. The metal chair chinks as I sit with my face towards the wall. It's cold. The room has no windows, one electric light hangs from the ceiling. A bead of sweat crawls down my spine. *What will he do to me? Hurt me? Grope me with his long fingers?*

Baël puts little stickers on my bare skin and at every one, a small electrical sensation stirs and goosebumps rise. His eyes shine with delight at my body's reaction. He attaches the stickers over my heart, on my shoulders, and on my back. I am attached to a machine through wires. A steady soft beep comes from the machine when he pushes some buttons. He orders me, "Look!" before he disappears from my view. It's impossible to turn around. My control over my body has vanished. A mechanical click goes off behind me. The sound makes me wince. Pictures appear in front of me, each with their own metal click. They are projected one by one on the wall. Each is more gruesome than the last. Metallic clicks dominate the room. I fight the urge to scream.

* * *

Monster bounds through the street towards me and sniffs at all the weird smells that cling to my clothes. My legs tremble under me and hit the paved road. I hug him. His warm tongue licks my ears and pushes me over onto my backside. I expect to see Gran, instead. Mrs. Hydris walks up to me. My heart sinks. "Where's Gran?" I ask with a sharper tone than intended, but I need her right now.

"Honey, she had a nasty fall, so I said I'd meet you. It's nothing to worry about, dear," she adds and waves dismissively with her hand. My jaw clenches in worry.

Darya appears next to me. "How did you do?" she asks, her cheeks pink with excitement, but her cheer seeps out of her when she looks at my face. I ignore her question. If I start speaking now, I will fall apart.

"Let's get going then," Mrs. Hydris responds.

The oil lamps are aglow, but there is no one downstairs.

"She's in bed, honey," Mrs. Hydris says as she wanders into the kitchen. Darya sits down and regards me with something new in her eyes. While Monster lies down next to the stairs. His big sad eyes watch me and he puts his head between his paws.

I run up the staircase to Gran's bedroom, taking two stairs at a time. She wakes up as I open the door. "Elara, hello my darling, how are you?" she asks in a hoarse voice. She sits up in her bed. Her pajamas hang loosely over her chest and her cheeks have sunken in.

"Gran, why didn't you send someone to get me?" I sit down carefully next to her.

"Do you think I can't take care of myself?" She laughs, but a horrible cough ends her laughter. "I've fallen before, darling, and I'll do so again. These things happen." She gives me a hug, the strength she had before seems to have left her. "How was it? Did you learn anything of value?" she asks intently, looking at me while cupping my face in her hand, and just like that, I fall apart.

* * *

Dies Martis

A depressing atmosphere hangs around the college building. It oozes all the way into the town. After class, I walk outside with some classmates. It smells slightly sweet but pungent. Miriam and Darya discuss the assignment we have to finish next week. Both are clueless about our new gifts, and it feels like there is a glass wall between us.

"They are killing us with all the work they give us," Darya complains.

"Maybe they prefer us dying from homework than the war," Miriam says softly.

Darya pretends not to hear and turns to me. "So, when are you finally going to start with my assignment?" Her joke doesn't break the tension. We exit the grounds and some of us cross the road.

Darya's gasp stops me in my tracks. I spin towards her. She stares at something behind me and I follow her gaze. Four tanks roll slowly our way, -metal glints in the sunlight.

Chapter 7

"So, you got rough with Mr. Sosa's kid," Gran says as she fills my plate for dinner.

"How do you know already?" I ask with a mouth full of cod cake.

"Because it's my business to know, and you shouldn't let him provoke you that easily. You can be such a hothead. Try to allow things like this to slide off you next time."

"Raph's a-"

"I don't care what you think of that boy or what he did. Now it's become an issue and Raphaël will answer to his father. Please take it easy on him." Gran sighs.

"Anyway, hurry up and eat. I'll be late for my meeting with the Foxes if you dawdle."

Nowadays, people stay predominantly indoors. Blue-gray uniforms stain Main Road. They stalk the street, with eyes no one can evade. Behind the counter of the bakery, I sit with my nose buried in my anatomy book, ignoring the rare passerby. There is great satisfaction in being able to study. Without it, I would feel quite lost and unsure of how to pass the hours. The only thing that breaks my focus is when I rub a cloth over the already shiny surface. "If there's time to lean, you have time to clean," Gran always says. The citrus of the cleaning liquid overpowers that of bread and, for the record, the shop is immaculate. She would be proud, but for now, she's staying in bed.

"Hello, my dear Elara," Mrs. Hydris coos when she walks in. "Your face mirrors the weather outside. Won't you smile for me to make my day a little sunnier?"

I lift the corners of my mouth and she smiles at me. "There we go. It makes all the difference in the world." She puts down her big basket of apples we use for our apple pies.

"What can I do you for?"

"A loaf if you will, darling, the one with sunflower seeds. And a pie, of course."

I take the dough and put it in the oven for it to warm up. She looks at me and her eyebrows crumple in sympathy. I hate it. "Is Nuriël still upstairs?"

"Yes." I turn my face upwards as if my gaze could penetrate the ceiling into her room. Mrs. Hydris waddles to the stair door.

"I'll find my way up, sweetheart."

Last night, Gran shouted for my parents in her sleep. Silence returns to the bakery. I pet Monster on the head and he thumps his tail onto the floor. He looks up at me with his big brown eyes.

Dizzle falls down from the heavens. The few people outside disappear into their homes. Monster leaves my side and parks his butt at the entrance of the shop. He gazes out of the glass door like he is waiting for someone.

A Dog passes the window. She peers inside and waves at Monster, who pants at her. The light rain turns into a steady pour. I listen to the sound of thousands of drops hitting the dirt. Streets turn into mud, pools appear in the potholes in the road.

Darya, appearing in the doorway, soaked and shivering, is greeted by Monster, who thumps his tail against the floor. She wraps her arms around him and gives him a firm squeeze. He isn't deterred by her wet clothes. "Who is a good boy?"

He looks at me with a questioning face.

Then she turns to me. "How's business?" She takes off her dripping coat and hangs it next to the door.

"Slow." I yawn and stretch, proving my point. "I'm finally getting my studying done."

"Mrs. Storm will be so proud. Mother wanted me to swing by. We're out of bread."

I stand up. "Yeah, sure, same order as always?"

She places herself on my stool and scans over the open pages. Monster settles his head on her lap. "Did you know that they're saying she has up and left?"

I stay quiet as I prepare her bread.

"We had a refugee at the door today who came from Laodicae. Apparently, there is fighting there..."

That's not even a three-day walk from here.

I shove the second loaf into the oven. "Why?"

Darya shrugs. "Didn't ask."

Gran is in bed and the war is on our doorstep. For the umpteenth time, I wonder if the one has something to do with the other. *They are ruining a perfectly good town and for what? What are they doing here?* Monster pads back to his blanket and curls up on it. As I clear out another drawer to clean, my eye falls on a folded piece of paper I missed earlier, and unfold it.

Join the resistance!

The same words I read before. *Gran kept this one. Did she want their help as a means to get away? Or did she fall ill before she could? I would love to show the Dogs they don't own us.*

I fold it back up and pocket it. I will ask about this tonight.

Night falls early. The rain continues. Water leaks through the ceiling and I place a metal pan under the leakage in my bedroom. Monster leads me to Gran, who's reading a book in the light of a little oil lamp.

"How was business?" Her voice is hoarse. She lays it on her bedside table.

"Slow."

She smiles at me. "Well, at least you got your studying done. I should be able to work again tomorrow."

I hold her hand in mine and she squeezes it. "Are you sure?" I ask.

"Of course!" she says, and stifles a cough. "I am not made of porcelain!"

I give her the piece of paper as I sit on the bed. "Gran... I found something..."

"Where did you get this?" She inspects it through her reading glasses, her green eyes darken.

"In one of the cabinets-"

She crumples up the note and puts it back in my hand. "Be a doll and burn it, won't you? What do you think will happen if a Dog finds it?" She adds the last sentence when she sees my face as she strokes my cheek.

I can barely contain my eagerness. "Of course... Do you know where to find them?"

She drops her arm and looks at me with a grimace. "I wouldn't if I could."

"Being in the resistance could mean doing something good for people." *And with the Military already butting in on our daily life, it's increasingly tempting.*

"I will hear no more of this." She cuts me off in a kind tone, but I know when to quit.

Dies Donaris

The sound of a sudden crack pulls me out of my focus and the water I was practicing with splashes over my desk. I curse out loud. Long shadows litter my room. Birds outside are silent. I hear it again. A dry snap that silences all the other noise. It's a shot! *Someone is shooting!*

I jump up and peer out of my window. The street is deserted. Afraid but curious, I sneak down the stairs. The planks are soft under my bare feet. Through the glass door, I see nothing. With the door open, the sound of shots grow louder. I close it behind me and focus on where it's coming from - the square. Immediately I run to it, my feet leaving prints in the cold mud.

As I get closer, the wind caries voices to me along with a mix of sulfur and charcoal. I sprint silently down towards the commotion, dodging pieces of wood and rocks, and keep low. I want to see what's going on. One part of the road is torn open as if a grenade has exploded there. I can't believe my eyes. *What devastation. Why didn't I hear this?*

The square is plunged into darkness. Deep shadows move along the walls. You would expect people to flee in terror, but there is none of that.

The shots cease. My heart beats in my throat and every nerve is telling me to run home. All the lights are off, but even in the absence of light, I can make out the Dogs in the square. They don't see me and point their guns at something outside my field of vision. Officer Winchester peers into the shadows. He holds his gun in front of him. There are more Dogs I do not know. *I should get out of here!*

A small girl's cries pierce the air on my left. The desire to help is greater than the one to stay safe and heedlessly I run to the source of the sound. A Dog shouts something behind me. A young girl with a white ribbon in her short brown hair clutches is visible in the moonlight. She holds her knees while she sobs. It's Daisy, the clothing store owner's kid. "Are you hurt?" I ask.

She doesn't seem to see or hear me and continues to cry. I crouch down to look her over. Her 'saviors' come running and a Dog shoves me out of the way and fusses over the girl.

"Hey!" I shout, powerless. *The Dogs shouldn't touch her.*

A hand lands gently yet firmly on my shoulder. The pressure makes my body tense in reflex. With a sharp inhale, I turn around. *Officer Winchester.* He smiles at me, but I move away reflexively.

"Thank you, Ms. Waywater, for your concern, but it's not safe here. Let me escort you home."

I step back to create more distance between us, but in doing so I also widen the space from the still crying Daisy. Without them, this wouldn't have happened. *You made this happen!*

"We got him," a short Dog reports to Officer Winchester, who nods while he keeps his eyes on me. I avert my gaze to find that Daisy is being looked over by one of them with a soothing voice. Angrily, I break into a run and hide in the shadows of the park. From the ruins of the temple, I see them fuss around. It is well after midnight before I return home exhausted. Feeling like a small child myself, longing for the safety of Gran's arms.

I toss and turn as my dreams are chaotic.

I am running through an endless alley, away from Dogs who are shooting at me. They don't show themselves, yet I know they are there. I'm terrified of that first bullet tear through my skin. I run and run, without ever getting anywhere.

Now, I am a Dog and break into an oddly familiar house. As I sprint upstairs, I see a woman. She is holding something and I shoot her. The bullet finds its mark. She turns around from the impact and drops an infant with a white ribbon in her hair. Her empty eyes stare at me. The baby cries.

I scream and wake up with a start. My heart races and sweat beads from my face. While I pant the nightmare away, I notice that the temperature in my bedroom is scalding. Monster leaps up on the bed and licks the sweats off me while he whines softly. He lays his heavy body down and the weight reassures me. His fur is soft under my fingers and his big brown eyes examine mine. Now that Gran is so sick, Monster seems to take over her care for me. I stare at the ceiling until I hear her bustle in the bakery. *I must have fallen back asleep.*

She's pale as she kneads the dough in silence. "Why was the door unlocked?" Gran asks in the way of a morning greeting.

"We never lock the door.."

She looks at me sternly. "It's high time we changed that. We will ask Zale to fortify it *and* the windows. Well! Don't just stand there!"

"I think he might still be asleep…"

She calms down a bit. "Oh. You are right. Forgive me." She takes me into a strong hug. I feel her strength from years of kneading bread and the scent of eucalyptus. She talks into my hair. "They shot Mr. Doldrum." We say nothing for a while.

***

Dies Veneris

There is no substitute for Mrs. Storm yet. The official reason for her absence is that she has left to visit her sick aunt somewhere in the countryside. No one buys it.

The weather has cleared up a little and I sing a working song from my stool. It is very early and only a few people have come in. Which is lucky for me, because I'm behind on making bread. The familiar smell is wonderful and I'm in high spirits. After several sleepless nights, slaving away in the bakery is a pleasant distraction. Hard work is good for one's spirit, Gran always says, and she's right. It seems that she has recovered from her illness, but she has to use a cane now for longer walks, as her hip gives her a lot of pain, and she tires quickly. Naturally, most of the work rests on my shoulders. Not that I mind.

The bells signal someone entering the shop as I place the hot bread into baskets with my oven mittens. I put on my most friendly face and turn around. A jolt goes through my body when Captain Hawkeye stands there in military uniform. He gives me a crooked smile and nods. "Morning, haven't seen you in a while," he says in his smooth voice.

I wait in silence and he sighs. "A lot has changed, hasn't it?"

"What can I get you?" I ask as my fingers fidget with the hem of my shirt.

"Five loaves of bread and two boxes of those tiny muffins," he responds. While gather his order, the hairs on the back of my neck rise up. He hesitates and then asks, "could I call on you sometime?" His tone is casual, as if he commented on the weather, but I freeze with the bag in my hand. "I would love to get an insider's view of the town," he continues, undisturbed. I study him -he looks unchanged while I feel like a heavy weight has my knees buckling all the time.

***

Dies Saturni

Darya, Lilly, and I make our way to the Lunchroom. The large windows let in the weak sunlight, which casts a somber light on the white tablecloths. Business is slow these days, only a few tables are occupied.

My heart sinks when a group of Dogs in high spirits talks animatedly over bowls of soup. Some of them drink beer. *Winchester*. With a jolt, I recognize Cas who sits beside him. *Not Cas, Captain Hawkeye.*

The waiter walks by and offers to refill their cups. He seems to be in on some of their inside jokes, laughing loudly and slapping them on the backs. *5 years ago we came to this city, naive, thinking we could run away from war forever and build a new home.*

"Shall we go somewhere else?" I ask.

Darya wants to stay. She glances uncomfortably at me as if I'm about to do something embarrassing. I have been staring at them a second too long.

"So, ladies, what may I serve you today?" The waiter asks.

When we all go for the soup and he disappears in the kitchen as the Dogs erupt in laughter. Officer Winchester has told a funny joke and Captain Hawkeye throws his head back, roaring. *One, two, three, breathe.* Without the uniforms, they could have been any Lunchroom guests. Lilly chats away about the graduation party, but I can't focus. First, my heart beats too fast. *One, two, three, breathe.* Then my vision narrows and all I can see are men laughing at the table. My scalp begins to itch. Finally I've had enough, so I stand up. My chair screeches on the tile floor and walk right out of the establishment. The heavy door falls shut behind me with a bang.

Outside, the birds sing and the air is a lot clearer. My lungs fill up with fresh air. I lean against the wall of a shop and let myself sink to the ground. Absent-minded, I scratch my head.

"Care for a smoke?" I look up in alarm. Winchester stands before me.

"Smoking is bad for your health," I say foolishly.

He holds a cigarette out for me, which I decline. "Yeah, so is stress." Even if I wanted to, I wouldn't accept anything from a Dog. He lights it and takes a long drag while he rubs his temples. "You were one of many victims of the Assault of Brudahr, weren't you, Ms. Waywater? I can imagine that makes it hard to trust the military."

How did he know? What else does he know?

He inhales from his cigarette and exhales the smoke out slowly, as if in thought and says, "I imagine you think we are oblivious. People put on a fake smile or try to kiss our ass for special treatment? We're only here to help and besides, it's nice to have a place where the host is-"

"Why did you come here?" I ask, done with his monologue. From behind the window, Darya peaks outside, her blue eyes betray worry. Before Officer Winchester extends his arm to me he throws away his cigarette. "C'mon, let's head back inside before your friends get antsy."

But I ignore his outstretched hand and rise from the ground on my own. Together, we walk to the entrance of the Lunchroom, Winchester a few steps ahead. The girls stare at me as I retake my seat, but are smart enough not to ask questions.

* * *

Gran has fallen ill again, she complains about the cold, while it's sweltering hot inside her room. Worry makes me frown. She is very weak. And lies in bed like a collapsed oak, buried under a thick maroon cover. The realization that she could die never seriously crossed my mind.*Is this what stress is doing to her?* I ask myself for the thousandth time as I open the window to let in some fresh air. The scent of fall enters the dark bedroom.

"How are things going downstairs?" she asks in a hoarse voice.

"Darya is doing her best." We both laugh, but the fragile sound of her chuckle frightens me. Gingerly, I sit down on her bed.

"I will be up and running in a jiffy, dear," she reassures me, but her apple-pie cheeks have gone soft. Concern is etched in her face. "Am

I asking too much of you?"

"No! Of course not!"

She smiles, followed by a coughing fit. "Could you be a sweetheart... and fetch me something to drink?"

Happy with this easy task, I jump up to get her a glass of cold water. She's sleeping when I return, so I place it on her bedside table. I chew on my cheek as I make the call Gran would have protested.

The doctor arrives and I wake her. "Dear, you look absolutely dreadful," she jokes, her eyes dull. As expected, she protests and sits up in her bed when she sees the doctor standing outside her room. "You needn't have bothered, I am already getting better!"

I let myself out, and he shuts the door behind him with a soft click.

Downstairs, Darya is covered in flour. Sweat has formed on her brow, trying to knead the dough and failing miserably. There is a parcel wrapped in tin foil on the counter. I linger on the stairs, watching her work as I regain my composure.

"My mom wanted to give this to you," she says, gesturing at the foil -it emits the smell of Mrs. Ballard's amazing cooking. But I don't have an appetite.

"Thank her for us," I tell her as I put it in a cupboard.

"How is she?" Darya whispers as if Gran can hear her.

"I don't understand. One minute she improves and the other she gets worse. The doctor will know what to do." We go sit in front of the bakery for quite some time, watching the rare passersby. Somewhere in our street, the wireless plays a song.

In this wild world, where everything rearranges its shape.

Our love stands strong, unaltered, like stars in their eternal tape.

It's a mad world, but that's alright,

My darling, my love, my heart's forever in your sight.

The comforting smell of baked bread wafts out of the store.

"Will you take over... if she... you know." Silence grows. The little bakery with its smells and its old furniture is what I adore, however, I am not studying nursing to work as a baker for the rest of my life. *Besides, I can't run it by myself. But do I still have the freedom to choose?*

To keep my hands busy, I stroke Monster's back, and he glances at me with sad puppy eyes. "I don't know."

Darya puts her arm around me and I cry.

Dies Solaris

The doctor gave Gran medicine, a few suspicious looking pills that she has to take three times a day. She has made it out of bed and we eat my special cream cake to celebrate. I assumed a weight would lift off my shoulders when the preparations for escaping were almost complete, but I cry into my pillow that night. The thought of missing all that we have built here tears through me like a knife.

Work in the shop continues but people buy only what is strictly necessary. Despite the factory being open for longer shifts, but the laborers are paid less. Rumor has it some of them have already been drafted. On the street, men and women wander around aimlessly. Gran is careful and is not spending a lot of money herself. We'll need it on the road.

* * *

Dies Donaris

I walk home after class, but before I reach the bakery, I spot Captain Hawkeye. He's not wearing his uniform. Instead, he walks in a suit that is clearly not machine made and must have been expensive. He sees me and there are no shops I can flee into, and turning back will be suspicious.

I'm trapped.

"Good afternoon, Ms. Waywater. How are you? I hope you're doing well today." He smiles at me and his eyes shine.

My automatic pilot kicks in. "Fine, thank you, Captain. How are you?"

"I was wondering if you might have some time to show me around Eden?" He falls into step with me and I accelerate like my heartbeat with my eyes on the door of the bakery. *Oh no. I didn't expect him to still keep me to it.* He keeps up with my pace without any effort.

"Now? I just got off from college and now I'm going home."

I can feel him watch me. "Of course, I understand if you're busy. If you have some free time, I would appreciate it if you could give me a tour."

He holds the door open and I'm painfully aware of his presence near mine. "Gran probably needs me," I say again as I walk in. His cologne is intoxicating and being this close to him flusters me.

"Hello dear, how were your classes?" she asks, but when the Captain steps inside after me and she halts.

"Nice to officially make your acquaintance. My name is Captain Castiël Hawkeye. Can I call you Gran? Everybody here seems to." Then he holds his hand for her and she shakes it. I draw breath, noticing the tension that immediately builds.

"You may not. I believe that Mrs. D'Archard would be more suitable in this situation." Gran's voice is raspy compared to his silky timbre.

But the Captain is not thrown off that easily. "Naturally, Mrs. D'Archard. I was hoping to get your permission to have your granddaughter show me around town? I'm interested in learning more about the local community and culture and I thought she would be a great guide. Of course, I understand if you have any concerns or reservations."

Please say no, please say no, please say no. Tell him I have to work, or clean or anything!

"Pleased to make your acquaintance," she answers with a smile I don't recognize- it makes me uneasy. "I'm sure Elara would be delighted to show you around our humble place."

If she could only read my thoughts.

"You have my word, Mrs. D'Archard. Have a pleasant evening."

Before he steers me away from the bakery I glance back at her. Gran gives me a solemn nod.

The outside air is still and eyes watch from every window. My adrenaline has kicked in and my pace is fast. His long legs easily keep up with me. "So... what have you been up to?" he asks.

"Study, baking, the usual." *Breathe!*

"Elara, please slow down. We have at least an hour or two until it gets dark." He blocks my way, and I am forced to stop. "Elara, I want to assure you I have no ill intentions." He sighs. "If I had known this would be so unsettling for you, I wouldn't have suggested it. Would it be possible to put our differences aside for a couple of hours and enjoy each other's company?"

His eyes plead and I take a deep breath. "I- I can try to."

He smiles, relieved. That smile, with those lips, it's distracting. He offers his arm. I pretend not to see it. "So, how are things going for you?" he asks.

"Well- it has been odd to have a new professor so close to the exams. Though I have to admit, Mrs. Applegarth is knowledgeable. You- you knew about her?" I ask with a sideways glance as we make our way down the quiet road.

"Yes, I handled her paperwork. I'm glad to hear y- that the class finds her competent. She was nervous to be allocated here." He smiles as he recalls it. "It was a big change for her coming from the Capital and teaching in such a... different setting."

My heart relaxes a bit. It's so easy talking to him, especially when he's not wearing his uniform. "How are you liking Eden thus far?"

"I love it! I had never seen the ocean before and most locals have been very welcoming," he says, giving me the same side wards glance.

A few people who are walking by shoot glances at us and I feel exposed. "You've never been to the ocean?" I ask.

"No… my family is originally from Kafernaüm, I was raised with mountains and little rivers. Not vast oceans and beaches… " Kafernaüm is a month's journey as the crow flies. On foot, I remember, it took Gran and me several.

"I decided what I want to show you," I say.

"Are you going to tell me?"

I smile, and he squints at me playfully. A cyclist passes us as we stroll towards the park. "You've been here, of course," I say. He nods. "Did you know in this very place, the First Men built their temple? You'll see the ruins in a minute."

We walk down a gravel path to the center of the deserted park, right there. If you don't know it's there, you won't spot it. The floor which is spread a few yards across is made of mosaic. There is still a stump left of what used to be a pillar and the wall. Finally we're at the right spot and I point at the left corner of the image. "Can you see the ocean with the dolphins? That's when they came over. Over here, in the middle, they arrive on land and start building and planting crops-" Little people are busy with pots, food, and cattle. "-and here on the right side they honor Quatahna." Men are standing by the sea, holding water over their heads. There is even one who appears to be dancing with it. *Powers that should only belong in legends.*

Captain Hawkeye stands in awe of Eden's treasure. "This town still worships her?"

"Most do, especially the descendants of the First People, like my friend Darya, Ms. Balard I, mean. Their ancestors could control the water, just like-" He turns to me and my breath catches in my throat. "You?" he asks.

A breeze plays with a stray lock of my hair and I desperately want to steer the subject away from me. "How did you end up here?"

He puts his hands in the pockets of his jacket and looks away. "I was drafted in Kafernaüm when I was 15," he says.

"How did you feel? About being drafted, I mean," I ask, barely audible. The question is too intrusive, too venerable, but I have to know.

His gaze lingers on the mosaic. "It was a different life. The capital, the training—it changes you. It gave me so much in comparison to what I otherwise would be my life. I would be married to my sweetheart and become a farmer, just like my father and his father before him, but instead, I've risen in the ranks and gained more control over my own future than I ever thought possible. It has been a challenging journey, but the end justifies the means," he says, the last part more to himself than to me and exhales. *Is that true? And who decides on the right ending?* "How do you feel about going?" he asks.

I take a deep breath and expel it slowly. "It's complicated," I admit, my eyes meeting his. I weigh my words carefully. "My gift could help so many people, but I never thought I would leave Eden. It has its own rhythm, its own heartbeat and I have grown fond of it." *And I would never willingly work for the military.*

"Home has a way of leaving its mark on us," he says. His body is too close for comfort. *And still, you force me to flee. Again.*

"Is Kafernaüm similar to Eden?" I ask and turn away. Despite having gone through it, my memories of that period are non-existent.

He stares pensively into the distance. "It's different but the same, when I was younger I would have told you the people are differ from town to town. But they are actually very alike and very predictable, even if they don't see it themselves."

I raise my eyebrows when he says that.

"A mother anywhere in this land will die protecting her child. A young boy will make certain mistakes over and over again. While a young girl who is expected to serve will always in some period in her life defy authority. However, here in Eden, I have noticed you lot are very hospitable, once you let your guard down." His eyes look into mine and he lifts up one corner of his mouth. I giggle. *What is up with this giggling!?*

"I want to show you something else," I say and lead him away from the park. I'm not sure why, but it's suddenly important. "There is a little spot that is beautiful this time of day."

"Alright, I'm curious." he says and I guide him to the beach where our shoes sink into the sand. The golden sun hangs just above the horizon covering everything in an orange glow.

"Darya and I discovered this place when we were younger. I don't think a lot of people ever found it. Or bother make the effort, 'cause it's not easy and you can only get there during low tide, or over the rocks." Waves crash on the shoreline as if it's happy to see me.

"So you're quite the adventurous type?" He walks close to me and I'm drawn to him.

I chuckle at the memory. "Gran used to say we were a perfect example of two boys. When other girls tried on dresses and learned how to dance, Darya and I were climbing trees and hunting for hidden treasure."

This makes him laugh, and it fills me with a pleasant warmth. "Did you ever find the treasure?"

"Well, we did come across some interesting stuff," I say, excitedly. "Some ancient coins, a pipe, an old blade, and even a love letter." The last item leaves me uncomfortable, there is no way I want to discuss romantic feelings with him and I wonder why I brought it up.

"A blade?" he asks to my relief.

"Yeah, it must have belonged to the First Men, because the metal was still smooth as the day it was made."

"I would love to see it... analyze it. I have studied some their weaponry and their craft was amazing."

"Well... I'm afraid we lost it." *I don't want to give him an excuse for him to come to me again. Do I?*

We arrive at the familiar site and I guide him up the rocks. As I help him up on the last ledge, he comes dangerously close. His cologne- the warm scent of mint, lavender, and vanilla- is like a drug. With anyone else, this could have been a moment. Now I'm painfully aware I'm in a remote place, with a potentially dangerous soldier and nobody knows where I am, but when he gazes into my eyes and butterflies soar. I turn away from him, steadying my breath.

I point to a less secluded spot. "And then we sit there, it's the perfect place out of the wind and in the sun. Right here is the best view for the sunset."

The sea is restless today, powerful waves crash onto the shore. Water spray shines golden for a second before it falls. We stand and look out over the end of the world. I swear he's radiating heat,like a campfire, his warmth is pleasant, but I move away from him.

"Well, we never had sunsets such as this in Kafernaüm. I'll give you that." Hawkeye puts his arms on the small of his back as he admires the view. The glow of the sunset lights up his face and tinges his Onyx eyes with gold.

"Why not?"

"It's a mountain city, it grows dark early, and the sun disappears behind the mountains."

"That's sad..."

"Sad?" He looks at me. "No, not sad. Different... You have a-" He lifts up his hand to my face. His cologne overwhelms me. As soft as a breeze his hands touch my cheek as he strokes a loose hair away. My breath quickens. He retracts and doesn't move closer. Instead, he watches the sunset, first the yellow, then the fiery red and pink, and even splashes of orange and gold paint the sky. The early stars of the Hunter blink and the star Mintaka shines the brightest.

The tension has taken residence in my stomach. It makes me nauseous.

"Let's head back, your grandmother will skin me alive if I kept you out after dark."

After a painfully silent walk, we are back home. Stars peek through the night's canvas and light from the bakery lights up the street.

"It has been a pleasure, thank you. I hope she doesn't consider this too late." He glances through the window.

"Don't worry. Gran is glad I finally have a man to go out with." *Oh, gods no.*

He grins. "That is very kind of your Gran."

"Well… she is… you know…. kind." I'm looking at his lips. *What the hell am I doing!?* "You know… she wants me well off before she passes on." My heart pumps rapidly. *Stop talking!* Staring into his eyes is definitely *not* improving the situation. "Not that she is dying." *Shut up!* "You know how old people are…" *Alright, go ahead and shoot me.* "Yeah sorry, got to run. She'll probably need me for making bread."

The Captain watches me with humor. "At this hour?"

"Well.. bread never sleeps." *I did not just say that.*

"I hope you do." His eyes bore into mine with a crooked smile.

"Yes… thank you… you too." *You too!?*

He bends over to kiss the back of my hand and the electric current settles deep in my stomach. "Goodnight, Elara." My name sounds smooth on his lips.

"Goodnight, Captain!" I flee into the bakery.

The light in the stairwell is still on. Gran's knitting in her chair, when she hears me she looks up with an unfamiliar look in her eyes. "Well?"

I sit down near the fire. "I have no idea," I say as warmth glows on the back of my hand.

"Why dear?" The klick of knitting continues, but I have her full attention.

The flames warm my cold skin. "I started blabbering and I couldn't stop."

"He seems quite taken with you."

I turn my head to look at her with exasperation. "How do you know?"

"These walls are so thin sometimes." Her voice trails off.

"Gran! You eavesdropped?" I say admiringly, turning back to the fire. "That's... well... wow!"

"You should go out with him more often."

A surge of energy goes through my body. "No! I didn't want to go out with him now, and I don't want to see him again!" I turn around and stare incredulously at Gran.

"Befriending Captain Hawkeye might save your life one day," she says in a matter-of-fact tone. It's like I've never met this woman before.

Chapter 8

Darya and I wander into the square, chatting. "-and for the ceremony-" she stops mid-sentence and we stop in our tracks. Six Dogs with guns are shepherding three men, clothed in gray jumpsuits, in chains to a wall. Despite everything, they stand tall and proud.

Gran presses my head into her side, trying to block my view. Through her fingers, a person in a blue-gray uniform with brown hair and black boots. They are holding a big rifle in their hands. They are aiming at something that is hidden by Gran's skirt. Someone shouts. Gun's fire. Followed by a heartbreaking wail from a lone woman. A lumpy red streak covers the wall.

I try to blink the image away. But this time the memory doesn't fade and I can't bury my face in Gran's skirts.

Two prisoners I don't recognize. The third is Mr. Sosa, Raphaël's father. His gray sideburns are unkempt and his eyes are dull. The Dog Baël seems to be in charge. His straight posture and wide smile send chills down my spine. He shouts orders to the other Dogs. And my mouth grows dry. A woman cries and it echoes on the desolate square. *It's our people. YOU don't get to do that to OUR people.*

My heart beats way too fast and I start to hyperventilate. So I close my eyes. *One, two.. One. Two. Breathe. Breathe!! One. NO... One.* But when I open them, the scene is still there.

Terror is visible on the captive's faces, though none of them attempts to escape. Lines on the men's faces are deep. A small crowd has gathered and looks on from a distance. A woman cries audibly, her sobs piercing my heart. The others are shocked in silence by the display in front of us. A few men in the crowd give the Dogs murderous stares but don't dare take action.

Then I see the impeccably dressed blond Dog who is leading the men. "For your part in planning to blow up the military base in Eden, you are hereby convicted of high treason and sentenced to death by gunfire. Any last words?" Baël barks.

Tears well up in my eyes and I envision myself standing there, bound in metal, waiting for the inevitable end. *Is this the path for me?*

Silence fills the square, but for one man who goes as far as to spit at Baël's feet. The sun beats down on us as we all wait. *No, not if I can stop it.*

I set to charge. But a grip on my shoulder startles me. In a reflex, I lash out at the owner of the hand. Blue of the military uniform enters my vision and I aim for the throat. Except the Dog is stronger and more practiced than me. His grasp tightens, and he pushes me away from the scene. Then the rough wood scrapes against my skin. My body is pressed against the wall, my one arm pinned behind my back. The smell of timber penetrates my nose.

"No! No! No!" is all I manage, blinded by fear and rage.

"Take a deep breath… go on." His iron grip is inescapable, but terror feeds me and I fight. "Calm down! Stop fighting me!" A groan of exertion escapes him, and he pushes my arm upwards. Until my shoulder is a moment away from dislocating. "Elara, don't make me hurt you."

When I hear my name, I lose all my strength. And if the hands hadn't held on so tight, I might have collapsed. The face of my captor comes into view, and I recognize Captain Hawkeye's onyx eyes. Angry tears roll down my cheeks and shots ring in the air.

***

I sit in an unfamiliar room with Darya. She stares blankly into space, while tears trickle down her cheeks, but she doesn't wipe them away. The smell of chlorine hangs heavily in the air. When a door opens, my body jumps at the sudden noise. The adrenaline has not left my system yet. Lieutenant Winchester and Corporal Baël walk in with grim faces. Acid burns in my throat and my scalp tingles.

"Calm down Ms. Waywater, we are not here to hurt you," the Lieutenant says, his voice patronizing. "Hello, Ms. Ballard."

They proceed to take a seat opposite us -Baël's aura is as foul as ever and I lean backward in my chair. On the table stands a jug of water and Winchester fills four cups. Then he takes one for himself and sips, then pushes two of them to Darya and me.

"Awful, isn't it? Watching your countrymen, all proud and better men, be executed by monsters like us," Corporal Baël says. "You could ask Miss Hydris about monsters."

It's a trap. But my eyes grow wide when he mentions Lilly.

Lieutenant Winchester sighs and says, "Ms. Hydris was in your class, wasn't she? She disappeared last night, so her parents reported her missing. Unfortunately, we didn't find het until this morning."

Corporal Baël takes over. "The little lamb walked right inside our base, in fact. Strapped in an explosive a courtesy of your countrymen. A lamb to the slaughter and a martyr to their cause."

I gasp and sit up straight, my eyes on Lieutenant Winchester. "Please, tell me-"

He looks even graver. "We couldn't prevent the explosives from going off. There were six fatalities, and more injured -Ms. Hydris was one of them."

Beside me, Darya lets out a strangled sob. My fists clench and I shake my head. "No, Lilly is a sweet girl. She would never-" *Could it really be? Did Lilly blow herself up just to get to them?* Winchester lets Baël talk, who peers at me with his dead eyes. "What you saw were traitors to the Nation. Murderers."

I clench my jaw, ignoring the incessant itch on my scalp. *Don't you dare blame this on us.*

Winchester says, "Do you know why I am telling you this? The military's paramount objective is to ensure the safety and well-being of all. But you see it very differently, right, Elara?" He glances at Darya, who sobs in her chair.

Then it's Baël's voice that penetrates the air. "Look at your friend. She froze when she saw what was going to happen while you were about to assault me. You got the Captain pretty good, by the way, he sends his regards." After that, he sits back and smiles. "Ms. Waywater, are you aware that attacking military personnel is a serious offense. Assaulting a Captain while attempting to strike a Corporal is even worse."

Winchester leans forward. "Elara, you are a decent young woman and I believe losing a friend is enough punishment for today. But remember, this is the only free pass you will get."

Baël continues in his sleazy voice, "Ms. Waywater, we are intending to let Ms. Ballard go. You, we have to keep you here a little longer."

Darya sobs. Her tears have left black streaks on her cheeks.

"Darya?" I want to touch her, but she turns her head away from me and my hand falls between us.

"Ms. Ballard if you can come this way." Baël proceeds to open the door and holds it as she mechanically moves through it. Then he leads her away.

Before he looks at me again, Winchester scans through paper documents he brought with him. "We got your results back from the evaluation. They were very good. Normally we would ask you to volunteer for the army, but I have a feeling you are not going to comply with that. Read through it yourself." He hesitates a moment after he hands over the paperwork. "Elara, were you aware they were planning the attack?"

Slowly, I shake my head. *I would never use a friend as a bomb. Not even against you.*

"What is your knowledge of a local resistance?"

I shake my head again, this time looking at Officer Winchester. *Thank the Gods that nobody will tell me anything.* He snaps his files shut before he shoves his seat back. "Ok. Good enough for me."

That's not much of an interrogation.

"You'd be surprised."

My heart turns cold and I look at him. *Did I speak out loud?*

He folds his hands in front of his chin while he studies me. "We need people like you on our side,-"

People like me?

"-, your scores were superb. The grades for your classes are excellent and the teachers see great potential in you. A word of caution, we won't give up on you this easily. Private Boyle will drive you and Miss Ballard home."

* * *

Darya and I sit in the back of a black automobile. The luxurious leather of the seat is cold to the touch. We move fast and the engine clicks almost hypnotically. This is my first time in one of these contraptions, and despite myself, I'm in awe. Our chauffeur swerves the automobile over the road, trying to avoid all the potholes and cursing when he doesn't succeed. His red hair complements the brass handles of the interior.

Darya regains some color in her face as we drive away from the base. While she stares forward, she feels for my hand. We find each other and hold on tight. Her fingers are ice cold. Private Boyle takes a left into Darya's street and her house comes into view. Her mother sits on the doorstep while her father is standing in the doorway. When they see the vehicle approach, they rush toward it. The automobile stops and their daughter scrambles out into her parents' waiting arms. "Are you alright?" they ask.

"We're fine," Darya says while hugging them. "We're fine," she repeats and sobs. Private Boyle closes the car door behind her and taps his hat to Mr. Ballard. He turns the vehicle around and rides carefully back to Main Road. I make a choice. "Could you inform Captain Hawkeye I have found the blade?" I ask over the sound of the engine. Private Boyle looks at me questioningly through the rear-view mirror and nods. The promise of seeing him fills me with a treacherous joy.

* * *

Gran closes her eyes and sits there for a while, when I share it all with her. There is no shouting, no tears and no prayers. My mind jumps from one thought to the next, but a few of them make it out. I feel absolutely drained. To have something to do, I prepare dinner, which we don't eat. And the heat of the oven doesn't warm me.

"We need to go see Mrs. Hydris," I say from behind the uneaten meal, breaking the loaded silence. Initially, Gran refuses to intrude on her friend in this time of grief. But eventually she agrees and comes with me. No one understands the loss of a child like her.

The wind is chilly, but it doesn't bother me. With every step we take, I pray I was wrong, that Lilly somehow survived and was eating dinner with her parents. We move forward slowly. The shadows grow deeper. Gran struggles to keep up with me, and she pauses regularly. But as soon as the orchard comes into view, she straightens her back and leans less on her cane.

The door opens on the first knock, revealing Mrs. Hydris's pale face. Immediately, she falls into Gran's arms. She grieves in a way only a mother can for her daughter and I can't pretend it's not true anymore. Her sobs tear through my heart as sharp as a knife. My lip trembles and I dig my nails into my palms to keep from crying. Behind her, Lilly's father sits at an empty table and he rises. "Hello Elara, Nuriël, tea?" Without waiting for a response, he walks to the kitchen and busies himself. Mrs. Hydris' eyes still search for her. The room is too big. It emphasizes Lilly's absence.

When Gran and I take a seat, Mr. Hydris puts a steaming mug in front of us. Lilly's presence is still tangible in every fiber of the house. I remember her dancing at Mr. Sosa's bar with so much life.

Mr. Hydris takes a silver flask from his jacket and passes it along the table. The sound of alcohol falling into the cups fills the room. Mrs. Hydris gulps straight from the flask before passing it on. We sit in silence for a while. Next to the fireplace lies a large anatomy book with an unfinished essay on top of it. I gulp down the burning tea to counter the cramps that clench my throat. It's impossible to speak.

"What happened?" Gran whispers.

Mrs. Hydris holds her hands in front of her face. "We're not sure -we pieced together.. yesterday Lilly went out with Tennin in the Lunchroom after closing time. After a few beers, they strolled along the beach. When it got dark Tennin headed home, and she joined him. After dropping him off, she took the shortcut through the fields, instead of going the long way around which-" Mrs. Hydris' voice fades, her eyes seeing imeages we can't.

Then Mr. Hydris takes over with a monotone voice. "This Second

Lieutenant Winchester figure told us Mr. Sosa seized her. The other men must have come from Alvor. And they lured her to a shed. You know, the one that used to be a pig shed before Doldrum got himself shot?"

Mrs. Hydris wails at the thought of her little girl being kidnapped. "We assumed it was a late night with Tennin, so we never made anything of it when Lilly didn't come home!"

Gran pats her friend on the hand while a tear rolls from her cheek.

"In the morning, they strapped her into a vest and told her to walk into the military base. She must have been so scared!"

***

The funeral is, despite this controversial subject, a busy occasion. Since all the victims will be brought to rest at the same time, the whole town has shown up. I even spot a few people from Alvor. It's so crowded that guests stand outside the temple during the ceremony. There is a sense of hostility in the air. *Would it have been better to have separate funerals?* But the Priest insisted on an equal burial. For the relatives' sake, we join in, though I rather not be here.

The all-too-familiar blue-gray of the Dogs uniform patrols the surroundings, their eyes on high alert. Clearly afraid of retaliation of some sort. For the first time in my life, I am not sure who to fear most. Gran's words ring through my head. *There is nothing more dangerous than an angry crowd.* If something starts, I don't know how to get out. My body is tense.

Raphaël and his mother stand next to Lilly's parents. Everyone looks awful. Mrs. Sosa is pale and seems to be on the verge of fainting. Raphaël holds her up. His eyes trained on the mosaic patterns under his feet. They are clad in their normal attire out of respect for the

Hydris family; only they are dressed in the traditional blue.

Gran stands front and center of the mourning crowd in support of her old friend. She has refused to sit on the chair offered to her and leans heavily on her cane. Relatives of the convicted men will not get to speak. Mrs. Hydris talks about Lilly being a friend to everyone, a good daughter, with a thirst for life. Raphaël's trembling arms support his mother as Mrs. Hydris talks about her daughter. Though his eyes are red, he sheds no tears.

After the prayers, the crowd makes its way to the beach. I walk up to Raphaël. "Raphaël, I am so sorry."

He looks at me blankly and nods. When he opens his mouth, he shuts it again without saying a word. Behind me, Gran pays her respect to Mrs. Sosa.

"How will we get by without him?" she moans as Gran holds her hand. Raphaël's body shakes with his mother's sobs while he supports her on the last stretch. The men won't have an honorable way -they are to be pushed into the ocean on their boats and be left to the elements instead of returning to Quatahna. An arm hooks into mine. It's Darya. She rests her head on my shoulder as we move in the crowd. Like drops of water, insignificant in the mass.

On the beach, the bodies are placed in the funeral boat. Lilly's boat is closed off. I shiver at the thought of what is left of her under the thin veil. The boat is crafted of flimsy material, made to be broken with ease. It used to be a tradition that when the spouse died, the wife had to join him to the afterlife. To my relief, Mrs. Hydris doesn't get onto Lilly's boat, although it's her husband that keeps her on dry land. In the periphery of my vision, I see both Captain Hawkeye and Second Lieutenant Winchester touch their hearts and let their heads hang low. Gran holds on to me as we gaze at the sea. The waves are choppy and the stars are hidden by dark clouds.

We chant as Mr. and Mrs. Hydris guide their daughter into the ocean for her final voyage. I sing for them as much as they sing for Lilly. They push beyond the waves and when they are far out, they make a hole in the boat. The water surges into the small boat and claims it. Mr. Hydris helps his wife swim back and on the shore, and their extended family assist them on the beach. The priest chants in the old language as we say our goodbyes. Raphaël and his mother heave the boat into the water, but don't join Mr. Sosa on his last journey. My heart breaks as I watch Raphaël's deflated figure push his father into the sea.

* * *

Dies Donaris

The weird thing about life is it keeps flowing. Our study group makes our way to the Lunchroom. I wave at Tennin as we walk in and take a seat. His little sister, Siti, is helping out today. She passes a table full of men swaying her hips, trying to get their attention. But Captain Hawkeye ignores her as she walks by and I grin. When I realize Quatahna will punish me for this, I think, *Keep your thoughts pure as water.*

Miriam checks her curly updo in the window before she says, "Isn't that the Second Lieutenant? I'm going to say hello!"

Darya tries to grab her hand, but Miriam dodges her and saunters off. "Miriam, no!" *Great.*

The Dogs turn around as she points in our direction. I would be ready to die on-the-spot right there and then. Nothing happens, of course. *This is Quatahna's punishment. Breathe... I'm not in the mood for this... Breathe.* I look through the menu as the unwelcome guests join our table. The Lieutenant Dog greets me with a little nod before he sits down in an empty seat next to Darya. With force, I pull up the edges of my mouth into a smile. My heart accelerates.

"This lovely lady offered us another beer," Officer Winchester says, smiling at her. "So we thought the gentlemanly thing to do was to keep you girls company while we drink it." He beams and winks at her. Miriam must be oblivious to the fact he's married and has a kid, or she simply doesn't care. Four soldiers sit down at our table.

I tense as the Captain sits down at the head of the table. He gives me his half smile in greeting. I'm trapped, and every fiber of my body tells me to get out of here. My heart thumps loudly in my chest. Before it reaches full-on panic mode, Darya grabs my hand under the table and squeezes it. I breathe out and take my cup of tea in two hands.

"Hey guys," Darya greets the other two soldiers, and it takes me a second before I recognize Zale's brothers. "How are you?"

"We were relocated here now we're done in the Capital. A great coincidence that it was just before Solemnitatum. And Wade-" Seger throws his arm around his older brother. "-even got promoted to Lance Corporal!"

Wade shoves him away playfully and shows me his badge with pride. "Yes, and it means you have to show me some respect!" My classmates ooh and aah as desired. The two Dogs exchange a look and I look at Winchester. *How much death has he seen to move on from the execution so easily?*

Winchester is an easy talker and before long, he has everybody wrapped around his finger. Wade and Seger know all of his stories and they fill in the gaps or laugh loudly at his jokes. He tells us about his daughter who turns five soon, and how he will visit her in the near future. I just observe them while sipping my tea. *This encounter could have been worse.*

Darya takes a sip from her cup before she asks, "So, what's the Capitol like?"

"It's mind-blowing," Wade responds. "It's as if you're stepping into a whole other world. They have all the modern luxuries and the amount of *people* is overwhelming. They are everywhere, all the time, like an ant hill. And a lot of these people own automobiles. Sometimes there are so many of them driving around that they can't go anywhere because they are stuck behind other automobiles and they stand there waiting to get unstuck. It's marvelous!" Wade beams. Again I notice the two Dogs exchange glances, Darya sees it too.

"What are you fellas conspiring about?"

The Captain sits back relaxed and says, "The first time in the Capital may be impressive, but the 'ant hill' comes with many downsides. There is a lot of *noise* and filth. We like it much better here."

"There's significantly less trust in the big city," the Second Lieutenant adds, finishing his second glass of beer. "Everyone always locks their doors. And they're right to do so -things get stolen."

Seger puffs out his chest, "That is where the Privates come in. We help the local police when they are short-handed… In other news, El, I heard you went to the Solemnitatum with our little bro." He wears a grin that reminds me of a cat. "How was that?"

I nearly choke on my tea and my face betrays me by turning red. And of course, at this point, all other conversations stop. So everyone turns at me, making it worse. Luckily Siti has decided this is her cue to ask if anyone wants another drink, saving me from responding. *I promise Quatahna I'll never think badly about her again.* I turn down the next drink and decide its time to leave. I need to clear my head. I say my goodbyes and step outside into the fresh air. But the door doesn't fall shut behind me like I expect it to. The Captain has followed me outside and is standing behind me. "I wanted to pay my respects. I'm sorry what happened to your friend." He pauses and I smell his cologne. "Private Boyle reported that you found the First Men's blade. Would it be alright if I borrow it from you?"

"Oh right, yes I did." I take a deep breath and study his face. *It's unfair how gorgeous you are.*

An eruption of laughter comes from the Lunchroom and he looks back before he asks, "When could I drop by to see it?"

"How about I bring it over to you?" I say with my mind on Gran.

The Captain is taken aback. "Ah- of course. You can visit to the military base. How about tomorrow at 15:00 hours?"

* * *

Monster has already heard me coming as I turn into our street and trots towards me. I hug him and he pants into my ear and tries to lick it. Laughter escapes me while I push him away from me. "Ah! Momo, no, that's gross!" Then he storms into the bakery.

Gran is sweeping the floor. As I walk in she looks up. "A letter came in for you." A white envelope lies on the counter, bearing my name and the military stamp.

"It must be the from evaluation," I tell myself as much as I tell her.

Concern: Military Conscription

Dear Ms. Elara Ariël Waywater,

It has come to our attention that you are a citizen of great physical and mental capabilities, which are highly sought after in the service of the Nation. As such, we are pleased to inform you that you have been selected to participate in training in the Capitol, as ordered by the Leader Suprema.

We strongly advise you to comply with this order. As it is of utmost importance to the safety and security of our great Nation. Your participation will enable you to acquire valuable

skills and knowledge necessary to serve our country in times of need.

You are hereby instructed to report to the Town's hall at 05:30 on the 13th day of the fifth moon, where you will be collected and taken to the designated facility.

We appreciate your cooperation and look forward to your participation.

Attached to this letter is the list of items you may bring.

In Unity and Reverence,

Captain Castiël Hawkeye
In order of the Leader Suprema

My hands turn white as I grip the counter. I blink the tears away. A word escapes my lips which normally would call for a broom over the head from Gran. But she lets this one slide.

"That's in one moon."

"Breathe." Gran puts her hand on my back. "You will be alright. We continue as if everything is fine, keep a low profile, and then…" she trails off. *We run.*

Chapter 9

Dies Lovis

We sit outside the school, while we enjoy the warm rays of sunlight. It reminds me of the time before the military arrived. But I munch on my sandwich with little enthusiasm. I haven't slept all night and my thoughts keep returning to the First Men's blade in my bag.

"Did you get the letter?" I ask Darya, who is sitting on a bench next to me, dressed in her favourite pink outfit. Miriam shifts uncomfortably at the subject, but I don't care. Raphaël is pale and dark circles hang under his eyes. He pays the conversation no mind and stares into nothingness.

Darya's hair is beautifully done, but a few loose strands wave as she shakes her head. "It's a request. If you choose not to go, don't. Tell them you're responsible for Gran's care, or that you have to keep the bakery afloat. Tell her, Raph!" Darya stares at me and continues when Raphaël is clearly not backing her. "They won't force you, Elara. You realize that... right?"

I'm not sure if she is doubting her own words or if she's checking in with me, but then she regains her composure and rolls her eyes like we're being silly. We're told not to tell anyone about our new-found powers because not everyone shall react 'pleasantly' according to Mrs. Applegarth. But keeping this a secret from Darya has been eating away at me, although she appears casual about me staying after school. We discuss questions like "What does it entail? What would they do if we collectively refuse to show up?"

Raphaël tells us he will go. "I d-d-don't want to cause t-trouble for my m-mother."

"Raph! Where's your lunch?" Darya asks.

"I forgot t-t-to make it t-t-today… it's alright," he says. We all share him a piece of our food and tears well up in his eyes, but he hides them by casting them down.

Darya leans towards him and places a hand on his knee. "How is your mother?"

"She'll g-get there," he says in a tone like an anchor scraping on an ocean floor.

"What about you?" Miriam asks with a sad smile, her red curls gleam in the sunlight.

Raphaël sighs in response. "I'm alright, things have b-b-been hectic now that I have to get all m-m-my dad's affairs in order. His finances are a m-mess and it's been a nightmare trying to sort through it all, k-k-keep up with lectures, and run the bar."

Darya gives him a pat on the knee, but he doesn't even seem to notice.

* * *

The walk to the base takes longer than I anticipated. The commandeered building looks like a ghost from a different time now that they have built so many concrete buildings around it.

With the car, it took us no more than 10 minutes to reach Darya's street. Walking it takes me at least three times longer. My chest tenses as guards appear at the entry of the base. Their black guns carelessly hang from their shoulders when they ask me what I'm doing here. I state my name and business. They call for an escort and hold me there while eyeing my blade. *As if it would win against your guns.*

Apparently, you can't just walk into a military base and expect the Captain to open the door for you. I'm glad when I see Wade strolling my way and I wipe my sweaty palms on my pants.

"Hey, El! Fancy seeing you here." He turns to the guards. "I'll take it from here." They nod at him, and I follow Seger through the gates. As soon as we're out of earshot, he asks, "Why do you have an appointment with Hawkeye?"

"He wanted to see this blade Darya and I found," I say lamely.

He peeks at it. "That old thing? Why?"

"I have no idea." I don't tell him that this is my weapon of choice, and I hope to use it as leverage.

We arrive at a desk where Seger, sorry, Lance Corporal Boyle, is bent over a stack of documents. Behind him is a door with a little label on it 'Captain'. Without taking his eyes of his work Seger says, "You are late. He expected you 15 minutes ago."

I'm like a nine-year-old getting a lecture.

"The Captain is a busy man. It is unwise to keep him waiting. Take a seat. Perhaps you'll be so fortunate that he frees some time for you.

"Do you think he has time now?"

Lance Corporal Boyle inspects me before he answers. "The Captain has an appointment with the Second Lieutenant right now. I believe that takes precedence. Thank you, Private. You may go back to your station." Wade salutes his brother and, with a quick encouraging glance at me, he makes his way out. My seat is next to the closed office and I place my bag on my lap and feel like a kid waiting to get scolded by a teacher. As I'm there, several Dogs walk by. *What would Gran want me to do while I'm here?*

I observe my surroundings with a fresh pair of eyes. Despite Lilly's failed attempt to blow it up, the place is low on security. The door has no lock, and Lance Corporal Boyle isn't visibly equipped with a firearm. Two halls lead here, but the one I came through was unguarded and unlocked. The door opens with a snap and I jump. Winchester walks out, followed by a waft of cigarette smoke.

"Thanks again, Captain!" He spots me. "Heya Elara, how are you?"

"Fine. How are you, Sir?"

He winks at me. "Ah, I thought we were already on a first-name basis. Don't let all this make you nervous," he says as he motions around him. "We'll be seeing a lot more of each other soon." He claps me so hard on the shoulder that the chair legs shudder. "See you later, alligator!" He strides up to Wade but before I can eavesdrop the Captain is standing in the door frame asking me inside.

He walks me into his room. "I don't accept tardiness from my men, but I'll let you off the hook." His tone is playful.

"I brought the blade," I tell his back as I follow him into his office that might be bigger than the entire bakery. It smells like cigarettes mixed with his colone and I bite my lip. He goes to stand behind his desk, something that obviously comes naturally to him. He nods. "Straight into business, I see."

Looking over at us is a marble bust of the Leader Suprema. Her white hair and golden-trimmed uniform gleam in the electric light. Avoiding her gaze, I place the blade gently on his desk, careful not to knock over anything. He contemplates me for a few seconds before bending over the blade. "So this is the famous weapon. It's definitely a piece of art, but what indicates that this was the First Men's era?"

"The blade consists out of light metal and unusual gems, and around the hilt here-" I point out the decorations. "- there are ancient symbols."

He examines the hilt. "It could have been produced later, could it not? I mean, this piece could be made by any blacksmith."

I make an effort to not let his statement offend me. "No, this type of metal is extremely rare in this area. Our Priest says that it had to be brought along with them on their voyage. In our entire Nation, the earth might have enough to make a single spoon."

"So that makes this blade invaluable…" His words leave me uneasy. But he glances up with a crooked smile. "Don't worry, I will not confiscate it."

I need to stop being so predictable.

He picks up the weapon and holds it in a fighting position. "This is a beautiful piece of craftsmanship- it should be exhibited in a museum. The gems on the hilt alone- May I borrow it for a while? Just to study it some more," he asks, studying the hilt again.

I don't want him to keep it, but being in my debt could work to my advantage- even though I trust him as far as I can throw him. A part of me knows I will never see this blade again. My fingers have found a loose thread on my dress and I fidget with it. His black eyes seem friendly and I sigh heavily. "Alright, but I expect it to be returned without so much as a scratch, and you owe me." I fold my arms and study the important pieces of paper on the wall. They seem to be some kind of honorary distinctions.

He lays the blade on his desk before he puts his hands on the small of his back. "Of course. What would you require from me?"

Oh! That went easier than I thought. I move forward, placing my fingertips on his smooth desk. "You to answer any questions I ask honestly from now on," I say, sounding more dapper than I am. My gaze shifts to the bust behind him.

He has a twinkle in his eyes. "I can do that. I'll answer four of your questions. Honestly. What do you want to know?"

"Why four questions?" I say without thinking. He grins, as if we're playing a game and I'm losing.

"Because I chose to. Now you have three left."

I gasp at the unfairness of it, but refrain from giving him the satisfaction of starting a discussion. "Why did you approach me, during at the dance?"

He cocks his head sideways before he takes a deep breath, and says, "Not what I expected, but is that what you truly want to know?"

I panic, expecting him to go back on his word. "A second ago you said-!"

He waves at me to calm down."Fine, fine. We had intel that you and some others were refugees, and I needed to scope out the situation before we came in full force. For all I knew, Eden had all kinds of nasty traps made especially for us."

My arms drop at my side. "That's unfair. You purposefully infiltrated Eden while you knew we wanted no part in your- whatever it is you're doing. What is your end-game?"

He laughs. "You didn't need to waste your question on that. Everyone here could tell you. My end-game is to land my promotion to become Major and after that I'll work my way up to General."

"That's unfair." I whisper. Of course I knew he was a Dog, that he worked in favor of the Leader Suprema. Her bust looks smug behind her Captain. Yet, a part of me held onto the hope of his character.

He has a bemused expression on his face. "Unfair, huh? For you, or for me?"

"Well, for both of us. Especially for you, because you still owe me one answer and... I don't have one right now, but I'll have it later."

He smiles to himself. "I can live with that."

* * *

Dies Lovis

The bedroom is quiet except for Monsters' soft snores from somewhere near my feet. I trot to the shower and turn the water to cold to wake me up. Then I realize how the sun is already illuminating the house. *Shit! What is the time!? Why didn't Gran wake me?* I search the rooms only to find Gran napping on the chair behind the counter. *Oh well.. they are not going to kick me out because I've missed a lecture.*

Monster watches me, sitting with his chest puffed in front of the door. "You want to go for a walk, don't you, Momo?" I whisper as I cuddle his head. "Let's go." He barks a cheerful reply and wags his tail. Although Gran shifts, she doesn't wake.

Through the overgrown paths, we wander inland. When I'm such a distance away, I can barely see the bakery. Someone moves left of me, and my heart freezes. I've never met anyone up here… and with everything going on.

"Don't look so startled!" Second Lieutenant Winchester walks toward me with a cigarette between his fingers. He takes a puff and blows a few circles. "It's a free place to walk."

"Are you… showing off?" I mock him.

He smiles proudly and falls into pace with me. Trailing his scent of tobacco behind him. "You caught me. I learned how to do that today. You have to admit that it is cool."

"I'm sure your wife and daughter will be thoroughly impressed." I search the surroundings, but there is no one else here. Monster walks up to the Second Lieutenant and pants at him, waiting for some pets.

"Yeah… They aren't aware of my habit…"

"How can you keep something like that a secret?"

With a hand, he rubs his temple. "To be fair… I haven't been home in a while, and it helps me alleviate stress. Stress is a concept I believe you're well acquainted with."

"Stress from what?" I ask, hoping he'll open up to me. *Maybe it could help us get out of here.*

He winks at me. "Wouldn't you like to know?"

For a while, we walk without speaking, but I wish he would go away. A little cloud drifts through the sky as the birds grow louder.

"Miss Waywater, I want to tell you about what the military has accomplished. Although I fear it might fall on deaf ears. You hate me for being a.. a… Dog. Yet we made many positive changes in the Nation." He gives me a crooked smile. "Still, you condemn us."

I open my mouth to interject.

"Don't bother denying it."

I exhale and cross my arms. "Alright, I won't deny it. And why should you care?"

"War is dreadful, but occasionally, those in higher positions find it as a necessary evil." His voice dies away. It is treason to speak ill of the military. Perhaps he did it on purpose to draw me out, but it grabbed my attention, nonetheless. The Second Lieutenant's silence is brooding, leaving me wondering if he will speak again. "Elara, we have given so much effort to restore peace in war-torn areas. Supply food and water to the needy and uphold the law. We are not all the same. Besides a few… unbridled types, a lot of good people work in the military. But I'm here to help." Another long pause follows. All we hear is the rustle of leaves and chirping of birds. He bends over to pet Monster on the head. *The law only serves the ones who make them.*

"You don't know half the grief most of us have suffered, still you condemn us. As if you're better than every soldier, solely because we believe in a cause bigger than ourselves."

This provokes a reaction- it hurts like a needle pushed a too far under my fingernails. "Oh, please! Spare me the self-righteous speech! A few good deeds don't absolve you of all the harm the military has caused." Tears well up in my eyes and I wipe them away angrily. "And me personally? If *you* weren't here, Lilly would still be alive. Gran would be fine, and I… my parents…" My words get stuck in my throat. The Second Lieutenant glances at me with pity. This only sets me off more.

I rage on. "I bet you sleep soundly at night, knowing you've ruined countless lives in the name of your precious law. You're no different from the rest of your military pals—blinded by your own delusions of grandeur!" The world falls silent after my last word. Monster looks up at me with frightened eyes and my anger breaks.

"Elara, I know about your parents."

I stare at him. "Wha- how..?"

"It might be a good to talk with your grandmother about who they actually were."

My throat constricts. "What? Why? What are you talking about? I don't understand what you mean?" Monster wines softly.

He smiles sadly. "It's not my place to tell you. And even if I did, why would you believe a Dog?"

I have to refrain myself from smacking that smug face. He taps his fingers to his head as a farewell gesture and walks down the grassy slope, taking the smell of cigarettes with him.

My eyes search for something to help me. When nothing comes, I sit down on the ground and sob. Monster sits next to me and I hold on to him. It's like everything the Second Lieutenant said just pulled the carpet right out underneath me. *The army is evil, war is horrible, and soldiers are your enemy. Then why are some of them warm and kind? What gives them the power to control everyone?* I breathe in Monster's scent and it calms me. *If it wasn't for them, my parents and Lilly would still be alive. They're evil.*

"She wouldn't have died if they stayed away." Somewhere deep inside, I know my reasoning is flawed. I push that notion far away.

* * *

Gran helps a customer as I enter the bakery, and I wait until the store is empty. "Why aren't you in-"

"Gran, who were my parents?"

Gran tenses up and avoids my gaze. "What? Whatever do you mean?"

"A Dog told me to ask you about mother and father. How could they know something about them that I don't?"

She still refuses to meet my eyes as she turns around. "Let me make you some tea." She's stalling, but I don't know why. With the kettle on, she limps to the front door, flips the 'open' sign, and locks it. We stand in the empty store and she gazes at me.

"Elara, sweetheart, why are you talking to Dogs?" I cross my arms and when she sees I'm not going to answer, she folds. "Don't think I've been maliciously keeping this from you. After your parents... I needed to keep you safe. That includes protecting you from certain... people." Sadness weighs on her every word. Even now, I won't be able to share everything with you. Some things I remain a mystery to me too. I need you to believe me when I say I am trying to tell you enough." She clears her throat and takes a sip of her tea to steady herself. "Your parents...they were brave, Elara," Gran says with force. "Your father was well known in the community as a doctor. Outside of it, people started perceiving him as something vile and dangerous. Their help was rejected more and more, because they were..." Her green eyes search for mine.

"Tainted. Gran, I already know all this."

She regards me for a while before looking into her cup. Then the lines on her face deepen. "They believed what they were doing was right. They- we... had faith that a group that we called the Party could save the Nation from its downfall when it became clear that Carpathia was gaining popularity."

I want to interrupt her, but she holds up her hand to silence me. Her lips tremble and her knuckles are white around her teacup. "Can you trust that I am telling you all I can?" I sigh and nod.

"They got caught up in the 'Cause', but in the end, they were forced into hiding because their lives, and by extension yours, was in danger. They left you with me and went undercover with the help of the Party- which later became the resistance. We all thought they were safe. Until they weren't. Priestess Carpathia made it her personal mission to eradicate those like your father." We drink the rest of the tea in silence. It's apparent Gran is still afraid of something, there will be no use pushing her. Before I go to bed, she says, "I thought we would be safe here in Eden. That after all this, she would leave us alone. I thought they couldn't find us here. Foolish people are rising up because they took her relaxing the rule for weakness, but they are wrong. And now there's not only war at the border, but within our reach." Her voice has grown small and fragile. I walk to her and give her a big hug.

"We will make it through, Gran."

"My dearest," she says as she hugs me back tightly. "The Priestess became the Leader Suprema, and she eradicated the elementalists in the Great Cleansing." Eels writhe in my stomach, I feel sick. *And the Dogs know. What made father so special? They have known for a while. Why haven't they come for me? But they have, haven't they.*

Chapter 10

Dies Veneris

With swift movements, Mrs. Applegarth sketches an odd shape on the blackboard. "This is a water molecule. It compromises two water atoms and one oxygen atom."

She draws two little H's and a single O in the strange-looking figure. Raphaël, Thalassa, and I are trapped in the classroom for our 'extracurricular activities'. These specialized classes have been a little ray of light in these stressful times. Through the windows of the building, we see dark clouds cover the sky. It has been days since we've laid eyes on the sun.

"Certain individuals possess a unique sensitivity to the pulse of the molecules and the ability to manipulate their energy. The reasons behind this skill's selectivity remain a mystery. Regarded as formidable, their potential is seen as invaluable in aiding the Nation's endeavors while ensuring their talents don't fall into the wrong hands."

I sit back and cross my arms in front of my chest, worried.

Raphaël raises one eyebrow skeptically. "Mrs. Applegarth, you're saying the m-m-military teaches us these techniques and by doing so doesn't trust us by d-default? Then why teach us?"

She intertwines her fingers. "Very perceptive. The army needs people with this gift to help win the war and aid the wounded.

But manipulating molecules isn't without risk, the energy has to come from somewhere. Please read Chapter 1 about the basics of Aquakinesis and because Raphaël was the only one making significant progress, we will continue to practice with the cork."

We gather the containers and Raphaël bursts with enthusiasm as he tries to explain what happened to him. "It's l-l-like the water came alive! It was like… there were t-t-tiny ants drumming to the same beat all over my hands."

Despite myself, I'm curious to get going.

Equally enthusiastic is Thalassa. She's the first back at her table. "Alright! Let's go!" She holds her hand over the bowl, closes her eyes, and smiles. I focus on the water and my breathing. But I'm squeamish. I don't fancy the sensation of bugs marching up my arm.

"I heard a soldier say they look for the right genes. Obviously, it means people with a good family line," Thalassa whispers, disturbing my focus. "My grandfather told me we are descendants of the First Men." She pokes herself in the chest with her thumb. She beams at Raphaël as if they're kindred spirits. Rain starts to tap on the window and I shut my eyes to increase my focus. My fingers turn cold, hovering over the stubborn liquid. "I'm n-not so sure if that-" Raphaël says and then falls silent. The tapping of rain on the windows grows louder.

"Hey! You got it!" Raphaël exclaims, and I open my eyes. But the water in my bowl is as smooth as a mirror. Thalassa has moved her cork, albeit not as impressive as Raphaël's waterspout. Her water sloshes left to right in the bowl, nearly tipping it over. Through my lashes, I glance up at Mrs. Applegarth. "Congratulations, Thalassa!" She exclaims and smiles. Then she turns her focus back to the books she's reading. Thalassa looks at my bowl, and she tries to temper her enthusiasm.

"Good blood?" I ask bitterly. "What are we, breeding stock? So because your ancestors married into the right family, you're better than me?" My frustration's misplaced, but I'm weary and on edge. Thalassa averts her eyes, clearly hurt by my response.

"I think what Th-Th-Thalassa meant is sometimes family history can give p-p-people advantages or opportunities. It d-doesn't define who we are as individuals," he says, his tone calm and composed like someone who is experienced in settling arguments. I'm in no mood to be shushed and I roll my eyes.

"Elara, I didn't mean to sound superior. I thought it was interesting what my grandfather said… I agree with Raphaël. It's not about being better than anyone else."

Raphaël nods in agreement. "It's our actions and choices that d-define us, not our family l-l-lineage."

"I- I guess I'm on edge with everything going on. I'm sorry." I take a deep breath and all the fight flow out of me.

Thalassa smiles reassuringly. "I understand. Don't worry, you'll get there."

"We'll continue with theory. In-" Mrs. Applegarth tells the three of us and I breathe a sigh of relief. Since the discovery of my gift, I have been torn between mastering the skill my father had to aid people, or purposefully floundering to be as uninteresting to the military as possible. Studying theory gives me room to keep my abilities veiled, if not hidden.

"Aww!" Thalassa exclaims. "I was really hoping to try to improve my Aquakinesis today."

Mrs. Applegarth smiles but continues undisturbed. "In Chapter 2 of your book, it states that in addition to their own energy, the First Men also used Crystals and plants as a crutch to do amazing things. The first Crystal I want to introduce to you is Quartz. I'll give you all your personal piece which are yours to take home. Quartz is a type of silicium dioxide-" She draws three circles on the board and connects them with a line. "-and is known as the 'Mother of all Crystals'. This specific one is proven to amplify your power, aid concentration, and help balance your stamina." She places a white, semi-see through, rectangular stone on the table. I pick it up and the Quartz is cool, and the surface is smooth under my fingertips. When I hand the crystal over to Thalassa, she inhales sharply. "I-, I can sense it!"

"Very good Thalassa, does anyone else feel it?"

I shake my head.

Mrs. Applegarth continues with her lesson and explains about various types of Quartz and we pass them around as if this is a version of 'show and tell'. There is Jaspis, which protects you from absorbing negative energies and expels neurotoxins from your body. The red stone is heavy and warm in my hand. It emits a little tingling, as if a small electric current runs through it. Next up is Obsius, which clears scars and removes certain poisons. The Crystal resembles a black piece of broken glass and sparkles as I turn it over.

"Interesting, but nothing is happening," I say and look around at my classmates.

Raphaël smiles at me. "Don't worry, Elara. It's n-not like we're expected to master it all in one day."

We spend the lesson learning how to use and care for Quartz, and I lose myself in the mystical world of energies and mythical powers.

* * *

Dies Saturni

With a deep breath, I push open the door of Gran's bedroom. Inside, it's dark inside and I squint to see the bundle of blankets go up and down.

"Gran?" I call softly and she stirs.

"Elara dear?" At that, I walk into her room and smell a sour scent I haven't noticed before. I crack open a window to let some fresh air in.

"Good morning, Gran?" She sits up and tries to flatten her hair and I realize I have never been awake before her. "How did you sleep?"

"I had the most peculiar dream last night. It was about Hera and Eros," she tells me sleepily. I pause. She rarely volunteers to talk about my parents. "They were both calling out to me, asking me to pay them a visit soon…" A sad smile appears on her face before she comes to herself. "Could you do me a favor and make me some tea, darling?"

I walk slowly downstairs, over the squeaking staircase, and wonder if there is a deeper meaning to her dream. The thought alone makes me shiver. Monster barks happily as he sees me and I let him lick my nose, his wagging tail sweeps over the floor as I scratch the back of his head. With big eyes, he studies me as though he knows there is something different about me.

In the kitchen, the sound of water pouring in the kettle is soothing and the familiar flutter comes through my hands. My fingers itch to manipulate it, the hairs in my neck stand on end and I feel like I'm being watched. There is a knock at the front-door and Monster barks in anticipation.

Outside, in the sun, Captain Hawkeye stands in dark pants and a white dress shirt, awkwardly holding a bouquet. I unlock the door. *Huh, Gran got the door fortified.*

"Good morning?" I say as I open it and try to keep Monster at bay. He motions the flowers toward me, uncomfortably. "Hello Elara, I heard your grandmother was ill and I- I wanted to check in, see how she's doing."

"Thank you…" I accept the flowers and inhale the sweet scent. *This is what Gran wants.* "Would you like some tea?"

"That would be nice," he says and his shoulders relax. He rubs Monster's head before he follows me inside.

"It's incredibly kind of you to have such an interest in Gran," I say as I search the cupboards for a vase. Monster thumps his back leg against the wooden floor as Hawkeye finds the spot behind his ear.

He clears his throat. "Yes, is there anything I can do to h-?" he starts, but Monster distracts him when he whines for more attention. He drops to his knees and scratches Monster's back. It is strange to hear phrases like 'Who's a good boy' from someone like him. And I have to remind myself that he is the enemy here. I put on the water for the tea and arrange the flowers. "He likes you."

Hawkeye beams at him. "Do you now?"

I place the vase on the counter, and the kettle whistles softly in the kitchen. "Let me see to that tea." I walk into the back and decide to make rose tea, something I learned is effective against infections and aids heart disease. *My extracurriculars have proven useful already.*

When Hawkeye can't see me, I take a few deep breaths before I return. The Captain has regained his composure. "Do you know what's ailing your grandmother?"

Sadly, I shake my head. "Would you mind if I bring her tea first?"

He reassures me it's fine and I bring Gran her steaming mug. Gran regards me with a doubtful expression when she smells it. The curtains allow for a ray of sunlight, but the lamp on her bedside table is on. I sit on the foot board.

"It's good for you," I press.

She blows it before taking a sip and her mouth wrinkles in distaste. "Do we have customers?" she asks me and sits up a little straighter in her bed.

"Captain Hawkeye is downstairs," I tell her in a hushed voice, "he brought flowers for you."

Her face hardens, and she tells me to go back down and 'tend to his needs'.

I quickly fix my hair, put on some makeup and then head down with an elevated heartbeat. Walking down the last steps, I study him. He is still sitting at the counter with Monster's drooling head on his lap and stroking his cheeks.

"Where did you get him from?" he asks me.

"I actually found him when I was little. He was hurt and alone in the hills and I couldn't leave him." I pet Monster's big head lovingly and he pants happily.

"You had a healer's heart even back then." He smiles at me before he steers the conversation to Gran. Her health, her friends, her weekly poker games. He laughs his brilliant laugh. "She sounds like quite the character!" and her position in the town board until our tea cups are empty and I offer him a second cup, which he graciously accepts. When I return with two steaming mugs of tea, I ask, "How are things going with my blade?"

"Yes, I have been keeping it a tad long now, haven't I?" He scratches his chin. "I will return it to you soon."

"About that. You still owe me, and I have questions." I sit on the opposite side of the counter.

Captain Hawkeye sits up a little straighter and his eyes grow alert. "Of course. I will tell you what I can." The wording he uses reminds me of Gran.

"How much do you know about A- the special skills we're being taught?" I observe him from over my teacup and focus on any hint that might betray how he feels about this- his poker face is better than Gran's. "I am aware you've had Aquakinesis lessons, yes."

My pulse beats fast, but I don't want him to know I'm nervous. I blow in my cup to buy myself some time. "Are there any more... skills like...?"

"You ask that because of your run-in with Corporal Baël?" His face keeps his carefully crafted neutral expression. My heart skips a beat and I hold on to my mug of tea as if it's an anchor and without it, I might lose control. "You knew?"

Outside, the wind howls through the street and the windows clatter up stairs. The tension in the bakery grows and a little muscle on his jawline jumps. "Of course, I make it my business to know," he says gruffly. We stay silent. More questions pop into my head, yet I sense I have to tread carefully.

"Yes, I am asking because of the… run in."

He studies me. "Yes, Corporal Baël possesses the ability to… control the movements of other people." He keeps staring at me intently and I avert my eyes. My cup still anchors me, but it's getting harder to play calm. "What about you?" I glance through my lashes at him.

"What about me?"

A grin plays on his lips and I realize he's not going to give up information without me directly asking for it. "Can you control water, or… control people's movements?"

"No."

"What other skills are there?"

"I am not at liberty to say."

I sense I'm out of questions, but push through. "What are yours?"

"I apologize you had the encounter with Corporal Baël like you did. It must have been frightening," he says, his eyes compassionate while ignoring my question.

I wonder for a moment if I should repeat myself, but I accept defeat and deflate."It was." The room gets colder. "I felt so powerless. I was lucky someone called him away…" I remember the frozen floor and the voice who called him. His footsteps crunching over the ice. He had to talk to someone.. he was summoned by… "You. He was there and somehow you knew. Did you send him after me?" Before I know it, I'm on my feet. Monster jumps up in alarm. "He followed me into the lady's room and… and… you sent him?" Tears brim in my eyes.

"No, of course not. But I was made aware that he was harassing a local and I sent someone to fetch him. Corporal Baël has been known to… be a bit of a lose canon." He does his best to appear unphased, but his face is tense. "I feel responsible for what happened. I should have never let him out of my sight. I apologize." His Onyx eyes are soft when he looks at me. A part of me wants to throw him out of my house, another part of me sees the regret on his face and wants to forgive him. But either way, if I want our relationship intact, I need to control my emotions. Pushing him away will displease Gran, and falling out of his good grace could hurt us. "Can we talk about something else?" Monster lies back down with a sigh.

"Of course," he says carefully. He must have seen the emotions flicker over my face, because he watches me for any sign of.. what exactly? I sit back down and take a sip of cold tea.

"Have you ever had the opportunity to venture outside of Eden before?" We talk about the towns around Eden, the differences in religion, and my heart slows down. Hawkeye seems fascinated by the legends and traditions we have. He asks a lot of questions about the ceremonies and lore. So many that I can't even answer them all and I'm reduced to 'that's just how it's done'.

"What about you?" I ask him.

He smiles at me with his crooked smile. "I was raised without the teaching of the Gods. It wasn't until I grew in ranks in the Military that I discovered places like these still revered them."

While I let that sink in, I place my elbows on the counter, my tea cup still in hand. He's close to me now and I smell his vanilla-lavender colone. "People in the Capitol don't worship the Gods?"

"Well, we know about them. They are more like children's stories." He finishes his tea.

I try to wrap my head around it. I've never been such a strong believer as, for example, Darya, not even believing a little goes beyond me. Our talk is disturbed when the door opens and a customer walks in. I feel like a teenager who just got busted doing something naughty. Captain Hawkeye thanks me politely for the tea. "See you, Blue Angel."

I bite my lip as I watch him leave.

After the customer, I run back upstairs to Gran, who's reading in bed. The book has a red cover with golden letters which reflect the sunlight creeping into her room. Fresh air cleared out the unpleasant smells in the room and the temperature is pleasant.

"How did it go, my dear?" she asks and puts her book on the bedside table. There is more color on her cheeks, but there are still bags under her eyes. I recount the questions he asked and what I told him. She listens silently but fidgets with the sheets. When I'm done recounting, I circle back to the thing that has been nagging me.

"Gran, I also wanted to talk to you about something else." For a moment, I'm unsure how to broach the subject. "I'm really enjoying the Aquakenisis lessons that we're being taught." I blurt out.

Gran sighs while she looks at her book on the nightstand. I wonder if she either misunderstood me or thinks I've lost my mind. Her body looks even more fragile than it did before. "Your father possessed the same talent."

"Father could heal with water?" I sit up straight in surprise.

"That, and many more things." She smiles sadly. "Your father was a gifted elementalist and his ability to heal was second to none. He was a deeply compassionate man, which is why his skills were so remarkable." Gran puts her fingers under my chin, her bottom lip trembles, and proudly she says, "You remind me so much of him." Those words make me swell with pride and a smile appears on my face. She lets her hand drop and closes her eyes. We sit in silence for so long, I begin to wonder if she has fallen asleep.

"The Leader Suprema has made the decision to cease the persecution of the Tainted and to recruit them instead, although I wouldn't trust she won't reverse her course, and the Dogs follow her every whim. Ensure your bag is packed. We might have to make arrangements at a moment's notice."

The conversation has tired her, so I go downstairs to clean the empty bakery. There are no people on the street. Eden seems abandoned. Dust floats through the cool air as my mind races. I sit down on the bottom of the stairs and Monster gets up and trots towards me, his warm body comforting my deflated state. Absentmindedly, I stroke his fur as I attempt to make sense of this new world I have been blind to.

The military knows I have the gift. They also know everything about me, my name, where we live, and what I look like. With Gran being as sick as she is, I can't imagine being on the run. How would we earn money on the road?

My body is flooded with adrenaline and I can no longer sit still. Monster's gaze follows me as I stand up and pace up and down the bakery. Which is, in fairness, not that big to walk around in. Floorboards squeak under my weight.

Would people take us in? How far could Gran travel when she gets better? Was Captain Hawkeye here to check if we were still here? Are they already keeping tabs on me?

My eyes dart toward the vase with the colorful flowers. My breathing is going too fast as I keep pacing up and down the bakery. The sensation of being watched overwhelms me. I glance outside, searching for any signs of surveillance. The street is deserted. *Am I being paranoid?* Monster lets out a small whine to let me know I am scaring him. *A black humongous furry companion is a dead give away and who could take care of him? Could the resistance help me disappear?* I crouch down before I jump up again. Feverishly, I search the cabinets.

Porcelain clinks as I go through the contents. *Maybe they left another card somewhere.*

There is nothing in the bread baskets, nor in the glass pots of sugar or cinnamon. There is nothing in the bin but trash and I'm so desperate I even try to find something in the ashes of the oven with the poker. Defeated, I sit back down on the stairs. "Do you know where to find the resistance?" I ask Monster, and he pants happily, licking his lips. "Right. Food." I push myself up again and prepare his food. *How would I ever get food for him on the road?*

I place Monster's bowl on the floor and sit down next to it. This is the scene Darya walks in on. She pushes the door open. "Elara?" Her voice is loud in the empty bakery. Her beige coat hangs closely around her. "Are you doing ok?"

I wipe my eyes dry. Without waiting for an answer, she sits down next to me and we look at the empty bakery together.

"Darya?"

"Hmm?"

"I need help."

Chapter 11

We sit at the counter while Monster sleeps in a corner. Darya listens, her eyes wide when I tell her about the Tainted, the Leader Suprema, the visit we had from the resistance, and the encounter with Baël. She doesn't flinch when I talk about my new abilities or the fact that this is what they are teaching me after school. But her jaw clenches as I share my horrific encounter with Baël. She sighs heavily and sets her priorities straight. "So, what's our course of action?"

Shadows grow longer as I start to sketch out the idea that has formed in my head, and Darya helps me with a few kinks. She offers to inquire if people in neighboring villages are willing to help, but she has no clue if there is a resistance member between them. After a lengthy discussion, we come up with something solid and I can relax. It has grown dark and in the bakery, except for Monster's snores.

"Do you think I will ever see you again?" Darya asks quietly, her blond hair hanging limply at the side of her face. Without answering, I give her a big hug. "You're an idiot," she says. "you know that? How could you keep that creep a secret? I would have…"

"You could have done nothing and apparently the Captain was aware of it from the beginning." We break loose and I study her. "We were outmaneuvered. But this time we're one step ahead."

Darya shudders and glances out of the window. "Imagine how difficult it would be to control someone like that," she voices my thoughts. "Do you think Hawkeye has something on him?"

* * *

In the evening, I enter Gran's room with a cup of tea that I boiled with just my hands. It gives me a sense of pride to be able to do this now. And because I don't know what's ails her, I have put everything in it. It is lucky we have most of the ingredients in the bakery. The Rosa, Lavare, Bellis Perennis, and Echinacea make it fragrant and for good measure, I let the Quartz well in it for a minute to boost the healing properties.

Gran comments about the odd aroma, but I urge her to drink it and she obliges. We talk about my studies and I treasure each second of it. When she falls asleep, I spend the night sitting by the window gazing at the street, and into the houses. Mrs. Gill closes her curtains at ten past eleven and a few minutes later, she turns out the lights. The empty street plunges into darkness and leaves scatter in the wind. Every movement grabs my attention and my breathing is shallow. My nerves are shot and I'm tired, but I have something to do.

Dies Martis

I wake up with my forehead stuck to the window. The sun hasn't come up when I brew tea for Gran. As soon as I hear the first carts going to the market, I grab my money and hurry along in the crisp morning air. Monster is walking with me. It's quiet again, and the atmosphere is tense. Hurriedly, I visit every stall in search of everything dried, salted or pickled and purchase a medium amount of it. If I buy excessively, people might get suspicious. I take the long way round back home and glance over my shoulder for any signs of someone following me. *The Dogs aren't up yet.*

To my relief, Gran's health has improved, and I pride myself that at least one part of the plan is going well. Darya comes in early, her eyes vigilant. "I haven't seen any… people outside," she reports and puts down her leather bag. I go through her stuff and grab what I need, dresses, bleach, a long pillow, and her big pink hat. Before long, we hurry to class and I loudly discuss the Hospital of the Sun with Mrs. Applegarth, considering it for Gran. She smiles and assures me some of the best specialists are there, though it'll be a tiring trip for her. As expected, she offers to join us. I politely decline, saying we will make other arrangements. Darya leave after the normal classes end and she gives me a knowing look.

When our extracurricular lesson starts, Mrs. Applegarth writes 'Water glove' on the blackboard. Thalassa excitedly claps her hands, and even Raphaël has an eager expression on his face. Mrs. Applegarth grins and says, "The instruction I am about to provide applies to bodily injuries like cuts, bumps, or muscular sores. Thalassa, come here for a moment. I require your help with the demonstration today."

Thalassa nearly skips towards the front of the class and Mrs. Applegarth offers her a seat. She lays one hand on Thalassa's shoulder. "Now, one can't mend a person without…" In a flash, she draws a knife out of her sleeve and cuts Thalassa deep across the arm. She gives out a yelp and would have fallen backward in her chair if Mrs. Applegarth wasn't holding her tightly. While my eyes grow wide in shock, Raphaël got to his feet, ready to… *What exactly?*

"Raphaël, *sit down!*"

A deep cut halfway down Thalassa's upper arm bleeds heavily. Red liquid races to the ground. While Mrs. Applegarth gets the container from her desk and soaks her hand in it, when her hand reemerges it emits a faint blue light.

"The glove is easier to shape when submerged than to dispense it over your palm and hold it there." The water has formed a glove, which she puts it on the bleeding wound. When she removes her hand a moment later, only an angry scar remains. She lets the water return to the bowl.

"First step is to envelop the water around your hand like a glove. Envision the molecules intertwining with your energy. Sometimes it helps to imagine it glowing light blue. You can proceed!" She lets a perplexed Thalassa walk back to her seat. I'm processing what I saw and, by the looks of it, so is Thalassa. Her face is pale. She holds her hand over her new scar.

"In the field, if the healing is ineffective, repeat, but it is crucial to change the water frequently."

I haven't absorbed any of this and sit dumbfounded, trying to process what I have seen. The only one who seems to respond accordingly is Raphaël. *How did he react so fast?*

Mrs. Applegarth sits down behind her desk. Consciously giving us a few minutes. "Get your bowls. You all know how it works."

I'm torn between being in total awe of the gift and the fact that she just injured my friend. *This can't be normal.* Mrs. Applegarth breaks the stunned silence. "Now go on! Make a water glove."

Raphaël carefully submerges his fingers and takes them out again. Water seeps down, back into the bowl. He tries again, but leaves it in longer this time. When he pulls it out, the liquid trickles down as quickly as before. He pushes the container my way. With a nervous glance at Mrs. Applegarth, my hand glides into the cold water, imagining it being drawn to my skin like a magnet. It flutters, but I'm used to the sensation by now. Like a fool, I reemerge, but to no avail. The room is quiet with concentration, only the sound of birds outside break it. As we're preparing to flee, I grow more and more dedicated to mastering this gift. Once more, I sink into the cold and try to imagine a glove. My hand grows warm and, excitedly, I pull it out. Nothing. Disappointed, I shove the container toward Raphaël, who regards it thoughtfully. He stares at the ripples. "Was there no better way to demonstrate how to heal a cut?" he asks.

"Would you have allowed me if I had requested?" Mrs. Applegarth asks.

"I would rather have you cut me than Thalassa," he shoots back.

"It's- it's alright," Thalassa says, still a bit pale. "It was more shocking than painful."

Raphaël bluntly drowns his hand and immediately yanks it out again, splashing water everywhere. Mrs. Applegarth observes us and moves behind Thalassa as she submerges her hand. "Envision the water moving around your skin then clinging on. Water is an extension of you. Take a deep breath."

Thalassa emerges her hand and there it is. The water glove distorts her hand a little, making it appear bigger. When she squeals excitedly, the water melts away.

"Excellent Thalassa, now hold on to that feeling."

Thalassa repeats her action, closes her eyes, inhales, and waits a moment. The water glove glows, leaving almost nothing in the bowl.

"Everybody, Thalassa has mastered it!" Mrs. Applegarth says and walks over to her table.

She's nearly jumping up and down in excitement. "It's actually really easy. Be nice to the water, relax, and ask it to help you."

Full of renewed enthusiasm, I redouble my effort. Thinking watery thoughts, trying to connect with it somehow. I reemerge my hand and look at it expectantly, but nothing happened.

I try again, and again, to no avail.

Apparently, Thalassa is the only one who has got any talent for this.

After a while, Raphaël whoops, he has mastered the water glove and Mrs. Applegarth praises him. My cold hand plunges into the water. "Come on, water, please help me."

Without success. And we make no further improvement. Frustrated, I am close to tears and my hands are freezing. I can't focus.

With every gust of wind, I imagine Baël bursting into the room. *I wish Darya was here. She would know what to do.*

In the end, my hand is wrinkled like an old lady's. Mrs. Applegarth gives me an encouraging smile. "Elara, sometimes when our focus wavers, it gets increasingly difficult. Good efforts you three! I will see you again tomorrow."

* * *

I walk to the new assault course at the back of the school grounds. The grass is damp, and it smells of mud. Quickly, I change into my workout wear and start running for the beams, then I do push-ups. Training has made me stronger, so I get through them in record time, but I am sure someone like Captain Hawkeye does them a lot faster. Squats are easy, but I fail at pull-ups. The bar is slippery from my sweat and without help, I can't accomplish even one. Next round, I will bring Monster so he can train with me.

On my route to the bakery I feel watched, yet there are no Dogs about, they are notably absent. When I arrive, Darya is sitting behind the counter and stays while I run up for a shower and check on Gran. She's upright in her bed reading and I kiss her on the forehead. To make the plan a success, she needs to be able to walk. This gives me time to get fit.

The Captain doesn't show his face today and I am somewhat disappointed. In the evening, I share another cup of tea with Gran. She smiles. "Dear, you look absolutely dreadful, but thank you for the tea. Are you certain you don't need an extra pair of hands?"

Before I speak, I sip my tea. "I'm fine. Darya is helping me a lot. Gran, I need you to focus on getting better."

She eyes me skeptically for a second. "Darling," she sighs. "could you send for Dr. Steel and Mr. Haymitch in the morning?"

I nod, a little confused, before I kiss her forehead and wish her a good night.

* * *

Dies Veneris

The days fly by. They're filled with acquiring necessities, physical training and attempting the water glove. Darya brings a variety of things and I take what I find useful.

"For some of these I'm unsure about the size, but try them on," she says.

I give her a big hug. We seem to be doing a lot of that lately. "With these two dresses, I have enough. Thank you."

Dogs patrol the streets. They don't betray any special attention, but their presence makes me clench my jaw, nonetheless.

Today, I have put on Darya's dress, this one shows way more cleavage than mine. My body jumps as I hear the bell go off, signaling a customer. A Dog walks in and I genuinely smile as I see the familiar black hair and onyx eyes.

"Good morning. How are you? I wanted to thank you again for bringing the flowers." I gush as I hold my arms folded in front of me to push out my chest out a bit more. *This feels so unnatural.* As a bonus, I glance at him from under my lashes. I've seen Darya do this many times, but for me, it is new territory.

Hawkeye pets Monster on the head before he turns to me. "Hey Elara, I was wondering if I could get a few cinnamon rolls?" he asks, while his eyes flicker to my cleavage for a fraction of a second. *Gotcha!* I look up and brush a loose strand of hair behind my ear. "Of course, anything else?"

He cocks his head and there is a glint of something new in his eyes. "What did you have in mind?"

My heart takes a leap and my mouth is dry. *Where do I go from here?* I smile innocently while my gaze keeps locked with his. The tension in the bakery grows. There is something here and it can't all just be in my head. "Do you have any plans for the weekend?"

"Are you asking me out on a date?"

My heart beats fast. *Shit. Shit. Shit, I am, aren't I?* "Depends,-" *ON WHAT!?* "on your answer." I end lamely.

The tension in the room dissipates. Hawkeye has a smile on his face, and I exhale. "Elara," he says, but his tone makes my heart drop. "I'm flattered, I really am. Don't take this the wrong way, but I'm currently in a position where I must decline." He takes the cinnamon rolls from me and turns to leave. "See you around, Blue Angel."

I turn away when he leaves and have to refrain from punching something. *This is not according to plan.*

In the evening rain falls and the streets are empty. Mrs. Gill closes her curtains at 11:00 and I berate her in my head for being a night owl. At midnight, I take Monster for a walk again. He begrudgingly goes with me.

* * *

Dies Saturni

The day passes and besides my hurt ego, everything moves on schedule. Gran even makes it downstairs this morning to welcome Dr. Steel and Mr. Haymitch. I am certain we will escape soon and to blow off some steam, I go out to train with Monster. I return sweaty and tired after training. Through the window, I spot Gran, who has fallen asleep in her chair, but when I open the door, she startles awake. "You're too skinny, honey. Are you eating enough? Let me brew some tea." She is already up before I can protest. Her walk is still pained and I second guess my plan as I sit down next to her. "Dear, we need to talk," she says, after she has come back with two steaming mugs. Outside, the wind has picked up, and the house creaks. "Honey," she pauses, and her green eyes find mine. "I had a talk today with Dr. Steel and Mr. Haymitch. Are you aware of what Mr. Haymitch does for a living? The lawyer made final edits to my will, while Dr. Steel ensured my sanity."

"I don't understand?"

Gran sighs and takes my hand. Hers are cold. "Honey, I'm ill-,"

Frustrated, I yank my hand back. "You're getting better, because of the tea I have-"

Gran regards me with a sad smile and intertwines her fingers. "I know, your father would give similar ones to his patients as well. However, this is nothing any brew can cure, my dear, and that's alright."

"No, Gran!" Panic builds in my chest. "No! We will flee and- and start anew."

"What are you talking about, dear?" she asks, surprised.

"I have planned our escape. Darya is helping me set it up and we will leave as soon as possible. I just need-" My tone has alerted Monster and he walks up to me and leans against me in support.

"Sometimes you are still a child," she says lovingly. "How did you expect to bring this old hag with you? The reason I'm in this damn chair is because I don't have the strength to walk back up. There is no energy in me anymore to run."

It's overwhelming. I break down at her feet and put my head in her lap. She shushes me and she strokes her hair. The small of eucalyptus tickles my nose.

"I can't go without you," I sob.

"You can, and if you are sure about this plan of yours, you will." She keeps stroking my hair. "And I shall support you as much as I'm able."

At the end of the day, I assist her up the stairs. Her arms are alarmingly thin and I berate myself that I didn't notice it before. She gives me a goodnight kiss and closes the door. I run to Monster and let tears wet his coat.

Dies Lovis

There is a letter for me. The military seal makes my heart drop. *So it's time.* It's lying there, a white square on a brown wooden floor. I don't want to open it, I don't want to touch it, I wait for it to spontaneously combust, or fly away. I do the mature thing and tear it open.

Attention Ms. Elara Ariël Waywater,

You are required to report to the Town's hall at 07:30 on the 13th day of the fifth moon, without exception. Second Lieutenant Winchester will escort you and your peers to the Capitol, where you shall receive further instructions and training.

Please ensure that you refer to the attached list for the items you must bring with you. You are prohibited from bringing personal belongings. All necessary supplies are provided to you upon arrival.

Your service to our nation is of utmost importance.

In unity and reverence,

Captain Hawkeye
In order of the Leader Suprema

My hand finds the vase with his flowers and I smash it as hard as I can into the wall. Monster jumps up, alarmed at my outburst and decides it is safer upstairs. I stalk to the kitchen, don't know what I'm supposed to be doing, and walk back. "Monster, we're going out!" Monster stands uncertainly atop the stairs, but refuses to come down, so I march out of the door alone.

Chapter 12

Dies Luane

Birds chirp outside when I wake. Monster has left my room. I watch Gran's door through the opening he left, it is still closed. So I decide to let her sleep in and tip-toe downstairs. To my surprise, the first customer is Captain Hawkeye who strides in his meticulous uniform. I'm in one of Darya's dresses and have my hair in a simple braid.

"Good morning," I say as pleasantly as I am able, my eyes flicker towards the place where I smashed the vase not days before. But Monster happily sniffs at him and lays down to invite him for a belly rub.

"Good morning, Elara," he says and complies with Monster's wish.

I fold my arms and try not to look at him. "What can I do for you?"

"Two loaves of bread, please."

I get to work.

"Are you upset with at me?"

"Why would I be?" I say with my back towards him and he sighs and holds out his hands in a ceasefire. When Darya walks in and Hawkeye's spine stiffens. She, in turn, halts when she sees the scene. "Oh, hello Captain Castiël Hawkeye. Hi, Elara. I-" Her eyebrows shoot up at me.

"Hello, Miss Ballard," the Captain says and nods in her direction.

"How's your day going so far?"

She gives him a tight-lipped smile. "Fine, thank you, Captain." Monster trots up to her and licks her hand and she gives him a scratch between the ears. I move to get Darya's usual order. The only sound is the slapping of Monsters tail against the wooden floor.

Hawkeye smiles at me. "I better be going, thank you for the bread."

Darya watches Hawkeye's retreating form and shakes her head. Then she turns to me. "How's Gran doing?"

"I haven't woken her up yet. She needs sleep." I turn to put bread in the oven. Darya stands in the middle of the bakery in silence, she inhales deeply before she says, "Oh, I nearly forgot, mother told me to give you these." She hands me a basket of apples. Then, for a strange moment, my mind goes to Lilly and I send out a little prayer for her. Darya sits on her usual spot and I pour two cups of tea. When a big thump comes from upstairs. My heart skips a beat and I freeze with the kettle still in my hand. Monster barks, panic tinges his yelps. Dread fills my chest.

Without a word, I fly up the stairs with Monster beside me. Gran lies on the floor, next to her bed. Unmoving. Her eyelids are half open. "GRAN!?" I sprint to her and my shout alarms Darya, who runs right up. Together we pull her frail body into bed. She really has lost a lot of weight, my hand can nearly close around her upper arm. I bite back tears. "Darya, get the doctor!"

Darya turns and speeds down the stairs. Meanwhile, Gran lies in bed like a rag doll. Her breathing comes out unevenly and her eyes stare vacantly to the ceiling. My hand touches her face, her skin is grey and cold. "Gran, Gran, please. It's me, it's Elara. Please look at me!" My fingers fumble for her heartbeat, but I can't feel anything through my trembling hands. I stroke her hair, making her look presentable for when the doctor comes. But it seems hours pass until the doctor arrives, while it has probably been mere minutes. He rushes up the stairs.

"She's not responding!" I howl as he enters the room. He has bags under his eyes, has forgotten his hat. But he goes to work, he checks her pulse, lungs, and temperature. While I watch his every move. Waiting for a signal that she's alright. Darya stands in the doorway.

"What do we do?" I ask.

"I can make sure she's not in any pain..." The doctor glances meaningfully at me over the rims of his spectacles.

"What are you saying?" My brain is not processing the way it should. Everything is moving too slowly.

"Miss Waywater, there is nothing I can do for your grandmother anymore."

My heart beats in my throat, my breath comes out in bursts. "What about medicine? It helped last time. She just needs more medicine. Give it to her medicine!" The doctor shakes his head foolishly. As anger fills my chest, Darya places a hand on my shoulder. I shrug it off "No! No! There has to be something, anything!"

"Elara," the doctor says in a steady voice. "I will give her something, to ease any pain, but it will not heal her."

Heal her... "Dar-, Darya, I need Mrs. Applegarth."

Darya's big blue eyes fill with pity, but she nods. But the doctor's face sours for a second and looks at me over his bag and lets out a deep breath. "Miss Waywater, this is not something even Mrs. Applegarth can fix," he says with strained patience. But Darya has already run out of the room. The doctor takes a vial and syringe out of his suitcase, and carefully searches for a vein. He injects the clear liquid into Gran. Her cold hand lies limply in mine. I hold on to her as if she is an anchor. The tips of her fingers are a feint blue. I plead with Gran, I plead with the Gods, nothing helps. I'm powerless. We sit in silence and Gran's breathing relaxes. Her fingers are like ice and the top of her hand is turning a dark shade of blue. Outside, a car drives by.

After a long while Darya returns, accompanied by Mrs. Applegarth. She is wearing a modest green dress that comes down to her ankles. Against all my training, I pray for a miracle.

The man presses his lips together and lifts his chin when he sees her. "I'm sorry you have come all this way, Mrs. Applegarth. I believe it's for naught." The doctor stands up, declares. "I'll be downstairs." And leaves.

I sit breathlessly as Mrs. Applegarth revieles out her flask and conjures the water glove. She closes her eyes as she focuses. *This has to work.* The blueish glow fills me with hope. Strands of hair fall down Mrs. Applegarth's face as she moves her hand over Gran's head, heart, and lungs. Her brow is furrowed. Her eyes find mine. "Elara, I'm afraid the doctor is right. There is nothing I can do he hasn't already done."

Chapter 13

Breathe, one, two, three, breathe. Standing before the crowd of blue-clothed people, I realize the whole of Eden has showed up. The flickering torches throw odd shadows on their clothes. Even Captain Hawkeye and Second Lieutenant Winchester have come to pay their respects, but stand out like a sore thumb. They moved a bit from the mass, as if they're uncomfortable imposing on something so personal.

My clammy hands shuffle the dry pieces of paper and read aloud what I have written before. Of course, I know it word for word, but I hope reading it makes the words come out easier. Am I sweating? Or are these tears on my face? Have I cried already? I search for Darya and find her standing next to a white pillar with her parents. Her blue clothes match her eyes, which are puffy and swollen. Faint scents of smoke enter my nose and I observe the flickering torches. Softly crashing waves are the only sound now that the crowd has become silent.

"In my birth city,-" I say hoarsely and clear my throat, with a louder voice I try again. "In my birth city, we lived as a happy family. I remember... when I fell trying to climb a tree and my knees were bloody, Gran lifted me up, brought me home, and held me until I calmed down. She cleaned my wounds with water and stitched me up, which are my first memories of her and made me want to pursue nursing." I smile at the memory of her no-nonsense attitude during

150

the stitching. "I must have screamed bloody murder. She wasn't deterred. My parents were alive then… But Gran's strength left a lasting impression on me." *Why didn't my father take care of me?*

A sound makes me look up. It's Mrs. Hydris blowing her nose. Beside her, Darya looks up at me with red eyes.

"We had it good, until unexpectedly, the war came on our path. Gran took me and we fled to Eden and we made this our home. I-" Breathe, one, two, three. My eyes flicker towards the Captain. His face betrays no emotion. "I never realized how challenging it must have been for you- I mean, for her. We all lost our lives that day." I swallow. And when I dreamed my scary dreams, about mother and father, and cried at night, you would come to sit beside me and stroke my hair softly. Telling me everything would be okay.

Now comes the difficult part. I take a sip of my water to wash away the gravel in my throat. It doesn't help. "Later, we didn't get along so well anymore. You were old-fashioned, and the lessons you tried to teach met deaf ears. I stopped sharing what I did or thought. Just recently, I realized how awful it must have been for you." I clench my jaw, pushing back the tears. "Now I long to talk to you, and ask for your advice, one last time because I'm so tired. All I want to say is, Gran… I love you so much. Quatahna will guide you to a better place. And where life may lead me, I ask you to be my guide. Please watch over everything we see because the future is so dark and confusing right now." I hold up my hands and everyone chants the holy words at me. They offer me no comfort. Oh, Gran… I am so indescribably lonely. The chant starts again and through my cramped throat I sing for her.

"You did great," Darya whispers after the speech. She squeezes my hand as she leads me to the beach for Gran's last voyage.

"Gran would be proud," I say with a dry sob.

We make our way to the beach, and Darya holds my hand as the crowd follows. The moon is full and the stars are shining brightly, glittering in the sea. Torches lead us to the waterline and Raphaël, Trent, Tennin, and Seger carry Gran. Seger has dressed appropriately, leaving his uniform at home, and looks like a respectable Edeneer. Gran is wearing her favorite dress and Mrs. Hydris has helped me do her hair. The crowd chants softly as Gran is carefully tied to her last resting place. Darya stands next to me as we watch. The scent of smoke from the lanterns calm me. I glance down the coast, where Darya and I hide at our secret spot, going for a swim, before the world collapsed.

"Gran was a wonderful woman," Darya says with a sad smile. "She was always so nice to me."

After they finish, the men walk back. They all nod to me and touch their foreheads as a sign of respect. Raphaël is last and as he touches his forehead, he says, "Gran was a woman with a h-h-heart of gold. She will be missed."

I thank him for his kind words, but can't manage a smile. He puts an arm around me. I lean into him as the Priest comes forward and we all listen to his funeral oration. Raphaël's shoulder catches most of my tears and I miss the Priest's speech. When it's time, Darya tugs my hand. With no other family member available, she volunteered to assist on her last voyage, which the Priest accepted. Sand tickles my bare feet as we walk towards the boat. Gran lies there peacefully. It's like she's sleeping. She still smells of eucalyptus. Breathe, one, two, three, breathe. The crowd behind me waits for us to make the first move. Torches cast an orange glow over their solemn faces. Mrs. Hydris cries with her husband's arm around her. Beside her are Raphaël and his mother, standing tall, with their heads down. How much is he reminded of his father?

"C'mon Elara," Darya calls me back to the moment at hand. We stand on either side and start pushing the vessel into the tranquil sea. It's like Quatahna has asked it to calm down just for Gran and I thank her. The second we touch the boat, the crowd chants and the sound makes the surrounding air vibrate. Gran's boat is heavy and we need to strain ourselves before it slides easily over the sand into the shallows. As soon as the waves touch my bare foot, the fluttering sensation starts. With a steadying breath, I keep on walking until my feet can't reach the ground anymore. Flutters surround me and when my arm pushes away the water, it glows as if I'm disturbing luminous algae.

The sea sloshes around me as we swim with one hand on the boat, further and further into the dark. It gets into my mouth, tasting like salt and seaweed, and I spit it out. We continue swimming until Darya says we are far enough. Then comes the next part. The knife loosens from my belt, the weight of it heavy in my grasp, and I watch it gleam in the moonlight.

"You can do this, Elara," she encourages me when I linger. She swims towards me and envelops my hand with hers. We both cut into the boat and water streams in. It engulfs Gran, and I gasp. It happens too fast, and before I'm ready, the dark welcomes her to the bottom. "Quatahna will look after her now," she says when we can't see her anymore. "Let's turn back."

The swim is far, and the tide is strong. When we hear the chanting again, and Raphaël is there to help me onto the sand- I can barely stand on my feet. For Darya, it's Alphonse. On the shore, we both get a towel and receive some dry clothes. The priest blesses us, but I can barely stand on my legs. Everyone comes over to give their condolences and touch their foreheads. Some hand me little gifts. It's all a blur, just one face stands out. His onyx eyes gaze into mine and he holds my icy hand in two of his warm ones.

"I am so sorry for your loss, Elara. Your Gran was a gem."

A small group escort me home, Darya and Raphaël both support me, while their parents walk silently behind us. The bakery is dark, and the moonlight throws cold shadows through the windows. Darya goes in and lights the lamps before I enter. Monster lies on his belly in the kitchen and rises slowly as we come inside. His tail stays still and his head is low as he steps towards me and that tells me he knows. I offer my guests tea, not wanting to be alone, but they excuse themselves, all except for Darya. She stands by the door, but I can tell her mood shifts. "Elara, you need to leave now."

"What?" I feel thrown off and my gaze is on Monster, who looks up at me with his dark brown eyes. "I only just got here."

She continues loudly, "Elara, if you want to run, now is the time. The…" She lowers her voice. "They won't expect it if you flee now and no one will blame you for not showing up anywhere in the next couple of days. It's perfect!"

"What?" I say again, Monster's eyes mirror my confusion. "No."

"Elara, you need to go *now*! I understand this is hard, but you won't have another opportunity like this one!"

She pleads with me while I shake my head and fall to my knees and tears well up in my eyes. "Darya, I can't. I can't!" She tries to drag me to my feet, but my legs give out from under me. "I'm sorry!" I sob, unsure of what I am apologizing for. With my face in my hands, I keep repeating it. "I can't, I'm sorry!" I wail. Monster forces his nose to my face and licks my tears away, his tail wags uncertainly. Darya puts her hand on my shoulder, "Are you sure?"

I nod, and she gives up and makes us some tea. We sit on the wooden floor of the empty bakery.

* * *

The first week passes in a blur. Darya doesn't leave my side during the day, Mrs. Ballard walks Monster in the early mornings, and Mrs.

154

Hydris helps me manage the bakery. At night it's me and Monster. Townspeople come and pay their respects, and some bring meals for me, but I throw most of them away because I'm not hungry. Some buy more pastries to help me earn enough money. No one comments on it, but they aren't as sweet anymore, no matter how much sugar I put in them.

Everyone has been understanding about me missing the last weeks of college and Darya has offered to help me clean out the house. It has been something I'm dreading.

I haven't entered Gran's room after the funeral, but the room is filled with the scent of eucalyptus. Her bed in the middle of the room still has the velvet green cover neatly draped over it and her slippers are waiting for her.

"It might be best if this is done methodically. Let's start with the big things," Darya says, putting down some bags. Outside, birds chirp happily and a cart rolls past as if nothing has changed.

Monster stands behind us, sniffing from his place at the door frame. I have to regroup for a minute before I begin. But when I move forward, he follows, inspecting the old room. Darya throws open the windows to let in the fresh air and I clean out the closet.

"Let's make three piles," she says briskly. "One with things that can be thrown out, one for items we can donate, and one for the stuff you wish to keep." She glances at me as I stand forlorn in the middle of the room. Her resolve softens. "Elara, you can do this."

I want her to get mad at me, because her caring voice makes me want to cry again. "Yes, I can do this." I try to sound as resolute as she did, but fail.

Gran's perfume fills the air, and it soothes me. It has the same effect on Monster, because he stretches, leaps onto the bed, and makes himself comfortable on the velvet duvet. Normally Gran would drag him off it and tell him a bed is not made for him, but I enjoy his support.

We work in a hushed silence. Darya and I sort her clothes first, the ones that still look good I place on the bed neatly folded. Worn-out garments, I shove into the trash bag. Next are her shoes, her stockings, and her nightgowns. I keep her white gloves because they remind me of her the most -she used to wear them on special occasions. Monster's eyes track our movements as we move around the room. Darya cleans and throws some old stuff away. This is the longest she's ever gone without talking. In episodes her eyes get misty, but she's holding it together. After what feels like hours, I break the silence. "I need a drink. You want anything?" Darya nods, and I walk to the kitchen.

Keep breathing... I have to get this over with.

We take a breather, drinking some tea and letting Monster outside to do his business. After the tea, Monster stays downstairs with his head between his paws and we clean out her make-up table and decide to throw the lot away. Next up is the bookshelf. We create two piles. Gran would not have believed the methodical way Darya was going through her belongings. After telling her off that she shouldn't touch her things, she would probably be proud.

There are a few diaries I want to read, biographies of people I never heard of, and history books. As I stack them on a pile, one book falls apart, and yellow pages flutter everywhere. It's like the drop that made the bucket overflow and I fall to my knees and cry uncontrollably. Darya sits down next to me. I bawl onto her shoulder and all the tension seeps out of me.

"I'm so sorry," she whispers in my hair, and she also cries. Together, in Gran's old room, we turn into a blubbering mess.

When we've calmed down, she stands and gets me some water. "Do you want to continue?" she asks after a while.

"It's getting late and I think I need to sleep a bit. Thank you, Darya, for all this." We say goodbye and I walk to my own bedroom, but I halt. Then I return to Gran's room, lie down on her bed and breathe in her scent from her pillow, bread and eucalyptus. Monster hears me move and trots upstairs. He joins me on the mattress and I hug him close as I fall asleep.

When I wake, it's pitch black. I turn, trying to catch some more sleep, but it evades me. Energy hums through my body, so I ignite the lamp. A film of dust is already covering the furniture. On her old teak wood desk, a bunch of envelopes lie next to the books. If Gran was here, she would tell me to tuck them away. *Geez, even when you're not here, you are still ordering me around. What letters did you find worth keeping?* In the warm light of the lamp I stand up, Monster shifts and continues to sleep. Feeling like a detective, I decide to open the first letter. A yellowish piece of paper falls to the ground. It's not Gran's handwriting.

Dear Nuriël,

We have made it safely to our new location. Thank you for getting us into contact with C., he has been marvelous. You are right regarding the Military. We will do all we can.

Eros.

P.S. Give Elara a big hug for me. Is she eating right?

Eros… I can't even picture his face anymore. His hair was dark. He had enormous hands he would use to pick me up. I sniff at the paper, but it just smells like paper.

How did father smell?

I grab the next letter. It's written in a different handwriting.

Mother,

It is now 3 o'clock at night. I am writing to you in secret because there's a leak in the group. Mom, everything is getting worse. Nine people died in battle today and the other two hundred are frightened.

We've been here for nine months. That is six months too long. The locals are tired of our 'help'. The military is coming from every side and this fight is not leading us anywhere. I can't contact you anymore. Please take care of Elara until I can get to you. It is really getting bad here, Mom. I want to get home, I don't care how. If you had any idea of how tired I am…

Love,

Hera

This is mother's. I never knew she was off fighting somewhere. A hollow sensation fills my stomach.

Why did Gran hide this from me? Apparently, my mother worried about me, otherwise, she wouldn't have left me with Gran, right?

There is another letter stuck to it. I pry it loose from my mother's letter. This new letter is blotched, as if someone has cried while reading it.

Dear Nuriël,

Last Dies Lovis, the resistance base got attacked. I am so sorry. Hera and 13 others did not make it. She passed away in the woods near Thebe. I buried her under an olive tree.

This will be the last you hear from me. I am going into hiding.

Please take good care of Elara.

Eros

So that is my father.

I want to throw up.

My parents were working for the resistance? My parents were with me when our house got attacked, right? Dad went into hiding? Does that mean he is still alive?

The last thought leaves me surprisingly untouched. I should want to go search for him. Reunite and hope for a happy family? But I don't. Above all, I'm hurt that Gran never deemed it fit to share this with me. I sit back on the bed and Monster looks up. *Wasn't I mature enough for her? Did she expect me to throw myself to my knees and weep for a man whose face I don't remember?* I listen to Monster's even breath. Was she afraid that I would hold out hope for a happy family reunion? I probe at my feelings, inspecting them from all angels. *I liked it better when he was dead to me. Dead to the world.* My body falls onto the mattress with a thud. *Would he be proud of me?*

* * *

I wait for Darya at the crossroads on our way to college. I really want to share this story with her. We hug when she sees me, something we have started to do recently. Her warm embrace is a warm current in an icy sea. The familiar scent of Jasmine and sea salt makes me smile.

I tell her about the letters. She gasps and holds a hand in front of her mouth. "Do you think she kept more?"

"I don't think so. I've checked the bookcase and all the drawers. Twice. Perhaps there was one in the clothes we discarded?"

"No," Darya says. "I checked all the pockets before donating the clothes. What will you do?"

"I stick to the plan."

"What do you think they meant with your Gran being right about the military?" Darya wonders. Her eyes are as large as saucers.

I look down, hurt. "I don't know. Gran shared none of this with me. Or she didn't trust me?"

"I don't believe it for a second. You two were closer than anyone I know. There must be another reason."

My fingers fidget with the hem of my skirt, and I shrug. "Perhaps she forgot?"

"Your daughter and husband dying while having figured out some dirty secret from the military? I don't believe that either."

***

The familiar ring of the bell goes off as I push open the door and nearly walk into a blue-gray uniform with well-defined muscles. Captain Hawkeye's smooth voice fills the bakery and Mrs. Hydris giggles at something he says.

"Ah Elara," Mrs. Hydris says, who now Gran has passed away insists I call her by her first name, Mauria. "You have a visitor."

He turns to me and she winks at me from behind him. I try to keep my expression neutral, but I don't have the poker face he does.

He places a hand over his heart. "I wanted to pay my respects. I haven't seen you since the funeral and I was wondering how you were holding up."

"I'm getting a lot of help running the bakery next to my classes. I've been keeping busy."

"Good," he says, more to himself than to me. "Anything I can do to assist you?" he inquires. A concerned smile decorates his lips. Behind him, Mauria nods her head enthusiastically.

I look at him with narrowed eyes. "Do you know how to run a bakery?"

"No," he admits. His hands grow restless and I see he has brought something. He offers me a long, thin wrapped parcel. "I had an ulterior motive to show, I wanted to return your blade."

My eyebrows shoot up, and my body relaxes. "I forgot," I admit while taking the package from him. "Did you get what you wanted from it?"

"I'm afraid it was holding no further secrets," he says and scratches the back of his head. "Maybe I was hoping to find something that wasn't there." He gazes at me and my heart skips a beat, very aware of Mauria standing behind him, and if I'm not mistaken, so is he. He clears his throat. "I better get going then. Thank you for the pastries, Mrs. Hydris." He flashes her a devastating smile as he leaves.

"Pleasure's all mine, Captain, truly." She waves at him, then she turns to me and hisses. "Elara, that was an open invitation! How could you leave him hanging?" She fusses over the counter. "How do you expect to find a husband if you don't make a move? Nuriël would be so embarrassed."

Did she hound Lilly the same way? Besides, what is the point of being with him if I have no one I can share my intel with?

Chapter 14

The house creaks in the wind. A light patter of drops falls on the window. Clouds cover the waning moon and I toss and turn. It feels haunted. Monster snores gently while sleep eludes me. In my head, I go through the list again and again. Meals, warm clothing, disguise, dog food, blanket. Until I am sure, I haven't forgotten anything.

Without having shut my eyes, I climb out of bed a few hours before dawn. I take a shower. Possibly the last one in a while. I enjoy the scent of soap and scrub everything thrice.

The ceiling creaks as the wind throws itself against it. I follow all the steps Darya and I have thought of so carefully. One thing I got from her is bleach and I apply it to my hair. The chemical liquid burns my nose. The goal is to become as blond as she is, while she will cut her locks to shoulder length like mine. Because the bleach needs to sit for a bit, I walk downstairs and peek through the curtains. It's deserted, and I steady my breath. Panic threatens to engulf me, but I need a clear head. Long shadows creep through the street as the moon fights the clouds. The water-filled potholes reflect her light.

My heart pounds as I wash out my hair and observe myself in the mirror. Blond wet hair falls down and, for good measure, I cut bangs for myself. Overall, I am quite happy with the result.

"Who knew I would look stunning as a blond?" I ask my reflection. I laugh, but it's joyless. Darya has given me one of her winter dresses.

It smells like her, Jasmine.

Some months ago this would have been too tight, now it falls over my frame loosely. *Gran was right, I am skinny.*

Downstairs, I make a big breakfast consisting of eggs and fried vegetables. Although the smell of food makes me nauseous, I force myself to eat every last bite. By the time I'm done, the first light is brightening the cloudy sky. I give myself permission to take one more peek into Gran's room, where I inhale deeply. Her scent is already fading. *I love you.*

With steady hands, I wake up Monster. He follows me down the stairs. The familiar squeak sends a jolt through my body. I fill his bowl and his gaze doesn't leave me.

"You need a nutritious breakfast as well," I say. He snorts and eats reluctantly. The oven lights and for the last time, I read the addresses Darya has given me. My first hideout will be closer to home. Just a few hours' walk. After that, I travel East-Northward, toward Quillan. I crumple the paper with the address on it up before I throw it in the fire. I warm my clammy hands in its heat.

Rule number one: Don't leave a trace. It should also appear like the bakery is running. Fire consumes it, hiding my secret.

The first truck slowly passes through Main Road. The heavy engine makes the floor tremble and the glass shudders in their frames. I focus on my breathing in order to calm my nerves and slow down my heartbeat. Any moment now, a Dog will come in and force me with them. None do.

Darya will be here soon. Rain pelts down. Monster stretches himself and looks at me, sensing this is not a morning like the others. We discussed a special knock to signal her arrival. But I recognize her frame through the curtains before I hear it. I let her in and quickly shut the door behind her.

Darya's eyes are wide in panic. "I don't think anyone followed me," she breathes. "Are you ready?"

Her platinum blond hair is dark with rain and dye. She is wearing one of my old dresses. It might not fool everyone, but hopefully, it will confuse people enough. "Bangs?" she asks as she studies my face and I shrug.

"Spur of the moment." I take a deep breath. "I'm ready." We hug each other and my eyes get misty. "Thank you so much, Darya, for everything," I talk into her shoulder and force back tears.

"I would do it all again," she says and sniffs.

The big bag stands impatiently next to the door. In it all the necessities I will need on my journey. I look around and say goodbye to the bakery. Before panic paralyzes me, I sling the heavy onto my back.

"Monster, c'mon, we're going for a walk."

Simultaneously, the three of us leave. I leave the door unlocked. The Dogs don't have to break down the door when they come looking. Darya turns towards the square where they are expecting me. With clenched jaw, I watch her go before I take off, with Monster, in the opposite direction.

The enormous sun hat I got from Darya hides my face from passing people. It also makes it impossible to see if I'm getting any strange looks. I probably am. It's no weather for sun hats.

Monster presses himself against me, feeling my anxiety. I dive into the first alley and climb over a wooden fence. He follows me gracefully. My first stop is the next town inland, away from the sea.

Now I'm off Main Road, I walk faster. Monster keeps to my hip. All the adrenaline makes sure I don't feel cold, wet, or the weight of the bag on my shoulders. I'm terrified of looking back and keep my eyes on my target. It would be unwise to break into a run for any attention I might draw to myself. My body begs me to. My boots leave prints in the mud. *They could trace my footsteps all the way to me.*

But I have to carry on.

Bushes grow high around me and wet leaves stain my dress up to my hips. I glance back once, there is no sign of Dogs.

"We did good, Monster," I say, and he lets out a small bark, which startles me. "Shhh! We are not there yet," I whisper.

On top of the hill, I cast a last look over Eden. Trucks litter the square. A crowd of people walks around like ants. *Darya is there somewhere.*

I send out a prayer for her well-being as I imagine her trying to flirt with some army official. *How will they react when they realize I'm not there?* Involuntarily, my mind goes to Hawkeye. *Is he going to get mad? Disappointed?*

I turn and observe the undergrowth in front of me. It's the safest place to run, no one can find me here. This path leads me to the house of the people who will shelter me.

Mr. and Mrs. Swallow are an older couple who have lived in this house as long as I can remember. The Swallows have been good friends to the Ballards for generations and have no kids of their own. They treat Darya and her sisters like their own grandchildren. It will take me until noon to get there.

The rain falls relentlessly, soaking my coat, but I focus on the target. Rain and wet grass are the overpowering smells here. The ground squelches underfoot and my legs grow tired. The mind wants to give up before your body does and with each step I repeat to myself, *my body is stronger.* Overhead, a deep rumble stirs the air and I quicken my pace. *I hope Darya is somewhere warm and dry.*

Monster is in front of me. He knows these woods better than I do and has less trouble making way through the undergrowth. My foot sinks farther into the mud, gripping it tight.

"Ah! What in the holy hell!" I mutter, but with every jerk I give, the ground greedily sucks it deeper. My heart races and I have to push myself to keep it together. I curse the Gods until eventually, I pull out my foot, lie on my belly in the stinking mud, and dig out the blasted thing with my bare hands. Smells of mud and dung penetrate my nose. Small stones and sticks graze my fingers. My boot is slippery when I tug it. With a loud squelch, it lets go. This is how Monster finds me. He is disgruntled at this misadventure, his thick coat wet and dripping. The hat falls from my head and I swear again. The pink clashes with the forest floor and I decide to leave it there. But now my head isn't protected and the cold rain falls on my exposed head and down my neck.

I try to clean myself on my dress. I might as well have used the mud itself. *Hopefully, the Swallows have a warm shower I can use.*

Thick droplets fall through the leaves as I put my boot back on, and I gasp when I feel cold water in it. Shivering, I push myself up. The chill has seeped into my bones. To make up for lost time, I rush through the thicket. I pant loudly, but if I stop now, I'll get hypothermia. After I have lost all sense of time, a road appears before my feet. "Monster! We found it!" I cheer. *I wish I could tell Darya!* But Monster cowers in the bushes. "It's alright Monster, come on."

He refuses. The whites of his eyes show. He whines and puts his tail between his legs. He's too big for me to drag over. *Stupid Momo.*

After I try for a minute, I give up. He'll follow me when he smells the food. I turn around and want to take a step. *Oh hellfire, I got my boot stuck again.* I pull at my boot, but that's not the only thing stuck. I can't move and it's an all too familiar sensation. Fear grips me. My eyes shoot from left to right. Searching. A small bit away, I see a green truck half hidden between the trees. Out steps a tall, blond man. He smiles like a shark. He slowly walks towards me, as if he is strolling on the beach.

"Tut, tut, tut!" He grins, his teeth bare. "We should stop meeting like this, hmmm?" Corporal Baël is playing with the gun in his hands. My eyes fly open wide in realization. *He is going to shoot me.* He waves it around. "Don't worry, love, I'm not allowed to permanently damage you. *You* are too valuable. The Swallows weren't so lucky."

I inhale. The house stands alone in the rain, the curtains are drawn. *No! No! No!*

"I do like this new color on you, hmmm…" He brushes his fingers through my hair. Adrenaline drives my heartbeat into overdrive. "Not the bangs though, darling, it doesn't suit you." His nose is now inches from mine and a warm water droplet makes it down my cheek. "Do you want to play a game with me?" His cold dead eyes stare into my soul. His face is all I can see. He grabs the hair at the back of my head and pulls down, leaving my throat exposed. My muscles scream in fear, longing to move. "What could I do, that would not leave you permanently damaged, but would be fun to do. Hmmm…"

Behind him, a truck door closes with a snap and his focus lessens. I scream.

That is a cue for Monster to fling himself at Corporal Baël. Who shouts in surprise and his grip on me dissolves completely. I collapse to the ground. The Corporal brings up his gun. I lunge at him, but he is stronger and more skilled. He tackles me to the floor, knocking the wind out of me. Then he aims at Monster. Shoots. The gun fires. Monster yelps and my heart turns cold -it has found its target.

"STOP!" I hear someone below. A young man with red hair runs towards us, holding his own weapon. "You were NOT to harm her!" Lance Corporal Boyle shouts. Soft whines come from Monster. His breath is irregular. With Baël's focus off me, I scramble to him. The ground under him is turning red.

"The Captain does like his little toy, hmmm?" he says with an amused voice. "Fine, I'll be in the truck." He spits, spins around and gives Monster a kick with his boot. A shriek fills the air.

"Elara," Lance Corporal Boyle's voice comes from behind me. "We need to bring you to the base."

My fingers search for the wound. The blood is turning his black coat slick. I find the entrance wound near his stomach. I try to feel for the metal bullet. "Just-, just give me a minute." With trembling hands, I attempt to remove it. But his pained shriek breaks my heart and I just can't. I catch rain in my palm and I want to conjure the glove. But it's no use. All the rain seeps out of my hand and I cry out in frustration. Nerves and the cold make my body shiver. *Work, damn it!*

With a long inhale, I force all the energy into my hand. The air grows cold around me and my breath comes out in white puffs. I place my fingers in a puddle and this time the water sticks. A blue glow lightens Monster's fur as I find the damaged area. His small cries fade with every inhale. My hand hovers over his wound. A sharp pain shoots all the way up to my elbow, but the bleeding ceases. Monster becomes quiet, but his chest still rises and falls rapidly.

"El, if you don't come now, he will step out to get you," he warns me with a slight quiver in his voice. I want to scream at them, claw at their eyes, try to inflict so much pain they'll hurt forever. The floor captures me as I collapse, sobbing hysterically. An iron grip pushes me into the truck. The metal grazes the palm of my hands. The vehicle roars to life and starts to drive, leaving Monster behind in the rain.

Chapter 15

Within the four windowless white walls, it smells like cleanser and lemon. My sense of time is distorted. I am wide awake and stare into nothing. At first, I screamed at them, banged on the door, and called them every name in the book, until my throat hurt. Then I fled into a corner. *Momo... my Monster.* Nobody has touched the door after they threw me in here. There are two chairs I've thrown across the small space. They lie uselessly on the floor. Footsteps outside the white room come and go. This is the second time someone walked by. *Will they punish me? Put me in jail? Will they go back and take Monster? Will they hurt me? Why are they not talking to me? Are they trying to scare me? Have they forgotten about me? Can I leave? Is this a test?*

My back aches. If this is a way to stress me out, it's working. I hear two pairs of footsteps coming towards the door. My eyes stay fixed on the floor. They stop and the door handle scrapes until the door swings open, letting in a gust of cold air, sending shivers down my spine. A pair of legs walk around the table. When I glance up, the Mountain enters my vision. From the floor, he's even larger. His small pale eyes don't look at me as he grabs one of the chairs and sits down. "Ms. Waywater, do you know why you are here?" His voice sounds like a crashing wave. I nod, realizing he is not looking at me, and he probably didn't see that I say, "Yes," I squeak. He motions his hand to the chair, but I'm too afraid to move from my spot in the corner. His ice-blue eyes bore into mine until I avert my own and I study my dirty shoes.

"Sit, Ms. Waywater," he orders in the same tone I use with Monster when he has been bad. My body protests, but I push myself off the ground. Once I'm upright, I shiver violently. I take two steps towards the chair and my wet shoes squeak on the floor. Carefully, I sit opposite the Dog. The cold metal presses through my wet clothes. I have to clench my teeth to keep them from chattering.

"Good. Now, you are going to fill out some documents." He places the paperwork on the table.

I am taken aback. His eyes meet mine, his blue eyes remind me of shards of ice- there is no trace of emotion in them. "You will sign these, in which you state you are volunteering for the army."

"But-, but I am not." I press my nails into my palms to keep from crying. The Mountain glances at me and slides the documents in my direction with one single finger. His big hands could probably crush my skull if he wanted to. "Read it, or not. You'll sign it either way, and then hand it over." He stands up and walks towards the door.

"What about Monster?"

He ignores me, or maybe he didn't hear my whisper.

"I'll return in 30 minutes." He locks the door behind him.

Without a clock, I have no idea how long it will take. The silence is deafening. My dry eyes focus on the minuscule letters on the white paper. I shake my head, as if that might make this nightmare go away. But I'm alive, and I won't get out of here without placing my stupid signature. I need to know if Monster's okay. *If I do this, I can get back to Monster. And Darya... what did they do to Darya?* I pick up the pen. It's surprisingly light in my cold fingers. I sign. *Oh Gran, Quatahna, anyone, please help me. I'll do anything if you just make sure they're okay.* My muscles are too cramped up for the signature to resemble mine. I breathe deep, as if I'm about to plunge into the abyss. And sign. Every document, twice. The rustle of paper and the scribbling of the pen is the only sound in the room. I sign my free will away, paper after paper after paper. When the Mountain returns my brain has gone numb. *I have sold my soul to the military.*

They dismiss me and the guards all but push me out of the building. One of them mutters something unintelligible about an escort, but I have no time to waste and I ignore them, having no choice but to travel on foot. There is a flash in the clouds, the bang follows a few seconds later. I stand frozen for a moment. *Do I head back to the Swallows?* It would be at least a three-hour journey up that way. The thought of their house, the chimney cold, and the lights off makes me nauseous. But it will be a half-hour walk to the bakery. It's in the completely other direction. Rain pelts down on me and my clothes are soaked, but that doesn't matter. *Monster would have gone back home if he could.*

I half run, half stumble over the muddy road towards the bakery. Gusts of wind push at me from the side and I slip. With my right hand, I catch myself. The rocks scrape my hand and knee, but I ignore it. Warm raindrops trickle down my cheeks. First, I pass the College building. There are no lights burning behind its windows. It reminds me of a carcass. A little further I see the street that leads to Darya's house. It's deserted. No one is out in this weather. I stop to peer at her windows, there's no light on behind them. *Did Darya betray me? Did they hurt Darya to get the information?*

Torn between Darya's welfare and Monster's I stand completely still on the crossing. The sky rumbles and I let out a scream in pure frustration. *Darya might be fine. I know for sure Monster is not.* Light flashes above me and the thunder is instantaneous. It's getting dangerous to be out here. It's just a short walk home now. *Have I made the right decision?*

My heart freezes as I see the bakery door swing on its hinges. As a gust of wind pushes it, metal screams. A tightness in my chest forms when I think of all the people I have put in danger in order to escape. Inside, the room is silent and empty. I don't bother to try to close the beaten-down door.

"Monster?" My voice is muted and frail.

No answer comes. There is no sign of life. In front of the counter, I see splatters of something dark. I can't tell if it's Monster's or someone else's. I fly upstairs to check the rooms, my bedroom, Gran's room, the hallway, and the closet. It screams the absence of Monster. A trail of water and mud shows where I have been. My chest squeezes together and I can hardly breathe. I check every place he could be again. *No, no, no, no, no... Did Boyle go back for him? Is he still lying there? What would the military have done with him?*

I run into the street. Hoping outside the air will have enough oxygen to ease the cramp in my chest. Rain pours down heavily and I slip over the slick stones. My knees hit the stones and I gasp in pain, desperately I glance left and right, for any sign of Monster.

"Momo!" Rain trickles down my brow and into my eyes. I try to stand up. My knee shakes under my weight. "Momo!?"

My body shivers and warm raindrops stream down my face. Despite my knee, I rise, and as I walk I feel like I am watching myself as I get up and limp down the street. From a distance, I watch the rain falling heavily on the muddy street as if I am standing in front of a foggy window. *Her- no- My knee is most definitely busted, how am I going to get all the way to the Swallows?*

I see myself sway on my feet and finding stability against a wall. On the wall, there is a muddy hand-print. *Is this my hand? Did I leave that print there?*

Her body moves sluggishly as if she's battling the tides, every step requiring immense effort. A black automobile slowly drives in the other direction. The sound of my name doesn't reach her, the slamming of the door makes her jump and she moves faster. But the pulling tides doesn't let her. She's not getting anywhere. I watch as a Dog walks towards her from behind.

In the distance, there is that voice again, but that is not important now. My knee buckles as I take another step and I watch myself yelp in pain. Two pairs of strong arms lift under my shoulder and pull me to the opposite direction. "No!" I shout, still underwater. "He's, he's-" *That way.*

They drag me back inside and I cry uncontrollably, my gasps for air wreck my body. I get picked up as easily as if I was a rag doll and a blue-gray uniform lifts me up the stairs. "Please-" *This must be Baël finishing what he started.* "Please don't."

The Dog puts me in a chair and the moment he turns his back I flee to the door, but another figure blocks my passage. I collapse to the ground. Dogs exchange words. He talks to me, but his voice is distorted and I can't make out what he says.

I'm being undressed and I think of the dolls I used to play with as a little girl. From a distance, I see the Dog walk out the door and leave my crumpled body. He comes back with a duvet, smelling of Gran, and covers me. The blanket itches and scrapes against my skin. The figure puts wood into the fireplace and lights it. Within seconds the hearth is ablaze with light. *Hmm, that was fast.* The warmth eludes me as I watch what is happening. One of them leaves and the other pulls up a chair and sits silently beside me.

After a while, the sound of the fire comes into focus and I absorb its warmth. An odd perfume hangs in the air. It takes a while before my brain registers it as Lavender. Warmth returns to my body, but my insides cannot be heated. I glance at the person sitting there. "Captain?"

His black eyes are filled with worry. "Are you alright?"

I shake my head.

"Did he hurt you?" he whispers.

Again, I shake my head and he sighs a sigh of relief as if he takes some comfort in my bodily well-being. "Did signing up for the military harm you that much?" *How does he know? Right, he probably knows everything.*

"He- he shot Monster." My voice is unsteady as I bite away tears and my throat is still sore.

"He fired at your bear?" he asks, confused.

"He is a dog."

"Are you sure?"

I stare daggers at him, but this news seems to bother him. He covers his mouth with his hand for a second and sighs. The crackling of wood fills the silence of the room. Now I notice he made me tea and I'm already holding the cup. *When did this happen?*

"I'll be right back."

He walks downstairs and I can hear the door creak. I calculate my next move.

Could I use his car? How do you drive one of those?

The fire crackles and I sip tea to give my hands something to do. An overpowering flavor of lavender enters my mouth, yet there is a flower added to it. *Maybe Monster found shelter in the Swallows' house somehow.* But even I know I'm grasping at straws.

Heavy footsteps walk up the stairs and I jolt back to attention. It's Captain Hawkeye who tells me he has sent someone to search for Monster. The fire begins to die and I want him to leave. But I have no energy to say anything about it. Suddenly the sound of screaming hinges comes from downstairs. Again my body tenses and I draw a quick breath.

"Relax, no one is going to hurt you."

"Clearly you can't promise that."

The Captain leaves his chair and the steps descends. The cup in my hand is empty, but I hold it tight. Subdued voices travel up the stairs and hurried footsteps run their way up them. This time more than one pair. The first person storming through the door is Darya. She sees me and falls to her knees and gives me a hug. I must look like a drowned cat.

"By Quatahna, Elara, what happened?"

I give a dry sob. "They found me... and Momo..."

"How did they- No, Elara, I, I swear, I-," Her eyes widen, and she goes silent as she realizes the Captain is listening in. She can swear all she wants, but someone told them exactly where I was going and it wasn't me. Her hands rub over my arms in an attempt to warm me up.

"They shot the Swallows," I tell the empty cup of tea I'm still holding, and Darya inhales sharply.

She takes a deep breath and tries to get me to make eye contact. "I know. Elara, I know where Monster is."

I snap to attention "What!? Where!? Is he ok!?"

"Seger came to my place as soon as they dropped you off at the base. He told me I should go and find Monster. Near the Swallows' house. He was injured, and you were gone. So I took him home..." Darya takes a deep breath. "He's hurt bad,"

My chest constricts. I throw the duvet to the floor and jump up. Darya coughs when I'm nearly through the door. "Uh Elara..." Darya's voice trails away. She glances pointedly at my clothing. Or lack thereof. I'm not decent. Captain Hawkeye clears his throat as he points to a pile of soaked rags lying discarded in the corner. His eyes are fixed on the fireplace. *What a gentleman.*

Then I realize he also took them off, and I feel violated. I run to my wardrobe, grab a dress, and yank it over my head. "Now we go!"

Hawkeye takes us to Darya's house in his car. Another Dog drives as we sit silently in the back. Rain beats loudly against the windows. For the first time tonight, I experience the cold. My teeth chatter. The automobile stops at the front door quicker than I could have run it. Before it stands completely still, I rush out of the vehicle. Darya is right behind me as she follows me to her door. I tug at the handle, but it's locked. *That's never been locked before.*

"My parents are off to Alvor to visit Dew and won't be coming home for a few days," Darya says as she opens the door.

"He's near the fireplace." I step through the doorway. Inside Darya's house it's toasty warm, still, a shiver goes down my spine. Monster lies in the living room. His paw is bandaged and so is his torso. His breath is shallow and fast, his tongue lolls out of his mouth and his eyes stare off into the distance. I wail as I fall to my knees to pet his gigantic head. He doesn't respond to my touch or my voice. I bury my nose in his fur and inhale him. *I am so sorry!*

"He has been like this for a while now," Darya says in a small voice. Captain asks to use Darya's phone and makes a quick call.

Time goes by and Monster doesn't move. Or blink. I stroke his thick fur, fiddle with his paws, and pick at his big ears, hoping something will get through to him. Darya has made the Dog some tea and they sit down on a couch. The fireplace roars and beside Monster's wet fur, I smell pine. Darya and the Captain are talking in low voices. I only have eyes for my friend. I hug his enormous body. "Mooomoo, it's okay, I'm here! I'm here," I murmur into his coat over and over again.

Another person walks into the room without knocking. It's Mrs. Applegarth, dressed in a long black coat that reaches her knees. Captain Hawkeye stands to shake her hand and they talk in hushed voices before Hawkeye announces he has to go. He turns to Darya. "Thank you for the hospitality, Ms. Ballard, and for your service, Mrs.

Applegarth."

Mrs. Applegarth salutes him before she sits down next to me.

"Oh my," she says as she sees the blood on Monster's coat and instantly goes to work. "Darya, could you be so kind as to fetch some warm blankets?" Darya runs up the stairs and Mrs. Applegarth asks me what happened. While I tell her he got shot and I tried to heal him, her fingers search for the wound. She only has eyes for her patient.

"You attempted Aquakinesis? It might have saved him from blood loss, although I need to open the wound again to remove the bullet." She retrieves a leather satchel from her coat and then her hand draws out her flask. Just as with Gran, she forms the water glove on her left hand. As she moves it over Monster's belly, a whine emerges from his chest. The high noise comes and fades. With her free hand, she opens the satchel and takes out a small surgical blade. My stomach turns. She cuts into his side and he lets out a yelp.

"Is he awake?" Darya's voice trembles from behind us, holding the blankets in her arms. Monster shows signs of life, but he is clearly in a lot of pain.

"Shhh!" I stroke his snout. "You are going to get better soon." Our teacher asks Darya to find him some food.

"Cooked chicken if you have it."

"Of course." She drops the blankets and hurries off.

Mrs. Applegarth focuses her attention on his soft belly and with tiny movements of her fingers, she conjures the bullet out. His shallow, uneven breathing turns into slow, deep breaths. His blank stare hasn't changed. "Elara, I'm unable to do this alone. Lend me your hand." She places hers under mine and leads it to Monster's side. "Channel any energy you sense in the water to my hand." The familiar flutter goes through my hands. With all my might, I try to do as she says. And Instead of a push, the energy is being drawn out of me. *It's fine, as long as it helps.*

She holds it there until some life comes back into Monster's eyes. It makes me tear up.

"Captain Hawkeye also expressed worry about your knee. Show me." Mrs. Applegarth turns to me. *Oh, right.*

Darya comes in at the moment I pull up my dress high enough for Mrs. Applegarth to examine the swollen joint. The skin has broken in a few places and streaks of dried-up blood run down my lower leg. It's a right mess.

She ushers me on the couch and binds the water around my knee for a good thirty seconds and before my eyes, the skin heals and the swelling goes down. Darya gasps as she sees it. My skin now has an angry red-purplish hue, but I can bend it without too much pain.

"That's amazing!" she whispers and sits next to me as Mrs. Applegarth fluently flows the water back into her flask. Darya stares at the gift she has witnessed. She hands me some chicken. My leg protests a little under my weight as I crouch beside Monster. I hold the chicken in front of Monster's nose. A flicker of recognition flits through his eyes and he carefully licks at the food and chews. After a few bites, he falls asleep.

"Thank you, Mrs. Applegarth!" I want to fling around her neck, but I'm exhausted and only manage to give her a thankful look.

"I am happy to be of service, but I can only do so much. You both need rest and regular checkups. I will return tomorrow morning."

Darya and I sit on the couch while we watch Monsters sleeping form. "Why did you tell them?"

Darya is shocked. "Excuse me?"

"What made you tell the *Dogs* where we were going?" I ask angrily.

Darya's eyes become white hot. "I know you have been through a lot today, so I will let this slide. But if you think for a *second-*" She stops herself mid-sentence and leaves the room. I want to believe her, I really do, but how else could they have found out? I sleep on the couch with my eyes on Monster and after a few hours, Darya comes by to see if I need anything. *Is she feeling guilty? Or is she just a good hostess?*

The following morning, Darya makes breakfast out of the things she finds in the house. I hear Gran's voice in the back of my mind. *They can figure it out without you ever meaning them to.*

Breakfast is two boiled eggs and Darya walks into the room with two mugs of steaming tea. "Captain Hawkeye said Lavender would be good for you," she says as she gives me a mug. The atmosphere is frosty. Monster hasn't moved from his spot near the fireplace, but eats his breakfast with mild enthusiasm. She has put a letter on the table. It's from the military again. "This came in for you."

Dear Conscript,

We are writing to confirm your successful registration for military training, as ordered by the Ministry of War. Your prompt compliance with this mandate is greatly appreciated.

As previously instructed, you are to report to the Town Hall on the designated date according to your family name.

Upon arrival, you shall be provided with all the necessary equipment for the training, and you will leave all belongings in the Logon Office. Please note this is a mandatory requirement and failure to comply may result in disciplinary action.

Following the ceremony, you will be joining your fellow troops on the journey back to the Capital, where you begin your training.

Thank you for your willingness to serve our nation in times of need. We look forward to your active participation in the program.

In unity and reverence,

Captain of Arms
J. C. VAHL
Head of Logon Office for War Volunteers

***

Dies Saturni

After 2 days, we move Monster back as Darya's two cats are not happy with the current arrangement. Zale drops by to fix the door. But Darya handles all that. She helps me keep the bakery afloat and I care for Monster. Mrs. Applegarth has come by every day as she promised. Monster makes progress, but slowly. He hasn't walked far yet and when he does he moves across the room with heartbreaking care. Darya takes care of us both, bringing us food and helping where she can. Monster's wagging tail is the first thing he gains full control of.

The duffle bag sits open and empty on my bed and the list of items we are advised to bring lies next to it. I stand observing it in only my undergarments, not ready yet to put on the blue-gray uniform that lies on my desk. The house creaks and the first birds are waking up. My feet are standing on the carpet, which was once green and now is black. Dust particles are drifting through the air in the candlelight.

First, I go to Gran's room. It smells like her in there, even though we cleaned out a lot of stuff. Her presence breathes in every nook and cranny. A few of her dresses still hang in the closet. Those were the ones I couldn't bear to part with. The fabric is soft between my fingers. There is a layer of dust on her bookcase and make-up cabinet. From one of the books, I grab the last letters my parents ever sent her and decide to take them with me. The crisp paper is dry in my clammy hand. Quietly, I say goodbye to the bed, the furniture, and her smell. Before I close the door behind me.

Next, I go to the bathroom and get two towels, lavender-scented soap, and toiletries that we are advised to bring for our journey and return to my bedroom.

Gran would have been proud of how tidy my room is, and I regret not having cleaned it properly while she was here to enjoy it. My skin is cold and I can see goosebumps forming on my arms. I cross the distance between me and the desk with one step. The uniform lies there, waiting patiently. It consists of two pieces, the pants, and the coat. The pants are blue with gray stitching on the sides and an elastic band along the waistline. There are big white buttons on both sides of it, making it possible to attach the overcoat. As I pick it up, the fabric is heavy and thick in my hands, putting them on is easy. They are baggy on my body and not feminine at all, which makes sense because all Dogs wear the same uniform. Looking down, my heart thumps in my throat. I sit on my bed and put on the black boots. They are high and lace up to halfway up my shins. They smell like new leather and I am sure I'll get blisters before we reach the Capitol. For a long time, I watch the dust settle in my pristine room before I decide what shirt I'll wear under the coat. My choice ends up being a maroon one that Gran bought me last year, that I barely wore. I tuck it neatly into the trousers. My mouth goes dry as I examine the coat. First, I carefully put one arm through the sleeve, as if it might bite me, then the next. The coat is heavy on my shoulders and it closes uncomfortably around my neck. One by one, I fasten the gray buttons that are placed on two-thirds of my left side. With a high heartbeat, I splash some water on my face. My hands grasp the sides of the sink as I try to keep my composure. Quickly, I pack the rest of the items into my duffel bag. Before I walk out of my door, my foot hovers and I decide to take the First Men's blade. I cover the sharp metal with a cloth and strap it to my hip under my uniform. The cold metal against my skin gives me a glimmer of confidence.

While I lean over to grab it from my shelf, I glance at myself in the mirror and my heart jumps. An unfamiliar face stares back at me. There are bags under her eyes, which are red and her face is pale and her hair blond. Most importantly, she's a Dog, at least on the outside. She nods, defeated, and I turn away.

Downstairs Monster waits for me. As I walk down the stairs a growl starts in his throat. With teeth bared and tail low, he looks at my uniform.

"Monster honey, it's me," I coo at him. Unsure what to think of the situation, he lies down, but the rumble in his chest doesn't stop. With my back against the counter, I let myself sink down to the floor with tears in my eyes. *They have taken everything from me.*

There is a knock on and with Monster's eyes fixed on me, I rise. Monster stands up too, not trusting the new me. My limbs are heavy as I move. His eyes following me. Behind the glass door, the image of Mrs. Applegarth appears as discussed. Behind her idles a big truck. She will be taking over the care of Monster while I go to the Capitol. She smiles kindly when I open the door. Monster has spotted her and greets her by banging his tail against the counter.

"Good morning-" She regards me in my uniform for a moment. "-Private. I had to pull a few strings, but Monster can accompany us to the Capitol."

I blink at her, my brain trying to process this information.

"Thank you." My arms grab her as I cry. "Thank you, thank you, thank you!" I manage to say between sobs. *When did I become this unstable snottering mess?*

She smiles warmly at me. "I'll think of a way you can repay me one day. In the Capitol, he will be solely under my care. You can come to visit him whenever you like. But I have no time to look after him on our journey, so you have to take good care of him."

She enters the bakery with a glint in her eyes. "It took me some convincing, but when I told Captain Hawkeye, you would be a flight risk if we took you without him, he caved! I think he is fond of you."

Mrs. Applegarth takes out her flask and goes over his belly again.

"Can I get you anything?" I say as she works. "There are still some muffins from yesterday..."

She declines politely.

We carefully load Monster into the truck Mrs. Applegarth brought along. I thank Mrs. Applegarth profusely and Monster lets me give him a hug, but not very enthusiastically.

Back in the bakery, my fingers trace the smooth wood of the doorpost and I lean my forehead against it. The house is eerily silent as if it is holding its breath. The perfume of bread lingers in the air. "I will be back," I whisper to the emptiness. "I will be back and I will have made them bleed."

* * *

Dies Martis

Mauria and her husband Angus, dressed to the nines, have come to the Town Hall to bid me farewell. Mauria has lost weight and her demeanor is subdued.

She must be missing Lilly.

The weight of my new outfit presses heavily on my shoulders and I fidget with the coat to make it fit better, though no such luck.

The engines of trucks roar in the dark of the early morning, but the chatter of the people is louder. All in all, it's a near-deafening experience and I am glad because this gives me an excuse not to speak too much. My jaw clenches and I find myself being glad Gran is not here to see this. An air of tension and uncertainty fuses with the fumes from the trucks and hangs heavy in the atmosphere.

The Town Hall's whitewashed tree stems shine in the electric lights. Quatahna's face watches over us as solemn as ever. Her ocean blue eyes watch our every move and her silver hair looks cold in the light. This early in the morning the shadows make it difficult to make out its intricately decorated walls. I take comfort in knowing the First Men are all around us. *Please watch over us Quatahna. I don't know what to do.*

I walk underneath the painting of the First Men coming to shore. Their journey ended here in Eden as we had hoped ours would too. My throat tightens and I focus my attention on the gold patterns painted on their arms. The eldest has white flowy hair eternalized on the ceiling. Their voices echo from the dome ceiling. The First Men gaze down at us, all-knowing.

The big round hall is packed with people. Most of them are from Eden, some from the next towns over. You can easily miss all the doors because of these murals. Dogs walk in and out of them. Behind these doors, there are smaller rooms, normally used for meetings. *What would the First Men do if they could see us now?*

Four Dogs in uniform stand on either side of the Hall. Each has a handful of people scuttled around them. My eyes flash over my form, and it tells me I am to report to Amber Little, there is only one female so that is easy. Amber Little is a young Dog, barely a few years older than I am. Her short auburn hair goes well with her bossy aura. I am the last to arrive.

Besides the 'volunteers', family, friends, and some curious people have shown up. I feel like punching these disaster voyeurs on the nose and I tighten my grip on my bag.

With so many people here it should be chaos. It's not. A buzzing sound like angry bees fills the air. People stand neatly in rows in front of the desks with a Dog sitting behind it. Every volunteer has a big bag, slung over the shoulder or in front of them on the ground. Thalassa already stands ahead in line. She doesn't see me and I stay back, reluctant, because I know, if she asked if I was alright, I'd lose that little bit of composure I have left.

The line progresses quickly and people are handed a form before they find their assigned group. Dogs walk around in their blue-gray uniform, 'keeping the peace'. Second Lieutenant Winchester stands on a pair of stairs gazing over everything. A big gun slung over his shoulder.

Uneasy, I swallow. His friendly demeanor is gone. He oozes authority. This version of the Dog scares me. I scratch behind my ear.

When it's my turn to fill in a form, it's only a matter of name and number. The soldier hands me another form. I'm so insignificant she doesn't even glance up at me. "This is your new number, your classes, and your food stamps. Your mentor awaits you in the Town Hall," she says for what is undoubtedly the umpteenth time. The paper is dry in my damp hand.

"Next!"

Thalassa greets me with a big hug and kisses me on the cheek. "We're assigned to the same truck! Our gang is going to be together again!"

She seems to shine in her military uniform and her hair is as frizzy as ever. Thalassa's pants are so big on her that it's borderline ridiculous. I manage a curt nod and clench my jaw. Thalassa's emotions are so far removed from my own I want to start bawling.

There is a stark difference between the people who are leaving for home and the ones who will be leaving home. Ones who are leaving home are all a bit pale and our eyes flit to every unknown sound. Maybe it's just me.

My new black boots pinch my feet in several places and I am sure

I already have blisters. Thalassa takes my arm and leads me back outside.

Our breath forms puffs of mist in the chilly morning air. Mauria sees me and hurries over. Her eyes are red and puffy, but she gives me a big hug and tells me to 'be a good girl'. She sounds so much like Gran that my lower lip trembles.

Thalassa's parents give her a hug, and a kiss on the cheek goodbye and repeat several times they want a letter from the both of us once we arrive at the Capitol. Mauria holds Angus when we get called to enter the truck. Mr. and Mrs. Ballard and Darya are there to see me off, and Mrs. Ballard gives me a big kiss on the forehead. "Take care of yourself, darling". I give her a big hug and promise I will. Darya gives me a hug, but it doesn't warm me up. The thought she would betray me like this makes me physically nauseous. *How can she be so cold?*

I leave with misty eyes, refusing to cry and it feels like someone is squeezing my throat. My hand travels to the blade tucked snugly against my hip. We walk to our appointed truck and I can see the Boyle brothers. They're not here to see us off, they are helping with the preparations to leave. They're loading heavy-looking boxes into the back of a truck. Wade sees me, smiles and mouths, 'He's in here'. I lift up the corners of my mouth and give him a thumbs-up. The brothers will be staying behind to 'assist the local police' together with a few other militants. On the other side of the truck, Raphaël gives his mother a big hug while she cries on his shoulder. There are 4 trucks in total to move all the people and all the stuff we need to the Capitol.

The Captain walks up the stairs and waits for the chatter to die down, a jolt goes through me as he looks in my direction.

"Attention, Privates!" he shouts and everyone looks up at him. His uniform is impeccable, and he holds his arm behind his back. It's impossible to combine the man who enticed me to drink strong alcoholic cocktails with this image of absolute discipline. He continues in a softer voice but I hear every word.

"As your Captain, it is my duty to address you before we embark on our convoy to the base. We expect to be on the road for 5 days. As we venture south, remain vigilant and disciplined. Our safety and security are of utmost importance. Adhere to the instructions provided, exercise caution on the roads, and maintain the highest standards of conduct. New recruits, please collect your items with Lance Corporal Little. She is also assigned to your truck, and she is responsible for you until we reach the Capitol."

I let out a shuddering breath and long for the power to turn back time.

"Our actions reflect not only upon ourselves but also upon the uniform we wear and the flag we salute. So I expect nothing but the best from you. Now, let us gather our belongings and make final preparations for our convoy. May our journey be safe, our spirits unyielding, and our resolve unwavering." He salutes the flag next to him. "In unity and reverence, let us raise our voices and hail the Leader Suprema!"

Around me, the Dogs stand straight and salute the flag. "In unity and reverence! Hail Leader Suprema Crestwood!"

Chapter 16

The engines make the sound of an angry sea and our new officer's voice is shrill as she barks over them. "Listen up, group 3. My name is Amber Little and you are to address me as Lance Corporal Little. You will end your sentences with Sir or Madam. I'm not picky. Understand this: I have no tolerance for stragglers, imbeciles, or jesters in my presence."

Her short auburn hair glows in the light of the truck, and her sharp nose casts a shadow along her face. Her words make me want to freeze her head into an ice block -if I knew how to do that. She goes on, undisturbed.

"Know that my face shall be the first sight that graces your miserable mornings, and you will obey my every command. Smoking, showering, brushing your teeth, or even defecating shall be done only with my permission. Disobey any of these regulations and punishments shall swiftly follow. Do not test my patience."

She raises a paper sheet menacingly. "The regulations are attached to your forms. Do not read them without my permission!" she barks when the sound of paper ruffling reaches her ears. Thalassa quickly puts down her hands.

"This wretched group shall become your so-called 'family' during the drive south. You are lucky to have the competent Corporal Applegarth for advanced healing. Frankly, I hold no expectations for any of you to do well, yet perhaps you will achieve a state of being slightly less inadequate."

If looks could kill, Lance Corporal Little would be a little heap of ashes by now. She goes on undisturbed. "Follow me!"

We make our way to a table, and to my surprise, Trent is here as well. He smiles at Raphaël as he slaps his shoulder.

"Good t-to see you," Raphaël says.

Our new officer barks, "Each of you shall have a pistol to call your own. Affix your signature to this document as confirmation that you have received them. In the next five days, we will master the art of cleaning, disassembling, and reassembling them. Before we arrive at the Capitol, I shall mold you into true soldiers, rather than mere..." She motions at us as if we're sea cucumbers now and continues to explain what is to be expected from us this trip. Lastly, she revises gun safety, she holds up her gun and I hope she shoots herself with it. No such luck.

"This," she says as she holds up her gun for us all to see. It's smaller than the ones I've seen the officers use. "Is a semi-automatic pistol. And this pretty lady is known as Beretta. It has 9 distinct parts, and this is the most important one for you, featherbrains. The *safety*. It makes sure you don't shoot yourself or your buddies."

The cold metal is light compared to the damage it can do. Trent and Raphaël handle the pistol with grace. We repeat the safety protocol like sheep and I shiver in the cold morning air.

"Exercise extreme caution at all times. If, by any chance, this pistol discharges without my explicit consent, rest assured that I will personally ensure you suffer the consequences." Her eyes blaze with fire. "Once we arrive at the Capitol, I shall be promoted to Corporal, and I expect none of you to tarnish my reputation with boorish behavior!"

With frozen fingers, I check the safety, take out the bullets, and am about to put the magazine in my other pocket.

"Private Waywater, what do you think you're doing?" she asks, venom dripping from her tone.

"I, err, thought it would be safer to keep these apart," I respond timidly while staring at the ground.

"What good is a gun without bullets!? Do you truly believe we issue these to you as mere fashion accessories?" she spits at me. "Put it back and secure it in your holster!"

I do as I am told while glaring at the floor.

"Alright! Ready?" We nod silently and she rolls her eyes. "When I ask you a question, you say *yes ma'am*, or *no ma'am*, WHILE you salute me."

Like all the other Dogs I touch my hand to my temple and chant "Yes, ma'm." *I'm disgusting.*

A short metal ladder helps us climb into the big green truck. The blade presses into my skin uncomfortably as I follow Thalassa in. The metal of the ladder is cold against my bare hands. Benches are made from metal and I sit on it, dropping my bag at my feet. I clench my jaw to keep my emotions in control.

Outside, the morning mist flees like ghosts for the sunlight. A small group of people stand close to the truck to be able to catch one last glimpse of us. Trent is already inside and I sit opposite him. He volunteered for the military the second he was escorted from training camp. He nods at me. Raphaël gets in last. He's pale and uncharacteristically silent.

Thalassa puts her head on my shoulder and this little motion causes my heart to shatter. Lance Corporal Little jumps into the truck with us and tells us she will be gracing us with her presence today. *Just when I thought it couldn't get any worse.*

The group all try to find a place so they can look out of the exit to give their family one final wave. Things like 'Don't forget to write!'

and 'Keep your nose out of trouble' are shouted to and fro, and I feel detached from it all. My loved ones have one by one fallen away, and I can't bring myself to look at Darya again. The truck is covered with a thick canvas which limits our view of the outside world. I focus on my breath to try to keep my mind from going into a downward spiral. It's difficult and my vision blurs and my teeth clench.

I'll come back, I'll make it back soon and all of this will be a distant nightmare. Oh Gran...

Time passes, I don't know how much. My thoughts spiral from Darya's betrayal to Gran to Monster.

At midday, Little is the first to jump out of the truck while we climb out of it with stiff limbs. She holds a riding crop and I have to force myself not to roll my eyes.

I should tell... Oh, right.

The thought of Darya is like a punch in the gut.

The ground is dry and trees are few and far apart. The ones that were once brave enough to grow are now stumped and crooked. It smells like bark and greenery. We learn how to march like proper soldiers because even a nurse should know the basics.

"Now, fall-IN!" I try to copy her movement. It's unnatural. She steps forward, so I rest.

"Private Waywater, did I tell you to stop?"

In the distance, Hawkeye and First Lieutenant Winchester look in our direction. Normally I'd feel humiliated, but I'm just too defeated to care. We turn left and turn right like good Dogs until lunch is ready. The Lance Corporal puffs out her chest proudly when we walk away.

I need to run before we get over the mountains. It will be nearly impossible to get over them on foot, with winter coming. But Momo is still hurt too bad..

Together with Raphaël and Thalassa, I search for Monster. The big truck we put him in this morning is at the back of the convoy. Through the canvas opening, his big relaxed form is visible. He sees me climb in and he licks my face and ears happily. I bury my nose in his fur and he pants like a little excited puppy. Thalassa plays with his ears. "Can't he come with us in our truck?"

Raphaël raises his eyebrows. "I don't th-think he'll fit."

He leans, raises his painful paw, and emits a low growl when Raphaël tries to pet him.

"Momo! Cut it out, he's friendly!"

Monster stops growling but whines nervously.

"Let him sniff your hand."

Raphaël calmly puts his hand in front of Monster's face. Carefully, he smells the hand and regards Raphaël.

"It's okay, b-b-buddy. I'm not scary." He turns towards me. "They m-must have hurt him pretty b-bad."

"They did. Would you- Would you take care of him if I-" I whisper to Raphaël. "Geez Elara, we're going to the Capital, not to the front!" Thalassa nudges me with her elbow, but Raphaël watches me in quiet understanding.

The smell of chicken soup makes my mouth water. A man is hunched over and cuts vegetables while a woman is bent over a large stove. Her face is flushed from the heat. Second Lieutenant Winchester walks in right after me, giving me no sign of recognition. I sigh in relief.

At the sight of Winchester, the cooks smile and the fattest of them jogs towards him. Sweat glistens on his brow. This man reminds me of a big bowl of jelly pudding. On the center of his fat face sits a big red nose that is almost purple, like a raspberry. Not as tall as the Mountain, but just as wide. A bit of white wispy hair above his ears shows his age.

"Chef-! How are things?" Lieutenant Winchester inquires. Apparently, Chef likes to complain. "Tha tent iz too zmall, tha cookz are zimpletonz, tha ground to muddy, tha meat in the village zcarse, and tha temperature too cold". He does this all with huge arm movements, his big belly moves up and down with excitement. After all this complaining, I decide I like Chef. He ends his tirade with, "And how iz tha little Winchezter?"

The Dog starts to talk about his daughter and how she is still struggling with the word potato. Chef asks him, "How long zince you zeen ha?" And a cloud covers his good mood.

"Not in months, Chef." They are silent and nod knowingly as I stand behind Winchester, feeling awkward. *I'm hungry!* Instantly, the mood shifts. "This is Private Waywater, my new friend." He motions towards me. *He knew I was here!?*

Chef gives me a big sweaty smelling hug and 'welcomez me into tha family'. "Zooooo –" he says with his voice climbing a few octaves- "Michael likez ya, hea? Then Chef likez ya too. Ya be good to old Chef and Chef'll be good to ya. Winchezter has a good noze for tha things," he says tapping his own. "Thiz lo-ve-ly lady iz called Zophiël, but we call her Zophe." She is also big, though not as monstrous as Chef.

"My name is Elara, Sir."

His eyes pop and his big belly begins to wobble. He makes a wheezing sound and I realize he's laughing. "She called me Zir! I do like ha!" He heaves. I glance over at Second Lieutenant Winchester, and he gives me a wink.

"Well, Chef-" Trying not to either push my luck or kill him. "I need… I would like… If you could. I need some breakfast," I end lamely.

Chef grins. "Of course! Here you go Babushka!" *What the hell is a Babushka?*

Not sure if I should be flattered or offended, I decide I don't care as

I end up with a big plate of the orange goo. High-ranking Dogs are seated on comfy stools, already eating and talking amicably. Baël, Hawkeye, the Mountain, and Mrs. Applegarth are deep in conversation and don't notice me. The sight of them being so at ease spoils my appetite. Raphaël nudges me and I break out of my trance. We go in search of a good piece of ground to sit on. Lance Corporal Little sits with a few others I don't know and I avoid eye contact.

Chef shakes his head when I ask for seconds. "Zorry babushka, it'z all gone." *Does Mrs. Applegarth have anything with her for Momo?*

* * *

The sun has set when we stop at a military base. I'm exhausted and sore. Lance Corporal Little leads us to a big stone hall surrounded by more military personnel. This time we get mashed potatoes, beans, and fish. I play with my mashed potatoes and fold the fish into a handkerchief for Monster to eat later. Thalassa glances at my handkerchief and winks at me. Our little secret.

Raphaël just takes a big mouthful of mashed potatoes and pats me on the back. The group leaves me to get seconds and I look around the stone hall. There is a big painting of the Leader Suprema on one side. She is wearing the same military costume as I am. Her white hair is tied back for the occasion and she is holding a long sword with its tip touching the ground. Underneath the painting, the line 'In reverence and unity' is drawn in golden letters. I have to consciously relax my jaw and eat a little to relax the tightness in my throat.

When the team comes back, Raphaël and Thalassa donate their second portion of fish to me. I thank them for their kindness while tears fill my eyes. After dinner, Raphaël and Thalassa take off to find their quarters inside the complex, while I walk back to the trucks.

In ours, I find a rolled-up mattress and then go to Monster's truck. His scent has overpowered the fumes of the truck and I lay down next to him. There is not a lot of room, but he keeps me warm. His thick fur is comforting between my fingers.

The floor presses hard against the bones in my hips and shoulders. Between this and my constantly buzzing brain, it's hard to find a good position to sleep in. I stare wide-eyed at the canvas ceiling of the truck while I try to order my thoughts. My first priority is to get both Monster and me through this journey unscathed and well-fed. After we get to the Capitol, I will find the resistance there. In the meantime, it's important for me to keep close and personal with both Winchester and Hawkeye. I turn on my side and Monster breathes a deep breath in his sleep. *How will I find the resistance in a city as big as the Capitol?*

I look in the mirror and admire my mother's old dress. It suits me perfectly. My hair is soft, and it gleams in the sunlight. Downstairs, I hear the bell ring - a customer. I walk downstairs and see Gran humming while she sweeps the floor. The customer is playing with Monster. His black hair causes a tingle in my chest. "Are you ready?" He is wearing a maroon dress shirt and dark slacks.

"No, I-I don't want to go." A fear hits me like a tsunami. If I step out of that door, I will never come back again. His hand grabs my wrist firmly.

"Come on, Elara. You are ready now."

I try to wrestle from his grip, but he is a lot stronger than I am. He pulls me towards the door.

"Elara honey." Gran is smiling while she holds a black piece of metal in her hands. "You forgot to pack your gun. You always need to carry your gun."

There is something wrong with her smile. It's like it's melting. Meanwhile, Onyx Eyes is trying to drag me out of the bakery. "GRAN! Gran, help me!"

She stands there waving happily at me.

* * *

A blink of an eye later, we are awoken by someone climbing into the truck. I gasp when I see a blue-gray uniform. Monster begins to growl.

"Who are you?" A blond Dog asks when he sees me lying there. It takes a minute for my heartbeat to slow down.

"Elara-sorry. I'll- I'll leave now."

He takes a step back as I roll up the mattress and kiss Monster on his nose.

"I think someone is looking for you…" He whistles between his teeth and an auburn-haired woman turns around. Lance Corporal Little's eyes are ablaze.

"Is this the one?" he shouts at her.

She is almost as red as her auburn hair and she marches towards me. "Private, where have you- have you SLEPT in there?" she asks, her eyes on my hair.

"Yes, ma'am," I say, not wanting more trouble.

"Ms. Waywater. It appears your incompetence knows no bounds. Be warned, further infractions shall not go unpunished. Your ineptitude has not gone unnoticed, and I will be keeping a watchful eye on your every move." She tells me as she wags her finger at me. "You are to be with your team at all times. What if something happened to you?" *In other words, what if I decide to flee?* "It would be MY head!" *Good.* "Now get in your truck! I won't have *you* make us late."

I'm the first one in our truck and from my bag, I get my comb and brush out the knots in my hair. I start when the truck jolts. It's Raphaël. By the time I'm back to my resting heart rate, Thalassa has also entered the truck holding a big plate of food. They're both showered and well-rested. Thalassa has brought me some breakfast. It consists of scrambled egg, two fat sausages, and greasy bacon. Before she is seated, the engine roars to life.

"That's great! I'll bring it to Momo right away."

"Elara, you haven't eaten properly since we left. This is for you!"

"No, no, I'm fine. Give me a second!" I tap on the window and motion to the driver to wait a minute. He taps his watch, but I get out anyway. Monster's truck has already started rolling for the outer gates and I run after it. It's a good thing the gates are still closed, so I catch up with the truck easily. I put the plate down in the truck. Monster sniffs at it and carefully licks the egg from the plate. He enjoys it so much his tail taps the metal floor.

Our truck passes me and I jump in while it drives. For once, I'm happy with my coordination. Some men applaud me. Second Lieutenant Winchesters smiles with arms crossed.

"Elara," Raphaël says, he's clearly uncomfortable. "At breakfast, C-Captain Hawkeye said we are driving through dangerous territory t-today. He ordered all of us to stay in the truck until someone of higher rank t-tells us it's safe to come out."

A spark of hope ignites while I wonder if that means there will be active resistance members about. "What dangerous territory?"

Raphaël shrugs. "That's all he told us."

The truck's even more uncomfortable than it was yesterday. The metal bench is pressing into my back and the absence of cushioning and constant jostling bruises my increasingly protesting bum. The roar of the engine is starting to hurt my ears. From the back of the moving truck, I try my best to brush my teeth, settle my hair, and make myself presentable.

The world around passes us by and I doze off until the truck screeches to a sudden halt. I've drooled a bit on Raphaël's shoulder in my sleep and hope he doesn't notice. The engine keeps running and we look at each other, unsure of what to do.

Through the opening in the back of the truck, there is a large, dense forest. I move closer to the opening of the truck to catch a glimpse of the outside. Bodies of both civilians and soldiers lie left and right along the road. Old men and children lie among them. I gasp at the nightmarish sight before me.

Near the tire of the truck, flies are walking over a girl's half-open eyes. She is wearing a violet dress with little black boots, and her hair is braided with great care. My hand covers my mouth, but I don't remember putting it there. Flies buzz into the mouth of an old woman, her fingers still reaching to a girl's hand. Nausea hits me as I stand frozen in place. Underneath them is a pool of blood with so many flies on it that it's more black than red. There are tracks of the truck where it drove through the pool, stirring up the flies. The sound of the engine covers the sound of the flies. In my mind, I can hear them buzzing. My heart beats loudly in my ears as I see a Dog propped up against a tree with a gun in his limp hand. *You! You did this!*

The gray sheen on his face tells me he has been dead for a while. His curly hair moves by the wind made by all the passing flies who try to reach his torn open skull. Burning acid creeps up in my throat while a part of me feels glad the Dog is dead. Like some sort of sick revenge for the woman and girl who were trying to get away. Hawkeye's voice shouts something, probably orders, somewhere out of my direct field of vision. More bodies are strewn over the road, some are not even recognizable anymore. Then the smell hits me, the strong sour smell makes my eyes water and I gag.

"What's out there?" Thalassa asks, holding her blue-gray coat over her nose. Next to her, Raphaël has a green hue and there's a sheen of sweat over his face.

"You really don't want to see," I answer, and something about my tone withholds anyone else from taking a peek. Thankfully, the truck sets into motion, away from this grizzly sight.

More than anything, I wish I was with Monster right now. I could bury my face in Monster's coat and press him close to me.

Hours go by and my eyes keep seeing the girl in the violet dress. The truck stops, and the driver kills the engine. We get the cue from Winchester to climb out. We make our way outside like puss oozing from a wound. The fresh air is a welcome change to the truck's fumes. My body has gone stiff and I am ready to stretch my legs.

We find ourselves in the ruin of a city. Smoke on the wind stings my eyes and wooden beams that once held up homes, have turned to black and are now headstones for the houses which once proudly stood there. Behind me, the others climb out of the truck. Someone steps next to me and grabs my clammy hand. Nothing higher than a person is standing upright, and a brisk wind blows through the torn streets. Whistling as it goes. *Why did the military do all this?*

My eyes search for Captain Hawkeye and his Second Lieutenant while I try to swallow. It feels like gravel in my mouth.

Raphaël lets out a dry sob and Thalassa whispers, "But- I don't understand?"

Bricks have been strewn over the streets, making it impossible to walk down it. I think of the people who used to walk down these streets. *Did the girl I saw dead on the forest floor live here with her mother?*

With that thought, my heart breaks and I have to use all my strength not to break out in tears, because if I start now, I don't know if I would be able to stop. I squeeze the hand that is holding mine while my vision goes blurry. My breath comes out shaky, so I try to hold it in before I lose control.

Pieces of fabric flap in the wind and I'm not sure if it's a lone dress or a pair of curtains. Something other than smoke finds my nose, a foul familiar scent makes the bile rise in the back of my throat. I walk to the side of the truck and throw up.

The high-ranking Dogs are muttering with each other. The Second Lieutenant is gesturing with both hands to his team while keeping his voice low. In the distance, there is the sound of a gunshot. Our heads turn in the direction of the noise. I take a step back. There are two more shots.

Hawkeye turns to face us, his eyes hard and imperative, his voice steady. "Everybody, get back into your trucks." For the first time, I can see how he made it so high up the ranks. He is calm and calculated and doesn't have to shout or flex his station to get us to do what he wants. His eyes meet mine before I climb back into the truck.

The engine roars back to life, before we drive off Second Lieutenant Winchester climbs into the truck.

He is calm as he sits down opposite me the second the truck begins to move. My body wants to get as far away from him as possible. My back straightens, my arms fold in front of my chest protectively, and my face turns away from him. My eyes are hyper-vigilant and scrutinize his every move.

Winchester's forehead creases, and he eyes us one by one. "I'm sorry you had to see that. Are you alright?" Raphaël sits with his head in his hands and Thalassa cries quietly. "This is probably the first time any of you have seen this type of violence up close." He leans forward like a father talking to his kids, his elbows on his knees. I shift a small bit away from him. Out of one of his pockets, he gets a white cotton tissue and hands it over to Thalassa, who accepts it with a sad smile.

"I remember my first time seeing what war does," he tells us as the truck jolts around on the broken street. In his fatherly manner, he puts his hand on Raphaël's knee, who is sitting next to me. "Let me know if you ever need anyone to talk to. War can mess you up, body and soul." He proceeds to tell us Hawkeye will find somewhere we can have lunch safely. Thalassa asks what it was we just saw. He tells us this area has been actively targeted by opponents of the military and the regime. *Of course, the military will shove all the blame onto the resistance.*

"After lunch, we will drive straight to the home of a baron in Valladolid. He has given us shelter before and will give us a roof over our heads. It will be a very long day today. At least you'll have a decent bed to sleep in tonight." He glances at me when he says that.

Thalassa offers the handkerchief back and Winchester refuses it. "I keep an extra set with me for any ladies in distress." He winks at her like they have an inside joke and Thalassa manages a smile. "Don't be so down, chaps! You are driving in luxury." He gestures at the truck that feels like anything but luxury right now. "In my day, the recruits had to *walk* all the way towards the Capitol. We were packed like alpacas and in the end, we even started talking like them. Spitting everywhere and moaning." The group laughs carefully. "Those were the good old days, if you ask me. You will grow soft!"

Raphaël cuts in, "I'm n-no softie, I swear I could fend for myself just f-fine." He puffs out his chest. "They want me to take care of this lot." He adds arrogantly, and to my relief, Winchester pokes fun at him and Raphaël deflates a little.

It can't hurt to have "friends" in high places, right?

I think and laugh at Winchester's jokes and even ask him about his daughter.

Delighted that I remember, he pulls out a picture he has of her from his wallet. He tells me she is now learning to ride a bike and how much she loves her new toy unicorn. Despite myself, I smile and feel a little more at ease. It's strange to go from seeing the horror of war to laughing and joking with a Dog, I guess it's just how things are here. It's a survival mechanism, I suppose. The picture goes around the group and Thalassa makes a big fuss about how cute she is. Time goes a lot faster now we are all talking.

Winchester tells us we have to eat inside the truck today for our own safety. My mind goes to Monster, who has been on his own in a cold truck all day. Chef walks by relatively quickly after the truck stops and I wonder if he already started cooking while the truck was still driving. He distributes a quick meal of rice, beans, and sausage. His usual jolly demeanor has vanished and his lips are pursed. As soon as we have full bowls, the engine roars back to life and we are on the move yet again. I feed Monster my bits of sausage and some dog food from my bag. He licks his lips when he's done and looks at me, begging for more.

"I'm sorry, boy, this is it." My heart breaks a little when I gaze into his big puppy dog eyes. Raphaël puts some of his sausages on my plate and nudges me. "We will find him some more food soon."

The sunlight leaves us again and we stop at a big mansion. The stone building is located inside a dense forest and it's even bigger than our Town Hall. It's made entirely out of a smooth type of stone. Lance Corporal Little doesn't show her face today, and we are led inside by Second Lieutenant Winchester. He also assigns us to our rooms. Men and women are sleeping separately this time. I scratch behind my ear. *Of course, we get salacious by driving in an uncomfortable truck all day.* I roll my eyes and it's like Winchester reads my mind because right then, he snorts. "Company, present arms!"

We all salute him and then he leaves the room silently. We barely have thrown down our bags when we are called for dinner. This time, it's some gooey strings in white sauce and tiny pieces of pork. It's not going to be enough to keep Monster's belly from rumbling.

Chapter 17

Full of dinner, the three of us are summoned outside to Mrs. Applegarth. Even during the trip to the Capitol, we are expected to follow classes. We get up and slouch toward the garden.

"Welcome back, all of you." Mrs. Applegarth beams at us. "I am pleased to see you. You have accomplished healing bruises and quickening the healing of minor flesh wounds in our last session. Tonight we will delve into the next subject. Take some days to brush up on it. By the time you're in the Capitol, you will be putting it into practice." The group gives a collective sigh at the thought of being tested on something we have to practice on our way to the Capitol. "Today, we will be trying to extract water from your surroundings. This is why we will be going outside."

She walks out into the darkening courtyard and, like a group of good little soldiers, we follow her. It's quiet outside. Only a few animals chirp in the dark. Orange lights are burning inside the houses. It has grown chilly, and the wind has picked up. There is a near full moon and we don't need extra light to find our way. Nobody talks, but we are very curious to see what is going to happen. We walk to a bunch of trees and gather around Mrs. Applegarth. "Gathering water here shall be a simpler endeavor compared to the challenges posed by arid regions. As of now, we find ourselves encompassed by water, quite evidently. Thus, the question at hand is, how shall we extract water from our surroundings?" The group stays quiet until a shy hand of Thalassa rises into the air.

"Yes, Private Rivule?"

"Well… I tried to do it before… extract water out of grass.. and I sort of grabbed it.. without touching it." She does a little motion, reenacting that moment in her mind.

"Very good, nice initiative. Can you describe what you did exactly?"

"Well, the water glove had a kind of pulse in it, right?" Thalassa looks at us to confirm her experience. "Plants and trees have the same feeling, the same pulse. It's more apparent with pure water, but it's there. Like a heartbeat. It makes it easy to grab hold of it. This time I didn't cover my hand. I could hold the water in mid-air."

Mrs. Applegarth folds her arms. "Very good. Have you mastered it?"

"Well.. Uh… I guess." Thalassa holds herself.

"Demonstrate." Mrs. Applegarth motions to the center of our circle.

Thalassa moves uncomfortably into the center. She breathes a few times. Then she stretches her arms to the ground, does a scooping motion, and lifts it up. A water sphere is suspended in the air. It glistens in the moonlight and distorts the view behind it. Then it quivers and collapses back into the ground. We give her a round of applause, which she accepts graciously.

"Good attempt, Private Rivule. Try again, feel the pulse in your body. Keep your motions fluid."

Thalassa does the same thing again, this time turning it into a kind of dance. The water sphere is bigger this time and is more solid. With some complicated hand movements, she can hold it up longer. It only disperses when she allows it to. When she looks up, her face is both proud and flustered and applause erupts from the class.

"Thalassa, you can assist me in educating the class. The rest of you, begin."

I quickly learn I am nowhere near as supple as Thalassa when it comes to hand-to-toe flexibility. The movements come surprisingly naturally, yet the water won't stay in my command. We practice for about an hour until we are all cold and tired. Raphaël and Trent can scoop the water up, but can't hold it in place. The water is not listening to me today and I'm a bit disappointed. Thalassa gives me a half hug as we walk back. "You'll get it. I didn't get it on my first try, either."

The breakfast tent is a cacophony of scents that assault my nose–sausages and sweaty clothes mingling in an odd symphony. We load our plates and I give Chef a little wave. Near the exit, the officers are seated, and then there are smaller tables for the groups. My palms grow sweaty when I see Corporal Baël sitting at the table next to Seger, Zale's brother, who also doesn't seem to agree with the seating arrangement. His whole body leans away from him. Corporal Baël looks in my direction. Immediately, the hairs on my neck and arms stand on end.

"You know everyone," Thalassa says admiringly

"What do you mean?" I ask, distracted.

"Well," she says as we sit down. "I've heard you're getting cozy with a Captain, during breakfast, Second Lieutenant Winchester knew your first name, and you seem to know the cook as well."

I turn red. "First of all, I am not cozy with anyone. And second Lieutenant Winchester introduced me to Chef when I was late this morning."

"Hmhm…" She definitely doesn't believe me. "And you being on a first-name basis with the Second Lieutenant?"

I fidget in my seat. "I have no idea how that happened," I say while I watch Winchester as he fills his plate and talks to Chef. *How did that happen?*

"Knowing someone's first name doesn't necessarily mean you're 'cozy' with them," I say, trying to provide some objectivity to the situation. "Sometimes it's a matter of circumstance or formality." *Thank the Gods they don't know about our 'date'.*

Raphaël interjects. "No Elara, don't lie. Zale told me you practically skipped home after Captain Hawkeye flirted with you during Solemnitatum."

I furrow my brow at Raphaël's words, filled with a mixture of annoyance and embarrassment. "Well, Zale is full of it," I say, my voice tinged with frustration. "Solemnitatum was a formal event, and the Captain happened to walk past when I was going to leave, anyway." I wave my fork at Raphaël to make him shut up.

Thalassa holds her hands up, signaling her defeat. "Sorry, didn't mean to stir up anything."

I fall back when we pass our truck and I whistle. Monster pokes his head out of the truck. "C'mon, boy, I'm going to sneak you in." By some kind of miracle, nobody spots me and this enormous dog sneaking into the baron's estate. Monster follows me into the room and then limps past me and claims my bed. I barely fit next to him on the bed, but we make it work.

The oven of the bakery is crackling behind me and Gran is kneading the dough. It smells like flour and sweet fruits. The morning sun is pouring through the windows and I see small dust particles float lazily through the air. Gran is humming her working song and I am sitting on a stool, just watching her hands work. Bells ring and the smell of metal enters the bakery as a mother and daughter walk into the shop. A faint buzzing sound comes in with them and the morning sunlight has been replaced with shadows cast by a pine forest. The daughter's hair is braided, and she is wearing a pretty violet dress. Somehow I can't focus on her eyes and an omnious feeling creeps over me. There are bad things happening.

The buzzing sound gets louder and louder until it drowns out all the other sounds. When I look back at the place Gran was, she is nowhere to be seen and my heart starts thumping in my throat. Flies are sucking at the moisture out of the daughter's eyes, walking into her mouth. The stool falls away from under me and with my hands, I try to scare away the flies from her face. The girl stumbles away from me, frightened by my Dogs uniform. Over the buzzing sound, I hear a dry click behind me. When I look back, Gran is holding a gun to my forehead. "All of them are Dogs" I hear in my head and she pulls the trigger.

* * *

We enter Achabi. The first big city between Eden and the Capitol. This is the first time any of our group has been here. It smells like wood and earth, just like Eden. The only thing missing is the salty sea smell.

Lance Corporal Little has us marching behind our truck like good Dogs. We have improved since the first time and Little marches alongside us.

She's showing us off like cattle!

It doesn't do my opinion of her any good, especially when none of the others are marching. It does allow me to take in my surroundings. While my head has to face the front, my eyes can wander all around. Roads are smooth and made of hundreds and hundreds of small white stones. Tall wooden houses are crammed on either side of the street. They are higher than any we have in Eden. The street has intricately decorated lamp posts, surrounded by fragrant flower beds. There are a lot of people walking up and down the streets. Some stop and stare as the trucks pass by. Some people give us a wave as we pass by.

We march past what must be the city square. I've never seen so many people in one place. They part for the trucks like water for a ship. The word 'ant heaps' crosses my mind. The square is full of flowers and the floor has been decorated with mozaik. An enormous building towers on one side of the town center. Its peaks reach high into the sky.

Here we will pick up more recruits and I see Lance Corporal Little shout at one boy so young it looks like he hasn't even hit puberty yet. Even through his uniform, it's apparent he hasn't had a decent meal in weeks. A girl with strawberry blond hair stands next to him. The difference between them is staggering, and I find it hard to believe they come from the same city. Little stands straight as she lectures the new ones, clearly enjoying her status. We observe the display from a distance in the safety of our truck before they come to greet us.

We introduce ourselves. The strawberry blond girl is Sheena Sinclair, and she volunteered because she wants to be a mechanic and the military has great study programs. Her parents are both veterans and she appears rather pleased with her heritage. The young man introduces himself as Leo, with eyes too big for his head. He tells us he has volunteered, and he is excited to 'make summing' of himself. Cynically, I wonder if Chef's cooking will be such a hit on his system he might implode before we get to the Capitol.

Monster stands up when he sees me walking towards his truck. He looks better than he has done in a while, though he still doesn't put a lot of weight on his paw. I scratch his ear and give him a hug. His scent and warmth comfort me, and I hold him just a little closer. From my pocket, I get a handful of dog food and throw it in the truck.

"He's big," someone behind me says and I turn around. It's Leo. His big eyes stare at Momo.

"He's enormous, but he's friendly," I say and we watch Monster happily lapping his food off the floor of the truck. "You can pet him if you like."

Leo walks over nervously and pets Monster's big head. Monster holds still, so he doesn't scare the kid. He watches me with his big puppy eyes as we leave. "It won't be for long, Momo." I give him a kiss and walk away.

* * *

A big lazy river runs through the city. People here have ferries to cross the brown water. A ferry can transport one truck at a time, so we are left to gaze over the river while we wait. Citizens in the city seem to be a very busy lot. Men and women in beautiful outfits pass us quickly and don't even glance twice at us. Women's dresses are beautifully decorated with gold thread and white little stones.

"Aren't the dresses pretty?" Thalassa chirps as an especially colorful one goes by. Big elaborate hats decorate their heads, which are thoroughly powdered. My Solemnitatum dress looks like a sheet in comparison. Men also wear hats. These are black, like the ones the doctor always wears. Over their checkered dress shirts, they wear short coats with the hem of their sleeves embroidered. There is a young boy near us trying to sell newspapers, shouting out the headlines. None of them are particularly meaningful to me. There has been an earthquake in a place I never heard of before and there is a famous festival near another place. The boy sells one of his papers to an older woman dressed in black. The boy doesn't wear a black hat like the men who walk around here, but a felt cap.

On the river there are people rowing little wooden boats, some are filled with supplies. The ferry reaches the other side of the river and the first truck drives off. A whole hoard of people gets on it before it makes its way back to us. The ferry belches out gray steam and there are big wheel-like structures on either side. They remind me of the wheels some farms have back home. *Home... But what do I have to go back to?* An ache forms in my chest and I lock my arm with Thalassa.

"How are you holding up?" I ask Thalassa softly. She gazes at the brown serpent, sunlight reflecting off the ripples in the water.

"I can't wait to get to the Capitol. Do you think it'll be like this?" She looks at me expectantly.

"I think so." My mind can't conjure up a more fantastical place than this. "I do think we will need to go shopping when we get there."

Thalassa gives a joyous squeal and squeezes my arm.

We walk onto the ferry with our truck and the ferry shudders before she propels herself into motion. We watch the bright sun sparkle on the water's surface and I wonder if the girl in the violet dress ever saw this river.

"How far do you think it would take to walk from here to Eden?" I try to ask inconspicuously.

Thalassa raises her eyebrows at me. "From here? Two weeks, maybe more."

The travelers of the elite truck are on the ferry with us. I see the Second Lieutenant talk with Hawkeye as they gaze at the approaching shoreline. Hawkeye stands tall and holds his hands behind his back. Now I know this is called Parade Rest. In his blue-gray uniform, he oozes authority and confidence. As we walk toward him, he turns his head and gives me a half smile. A little spark burns in my chest.

***

An unseen yet generous baron lends us his estate and I wonder if that's a nice term for 'commandeering'. As we walk through the stone walls, I can see two giant stuffed cats with long fur around their heads.

"Lions," Raphaël whispers to Thalassa. The animals look very unhappy and I quickly move away from them.

We are called to dinner in the Baron's Great Hall, who shines by his absence. "Do you think the Baron let us stay here by the kindness of his heart?" I whisper to Thalassa while I look up at one of the crystal chandeliers.

She shrugs it off. Our group sits down at one of the round tables. The high ceiling is painted light blue, with birds flying over and clouds drifting by. Three big chandeliers are hanging from the ceiling and I can see them run on electricity. The lamps emit orange light that makes the crystals sparkle.

Exotic plants next to the doors and along the walls give the whole place a botanical ambiance. Servants wearing black and white suits and white gloves rush in. Not one of them speaks to us. We thank them for the food they serve, anyway. When they are out of earshot, Raphaël complains, "this isn't enough for me! Do you think we could get seconds?"

His worry is unnecessary because after this meal we get three more courses. When we are all full and tired, Second Lieutenant Winchester approaches us. "The baron is pleased with our presence and has offered the men to have a drink with him in the sitting room."

"Just the men?" Thalassa asks, insulted.

Sheena rolls her eyes but stays silent.

He holds his hands up. "Hey, don't shoot the messenger."

Leo, Trent, and Raphaël decide to go. When the servants mutely take away the last dishes, we go our separate ways. Thalassa is fuming. "Really!? Just because I don't have a pecker, I can't go?"

My head goes red when hearing the word 'pecker'. Sheena snorts and walks past us.

"Why do you want to go to talk with some balding sweaty baron, anyway?" I ask.

"I don't! Yet I refuse to be ignored because I have a quim."

"SSShhht! Thalassa, keep it down!" I hiss, embarrassed. "Someone might hear you."

She snorts with laughter loudly and says, "Oh, Elara, you're such a prude!" And gives me a big hug. "But I love you for it."

I push her off me, even more embarrassed, and mutter I am not, in fact, a prude. To which she raises her eyebrows. She opens her mouth to say something, but I cut her off.

"Anywaaayy, I need to go out and find some food for Monster."

"Shall I join you?" Thalassa offers.

I decline, stating I don't want my prudishness to rub off on her.

Laughing and shouting creative alternatives to 'pecker', she walks off.

Monster bangs his tail loudly on the metal floor when he sees me and forgets he is still healing from his injuries. I try to calm him down as fast as I can, but not before getting pushed over and a face full of tongue. Monster pants happily as he lies down.

"You must be so bored being cooped up in there all day. Let's go for a walk!"

At the word walk, he rises gingerly and barks once. I stroke his fur, which used to shine, now a dull black.

Monster keeps next to me as we walk down the stone street to the walls of the baron's estate. My fingers play with the hilt of the blade that is hidden under my uniform.

Electric light from inside the house makes everything outside seem a lot darker. Shadows are deep, and the parked trucks remind me of a pack of sleeping giants.

A low rumble comes from Monster's chest. My wide eyes try to spot any danger in the night. He puts his head down and stares at something close to the metal gates. A little dot of red light breathes on and off.

"Second Lieutenant Winchester?" For a second I wonder if I should salute him.

"At ease, Private." The red dot shines brightly again. "Where are you sneaking off to in the dark?" He walks forward as he exhales a big cloud of smoke.

"I'm going out to find some food for Momo," I explain. "He hasn't had a proper meal since we left Eden."

He doesn't look at all surprised and nods as he sucks on his cigarette.

"We can't give him food that is meant for us. But-" He cuts me off before I get to open my mouth. "I think maybe we can feed him without using our food meant for the military. Let's begin with our friends in the kitchen. Why don't we? Chef tends to throw bits of second-grade meat away." He gestures his head towards one of the trucks. Chef may not be the friends in high places I had in mind, but it certainly helps.

Steam drifts up through the cracks of the canvas and for a second, I think the thing is on fire. We walk towards it in silence. Monster limps carefully along with us.

Winchester pushes away the flap of the truck and reveals Chef cutting vegetables and a woman bent over a large stove.

"Hi, Crew!" Winchester says loudly to get their attention. At the sight of him, they smile. Chef's brow shines with sweat and his white clothes are covered in stains in all textures and colors. His black curly hair is stuck to his forehead. "Chef! How are things?"

Chef is happily complaining; tha truck iz too zmall, tha kitzen in the eztate too clean, tha bedz too hard, tha meat in the city zubpar, tha temperature too cold and tha breakfazt startz too early. His big belly moves up and down in all the commotion.

"You remember Private Waywater, my friend?" Winchester cuts in.

"Of curz!" he says as he boops my nose. "Such a little treasure, this one!" Unsure how I feel about getting my nose booped as an adult, I smile at him.

"Well Chef, Sec-, Win- I mean, uh, Michael said-" I am painfully aware this is the first time I use his first name, and it feels wrong. "You might be able to help me out."

Chef grins. "He zaid zo did he? What can I do for little Babushka?"

I really need to figure out what a babushka is.

"I need… I would like… If you could-" I am not sure how to broach this subject.

"Private Waywater here has a problem. She has… something like a bear and she can't find enough food for him."

"A bear?" Chef raises his eyebrows. I whistle out for Monster and up jumps my humongous friend. Nearly knocking over Winchester and his head sniffing Chef's red nose. For a moment, Chef observes Monster through narrowed eyes, breathing in and out. Then he regains his cheerfulness. "Zabakah! You iz almost as big as Chef!" And with that, Monster and Chef are thick as thieves. Monster loves Chef, though I am not sure if it is because he smells like food or because of his cheery aura. And "of courze Zabakah can have some spare food!"

Today is the first time on this trip he eats a proper meal. Chef enjoys Monster's enthusiasm for the food and keeps giving him more, shouting things like, "Ya eat Zabakah!", "Hungry Zabakah?", "Good bear!". And from then on, Chef helps us out with food and Monster is known as Zabakah.

Chapter 18

The world is gray yet weirdly warm. I try to move, but I am trapped. I'm lying in a beautifully carved four-poster bed with Monster on top of me. Hence the unusually warm feeling.

Early birds have woken up and have begun to sing to give color in this gray world. A song of three sleeping beings sing through the room. Thalassa's soft, deep snores combine with Monster's heavy sighs and Sheena's fast breathing into a lullaby. Thalassa's frizzy hair frames her head like a cloud, while Sheena's sleek hair flows down her pillow.

The room is grand, but with all the furniture crammed inside it, it still feels cozy. After a while, the quiet gets disturbed by a knock on the door and the spell breaks. It's time for us to get moving.

The heavy wooden door only opens when I push with my whole weight against it. Monster bounds right out and storms off to Chef's truck. A frosty breeze blows through my hair, and I hug myself as I walk down the steps. Walking down, I see Winchester having a smoke. *Will you be able to stop before you see your daughter?*

He looks up at me with a snap. "Ah, good morning, Private Elara." He throws the cigarette away and mutters. "I should start quitting."

I look at him and hold my hands up. "I didn't say anything."

He grins at me. "But you were thinking it, weren't you?"

"Ah! Good morning little Babushka." Zophe's bronze skin glistens from sweat despite the morning cold. Her hair is tied back with a red bandanna. A few curls still escaping its confines. "How iz my favorite pair?" Her accent is as thick as Chef's.

"We are fine. I missed breakfast in the big hall. Is it possible to get some from you?" She gives me a booming laugh before she responds.

"Ya lazy, lazy, lazy babushka!" Her voice goes up an octave with every 'lazy' and she wags her beefy finger at me. "Of courze we have-e something for ya!" She swoops a clean dish of a pile and pops her head in the truck. I get some sugar bread with butter and a banana. Monster's head pokes out of the truck and by the movement of his torso, I can see his tail is wagging.

"How are you doing Zophe?" I ask, thankful she would help a stranger like me.

"Zophy is alwayz buzy, az buzy az a bee!"

"Can I help you with cleaning?"

"Ah no, ya zilly Babushka. Ya are too kind. But zit down while ya eat. Ya want tea?" She waddles towards the truck without waiting for an answer and shouts something unintelligible to someone inside, and a male voice shouts back. "Ya like honey?" She gets me a big mug filled with herbs, and it smells a bit lemony.

"I won't say no to that."

She sets her heavy body on a small stool and motions me to sit down with her. "Zoo Babushka, what are the rumorz?" I tell her I am not in the loop of anything. "They are ztill training ya?" She rests her elbows on her knees. Through bites of breakfast, I tell her about self-defense, shooting practice, and our nursing classes that are put on hold for now. She tells me about the military training in the Capitol and we compare that to what I've already done.

Her eyes have a mischievous gleam to them. "We all have our own abilitiez." *Does she know?*

"Iz it water?" Her voice has dropped, and she is eying me as if she sees me for the first time. I look away and my eyes fall on Monster, who is happily munching on a soup bone. *Do I deny it?*

"Don't ya worry, babushka. Military alwayz takez gifted. Zo, water?" She smiles at the shock on my face.

I nod, checking there is no one else in earshot.

"Have ya figured out the rezt?"

I bite my lip at her question, unsure of what I want to share with her. She straightens up with a big smile, like she's a teacher who is curious to know if her student has been paying attention.

"Well... I know Corporal Baël can do something..." I shudder, thinking about my run-in with him not long ago.

Zophiël fidgets uncomfortably for a moment and waves her hand. "We do not talk about Baël. No, no, no babushka. You are a elementalizt!" Her hands gesture at me like she is giving me a present. "There iz not many of uz left after... but we zurvive."

A thousand questions explode in my head and I sit in silence with my mouth open, trying to organize my thoughts. With a finger, she pushes my jaw up and she snickers. Zophiël lets me ponder this and I drink my tea, trying to buy myself some time.

"The Leader Suprema..?" I wish my first question was something a bit more profound, but this one is the most encompassing.

Zophiël raises her eyebrows. "Wantz more land and she knowz gifted can help ha. Juzt be careful when the fight iz over." She taps her nose.

"Why tell me this?"

Zophiël takes my now empty teacup from my hands and stands up. "If ya and ya friendz are the only ones not knowing, it can make things... dangerouz."

"How do you get these gifts? Can you learn everything?" I ask her coming to my feet.

"Zome zay ya get the gift from mamah and papah. Otherz zay the Godz have chosen ya. It only comez to outing when ya are in great danger or distrezz."

I think of my group. For Raphaël, it's probably one of the times his father disciplined him, but Thalassa... *I guess I don't know her as well as I thought.*

"So, besides water... People can manipulate...?" All this new information is dizzying to me and I rub my eyes.

Zophiël smiles and nods. "What do ya think I am?"

"Stone," I say at once. Somehow, this feels totally logical.

"Clever babushka!" She winks at me as she cleans our teacups. "And our friend, Michael?" As obvious as stone was for her, somehow I can't place Winchester in one of the four elements. Monster chews on his bone loudly and a slow fear bubbles into my stomach. "No idea..."

"Michael is a mentalizt. He readz mindz," she whispers as she taps her forehead.

"He can read minds? Like a book?"

Oh my Gods, Darya never said anything. He read her mind. She told me the truth, and I didn't believe her.

* * *

Because one of the trucks has broken down, Lance Corporal Little has decided to fill the time with target practice. The ammunition gives a dry click as we push it into the gun. Nervous, I glimpse over the makeshift shooting range that stretches out before us. In the distance, a few makeshift targets stand in wait.

Lined up in perfect formation, we hold our pistols in front of us, aimed at the ground. I hold the pistol with trembling hands, my knuckles white. Lance Corporal Little stands before us, her gaze stern and unwavering. Her voice cuts through the silence like a sharp blade. "On my mark, and my mark alone, you shall shoot. One shot, and then you shall await further instructions. Understood? Focus your mind and steady your grip."

Her short hair is as prickly as her demeanor. Raphaël shoots a glance at me and we lock eyes. His jaw is clenched shut. Just like me, he seems to feel this is a point where things happened before and things happened after. Nervously, he brushes his fingers through his hair.

"Align your sights with the target. The target is your focus. Nothing else matters," Lance Corporal Little continues, her voice steady and unwavering. "Shoot."

With a deep breath, I close my eyes and squeeze the trigger. The sounds of the gunshots shatter the silence. The recoil of the pistol jolts through my arms and catches me by surprise. An acrid smell of gunpowder fills the air. It smells like cheap cigars. I open my eyes. From this distance, I can't see if any of our shots have met the target.

"Keep both eyes open. If I see anyone close their eyes during a shot again, you will do the morning run twice. Now, reset positions, shoot!"

Another round of bangs and sound and the smell of the gunpowder grows stronger. Lance Corporal Little moves among us, her watchful eyes analyzing our every move. At the end of the session, my target is the only one with a small hole in it. I'm uncertain if it's from my pistol or if someone shot way out of their range. But I'm pretty pleased with the result.

"Congratulations, Private Waywater. It seems you are not a total waste of space." Lance Corporal Little nods at me while I rub my sweaty palms against my uniform.

* * *

Through the slit of the canvas of the truck, the sky is clear and the mountains loom above us. Their bodies are covered in green and their hats are white with snow. I must have traveled over these mountains once upon a time with Gran, yet nothing looks familiar to me. Gran always said if you stand on a mountain you can gaze over the clouds. It seemed like magic to me, though that doesn't rule anything out these days. The whole day we drive northwest to what is going to be our last stop, and my last chance, before we cross the mountains.

I take Monster out for his afternoon exercise before we take the windy roads into the mountains. All the military personnel and drivers are in a tense mood. Crossing these mountains is apparently quite the ordeal. There are no roads the trucks can ride comfortably on and there is always the chance of avalanches. Everyone deals with stress in their own way. Raphaël has gone out of his way to annoy Thalassa. "I'm the s-spark that lights your f-f-fire sweetheart!" He sings as he follows her around.

"It must be hard with your sense of direction, never being able to find your way to a decent pickup line."

I smile as I hear them bicker.

Winchester and Hawkeye stand side by side, gazing at the mountains. They murmur softly while Winchester smokes a cigarette and Hawkeye waves his hand in an attempt to wave the smoke away. Winchester breaks off the conversation when he sees me. "Private Waywater." He nods at me.

"Second Lieutenant," I say in the same official tone.

"Private," Hawkeye says stiffly. His eyes trained on the mountains.

"Captain," I say with my heart beating in my throat. *This is weird, right? Did I intrude on something?*

"Just out for a stroll." I explain myself and am ready to hit myself for being so transparent.

Do they know? They know.. Do you know?

I wander away within a respectable distance with my back to them, my face burning and adrenaline shooting through my system. My fingers absentmindedly play with the hilt of the blade under my uniform. Mere weeks ago I would either have not dared to do this, or would not believe it, but here and now I give it a shot.

The green grass moves softly in the wind and Monster sniffs at a few interesting blades of grass.

So Michael, how are you doing?

I glance over my shoulder. He doesn't look around or respond in any way. The cool wind blows my hair in my face. Maybe if I stand a step closer. *Hello!?*

A few seconds pass and the only change is he takes another drag and blows it out in circles while Hawkeye points at something in the distance. *Speak when spoken to!*

I scream in my head as loudly as I can, still no reaction. Maybe Monster is telepathic because he walks back up to me with a barely noticeable limp and lies down. *I'm not wearing underwear today!*

Still nothing. An unseen duck laughs at me and I sigh at my own gullibility. Monster sniffs at a rock a small distance away from me. With Monster on my heels, I head west down the hill, careful to keep a relaxed pace and not break into a run like I want to. I have no plan, no supplies, and nobody that can help me, but I have Monster, I have the element of surprise an-

"Private!"

I jump as Winchester calls out to me. He strides towards me with a brand new cigarette in his hand. "Shall I join you on your walk? Don't want you to get lost now, do we?"

Taken aback, I wipe my bangs out of my eyes. "Uh, yeah.. sure."

We walk in silence down a dirt path, Monster on our tail. Smells of sweet flowers blow towards us on the breeze and the birds chirp.

"You know, it's incredibly important for girls like you to wear proper clothing in places like this. Eden might have been nice and warm, but wearing no underwear in places here can get you nasty bladder infections," he says seriously. *Wait, what?*

My face goes pale and my eyes open wide in shock. he doesn't need to be telepathic to read what I'm thinking this time.

"Yeah, I heard you." A solemn expression on his face. The tip of his cigarette lights up as he inhales deeply. "Don't you think years of this ability taught me to keep a straight face? It's also why I need these to keep me sane." We walk past a flower bush and a few birds take wing. "And I don't have to read your mind to figure out what your face means."

He has turned on his fatherly aura again and I feel safe, but maybe that's a trick? I turn to study his face with a pounding heart.

"It's the policy only a strict few know. There is a hefty penalty for telling someone, so I forbid you to tell anyone else about this. And of course, I will know when you do tell someone." He takes another drag while I think about Darya. "Do you know what sometimes goes on in people's minds? Think about all the thoughts you have had versus how many of those you actually say out loud. Hearing what people think can be... disturbing."

We follow the dirt road to a slow stream and he motions for us to sit down.

"Could you always do this?" I ask as I study his five o'clock shade and the gray tufts near his temple.

He sucks on his cigarette and blows out the smoke. "Not this strong, no. I could pick up vibes, feelings, the sort that most people can. Hearing actual thoughts took many years of practice. And once I could, I regretted it." He grimaces. "It is extraordinarily exhausting."

"The thing with Baël-"

"Corporal Baël," he corrects me while studying his cigarette thoughtfully.

"The thing with… Corporal Baël, you, uh, heard my plea for help?"

He nods, looking grim. "You were inside my 'radar'." He makes air quotes with his left hand, "I could hear his thoughts too."

I grimace and feel a little sick while I mull this over. *Then you know about my feelings for-*

"Of course I do!" He smiles and nudges me with his shoulder while I turn bright red. "I can feel *that* warm fuzzy feeling from a mile away. Go talk to him sometime."

I ignore the invitation and ask, "So, how does it work?"

He waves his hand like he's waving away an annoying fly. "None of your concern, Private."

The trucks drag us into the mountains, and they battle the strong headwind that whistles through the truck and our breath forms big clouds in the frosty air. I'm trapped in my own head, thinking about our conversation. I am huddled against Monster whose thick fur I have never appreciated as much as I do now. Despite Winchesters fatherly exterior, he might be the most dangerous man in our convoy. It's no wonder Hawkeye keeps him so close. *Can I control my thoughts to such an extent I can trust to be around him?*

That he hasn't found out my drive to run away is probably sheer luck and I don't want to push it. I missed being executed for treason by a hair. Still, the thought of Darya being truthful makes me feel lighter. *I need to go back to her. I need to make it right. And I will. In person. I just have to be smart about when. So.. when?*

Snow falls in heavy clumps, limiting our vision of the outside world. The first sight of the mountains was impressive, and now all I want is for it to be over. Raphaël and Thalassa are practicing their water skills and Sheena looks on with pursed lips, reminding me that this gift is not accepted by everyone. Leo, on the other hand, looks on open-mouthed as he watches the water hover between my friends.

Thalassa looks at her own water glove, her hand distorted. Raphaël and I look at it as it gives off a soft glow and distorts her hand. "Let me try something." She grabs my hand with her water glove and lets the water cover mine.

"Now hold it," she whispers, all concentration. I try to match her concentration. *Water glove, water glove, water glove...*

The water that envelopes my hand is near freezing and my arm screams from the cold. Water splashes on the floor of the truck. Monster looks up at me grumpily. Leo winces and Raphaël makes a horizontal movement with his hand. The water splashes back in its bowl. Sheena looks on with pressed lips and a tight frown.

"Try a-a-again!"

Thalassa turns to me again. "Think of the gift the first men received. The moon was their teacher, pushing the tide and taking the water with it wherever it went." My mind goes to the sea. It's never-ending tide, the push and the pull. A fluttering feeling starts in my fingertips and fills my entire hand. With the same calmness, I put my hand in the water and take it out.

"T-T-Took you long enough!" Raphaël smiles at me and Thalassa gives me a hug. Leo applauds as if I just conjured a bunny out of a hat. Sheena's response could not have been more different from the groups. She wrings her hand and disappears deeper into the corner. I look at my hand and breathe out slowly. I have finally mastered the Water Glove.

The moon is hidden behind the clouds and the waves are higher than I've ever seen them. Thunder clashes somewhere up ahead and lights the beach. White sand contrasts sharply with the black sea. Cas is standing beside me. He's wearing his uniform. His eyes are as black as the sea. "Why did you bring me here?" he asks me and I draw a blank. Why did I bring him here? He morphs from Cas into Winchester.

"So you are going to cozy up to Onyx Eyes?" He takes a drag from his cigarette. *No, no, that's wrong. He didn't say that. In my head, I hear her cough. For a fraction of a second I'm in the bakery flooded in warm light before a wave crashes and it's all dark again.*

Winchester keeps morphing to Cas and back. "Can I trust you? There are hefty penalties if you tell anyone."

Gran is standing behind us in a violet dress. "You need to cozy up!"

* * *

The wind has blown itself out and an eerie dull silence has replaced the howling. The snow is brown and forms an ugly road back from where we came. I walk alongside it a few dozen steps. Dark gray clouds cover the sky, holding even more snow. Down here, the snow already reaches halfway up my knee. *I could never survive the mountains alone. I would have to wait for summer to cross...* I walk back to our circle, uselessly looking at Raphaël. The driver huddles up against a tree, breathing white puffs into the air. He examines the engine, shouts something in a walkie talkie and the verdict is, 'we wait'. Leo and Sheena are still in the truck, and the rest of us are sitting in the snow with the driver.

"Why are ya'll l-looking at me like this is my f-f-fault?" Raphaël indignantly asks Thalassa.

"Because it is your fault!" I throw my hands in the air in frustration.

"Yeah, you're probably right," he admits while looking at the truck. Leo giggles and Raphaël shoots him a small wink.

"This," Thalassa says, "is without a shadow of a doubt,-" and makes snowballs and throws them at him at every second word. "the dumbest thing you've ever done."

Raphaël protects himself from the incoming snowballs while he shrugs. "I-I don't know about that. Remember the w-w-waitress in Ach-gggg!?"

The last snowball hits him right in the face.

The truck has broken down after Raphaël claimed he could let the truck run on water and now we can't get it to work. All the trucks have passed us already and we are losing daylight.

"Well… Let me give it a try," Sheena says bravely and jumps out of the truck. Thalassa looks impressed.

"We should try and find an engineer," Raphaël suggests.

"We are hours away from anything!" I huff and throw a snowball at a tree.

After a while, Sheena sits down with us with a big black streak on her forehead.

"You sure t-t-took your sweet t-time," Raphaël says when she sits down. "D-Did you make any headway?"

"Well, I'm afraid not. I couldn't manage to get it up and running," Thalassa replies with an exasperated sigh.

"W—why not?" Raphaël asks.

"I had a bit of a fight… with the engine."

"You had an argument with a machine?" I ask bewildered, and Sheena shoots me an annoyed look.

She looks at me with a sour expression. "More like I was the one doing the arguing, while the engine just sat there, stubborn as ever."

Leo laughs and Raphaël gives Sheena an awkward pat on the back.

The light fades when the snow stops falling. The landscape is silent, and the frost has made my nose and lips numb. Big lights illuminate the trees and the sound of a truck meets us. Winchester's head pokes out the window of the moving vehicle.

"The truck won't budge," Sheena raises her voice to be heard over the engine. Winchester's eyes linger a moment on the black smear across her face and nods.

"Well, come with me then."

We climb into his truck, I shout for Monster but he refuses to get into the new truck and trots behind us instead, leaving big paw prints in the brown snow. I climb in last and the only free seat is in front with Captain Hawkeye.

"Thank you for coming back for us," I say while sitting on my hands, trying to regain some feeling in my fingers.

"Yeah… Don't make me do it again." The Captain presses his lips together. His eyes are focused on the snow-covered road ahead of us. With one hand, he offers me a fleece blanket and his face softens.

Our truck arrives at the last stop of the day and Mrs. Applegarth is waiting for us. As soon as the truck stops, she tells Raphaël, Thalassa, and myself to hurry. In the moonlight, she looks pale and her movements are slow and heavy.

With our black woolen coats over our uniform, we trudge through the snow-covered landscape. Snow crunches softly underfoot and is the only sound breaking the silence on this night. The air smells like metal and pine and something hums uncomfortably in my chest.

We pass a tent and wounded soldiers come into view. They are either being tended to or are as pale as the surrounding snow. There are so many of them that the tent is full, and they are left outside. Noises of shouts and moaning belches into the air. Mrs. Applegarth leads us to a soldier who lies a little distance from the rest. Moonlight lights up the soldier's features and I recoil.

Someone laid him down on a stretcher, a luxury not many of his team are permitted. His blue-gray uniform contrasts harshly with the red of his blood and the white of the snowy ground. I'm not sure if it's purely for us or if they've given up on him. His hair is caked with blood and I can't even imagine what he looked like before he got hurt. The man is unconscious. His leg is sticking out at an odd angle, his hands are crushed as if something heavy fell on them, his face is a bloody pulp and he is breathing shallow and fast. *What the hell happened to him?* This comes close to one of the men in the pictures we got in our cognitive exam and my heart begins to race.

"Class, you have put in commendable effort during our lessons. Although you still have a lot to learn, it's time to gain practical experience. Tonight, you will be assisting me in healing this man. As you've learned, the process can be energy intensive. So, for little things, we use crystals to strengthen our skills. This man is in such a dire condition I could not heal him without causing serious harm to my well-being. So this is where *linking* comes into place. Ordinarily, this would be way above your skill level, but under the circumstances, we have no choice." She sighs and purses her lips together.

"Raphaël, because you did such a good job throughout the lessons, I want you to assist me first. We will sit down on opposite sides of the patient."

Raphaël does what he is told and sits on his knees in the snow. I move a bit closer so I won't miss what they are doing. The labored breath of the man continues.

"Right here I have water that I have just cleansed and infused with the appropriate crystals. Raphaël and I will make the water gloves at the same time. Raphaël-" She looks at him as she explains the steps. "You are to channel your healing energy into my hands. Nothing else. Do you understand?"

Raphaël nods and swallows.

Mrs. Applegarth pours some water over her hands and it attaches to her like some living thing. "Now put your hands on mine and guide the water off your hands. There is enough for the both of us." Raphaël does what he is told and the water attaches to their hands. First Mrs. Applegarth moves to the man's face. She puts her hands directly on the skin and before our eyes, the man's brow and nose begin to heal. With a nauseating pop, the nose snaps back into position and the split brow heals, leaving a thin red scar. Cold air gets a hold of my lips and nose. It reminds me of being drunk all those moons ago.

"Yes, good, good." Mrs. Applegarth smiles at Raphaël. "Now we focus our attention on his broken leg."

Raphaël closes his eyes in concentration, following Mrs. Applegarth's impressively fast movements with his hands and the leg snaps back into place with a sickening 'crunch'.

"Well done, Raphaël, you can go." Mrs. Applegarth lets the water wash away. As he turns around to face us again, he rubs his eyes and lets out a tremendous yawn. I'm pretty sure Raphaël didn't look tired during dinner.

Thalassa is called forward and together with Mrs. Applegarth, she heals the rest of his face, her brow furrowing as she does so. Slowly and carefully, this man becomes recognizable as a human being. Still, the man's breath is shallow and fast. Thalassa evidently has more energy remaining because she feels well enough to heal his left hand.

I hadn't noticed she got this good.

"What about his right hand, Private Rivule?"

Thalassa's eyes slide to me. Her eyes are tired just as Raphaël's. "But Elara hasn't done anything yet."

"She will."

Thalassa does as she is told and after she slouches away from the man. Big bags have formed under her eyes within minutes.

"Now, Elara." Mrs. Applegarth turns to me. "What have the rest of the class overlooked in the healing?"

"Well… The man is still breathing shallowly." My words rise up like puffs of smoke into the air.

"Very good. And what do we do about it?" She asks.

I glance at Thalassa and she's as nonplussed as I am.

"Heal his inner structure," Mrs. Applegarth says in a tone that makes it clear she thinks this is obvious, but ends her sentence with a warning. "Don't drown him."

I walk towards the man, my feet leaving dents in the snowy ground and the hairs on my neck stand on end. Mrs. Applegarth empties her flask over her hands and holds them above the patient. My hands are placed on hers and she guides the water to cover mine. The water is very cold and the fluttering feels faint. The breathing of the injured man fills my ears and I glance uncertainly at Mrs. Applegarth. She nods her approval. "Elara, concentrate on my hands and don't break the bond." She moves her hands towards the man's face and I move along with her. She swoops her hands down quickly, flowing the water into the man's mouth.

I close my eyes to be able to focus fully on our bond. Water flutters more pronounced and it becomes warm between our hands. *Concentrate!*

I imagine the water going down his throat, then entering the lungs and healing it there. Sure enough, the man's shallow breathing subsides and the pained expression on his face soothes. With another movement, Mrs. Applegarth moves the water out of the man's mouth. I notice the water now has a pink hue to it and before Mrs. Applegarth drops it on the ground. The snow becomes pink before it melts. Mrs. Applegarth smiles, and the class applauds. "Well done. This is advanced Aquakinesis and you all have done expertly."

I nod, exhausted. Within I feel ecstatic. This is the most amazing feeling ever.

I'm sitting in the bakery, outside there is a thick layer of snow. The oven behind me is giving off a pleasant heat. Behind me there is no wall, but a big pine forest. Gran is somewhere in there and I have to go find her. She forgot her black coat and she might get cold.

I walk into the pine forest. Moonlit snow guides me. I start when I see a Dog propped up against a tree. His gray sheen tells me he has been dead for a while. He feels familiar, but his face is so messed up I can't make out any features. I walk faster and in the distance, I can see the bakery again. Gran is right there. At first, it feels like I'm walking through sludge, and I'm back at the bakery. Orange light from the oven makes me smile. Gran is braiding someone's hair with great care. I see a fly on the counter before I see the violet dress. A terror comes over me and I stumble away. More flies fly around me and they want to suck the moisture from my eyes. I bat them away screaming, but they get into my mouth. Gran keeps braiding the little girl's hair as my vision gets blurred by black patches. She doesn't see me. She doesn't hear me scream.

* * *

Dawn breaks and a sliver of warm sunshine bravely shines through the thick clouds. For breakfast, we get warm chocolate milk and a pat on the shoulder. Second Lieutenant Winchester pours something from a silver flask into his chocolate milk before taking a sip and passes his flask to others. With a full cup, we clamber into the truck, which slips and slides its way down the narrow streets.

Raphaël holds his cup and tries to keep its contents in it despite the choppy moving truck. "What about b-b-breakfast?"

"Ha! You want more soup?" Thalassa teases before she accidentally throws a large portion of the warm chocolate milk over herself and curses.

"Hey guys, I picked up a little something something," I whisper and everybody leans forward. "There are more like us, they are called elementalists."

I could tell them this, right?

I second-guess myself and my eyes flash to Winchester, who seems happily distracted by Chef. Chef uses big arm movements to explain something to a snickering Winchester.

"I knew it," Raphaël boasts. "In w-w-what kind of messed up world would we be allowed to b-be the only ones?"

"How do you know this?" Thalassa asks.

Shit... I don't want to rat Zophiël out.

"A little birdy told me."

We have a longer break for lunch and L.C. Little joins us and helps us make a fire. She shows Leo how to start with small twigs and then allows him to place some bigger branches on them. The wood he uses is wet so thick dark smoke comes from the fire as it sizzles and spits. My eyes begin to water from the sharp smell of smoke and I cough. Footsteps crunch in the snow signaling someone is approaching our little fire. Captain Hawkeye sits down on a log next to me, his big black coat goes well with his onyx eyes.

"Privates, Lance Corporal." He nods at us in greeting, and when he looks at me the familiar electric current runs through me. My eyes flit to Raphaël to see if he has noticed, but he's preoccupied with his conversation with Thalassa. Captain Hawkeye puts a bit of meat over the fire which sizzles and crackles as the fat seeps out of it. He appears happier today, but he is still silent.

You should cozy up to the Captain, I hear Gran's voice in my head.

I smile at him warmly. "Well, thank you for joining us, Captain. We appreciate the meal."

"As Captain, I am supposed to watch over my privates," he says stiffly. Raphaël snickers. "Ha! Privates" and gets a stern look from Hawkeye. I feel taken aback and don't know how to proceed.

"Ah! Captain, can't you be l-less frosty?" Raphaël looks around at us to see if we have caught on to his dad-joke and Leo and Sheena laugh.

Leo tries to help his new friend. "There is so much to enjoy!" All of us face him disgruntled. "Sorry..."

"I hate these mountains!" I vent in a burst of anguish. "They were so pretty from afar, but I can't wait for us to be done here." Hawkeye seems to have forgotten his stiff upper lip and smiles at me while I vomit my frustration all over them. "I have been thinking about the mountains since the first day we left. Seeing such unbridled nature. Gran once told me you could see the top of the clouds from the top of a mountain. Now I'll be happy if I never have to climb another mountain again."

The team is quiet for a minute, stunned at my outburst, but it has pushed Hawkeye's buttons and he joins me in the venting. He motions to the trucks. "The mountains are terrible, two trucks already died on us-" Raphaël peers at the sky and couldn't have looked more guilty if he started whistling. "-and we are a day behind schedule. I just want to get it over with." He sighs and turns to me. "Have you ever seen the other side of the mountains?"

"No... We never left Eden," Raphaël speaks for us and Hawkeye looks at the group.

"You will love it," Hawkeye says with a spark in his eyes. "The grass is literally greener on that side, with more flowers and wildlife." His excitement is infectious and before long we are happy to climb back into the truck for the next haul. He walks away with Winchester and flashes a smile back to me before I climb into the truck again.

"Sooooo," Raphaël begins, stretching out the o's. "Someone's got 'high ambitions'." He teases making a vulgar movement at me.

Thalassa punches his arm. "Shut up Raphaël."

I turn away my flushed face.

A cheer erupts from our truck as we finally ride off the mountain-side. Monster trots behind the truck again, his limp is gone and his eyes are wide and observant. The drivers are tired after the long day's ride and in the orange glow from the setting sun.

I climb out of the truck I see Hawkeye was right, Kafernaüm is one of the most beautiful places I've ever seen. Hills are alive with countless flowers in bloom, the green hills are covered with yellow, red, and purple. The breeze is full of a sweet lavender smell and fills me with joy. We are permitted to walk the rest of the way to our lodgings. Monster bounds through the flower fields, scaring unsuspecting birds and farmers. I glance back at the mountains with a heavy heart, they pierce the sky like knives.

I can't pass over them without any help.

Thalassa and I walk a while side by side while she points at the flowers, the colorful birds, and the Capitol we can see in the far distance. The sight of the Capitol makes my heart race and my mouth turn dry. It is built inside a crater formed by a meteorite that hit long before the First Ones came. From here we can see the dark walls. We are still too far away to hear the noises or smell the smells from the city, we can make out the tall buildings that reflect the light from the setting sun. Thalassa follows my gaze and squeezes my hand. "It doesn't look that scary from here, does it?" she asks.

"The beds must be softer compared to sleeping in the truck." I attempt to joke a ray of hope hills my chest. *There must be people in the Capitol who can help me. I just have to find them... Somehow. Maybe there is still some form of resistance. How can I find them?*

A little way in front of us Winchester casually striding with Hawkeye and we catch up. Thalassa talks to Raphaël happily, but I slow my pace, afraid to come into too close a range with the mind-reading Second Lieutenant. Raphaël bumps into me because of my sudden change of pace.

I mumble, "sorry," as I kneel down and pretend to tie my shoelaces.

Hawkeye is certainly happier on this side of the mountain. He is talking animatedly with Winchester and they both laugh loudly at something he said. When they come into earshot Captain Hawkeye is telling Winchester about how a few of his crew went crazy about a flower girl in the Capitol and how he was eventually the one that took her out for a rendezvous. *I didn't need to hear that.*

Around us, the first crickets are starting to sing. Winchester turns around. "Ah Private Elara, don't you go sneaking up on us like that!" He looks at Hawkeye for a second then nods. "I got somewhere to be, bye!" He waves awkwardly and stalks off.

I raise my eyebrows and murmur, "Uh, he is not very good at making an unsuspicious exit is he?"

Hawkeye smiles as, and eyes follow him too. "No. But he is a good man." His demeanor is relaxed now we are over the mountains.

"So… Are you happy to be in your hometown?" I decide to jump in the deep end, he looks surprised that I remember and he smiles.

"My three sisters and two brothers still live here. So I will join them for a big family dinner tonight," Hawkeye says and tells me about his mother's cooking, and how he used to help his mother take care of his siblings while his father was away working on the field. He laughs about the time his sisters played dress up with him and forced him into a pink frilly dress. I wonder what kind of person he was when he was a young boy. It's impossible to see this man as anything else than surefooted, confident, and purposeful. "Do you miss Eden?" he asks in his wonderfully warm voice.

"I miss the heat, I never thought I would, but I do. And being able to stroll to the beach, and the bakery-" The thought of the bakery brings tears to my eyes. I cough to cover up my emotional hiccup and apologize. Frogs join the cricket chorus and it feels like we are alone in the world.

"I understand." His face is grim and his eyes gaze into his memories, the lights of Kafernaüm reflected in them. "I know what it is to feel like a prisoner."

My eyes find him and for a moment he looks exhausted. The sun disappears behind the mountains, leaving us in the near dark. "It's okay, you didn't make it a secret you didn't like us in Eden. I expect nothing else now." He turns towards me and his Onyx Eyes drink me in. *That's why he is so hesitant.*

We stand still and I long for him to touch me, to break this invisible barrier that stands between us.

A bark from my left snaps me out of it, Monster has come to find me and wags his tail happily. Hawkeye puts his hands behind his head and starts down the road, leaving me breathless.

"We fled from the war when I was little. Gran always blamed the military for my parent's death. I think it's not black and white." I don't know why I feel like I have to explain myself to him, but I do. Maybe it's because now I can put a human face to the military and I can't hate them the same way I did before, I catch up to him.

"You have a very mature view of the world. I think you're finally growing up," he teases and looks at me with a cheeky glint in his eyes.

Despite myself I try to make myself taller. "Hey! You are not much older than I am!"

He grins and my heart flutters. "I have a decade over you."

I never asked him his age, but with his military rank, it makes sense. "Really!? You are that old?"

"You are that old, *Captain*," he corrects me. We look at each other and I giggle. *Why do I giggle? I never giggle!*

"I have matters to attend to, until we meet again, Blue Angel." His eyes search my face at me and a muscle in his jaw twitches before he gives me his half-smile and leaves me. It has been a while since I saw this smile and my insides are buzzing. *And Winchester can feel it from a mile away.*

Chapter 19

The trucks screech to a halt and multiple Dogs remove the canvas of the truck. For a moment, we are blinded by the bright sunlight. My eyes flit from Winchester's face who is sitting opposite me and my heartbeat quickens as the Capitol looms over us. Menacing iron-wrought doors come into view and my heart drops as I see how well-regulated the exits of the city are. *You can't easily stroll out of here. I really will need help.* Dogs with stern faces interrogate the driver. The sound of their boots stalking the truck makes me grind my teeth nervously. Their prying eyes peek inside the carcass and see us sitting there. Thalassa nudges me, and I remember to breathe. The Dogs are done inspecting the belly of the truck, before it dawns on me they are searching for bombs. *That means that the resistance has a presence here, right?*

Lilly enters my mind involuntarily and cold sweat breaks out all over my body. It's of utmost importance I keep my thoughts straight because Winchester is sitting too close to me. My hands find Monster's thick fur and I scratch his head. He looks up at me with a heavy sigh, as if he knows something unpleasant is coming. *Could they be my way out?*

I dig my nails into my hands as a punishment.

Our group feast their eyes and Leo is pale as he takes in the immensity of the city. Having lived in the slums all of his life, this splendor contrasts heavily with everything he knows. After the first checkpoint, we are swallowed up by the outer defenses. Behind the iron wrought doors is an ancient bronze arch decorated with bronze flowers, grapes, and birds. An ancient remnant of the day before the Leader Suprema. I'm surprised it hasn't been taken down. Sheena crosses her arms and leans against the driver's cabin, imitating Winchester's pose. But where he just seems to entertain himself by observing our reactions, she tries to seem unimpressed. He looks at our faces and grins as we point at the houses, people, and passing cars.

We drive through the street, all of our heads peek out, trying to see as much as we can from this city I never thought I'd see again. The eels in my stomach slither. *Was this the gate Gran smuggled us out of?*

I don't remember. The iron gates must have been placed here shortly after. Did I think I would feel closer to my parents, here, the place where I lived with them? The streets are paved with big white slabs of stone sterile enough to eat off, replacing the little tiles that I have run up and down as a small child. There is no broken glass that used to litter the street.

Thalassa stands in the truck to get a better view and Raphaël follows suit. The ease they move in each other's presence is something I only ever saw Raph have with male friends. Thalassa points excitedly at the flower beds and flowers that decorate the walls of the houses, the lampposts, and the iron gates in front of the houses. *Did we have a gate like that?*

The scent of the flowers is nauseatingly sweet. Sweeter than anything we've ever made in the bakery.

"How do they feed all these people?" Leo wonders with big eyes, so far removed from the soldier he wants to be.

"Don't worry, Leo, I'm sure they'll have enough for you," Raphaël says with an encouraging smile. Leo stands up to stand next to him and together they look out into this ant hill. I smile to myself as I realize Leo has adopted Raphaël as a big brother.

People clad in white crowd the streets; men wear white slacks and very light-colored dress shirts and the women are in all white, many of them are carrying a white parasol to keep the sun out. The fake 'pureness' of it fills me with bitterness. With all my might, I try to control my thoughts.

It's not even that warm.

The houses defy gravity on either side of the sterile road. There are houses with three or even four floors. I will them to topple over to break this abhorrent facade, but of course, nothing happens.

A young woman waves at us politely as the convoy drives by. Every single inch of her dress is covered in embroidery. I stare at her magnificent dress as we drive by. *Flowers. What is the people's obsession with flowers?*

Raphaël gives her a little bow, and she smiles coyly behind her hand. *Tart.*

Winchester points out a man-made park where people leisure on benches. He smiles at our expressions. "Welcome to the posh part of the Capitol."

Past colorful shops and more flowers, we are brought to the center. A glimpse of water spouting up in the air gets me excited. I jump up to have a better view, but we are already past it. *Was that a fountain?*

Despite myself, I'm in awe. I have heard about them, of course. I have read about them in books. Yet I have never *seen* one. These must have been installed after the Leader Suprema seized power. Conflicted, I rest my forehead against a cool metal beam. Thalassa looks excitedly at me and reaches out for my hand. I smile my bitterness away. Raphaël talks to Winchester about the cars we see on the road. Sheena remarks she has always wanted to visit the Capitol's famous mechanical shops. *There are famous mechanical shops?*

We arrive at an open square that dwarfs Eden's park. It's surrounded by magnificent houses, with wide stairs leading to the front doors and gold-colored fences dividing their territory. Did Gran love it here? *Gran would call these houses Grand and pronounce it with a capital G.* She would wink at me and we would think about all the things that could fit in such a Grand house.

"This is the Leader Suprema's palace," Winchester says as the truck rolls to a stop. My heart skips a beat and my anxiety makes me fidget with the hem of my sleeve, but my scalp stays calm.

The Leader Suprema's palace is the most grotesque, opulent house I have ever seen. Despite the lack of tingling on my scalp, I focus on keeping my thoughts in check.

Extravagant golden fences gleam in the sunlight, the stairs are made of marble and there are little towers on four sides of the building, their roofs gleam like gold in the sun. It must have cost a lot of money to build it. Money that could have fed children like Leo. *Is she there right now?* The windows, as large as doors, look vacant over the square, like the eyes of a whale carcass. Two doors make the main entrance and are so large the whole bakery could have fit through there. A garden the size of a park lies before it. The garden is impeccably maintained, symmetrical, and surrealistic. In the center of the garden is a fountain. Marble mermaids throw water at each other with their marble hands. Standing upright and taller than any man, is a male mermaid, with a golden crown and staff. I'm just like a speck of dust in a world that's too big for me, too insignificant to notice, let alone make a dent.

Did my father ever walk by these fences? Did mother and father stop and stare at the palace? Unease trickles down my spine.

"Do we get to see the great Leader Suprema?" Thalassa asks in awe, and I feel nauseous. *My opinion of Thalassa may need some adjusting.*

Winchester chortles at her naivety. "Not today, Private, maybe some other time."

A wave of draftees clamber out of the trucks for the welcome ceremony. The people who joined us in Achabi are a bit fresher than the rest of us. The stark difference with my surroundings makes me self-conscious and I try to wipe the dirt from my knees. Monster stays in the safety of the truck, clearly not sharing in the awe and missing woods and grass. *Would mother and father have liked Momo?*

A stage, draped in red velvet, is dwarfed by the golden gates. The flag with its gold sun chaliced by black hands on a blue background waves behind it. We stand in neat rows with our hands on the small of our backs. Locals have come to watch this charade and surround us like sea foam. Hawkeye, the leader of the 'expedition', strides on the stage, with an aura of great importance. Not for the first time. I have trouble picturing him at the bar in his dress shirt and a crooked smile on his face. This man never seems to smile.

"Welcome to the esteemed Capitol, where our long journey has finally concluded. Here, you will experience the comforts and privileges our great nation, under the guidance of the Leader Suprema, has to offer. The Leader Suprema expresses her utmost satisfaction at your arrival and extends her warmest wishes for you to feel at home within these walls." *Like we had a choice.*

"Your assigned Officer will now guide you to your designated quarters within the military base. Upon arrival, you will be provided with a fresh uniform. Additionally, you will receive your first salary." Some people cheer and he waits a moment for the crowd to quiet down.

"For the remainder of the day, you are granted leisure time to familiarize yourself with the base. However, it is advised you exercise fiscal responsibility. Tomorrow, your training will resume." He snaps his feet together and salutes. "In unity and reverence, let us raise our voices and hail the Leader Suprema!"

The intense Hail the Leader Suprema that bounces back at him saddens me. My lips move, but no sound comes out of them. My silence is like a small pebble of rebellion in a vast ocean of compliance. *I may be a Dog, but I'm not trained yet.*

We clamber back into the truck for the last stretch. Something racks my nerves that I can't quite pinpoint. Others chat away happily while my fingers fidget restlessly with my sleeve. Driving through another set of iron gates makes me gasp as a memory hits me.

A woman comes out of a big house, through the gates with her bodyguards dressed in blue-gray, and she steps onto the stage, opening her arms wide. Her blue uniform is laced with pretty gold lining. From Daddy's shoulders, I can see her white-blond hair she has braided intricately. Daddy says this is a big moment for all of us, that's why he brought me here.

For a moment, the Leader Suprema smiles at us and the crowd we are standing in falls completely silent. It's like everyone is drawing their breath. I don't understand why the pretty lady makes the people so nervous. All the uniformed men and women don't smile and look sternly into the crowd, their guns in their hands. Daddy wants to put me down and I refuse. "Elara, dear, Daddy wants you to get down now."

"No," I say. The lady with the white hair is pretty and I want to look at her.

Pretty lady is speaking and I want to watch her. She talks with a fake cheeriness and I play with Daddy's ear.

Under loud protests, he puts me on the ground and berates me for not staying quiet. We get a few angry glances from unfamiliar faces in the crowd and I squeeze Daddy's hand. Pretty lady's voice is still echoing over the square. Now muted because of all the grown-ups.

I grab Daddy's leg, afraid of getting separated from him, when an enthusiastic roar comes from the crowd. Daddy takes steps back as others are pressing forward. "Elara," he says as he crouches down. "we are going to go now. You need to hold my hand tightly, ok?" His eyes shoot from left to right. He grabs my hand too tightly and walks away from the stage. A woman in a green dress follows us. Daddy is running. He drags me with him, my feet barely touching the ground.

At that moment, loud cracks go off behind us and people scream. I want to turn around at what is happening, but Daddy keeps on running holding my hand. Next to me, the woman in the green dress runs too. She falls and I can't see if she gets up again. There is more screaming and people are crashing into us, trying to get away. The smell of metal hangs in the air.

My breath comes in shallow bursts. Fear envelops me as I recognize the square. My hands become moist and my heart thumps loudly. My eyes search for the road we ran through, escaping the slaughter. But I can't remember. The square looks smaller now. Did we run left or right? The memory gets vague there. Monster whines nervously at my feet. My nails dig into the palm of my hand.

I need to get myself together before Winchester inspects my mind!

The gates close behind us with a crash and I jump. Monster barks once before he falls silent, his tail tucked between his legs. The trucks all come to a halt, and we are ordered out. I'm lightheaded as I see more Dogs, these have impressive guns they hold at the ready. *I'll be dead before I reach the fence.*

Raphaël watches me with a concerned frown on his face and approaches me. "Are you alright? You look like you've seen a ghost." He holds his hand up and leads me out of the car. "Automobile sickness is not a great thing to have when you need to be driven everywhere."

I nod, thankful for the excuse.

Every step my feet take feels like I'm wading through water. I hold his hand as if it's a lifeline.

We are to stand in line, and I stand between Raphaël and Thalassa. The Officers have put on their berets now, their faces grim and their bodies tense. A Dog with dark hair stands in front of us. Welcoming us to the Capitol, but most of the things he says I don't register. *Bringing my parent's letters wasn't a good idea. What if one of these men finds them? They will surely execute me.* Cold sweat covers my back.

I am assigned to follow Winchester with a small group. Lance Corporal Little was a pain in the ass, though I am certain Winchester is far more dangerous. He looks at me with worry in his eyes but doesn't say anything. *Does he sense my distress?* This thought cripples me even more.

The base smells overwhelmingly of pine-scented soap, like they have crammed the smell of a whole pine forest into this one hall. Winchester leads us through white floored halls, with barred windows on either end before we find our barracks. A shiver runs up my spine.

This is 'home' now.

Winchester calls our team to him, his body tense. "Privates, we have arrived successfully at the Capitol, and it must have been an exhausting week. Take a clean uniform, put your bags away, freshen up and I'll meet you back here in 15."

On his right, there is a table with clean uniforms. I search for a female medium and take it with trembling hands. I miss my shoulder to cry on. *Oh, Darya.* Thalassa picks up a uniform and we walk to our assigned room. Footsteps from our heavy black boots echo through the sterile hall.

Thalassa looks at me. "Are you alright? You're so pale..."

I shrug her off. Now more than ever, I am in enemy territory. I don't know who I can trust. The metal click shoots my nerves and my knees give way from under me.

Thalassa looks alarmed and gets me a glass of water. "It will be alright. I'm sure you'll feel at home here soon enough," she says, mistaking my despair for homesickness.

"Thank you." I take in this prison cell. The only window is barred and dirty. It doesn't open, and the air is stale. A single bunk bed stands against the right wall, opposite it is one sink. Two tall narrow cabinets are put down alongside it. One for me and one for Thalassa. White walls are bare and a single light bulb hangs from the ceiling. *So, it's luxurious enough to have electrical lighting.*

Winchester has put on a clean uniform and an official-looking hat. The outfit goes with his solemn face. I would have paid him in gold just to smile the way he used to. He shaved and his 5 o'clock shadow is gone and his fatherly manner has disappeared along with it. He's intimidating. I stand close to Raphaël as if teaming up will make any difference, but he makes me feel safe.

"Privates. Pay close attention and follow me." This new Winchester is paired with a new voice. His joyfulness is gone. Here, he's a real Dog again. Nervous jitters dance within me and I clench my fists to calm them down. He leads us into a room the same as ours. "You are to make your bed every morning. That means there are no creases in the sheets, the covers are thrown back to this exact line, and the pillow is fluffed. Nothing except your covers and your pillow is to be on the bed. Understood Privates?"

We all nod.

"There are rules you need to follow here. One! Whenever someone passes you that is higher than you in rank, you will salute them. You all being Privates, just assume everyone is higher in rank than you and you will be okay. Two! Don't speak unless spoken to and always end your sentences in Sir, Madam, or their rank. Unless instructed otherwise. Three, remember that men are not allowed in women's chambers without an escort, and vice versa. It's essential to respect that boundary. Is that clear?"

The group chants back. "Yes, Sir."

"Alright. Do you all understand how to make your bed?"

"Yes, Sir!" The chant is stronger this time around, and I watch

Winchester as I say it. There is no trace of the man who helped me get Monster some food or who would gush about his little daughter. To keep my mind from wandering, I hang on his every syllable.

He continues to explain how we should use the cabinets, that we need to leave dirty laundry on the floor outside our door, and it will be picked up in the morning between 09:00 and 10:00. We are to bring any personal clothes to the in-house tailor who will embroider our names in them so they don't get lost. He walks out of the room while he keeps talking.

"Good! Always wear your uniform. This goes for when you are on the base, but also when you are out. The uniform is your primary form of identification and protection." *No one from the resistance will trust me if I walk around looking like a Dog.*

My eyes fly up to see any change in Winchester's eyes. There is nothing. *But years of this gift have given him a great ability to keep a straight face.*

"Listen up, recruits! Here's rule number eight, and it's a crucial one. Whenever you spot a black automobile rolling down the street, you better make sure you're nowhere near it—the street, I mean. The Leader Suprema, she's the one being chauffeured around in those black cars, and if anyone's caught on the street who shouldn't be there... Well, you don't want to mess with that, so just steer clear, no risks!" He looks uncomfortable and there is a little flicker of his fatherly manner. He takes little red books out of his pockets and starts to hand them out. "These are your identification. There is a hefty penalty for anyone who loses it. Keep them in the inner pocket of your trousers. It has a zipper right here, and take them out before you send them to the laundry. Are you still listening, Privates!? Good!" He continues to explain how life works between these walls.

"Private Sosa, Rivule, and Waywater after the first two weeks you will be assigned to a squad where you will help in the military hospital or the ambulance." This gets my attention. Putting my gift and study to good use is a flicker of light in this gray place.

"All of you! I suggest in the first few weeks, you do NOT go into the city alone at the risk of getting lost. The outer rings of the capitol are off-limits for recruits and you have no business there in the near future. At 21:00 you are inside the building and ready for bed."

My heart leaps, but I force myself to not let my mind wander.

"Punishments for not complying or being disloyal in any way will lead to retractions of your time off, limits to your time outside the base or confinement." I swallow audibly. "Any questions?"

Raphaël raises his hand. "When do we get days off?" Winchester raises his eyebrows, and he hastily adds, "Sir!".

"You can find your schedule for days off in the canteen, Private Sosa. Is that all? Good. It's already noon now, so you can either go to lunch or relax. Privates, presents - ARMS!"

We all jump up and salute him. He turns to me. "Private Waywater, walk with me."

But I didn't think it! Alarmed, I glance at my team, but don't see any way to get out of this. "Yes, Second Lieutenant, Sir!"

He walks me through the halls we walked through to get to the barracks. His rigid body seems to relax, and he glances sideways at me with a sad smile. "Your furry companion isn't allowed in the building and I understood from Mrs. Applegarth she has adopted him. So, hurry now to say goodbye before she leaves." *Adopted, he's not mine anymore.*

"Second Lieutenant Winchester?" He stops and turns to me. His solemn face makes me nervous. The man I had gotten to know must still be in there.

"Yes, Private Waywater?" he says stiffly.

"Thank you," I say while my eyes fill up with tears. Emotions and exhaustion get the better of me. He quietly lets me regroup.

We walk out the front doors and Winchester lights a cigarette while we walk to the truck to find an impatient Monster waiting for me. He paces through the truck and the whole thing moves under his weight. Mrs. Applegarth leans on the side of the truck. Monster whines with excitement when he spots me. His tail wags so hard that his whole body sways. *How can I just let him go?*

Behind the truck are the Iron gates and the square. I swallow my tears away and clench my teeth. Monster steps left to right in the truck. He jumps out gracefully when I call him. It's unbelievable how much he has recovered. A small limp lets me know he will never fully heal. Just like his master, he is permanently damaged. I fall on my knees and let him lick my ears and my face. Monster senses my tension and wines. My arms hold him close to me as if it will keep my heart together.

"All pets are to be leashed within this city," Winchester explains, and holds out a short leather leash.

"Of course they are," I say, trying to keep the bitter tone out of my voice and put it around Monster's neck, who shakes his head at this unfamiliar sensation. "Sir."

I give the leash to Mrs. Applegarth. "He isn't used to them, so please be patient."

She smiles at me. "I will take good care of him."

I believe her. Their friendship has grown over the past few weeks. My heart aches when she turns around and crosses the property. Monster looks back a few times to see if I'm coming with them. I clench my teeth. Tears escape regardless.

A small metal door opens in the enormous gates and then they are gone. Barbed wire glints in the sun and decorates the fencing like lethal icing. In my mind, I can see my father standing on the other side of the gate, with me on his shoulders. *You've successfully taken everything from me.*

Winchester puts a hand on mine, and I close my eyes. "You'll see him soon."

Like a Dog on a leash, Winchester leads me back to the big building. My scalp tingles, but I'm too exhausted to care. I notice barred windows. *This place is intimidating.*

Winchester gazes up at the building. "That it is. Oh sorry, didn't mean to pry." He scratches his neck and the tingle ceases. "I'm happy to be on leave soon."

"You're leaving us?" I ask, keeping my face in check.

He stretches himself and smiles at my shock. "It's not only exhausting for you, Private Waywater. I need a week or two to recharge. All those thoughts you and your friends have are draining. Don't worry, I'm going to stop listening in. Sometimes it's hard to turn it off." He pinches the bridge of his nose. "Until I get a reason to start listening in again. So keep your nose clean, Private!"

I enter my new prison and a small book lies on my bed that reminds me of a small newspaper. "What's this?"

Thalassa sits on the top bunk, reading her own copy. "The State Newspaper, a girl called Audrey, I mean Private Audrey, handed them out. She also collects your post if you have any." She turns a page.

I pick up the thin paper book. The first page is a headline about a catastrophic earthquake far to the east. Apparently, the military was the first to help on the scene, giving away free food and health care to anyone who needs it. I leaf through the flimsy thing until on the last page it ends with a quote from the Leader Suprema, 'Lucky for them we had recently improved their roads so we could offer help when needed. This is what I want for the whole nation, proper infrastructure. So we can offer help quickly when it is needed.' *Or send your Dogs wherever you feel your power is dwindling.*

The next page is a reminder of all the rules and regulations. My eye falls on a sentence written in fat letters:

Conjuring is only allowed under supervision.

She's still afraid of us? The rest of the newspaper appears to be filled with trivial things like, 'Lance Corporal Dave saved a scared cat out of a tree,' or 'Mr. and Mrs. May thank General What's-his-name for finding their kid!'. I throw the whole thing in the bin under the sink. Thalassa glances sideways at me before she continues to read.

Chapter 20

Shouts in the distance, a dream… or real life. From underneath the door, lights suddenly flood into the room and I'm wide awake. Shouting grows louder outside our door and I sit up. The door crashes open and the light bulb turns on. A burst of light hurts my eyes.

A fierce female voice shouts, "Get up, you maggots! It's time for hazing! Change into your uniform and stand outside your door in 5!"

Thalassa and I scramble out of our bed in alarm. There is no time for decency, so we rip off our pajamas and shoot into our uniforms. *Should I change into clean underwear?* There is no time. Unsure, I stuff a pair into a pocket just in case. The boots are a bit harder to put on. The leather hasn't softened as much as I would like and I struggle to loosen the shoelaces. I wonder if I should bring some clean socks. I shrug off the idea. We leave our room in time to see the woman march by again, like a bull on a rampage.

"Atten - TION!" she yells and even if we hadn't known what position to stand in, I believe in this tone I would have stood up straight no matter if I was military trained or not.

"If Lance Corporal Little has done her work right, all of you now know what to do. Present - ARMS!"

We salute.

"Parade - REST!"

Thalassa and I stand on either side of the door with our backs straight and our arms behind our backs. Opposite us are Sheena and her bunkmate Beatrice, both pale in the harsh light of the lamp.

"Forward - MARCH!"

We walk forward in sync and when we are in a line, the bull stops us. "Face -ME!" We stand to attention.

What time is it even?

"Privates, my name is Sergeant Aric and I will be your drill Sergeant for the upcoming six weeks. It is my job to make you survive as long as possible when you are at the front lines. My word is gospel to you. Do you understand Privates!?"

"Yes, Sir!" *Or should I have called her Ma'am?*

She walks around us, her steps echo through the hall. Her eyes notice every detail and I pray this won't take long and I can go back to sleep. The bull disappears from my field of vision.

"What is your name Private?" she yells at someone.

"I- I'm Mary Walker, Ma'am." A voice trembles.

"Are you slow Private Walker!?"

"What?" Mary asks in a small voice.

"ARE. YOU. SLOW. Private. Walker!?" I take a deep breath.

What a power-hungry -

"Why are your shoelaces untied!?"

"I-, I didn't have time, Ma'am," a new voice answers, barely a whisper.

"Your squad had the same time. They all have their shoelaces tied. While you tie your shoelaces, your squad will do 10 squats. NOW!"

We do squats as the poor girl in the back of the line ties her shoelaces before the Bull moves on to the next girl.

"What's your name, Private?" she barks.

"I'm Private Reyes, Sir!"

"Where is your gun, Private?"

My eyes grow wide.

Oh blast, I don't have it either.

"It's in my closet, Sir."

"Everyone, go get your gun! Privates that have theirs do three push-ups PER PERSON who forgot to bring it! That means 42 push-ups!"

More than half of the girls run back inside their rooms, Thalassa and I included. Hate radiates from the other girls who had thought of bringing it with them.

The first eight go smoothly, the smell of floor cleaner fills my nose and my hair flies in the wind. The others I have to break up. First in sets of four and my arms begin to burn. Then in sets of two before my elbows begin to tremble and for the last few I do, one at a time.

"PATHETIC!"

The next two girls, called Reed and Cook, have done everything right and we get to catch our breath. The next girl, Brooks, has forgotten to tie her hair back, and we get penalized with a one-and-a-half-minute plank. I lose track. There are more push-ups for something and more squats for something else.

"What's your name, Private!?" she shouts behind me.

"Sheena Sinclair, Sir!" Sheena shouts behind me, a shrill edge to her voice.

"If I were to go into your room, would your bed be tidy and your closet well organized?" *We had to do that?*

It stays quiet for a second too long. "Answer me, Private Sinclair!"

"N-No, Sir." Uncertainty creeps into her voice.

"Is your name *princess* Sinclair?"

"No, Sir," Sheena's voice is softer this time.

"Do you have *maids* who come and clean up after you, *princess* Sinclair!?"

Sheena gives a dry sob. "No, Sir."

"Who *else* thought they were a princess today!?"

I train my eyes downward as I raise my hand.

"Go make your bed. 50 Burpees for every princess."

Thalassa and I bolt to our room. It's easier for me to make the bed, but her bunk bed is high and Thalassa is short. She struggles to get the creases out. I climb on the bed to help her out and when we are done, we run back to the line.

"So, we have another Princess over here," she says as she moves close.

Gun, shoes, hair, uniform, posture, bed. Everything is done.

"What is your name, Princess?"

"Elara Waywater, Ma'am."

She looks me up and down. "What are you packing?"

Caught off guard, I look at her. "Sorry?"

"Stand to attention PRINCESS and you WILL end your sentences with SIR or MA'AM. Do you understand!?"

"Yes, Ma'am. Sorry, Ma'am!"

"Now let's try that again, you maggot. What are you packing!?"

"I don't know, Ma'am."

"So *princess* has *amnesia*!?" She plunges her hand into my pocket and pulls out my simple, pink drawers. My muscles lock into place, humiliated.

"Do you still *wet* yourself Princess Waywater!?" She looks around as if she is waiting for laughter. Silence. My mind is torn between keeping my head down or speaking up for myself. She circles my drawers around her fingers and holds them up like a flag.

"Do you think that wearing these will get you a fast promotion?"

"Give them back," I say, barely audible over my heartbeat.

She puffs out her chest and her eyes grow dangerous. "Excuse me!?"

I'm close to tears but won't cry in front of the Dog. I can't. "Please."

She looks like she is about to hit me, but I lunge towards her hand again to take back my crumpled-up underwear.

She takes two steps back. "*Private Waywater*! Get back in line!"

"Give me back my drawers!"

"Private Waywater, if you don't listen right now, there will be consequences!"

I walk right up to her and don't care if she hurts me. "Private Waywater, take one more step and you will answer to the Disciplinary Committee."

Two more steps forward and we're wrestling for my underwear. She grabs me by the scruff of my neck and throws me into my bedroom. My knees crash on the floor, and with a deafening bang, the door slams shut behind me. She still has my underwear.

** * **

Nervous eels swim in my stomach. I stand at attention next to a wooden door in a white hallway. The hallway smells like soap and the floor is still wet from mopping. Thalassa and the others are out on their training right now. I, on the other hand, have a disciplinary hearing. I realize I would rather be out there with them than in here with my chaperon. Lance Corporal Little is standing opposite me and has prepped me for what awaits. The door opens.

A Dog with blond hair stands in the doorway. A pen is tucked away behind her ear and a golden necklace hangs around her neck with a stone in it. "Private Waywater, enter the room." *Blue lace agate. Why do you need help to communicate?*

Behind a long desk, both the Mountain and Hawkeye sit on their chairs, looking straight at me. Hawkeye's black eyes regard me questioningly, with his hands folded on the desk. He breathes in deeply as he sees me. An electric current goes down my spine and my heart is caught by the tendrils of a jellyfish. *It had to be you, of all people.*

The Mountain's face is devoid of any emotion and towers over everyone, even while seated. His light blue eyes stare at me as his fingers absentmindedly stroke his mustache.

There is no chair for me to sit on. I am left standing. The blond Dog walks behind the desk and sits down. "Stand - at ease," she says. "Present today are First Lieutenant Wilson, First Lieutenant Klippa (present), and Captain Hawkeye (present). We are here today to discuss the penalty for insubordinate behavior. Please state your name and rank." She looks at me. Her pen hovers above a sheet of paper.

"Uh, Elara Waywater... Private."

The pen scribbles as soon as I open my mouth and for a few seconds, it is the only sound in the room.

"Private Waywater, you have been accused of inappropriate behavior towards Sergeant Aric, defying Sergeant Aric's direct orders, and using force against your superior.-"

Well, if you put it like that...

"Do you have anything to say in your defense?"

The Mountain stops stroking his mustache and Hawkeye leans forward ever so slightly, his eyes ablaze. I can't suffer their eyes and I cast my gaze down at the floor. It gleams and reflects the electric light hanging above my head. I dig my nails into my hand to keep control over my emotions. "She was humiliating me... and the other Privates."

"She *is* your drill Sergeant, are you saying she acted outside of protocol?" The Mountain asks in a rumbling voice. *You're men, I can't talk to you about her showing my pink underwear to everyone...*

"Well?" First Lieutenant Wilson asks.

"She was... nothing."

"She was nothing?" Hawkeye squints at me while his black eyes bore into mine. I look down at the floor again and take a deep breath.

"Private Waywater, is 'nothing' your final answer?"

"It's my final answer, Sirs."

"Wait outside while we discuss your punishment," Hawkeye says.

I salute them, turn on my heel, and march out of the room. Outside, Lance Corporal Little stares at me. "Nothing? Absolutely nothing to offer in your defense? If this matter has even the slightest influence on my promotion, rest assured, I shall derive immense pleasure from inflicting misery upon you. Consider it a personal guarantee!"

Lance Corporal Little is livid, and I count that as the only positive point of today. Muted voices come through the door as they talk about my case. I can't make out any words.

The Mountain opens the door. "We are ready for you, Private Waywater."

With great reluctance, I force myself to the door. Little is a little too pleased as I pass her by and I think of names for her that would have made Gran blush. My throat is dry and my hands are clammy. In the middle of the room, I stand still with my hands behind my back. *This is such a sick facade.*

The woman talks again. "Private Waywater, considering this is a first-time offense, we have decided to let you off with a mild punishment," she says with a sour look on her face. "You are to complete the haze with your fellow Privates, and when you return you will clean the officer's bathroom for a month. Keep in mind not all punishments will be this light, Private. You are dismissed!"

"Yes, Sirs!" I salute and get out of there as quickly as I can, relieved to get out of it relatively unscathed. When I'm a good way away, I allow my mind to wander.

"You only got off easy because of your powers," Little says bitterly as she leads me away. *I will make sure I won't be here after the hazing.*

Chapter 21

With my uniform on, shoelaces tied, hair done, and no underwear in my pockets, Lance Corporal Little drops me off. Back to my team. She all but throws me out of the car, into the woods. They are dense and no sunlight makes it down to the ground. Ferns and moss cover the floor. The Bull shouts from somewhere in front of me. For a fraction of a second, I think to run away, but under the unwavering stare of Little, I go straight through the bushes towards the Bull. My leather shoes keep my feet dry. A giant spider web catches my face and both the spider and I are not thrilled about it. I try to get the strands of spiderweb off of my face. The spider is long gone. A bit more careful, I walk towards the crew. As I get closer, puffs and moans come from the undergrowth.

Sergeant Aric has her back turned towards me. Her hair forms a black halo around her head. In front of her, not only the female recruits, also the male recruits work out. It seems they are playing some kind of game, but it doesn't appear to be fun at all. Raphaël is trying to drag himself to the other side of the field while a young boy tries to drag him back. The young boy has gotten a hold of his leg and pulls him in the other direction. Raphaël sports a bruise on his forehead. *Did he fall?*

Dirt and dead leaves cover Sheena's strawberry blond hair as she wrestles a man to the ground. Thalassa has disappeared in all the moving bodies.

I salute, and a part of me wants to kick myself. "Reporting for duty, Sir."

The Bull glances at me, puts a whistle in her mouth and blows. The sound pierces through the air and hurts my eardrums. "Good, I have been waiting for you."

At the blow of the whistle, the boy dragging Raphaël drops his leg and Sheena peeks up from the man she has pinned down.

The Bull walks around me, inspecting every inch of me. "Look who has graced us with her presence. Do you see how clean and refreshed Princess Waywater is after her beauty sleep. I'm sure she also got a fried chicken breast before she was *chauffeured* here. Privates, bow for *Princess Waywater!" She is setting up the group against me!*

The whole group gives me a grim nod, like good little pups. Sheena's face tells me she is out for blood. My heart pumps fast when I can't spot a single friendly face. Sergeant Aric feels inside her pocket and takes out a red handkerchief. "Who would like to sleep inside the base tonight instead of on the forest floor? Whoever brings me the Princess's red handkerchief to me will sleep in their own bed tonight." My eyes dart between people. They all eye me like I am prey. In this mob, I can't make out Thalassa's or even Raphaël's face. Sergeant Aric ties the handkerchief to my wrist. The first knot pinches my skin and she ties the second one so tight I worry she restricted the blood flow. I swallow hard. The squad eyes me like a pack of hungry wolves. "We will give Princess Waywater, what, say… six seconds, head start before you can follow her. So Princess, before I set this pack loose on you, you better run."

My mouth is completely dry when I turn right around and run in the direction I came from. Terror fuels my legs and I sprint away. My black leather boots beat heavily on the forest floor. Behind me, the blue uniforms get up. Only a tiny whistle protects me from them.

With one hand, I fumble with the knot the Bull has used to tie the handkerchief to my wrist. Fear of them ripping me apart, for the blasted thing fills me and I want to get it off my body as if it were the tentacles of a jellyfish. For the second I glance away from my path, a wet branch smacks me right in the teeth and I can taste metal.

Far too close. The whistle goes off and I fly over the undergrowth. I veer off to the right in the hope I can shake them off my trail. Bushes and small branches hit me, but I am protected by the thick material of the uniform. Behind me, voices shout. It's the same tone hounds use when they have smelled a fox. Breathing erratically, I make my steps wider and my arms swing around me. More branches slap me in my face as I pelt by. A bird takes to the air and causes my heart to skip a beat. Sweat forms on my skin. In front of me, a hill dooms up. I run up it. I hope at least some will be too tired to come after me. The soft moss makes me slip and I crash painfully on my hands. Smells of wet earth and rot fill my nose. *Just like when I was running from them for the first time.* Memories of Monster being shot overwhelm me and push my heart to its limit.

On all fours, I climb up the hill, every place my hands touch freezes over, leaving small patches of white frost. My breath comes out in frantic bursts as I try to listen for voices. At the moment, they are all silent. Again I fumble at the knot the Sergeant has put in the handkerchief. When that doesn't work, I try it with my teeth. The second knot loosens a little, but steps sound from below the hill. Like a wild deer, my eyes dart around me. There's not a single soul here. With my blue uniform, I must stand out like a parrot fish on the sand. My eyes dart around. *Maybe there is a pool of mud somewhere.*

I stand up and observe the area. There are dead leaves and moss. Missing any inkling of direction, I take a right. The spine of the hill leads me upwards. I nearly break my ankle when I step into a fox's den. With razor-sharp reflexes, I catch myself. The hill slopes down and I slide down it faster than I have ever before. Wind rushes past me and I pray there aren't any more rabbit holes or fox dens for me to step in. At the bottom of the hill, the sound of running water meets me. *Water means mud! Mud means becoming less visible.*

Crashing through the bushes, a waterfall greets me. With a wet thump, I fall to my knees at a place where the water is still. With a trembling hand, I reach to scoop up some mud when I pause. The water is flat like a mirror and I study my face. My hair is all over the place. My lip has split. There is a dark smear of dirt on my left cheekbone and my eyes are wild. My eyes blink once, twice. *I'm like a wild animal. What am I doing? They want to sleep at the base, not kill me.*

I sit back, crossed-legged. My chest rises and falls. Smells of earth and water fill me. My heartbeat slows down. Birds chirp not far away from me and the tension in my shoulders vanishes. In my new calm state, I easily loosen the knot in the handkerchief. *Now I can just give it to anyone who finds me first.*

Around me, there is the tranquil sound of running water and a bird sings in a nearby tree. I move to my knees and examine the broken skin of my hand. The cool water flutters as I put my hand in it.

The water glove covers my hand as I remove it from the water. My heartbeat quickens. Despite myself, I glance over my shoulder. Half expecting a 'hmmm?' to come out of the woods somewhere. No one's here. With my sore hand, I get the clear Quartz out of my pocket and let water run over it before I form the glove. My hands are gentle when I heal my broken skin. It works, however, it feels wrong. It feels like I accidentally swallowed a bug. Ignoring it, I study my split lip in the water's reflection. In this mirror, the soldier puts a hand covered in water on her split lip and a wave of nausea hits me. Again, the healing worked. Proudly, I look up. Leaves and branches keep the sun away from me.

I study the river and the waterfall and wonder where the water is coming from. There is probably a town somewhere upstream, but with no idea of what direction it would lead me to, it's foolish to walk. I could end up going towards the front instead of Eden. Could I figure out on the run how to get over the mountain range, or could I get a boat and bypass them altogether?

Behind me, the heavy sound of boots on the wet ground thumps loudly, and I'm disturbed in my pondering.

"Elara?" It's the voice of the sweet, young Leo. "I-, I found you."

And now he doesn't know what to do. He is no Dog. "Leo, here is the handkerchief," I say and hold out my hand with the red handkerchief. His footsteps come closer to me, but he's cautious. He pulls the handkerchief from my hand ever so softly.

I smile. "Let's get back to Sergeant Aric to tell her the good news."

I stand up and study young Leo. His dark blond hair is a mess and there is a bruise on his chin. Other than that he's fine. Leo takes the lead, and it's a good thing because I would have gotten lost.

"How did you find me?" I ask as he pushes a branch away so I can pass.

"By chance, I was looking for some mushrooms," he says. I'm not sure if I believe him, but what a wonderful world would it be if it were true. We wade through the undergrowth.

"Did you know I found at least four types of edible mushrooms here? There is one we should cook first. They are very tasty." Leo points at his full pockets and beams at me. His innocence makes me tear up. Behind us, there is the sound of someone trampling through the forest. Not just one pair, many boots fall on the ground.

"Run," I say.

Leo looks at me with big eyes, hears the boots, and scuttles off into the undergrowth. My feet itch to move, yet I hold my ground. The hit comes faster than expected. A heavy weight crashes into me and I slam into a tree. Something in my shoulder cracks, shooting a sharp pain through me. A curse comes out of my mouth. Somebody grasps my wrists.

"Where is it!?"

I grin at a man with olive skin and a bit of stubble, Private Eliyah, who looks infuriated. "You're too late. I don't have it anymore."

My hands push me off the tree, and I launch at him. Not because I think I can win, I don't, but because it will buy Leo time. Eliyah's knee catches me in my gut. All the air leaves my body in one grunt. With sparks in my vision, I fall to the ground.

He looks down at me. "Dumb move, Waywater," he says before he and his cronies begin the chase of Leo. *Fly, little one, as if the devil is on your heels.*

Judging from Eliyah's expression, it wouldn't surprise me if it turned out to be true. From the picture that greets me when I get to the camp, it's clear that Leo got there on time. Eliyah looks annoyed, and Thalassa gives the young boy a big hug. Raphaël walks up to me.

"I heard what happened from Leo, d-d-did you really just let him t-take it?"

Leo waves happily at me as he gets on the truck base ward.

"He deserves it most," I say, and I wave back.

Sergeant Aric put me in team D. "This will be your family for the rest of the hazing. Good luck." Her voice is as warm as a blizzard. The Privates sit on the floor. I recognize Sheena, her roommate Beatrice, Raphaël, and to my utter dislike, Eliyah. Raphaël is the only one who smiles at me as I walk toward the group. Sheena gives me a sour look. Eliyah still looks at me as if I'm his prey and Beatrice straight up ignores me. Not everyone is happy that Leo got a night on a warm mattress. In between them is the bulky bag we got from Sergeant Aric. I stare at it as I sit down, avoiding unfriendly eyes.

Thalassa smiles at me with a cheeky grin that seems out of place in this dreary world. "Right on time," she whispers. Despite myself, I smile back at her.

Lance Corporal Little points to the top of a steep hill. Wet grass glistens in the morning sun. A few drab gray uniforms already struggle up it and evidently, it's quite the battle.

"You will follow the other trainees on their route." Trent already wants to get a head start. "Wait! You forgot something." She barks and motions towards a pile of very heavy-looking bags, and one by one we pick one up with our name on it. "You must finish as a team. There are no lone wolves in the military."

There must be at least ten kg in the bag, no heavier than a big bag of flour. We sling it over our shoulders and move our feet. Trent leads our little team. The hill is even steeper up close, and I follow my team begrudgingly. Despite the early morning cold, sweat forms on my forehead. Before I am full and well up the hill, Thalassa and I already trail behind Raphaël and Trent. Her frizzy hair bounces up and down with every step. A forest appears before me.

Thalassa pants heavily. "You. can. do. it!"

I give her a thumbs up, unable to speak. We fall to the same rhythm. A faint path of knotted pieces of blue fabric leads our way into the forest.

At the end of the track, Raphaël and Trent wait for us at the Nation's flag, which hangs limply from its pole. The ochreous sun star, with black hands around it like a chalice on a steel blue canvas, wilts around its pole as if ashamed to be there.

"Alright girls, let's pick up the pace. I want breakfast," Trent says as he spurts off. Gasping for air, I watch him go with Raphaël and Thalassa in tow. I turn my back to the flag and spit over my shoulder.

The stiff uniform has loosened up a little. Now the bag chafes painfully into my shoulders, tugging on them with every step. Before we get to the end of the hill, I can't force my legs to go on anymore, and I stumble to a halt.

Thalassa glances back at me. "Come on, Elara, you can do it!" Her voice is raspy and tired. Alerted by the shout, Raphaël looks over his shoulder and slows down. Trent is nowhere to be seen.

After taking a few deep breaths, I follow her. My eyes on her moving feet help me keep to a rhythm. The ragged outpost comes into view and a pain pierces through my side.

"Wait!" I gasp when my sides cramp up. Where in the physical test I was average, I am the worst now. The sun is climbing, and it burns the back of my neck.

Thalassa walks back towards me, her face flushed and her frizzy hair limp around her face. "You can do this, Elara. Come on, we'll be late for breakfast."

My uniform is soaked as we return, and Thalassa's uniform also has dark marks around her neck and under her arms.

"Breakfast awaits," Lance Corporal Little says.

The wretched bag falls off my shoulders with a heavy thud. With my hands on my knees and my head hanging, I try to inhale as much oxygen as I can. "I need a shower!" I gasp.

****

Our babysitter awaits us outside our tent. Her rigid posture reminds me of a marble statue: cold, soulless, and unyielding. She peers at the clock in her hand when we appear. To my disdain, the schedule works for me and my loathing for Lance Corporal Little grows every time she shepherds us to our next assignment.

At the hectic pace that is breakfast, I spot Thalassa. Delighted to see her friendly face, I make my way to her. Bags cradle her eyes and she has a light bruise on her jaw. However, her dazzling smile hasn't left her yet. She goes into full gossip mode the moment I sit down. As if it's another day in College. From her tone, I gather Thalassa is having a blast at the military. Specifically, during self-defense. "Winchester looks fantastic without his shirt on, even for his age." She giggles and watches me for a reaction.

"He does appear... to work out a lot." My eyes flash involuntarily at the Second Lieutenant as he smiles into his breakfast. *Did he hear that?* I shrug off the idea because we are too far away and it's too loud in here for him to have eaves-dropped.

Thalassa leans in closer and whispers, "Oh, you won't believe the stories about the officers' antics during training. They say Second Lieutenant Winchester once challenged First Lieutenant Klippa to an arm-wrestling match, and it turned into an all-out competition among the recruits!"

I chuckle at the absurdity of it. "Really? I wouldn't have imagined the officers getting involved in such things."

Thalassa nods, her eyes sparkling with excitement. "And you know who's been keeping a close eye on all this? Lance Corporal Little, she was taking notes during the whole arm-wrestling fiasco! She even accepted money when she won the bet on who would win from the Captain."

"Captain Hawkeye's here?" My eyes glance over the Officer's table.

"He left," Thalassa says and follows my gaze. "But Little is not all stern and serious. I caught her cracking a smile during the whole thing, believe it or not."

I smirk, finding it hard to picture the stoic Lance Corporal Little cracking a smile. "Well, I'll take your word for it."

Thalassa leans back and takes a bite of her food. "Oh, and speaking of Little, have you seen how she looks at Lieutenant Winchester? The poor thing is so love struck, I swear she brightens up every time Lieutenant Winchester talks to her." For the first time, I see Lance

Corporal Little is all awkward as Winchester talks to her.

How does Thalassa notice all these things?

Thalassa winks playfully. "You've got competition."

"I do not have a thing for the Second Lieutenant!" I say just a bit too loud and the table becomes silent for a second. Thalassa giggles as I bury my face in my plate in embarrassment. Despite the mortifying display, I feel comforted in Thalassa's laissez-faire attitude amidst the chaos of military life. As Thalassa shares more gossip and stories, I forget about my worries for a moment.

It gets dark early in the forest. As the light fades, the animals grow loud. Sergeant Aric has us marching with an enormous tree trunk on our shoulders. Thalassa, who is too short to carry the log, is given two bags full of sand to carry. The big straight trunk weighs on my shoulder. When someone marches out of order, the rest of us get a painful jolt through our shoulder. My socks are wet, not from the ground, but from the sweat. My breath comes out in sharp bursts. Somewhere in front of me, someone stumbles and the tree trunk falls on the bones of my shoulder and I grunt. In front of me, Sheena lets out a high-pitched whine that reminds me of Monster. In my mind, he's in a warm bed near a fireplace. Mrs. Applegarth has just brought him some nice food and strokes his nose. I smile. A mosquito lands on the top of my hand and I squish it. *Hah! Got you, bugger!*

That was the first of many. It's impossible to get my bearings in this thick forest and the only thing I know is that we're nowhere near the waterfall. But I could be wrong. The thick foliage blocks out any means to discover which way is which.

Soon, mosquitoes hound us, and the high buzz surrounds me. I try to blow them away from my face, to no avail. After we march for what feels like hours, we are allowed to drop the log. I suspect that with this dark, it's too dangerous to keep us moving like this.

With my team, we return to the bulky bag. Sheena gets there first and zips it open. She hands out a sleeping bag each. All but Leo, who will sleep in the base one more night. Sergeant Aric takes him back, and he gives us a small wave when he leaves.

The rest of us investigate the surroundings for a good place to sleep.

"This is a good place." I point at a dark patch between some bushes. "Nice and sheltered."

"No," Sheena says, "we need something on a hill where the rain won't collect. If we sleep here and it rains, the rain will soak us by morning!"

After a few minutes, we compromise on a place we all are unhappy about. Sheena appoints Eliyah and me for the first watch.

Eliyah and I sit on a mossy stone as the others make themselves comfortable in their sleeping bags. Eliyah takes something out of his pocket and lights it.

"You were allowed to bring that?" I whisper.

He snickers, "No, but I wasn't foolish enough to put it in my pockets."

I'm glad it's dark so he can't see me blush.

"Do you want one?"

I decline.

"So, what are we supposed to be doing?" I ask while I stare into the black of night.

"Alright, you missed it. Okay, Princess, so everyone has a flag."

Did everyone forget Sheena was called Princess too?

Annoyed, I shove the long bangs out of my eyes.

"The team with the most flags after the hazing wins and the team with the least amount of flags gets punished. Don't ask me how, they didn't say. Anyway, we may steal it at any time and by any means. Except right out killing each other, of course. We already have two, so we need to keep an eye out for anyone who wants to steal our stash."

The sounds of the surrounding woods instantly feel less comforting.

"Where are you from?"

"From here. I was raised on Carpathia Lane. Have you been?" I say I haven't and he asks me where I'm from. He hasn't heard of Eden before, and I try to describe it.

"I think around 500 people live there, so it's small. My Gran and I used to have a bakery on Main Road. That was until they drafted me."

Eliyah says Gran must miss me and I tell him she passed away shortly after the military came to Eden. I ask him how he ended up here.

"My dad is friends with First Lieutenant Klippa. He used to come by all the time and tell me stories about the military. It made me want to enlist. My mother wanted me to finish my education before I started here, though. I haven't seen him around much since, but I'm sure I'll see him soon. What do you want your expertise to be? I want to be in the Special Forces. My mother would rather see me have a desk job."

I'm happy I don't have to respond and let him chat away while I listen to the sounds of the night and wonder if he might fall asleep so I can get a good view of the night sky. *Maybe the star Mintaka can guide me home.*

Eliyah lights up another cigarette, and the stink of the smoke bothers me, though not as much as the cold does. We fall silent for a while as the animals scurry around us. Once I hear a twig snap and we jump up. After that, nothing happens. Eliyah yawns and stretches his arms. One lands over my shoulder and I tense up, unsure of what is happening. *Is he doing this because he's cold?*

We sit there for a while, and he doesn't move. My body aches from exhaustion and the cold, but I feel trapped inside his arm, but he makes no further move and I decide it must be amicable. At the end of our shift, Raphaël and Sheena take the next watch.

"Do you want to lie next to me?" Eliyah asks and my instincts immediately respond with a loud no. Perhaps I have hurt his feelings, but I am proud I have stood up for myself.

Thankful for the soft ground, I zip up my sleeping bag and hide my head inside it. I'm so tired I fall asleep almost instantly.

The next day, the weak sunlight wakes us up and Sheena announces proudly we haven't lost our flags. She shows us an orange and purple flag. The two flags are too big to hide under our clothes, so we can't take them with us.

"We need to hide them somewhere that is not the bag," I say, and Sheena eyes me with disapproval. "It would be the first place I would look. Let's hide them somewhere, like, up a tree or bury them in the ground."

"We're not allowed to bury them," Eliyah explains. "But we can hide them somewhere else." We explore our campground and find a hollow stump. The orange flag we put in there and use leaves to cover it up.

"Let's hide one way up high in a tree," I suggest again while looking for one that looks sturdy enough to climb. Sheena gives me the flag and crosses her arms as if to say, 'I dare you'.

"I'll help you," Raphaël offers. As we walk around the campsite, Raphaël nudges me with his shoulder. "I thought it was a g-good idea. Don't let Sheena get you down. She's just tired." The words are sweet and I have to remind myself it's Raphaël who says them. Yet he has been kind since we arrived in the Capitol… possibly even before that.

We find a tree that seems sturdy enough to climb into, and Raphaël gives me a leg up. The bark is slippery under my fingers and I clasp on tight so I won't fall. I have to climb all the way to the top if I want to see something useful. With careful pace, I climb higher and higher, until the branches bend dangerously beneath my feet.

"I think that's high enough!" Raphaël shouts from below, but I still can't see enough. While my heart beats in my throat, in clear agreement with Raphaël, my determination pushes me forward, my gaze fixed on the pale sky above. My boots slip on some moss. My hands prove to have superhuman strength as I grasp onto the stem. Tearing a few nails in the process. I need a minute to regain my composure before I break through the canopy.

Out of breath, I reach the top and look around, my hand blocking out the bright sun. The canopy blocks my view to the sides. The foliage doesn't betray the place of the waterfall or the end of the forest. No mountains show themselves on the horizon. The sun is out; it hangs halfway in the sky, but I'm unsure what its position means. I curse myself all the way down.

* * *

In the morning Leo, all rested and clean, walks up to us with a big smile on his face. When he stands next to me, he whispers, "I smuggled in some bread sticks if you want something to eat." We sit with our backs to the group as we sneak pieces of the bread sticks into our mouths.

Our challenge today consists of an obstacle course. All the teams have to take part. We have to compete in teams of three and every winner has to compete again. Until all 10 teams are ranked. Team G is our competitor for 4th place. We are absolutely exhausted after our teams have endured the course twice. Raphaël proves to be an excellent runner, yet misses the marksmanship. While Eliyah shoots as well as I, but lacks team spirit. Leo is a great team player but runs quickly out of juice, and Sheena is strong, but causes the others stress by screaming at the marksman.

At the starting point of the obstacle course, we all get heavy bags of grain we have to hold in front of us while we run. The whistle sounds and we run. The big bag restricts my breath and, after a dozen paces, I struggle to keep up with the group. I gasp for air while the bag crushes my chest. My legs carry me over the familiar track. Group G is in front of us and is making good time. The next obstacle requires us to all shoot our guns at the target. Better shots here will mean more points at the end. We can't begin until we have all arrived at the marksman point. As soon as I drop the bag, Eliyah shoots his four shots in quick succession. The group goes by one by one as I lean on my knees to get some oxygen back into my lungs.

"Great, next!" Eliyah says, as he moves away from the ring. Raphaël walks up next and shoots the shots one by one with great precision. Sheena walks forward and shoots. She suffers from the pressure and misses her first shot. The other group is faster than us by two people. Sheena shoots the target the second time, but only just. Last two are fair, though nowhere near where they should be. She nearly throws the gun at Leo, who quickly recharges it. I hear the gunfire in quick succession. We are closing in on the other team. They are arguing in prominent voices and I hear someone curse. The gun they are using has jammed. If we win because of this, it won't have been fair. Leo gives the gun to me and the metal is warm under my fingers. *One, two, three, breathe.*

I switch the clip for a new one and time slows down. The target is a cardboard cutout in a human form. My hands go up and I point. There is one set of rings on the head and another on the torso. The figure already has bullet holes in his arms, neck, and a few around his belly. Eliyah has shot him right in the head. That on its own is 10 points. I remember being so proud when I told Gran I was a great shot. Never did I ask myself if she was proud or frightened of it. Just like the little hole in the middle of the head makes me frightened of Eliyah. My finger pulls the trigger and the first shot goes through the torso. I take another deep breath and I shoot two through the head, right next to Eliyah's bullets. If I ever need to take him out, all I can do is to be faster. The last bullet I aim straight through the heart. *Bullseye!*

I smile as I put the gun down and Leo thumps me happily on my shoulder blade. My eyes search for Sergeant Aric. They find a pair of onyx eyes instead. Captain Hawkeye looks right at me with a slight smile on his lips.

"People! MOVE!" Sheena screams at us. I tear my eyes away from Hawkeye and focus on the task at hand. The last crawl covered Sheena's uniform in mud. There is a dried-up smear on her chin, which makes her look as if she has a partial beard. She motions towards Eliyah, who is already on his belly. He crawls up the muddy hill with barbed wire over his head. Raphaël is a close second and, on the other side, our rivals are catching up again. Leo goes left while Sheena takes the right side.

I crawl up through the mud, my shoes slipping on the ground and my legs are already damp. With my hands, I search for anything to hold on to. Sheena's shoe almost kicks out my teeth as she slides down.

"Hey!" I shout at her and take hold of her boot before she can do any damage. I push her boot up and she uses it to propel herself forward. In the meantime, she pushes me back quite a distance and I huff in annoyance. Leo doesn't seem to be making a lot of headway. I catch up with him. His uniform is caught in the barbed wire. I turn towards him. "You're stuck. Come up a bit."

He does as he is told and my fingers release him.

"You're good, go!"

We crawl forward. We are equal with the other team and I want to win this thing. On the other side of the wire, Raphaël is on his belly towards us, sticking out his hands. Eliyah and Sheena are holding onto his legs. We each grab a hand and he pulls us smoothly through the remaining crawlspace.

"Good thinking!" I pant and give him a thumbs up.

Raphaël smiles at me. "Us E-Edeneers have to look out for each other."

We make our way to the last obstacle. There are two ropes hanging over a mid-sized pond and we all have to make it across. Falling will result in immediate disqualification. Thalassa already fell in and her team sits on the side. After she fell in, three other members fell in after her. Their bodies tremble uncontrollably in the frigid air as Hawkeye guides them towards a truck. *Probably to get clean clothes.*

One by one, we step onto the rope. Eliyah told us the trick is to hold your gaze straight forward and step at the same time. It gave us an edge in the first rounds. The other groups caught on quickly. This time, Raphaël goes on last. He is heavier and his weight makes the rope easier to stand on. As I get on, Raphaël whispers, "When you're on the other s-side run straight to camp to steal a flag while everyone is b-busy watching the finals."

I raise my eyebrows in surprise. "You- you are one calculating mastermind." I step on the rope. It sways a little under my weight and my body tenses. Eliyah told us to relax, so I muster up all my willpower and relax in the ropes. Leo's feet take steps, one small step at a time. Team G is already on the rope and might beat us. Their rope already wobbles. The wobble is dangerous as it might go out of control and throw everyone off. Raphaël's weight lands on the rope as we carefully make our way forward. Someone from Team G jells and my ears focus on a splash. If I glance towards them now, I might cause a wobble in our own rope. A yelp makes me lose my focus for a fraction of a second and a small wobble goes through the upper rope.

"Focus!" Roars Eliyah from up ahead. I do as I am told and block out all other noises. My world exists out of the rope and the feet in front of me. Step by step, we make our way forward. The rope rises as the first person steps off the rope. As we have seen in other teams, you are not safe because the first person has hit dry land. We step forward and I hear a big scream. *Don't look, don't look.*

Another weight comes off the rope and this time it destabilizes. We wobble and my body tenses up. I breathe in order to relax and the rope calms down, but it stays fickle. The feet in front of me step on dry land. *I am so close!*

"Easy there Princess," I hear Eliyah call to me.

"Focus, El!" Raphaël shouts from behind me as the rope shudders. It's a miracle I make it across. I thank Quatahna as soon as I make it on steady land. Our rivals have lost one person to the water, and she swims out of the muddy lake. Leo and Eliyah give me a high five, Sheena congratulates me with her eyes focus on Raphaël- a bit too eagerly. Suddenly I feel very protective of him as a fellow 'Edeneer'.

Raphaël struggles on the last bit and, as I remember his words, I bolt towards the camp. People ignore me and I almost crash into Hawkeye.

"Well hello, Private," he says with a solemn face, but there is a small spark in his eyes.

"Can't wait, flag!" I say and pray he won't punish me for not saluting him. He doesn't call me back and I breathe a sigh of relief. Camp B is the first one on my path. In the distance, another Private goes through Camp D. If I'm correct, he's from camp E. We both stop what we are doing as we see each other. I hold up my hands in surrender and the man nods. This will be our little secret.

I zip open the bag of Camp B. There is no flag in there. I inspect the camp and notice a few rocks piled up and a bit of red pokes out. One by one, I remove the rocks from the side and hold the rest up.

With my other hand, I tug the flag out of it. It comes out in one go. *Ha! Suckers!*

I run to my camp and check the bag first. The flag is still in there. I hide the red flag in the tree stump with the other. We need another place for it to hide, but now is not the time. I sprint back to the crowd near the lake. Hawkeye is gone. And Sergeant Aric has her eyes on me.

Lunch is a merry affair. We drink big mugs of tea to make us warm. After I show them the red flag, even Sheena seems to have defrosted a little towards me. She gives me a nod. Leo sits next to Raphaël and asks him a ton of questions about how to build impressive sandcastles, and Raphaël, with a warm smile, patiently shares his secrets. From my side of the ring, I see Sheena's eyes flutter to Raphaël a lot. When he makes a joke, she laughs and plays with her hair. *Oh, girl, you got it bad.*

I have to prevent myself from rolling my eyes. As if Quatahna herself thirsts for revenge, Hawkeye appears. There is a clatter of plates and a rustle of clothes as we hurry to attention and salute him.

"At ease, Privates," he says. "I gotta say, I'm proud to give you a shout out for your fourth place today. I've seen some serious growth from each and every one of you. And it's worth celebrating. The first weeks are tough, it's gonna push you to your limits. Mark my words, when you come out the other side, you'll be stronger, better, and ready to take on whatever comes your way. Remember, we got our eyes locked on you, making sure you're heading in the right direction." He meets my eyes when he says this. "So keep pushing yourself, keep striving for greatness. You've come a long way in such a short time, and that's no small feat."

Raphaël puffs out his chest. Hawkeye salutes us and we salute him back.

"Thank you, Sir!" we chant at him. He takes one more glance at me before he turns around to talk to the other group and I watch him walk away.

Sergeant Aric keeps us busy with marching and target practice until it's too dark to do either safely. Before bed, Sheena dictates I should have the first watch again. A part of me wants to argue I did that last time, but I'm too tired to fight with her about it.

"And I'll take the last watch with Raphaël," she says and walks towards him. It takes me a lot to not roll my eyes at her. Eliyah throws his arm around me, and I tense up. *Please don't touch me.*

"Actually," Raphaël says gently. "I think it's a g-good idea to switch around every night. This way we get to know everyone. How about L-Leo teams up with Eliyah and take the first round and I will take the second r-round with Elara. That way, you can get your beauty sleep tonight."

Sheena pouts her lips in disappointment but won't say no to a beauty sleep.

"What about me? Don't I get a beauty sleep?" Eliyah teases.

"There is n-no amount of sleep that can make your ugly m-mug beautiful," Raphaël says playfully. "You can have your sleep tomorrow."

I make myself ready for sleep.

Maybe I can convince the team to let me watch by myself. I'll have hours before anyone notices me. But what about Monster?

I stand behind the counter. The bakery is lit by a warm orange glow and the scent of warm bread fills my nose. An urgent feeling I have to find Monster boils up in my chest. He seems to be just out of my vision every time. It makes me restless. I hear him walk around and sometimes he growls. I call out his name, no sound leaves my mouth. Gran walks down the stairs. "Dear, what are you doing?" I tell her I'm looking for Monster. She gives me a puzzled look. "Monster? Who is that? Honey, we don't have a pet. Are you sure you are alright?" I try to tell her Monster is my pet. *The words get jumbled, and she doesn't understand me. I hear Monster's footsteps go up the stairs and I follow him into my room. There is a violet dress laid out on my bed. This means trouble. Yet I can't remember why. A buzz seems to emanate from the walls and it makes me queasy. I run to Gran's room and it's empty. Gran's dead, I realize with an ache. How was she just in the bakery? A hand grabs my shoulder.*

I awake with a gasp- someone has put their hand on my shoulder.

"Shh, it's alright," Raphaël says, "It's time for our watch."

The forest is full of little sounds as I struggle out of my sleeping bag. It's cold and my skin is damp from the damn forest and a shiver runs through me.

"I miss the beach," I tell no one in particular, while I lace up my boots.

Raphaël's outline chuckles and I sit down next to him. "I miss sleeping in a normal b-bed."

"Don't you miss the bar?"

"I hate the bar. Nothing good ever came out of it." He says bitterly, and this takes me by surprise. "It was my Dad's excuse to be a d-d-drunk, and when he was drunk, he would get angry. And when he was angry… well… you know."

"No… I don't," I say, wanting to hear more.

"Gran would come over after all was d-d-done and help us clean up the mess while my Dad slept off his b-b-buzz. Darya was the only person I could t-t-talk to about this. I reckon one of them would have told you."

I shake my head and a pang of guilt travels through me about telling Darya to drop Raphaël as a friend. "No, they never told me a thing. They kept your secrets well."

Raphaël laughs bitterly. "We were g-g-good at keeping up appear-ances. Mom was so afraid of being seen as a terrible wife, it almost k-killed her. That's why I wanted to study Healing; someone needed to take care of her when things got out of hand. Again. Now she has to run the bar on her own a-and I'm afraid she…" He takes a deep breath. "Can you keep this between us?"

"Of course." We sit in silence for a while. There is the occasional sound of something small scuttling through the bushes, alternating with Eliyah's heavy snoring.

"How did your mother take it that you were drafted?"

"She's afraid for me, of course, b-but she understands it wasn't much of a choice. Did you run away during the d-draft? I heard rumors but…"

"I- I don't want to talk about it."

"Is that the reason you suddenly had b-blond hair and bangs? It suits you."

"Thanks, I hate them," I say awkwardly while I brush the hair out of my eyes. "I have dreams about Gran. In my dreams, she is still with me in the bakery. It's like I'm still communicating with a piece of her."

"Maybe Qautahna has left a little door open for you t-two to communicate. Do you tell her about the C-Captain?"

"What!?" My voice is loud in surprise and I slap my hand in front of my mouth. Eliyah's snores continue uninterrupted, and I sigh in relief.

"He hides it a lot better than you do, but there is unmistakably something there."

I whisper, "No-, no! There is nothing going on between us. What- how?"

"It's one of the side effects of b-being a Sosa. We are very perceptive to other people's feelings," he says matter-of-factly. "Don't worry, you're n-not as bad as…" He motions his head towards where Sheena sleeps.

"Ah, you caught on to that," I say with a smile.

"Couldn't miss it if I t-t-tried."

* * *

Sergeant Aric's whistle wakes me up in the morning. I must have fallen asleep sitting against the tree trunk. Raphaël stands in front of me. *He let me fall asleep?*

The Sergeant stands underneath the cover of a small shed and to my dismay, Corporal Baël stands next to her. His eyes wander through the teams until his cold eyes find me and he winks.

Raphaël obstructs my view by taking a small step to the right. He turns around and helps me up. "What a c-c-creep," he whispers in my ear.

The morning starts with a march through the soaking rain. A full round will take up to around an hour. Thalassa has fallen in line next to me and I smile at her friendly face. Her hair is heavy with rain and her complexion is pale. Our heavy boots leave deep imprints in the mud.

"How are you holding up?" she asks

"I'm still here," I say. "You?"

"I'm maintaining."

Corporal Baël marches along with us, and I'm afraid to talk to her too much. His tall blond stature is marching a few rows ahead of us. I take solace in the fact he must be as miserable as I am. Everything has gotten so uncomfortable I can't banish it out of my mind anymore. With every step, my thighs chafe, and the fabric of the uniform weighs down heavy on my shoulders. My body shivers.

When we get near the campsite, my stomach all but collapses in itself when I smell something. For a moment, I believe my mind is making things up, until Thalassa groans and whispers, "I think that's bacon!" I don't respond. Corporal Baël has fallen back, and he is dangerously close to hearing range.

When we get back, Chef is handing out plates of food to the first troupes.

When he sees me, he tuts. "Oh no, my little Babushka. You look like a drowned cat."

He places pancakes on a plate and I see him put some extra bacon on mine. He puts his fingers to his lips to tell me to keep quiet. I mouth, 'thank you'.

The rain stops after lunch. We are all wet and cold. They ordered us to wash by the river and get a dry pair of uniforms and a towel each. Per team, we are assigned a time slot and we all get fifteen minutes. Team A gets back before their time is up, their faces flushed from the cold, their uniforms dry and clean. Sergeant Aric hovers over us like a watchdog. *But it has to be impossible to know all our whereabouts all the time. I just need to find the right time.*

Pretending to readjust my shoelaces, I let the others walk towards the river ahead of me as I try to commit the area to memory. *It will be harder to find my way in the dark.*

With a dry towel, I follow them to the waterfalls.

The men have no shame in taking off their clothes. They throw their uniform on a pile and their shirts along with it. Eliyah strips off his pants first. At least Leo has the courtesy of looking a little shy when he takes his undergarments off. As the three naked men make their way into the icy water, I make a conscious effort to keep my gaze fixed on the waterfalls. Sheena has stripped herself from her uniform and stands there unabashed in her lingerie before she steps into the cold water. She hugs herself as she slowly wades in.

Eliyah snickers at her and says. "I know honey, it's about this cold." He holds his fingers apart the size of an egg. Laughter ensues and

Leo says, "He's lying. That's what he started with this morning. Now I think it has crawled back inside!" They all laugh again.

"What about you, Raphaël?" Sheena asks.

He winks at her as he washes his hair. "My length has never c-caused any complaints, warm or cold." *Ugh.*

"Now you Elara, what are you hiding under that uniform?" Eliyah asks, and Raphaël splashes him with water.

"Nothing that will do you any g-good!" He laughs, and his melodious voice sings through the forest. *Sneaking away from the group might prove an even bigger problem than the Sergeant.* A bush gives me cover and I undress behind there. Painfully aware I will have to go into the water, I dress myself down. Too shy to take off my shirt and underwear, especially with Eliyah's eyes on me like I'm a piece of meat, I sneak in.

The familiar flutter of the water greets me like an old friend. It's not as cold as I thought it would be. Sheena looks at me with raised eyebrows as I swim towards the group. "You're still wearing your shirt, really?"

"Leave her alone, she'll figure it out," Raphaël says as he floats through the water towards me. I keep silent as Raphaël hands me the shampoo bottle. The scent of the soap is heavenly, a massive change from all the mud and damp. I close my eyes and my fingers massage my scalp. Before I'm done, Leo is already out of the water. With bare feet, he runs to the towel and covers himself with it. I can't soap up myself while I'm wearing a shirt. *Oh no, why didn't I think of that before?*

I remove my shirt and throw it to the water's edge. With a 'shlup' it lands in a pool of dirty water. Sheena hands me the soap and her eyes say 'I told you so' louder than she could with her voice.

I soap up as efficiently as I can without being seen. Eliyah is the second one to get out of the water and his pale behind is almost blue from the cold. I turn my back to them as I enjoy the flutter of the water.

"You feel it too, right?" I whisper to Raphaël, and he nods. He makes tiny scuttling movements with his hands.

"Let's get out. Do you want me to get your t-towel ready?" I nod and he walks out of the water with no shame. *I have seen enough asses to last me a lifetime.*

Sheena sneaks a peek and I'm disgusted. Raphaël gets my towel and holds it up wide, blocking the view for any peeping Toms. With both hands, I wring out as much water as possible from my maroon shirt. Raphaël looks at me when I glance up and I'm about to give him a proper scolding when I see his expression. It screams; are you kidding me?

"Oh, right," I mumble as I stroke the water out of the shirt. In the corner of my eye, I can see Sheena freeze, but when I turn my head, she's going about her business. *Must be my own paranoia.*

"There you go, C-Cookie."

The water flows from my shirt and after a few times, the shirt is dry on my hands. My hair is next, while Raphaël focuses his attention elsewhere. I take the towel from his hands and wrap it around myself. With a smirk, I realize the other's hair is still wet. *Definitely not elementalists then.* I'm proud as I put on my uniform again.

A high-pitched scream wakes me. I draw in my breath and try to see in the dark. It's a pitch-black night. The woods are silent. Even the nocturnal animals hold their breath.

"What was that?" Leo's voice whispers from my right.

Raphaël turns on his flashlight and shines into the thick velvet of the night. Instead of aiding, it blinds us.

"Turn it off!" I whisper to him. A click and it's dark again. Voices mumble overhead.

"Ladies and Gentleman," a voice bellows through the silent woods. My heart freezes and my eyes go wide. "One of your squad has been abducted, and it's your duty to find and save her! Make groups of four and come to me for further instructions." I expect him to finish that sentence with a 'hmmm?', but he doesn't. The others jump out of their sleeping bags and put on their shoes. I follow their example, but I would have liked to disappear in the bushes instead. The air is chilly and I notice our sleeping bags are soaked, so are my socks.

A flashlight illuminates the forest around Corporal Baël. His blond hair is impeccable. He hands out a map, a pen, and a compass to everyone. *If I could get my hands on those, I could figure out where to go.*

I stay back while Raphaël gets our stuff. I shiver. My heart beats fast when Corporal Baël looks my way. But he can't see me in the dark.

"Who of you is decent at reading maps?" Asks Raphaël.

Sheena rubs her eyes and yawns. "Even if I once was, I don't think I could anymore."

"I am, I can do it," I lie.

Private Eliyah puts the map on the forest floor and we gather around it. It's a large piece of paper and I can't make heads or tails of it, ending in a discussion of what north and south must be with an annoyed 'tssk' from Sheena. When we concur, we all huddle on one side of the map. I can't concentrate because my mind is so preoccupied with Baël's potential victim, but I can see some farms scattered to the East, not too far from here.

"The Corporal gave us c-coordinates to find our kidnappee," Raphaël says.

The group is too big to find one missing person. But the scream… "Who did he take?" I ask, feeling queasy. *Was that Thalassa?*

The camp is one big, chaotic mess. Groups of people walk in different directions. *I have a map... I might not get a better chance to run.*

"The point we n-need to go to is here, I think." Raphaël looks around for anyone to either concur or disagree. "Alright team, let's get our t-teammate back and go back to sleep."

We walk what we assume is Westward. Raphaël in front, me close behind. The thought of being caught alone in the dark forest by Corporal Baël makes my hair stand on end. I don't know what he would do if there was no one to stop him. Reluctantly, I have to admit that it's safer here with my group than out there alone.

It's a nightmare to stumble through the dark woods. Lucky for me, Raphaël is the one who catches the most spider webs, though he is also the only one with a light. My foot catches behind a branch. I stumble and fall against Raphaël, who drops his light and curses.

"Elara! Would you watch where you're g-going!?"

A part of me wants to pick a fight with him, but I think better of it. Cold bites into my feet and hands, and I shiver. He halts and rechecks the map, mumbles, and goes on again.

After a while, we arrive at the river and inspect the surroundings. "Anyone here?" Leo asks in an uncertain voice. There is only silence in return.

"Are we even in the right place?" Private Eliyah asks as he walks past me.

Raphaël shines his light around the river bed. It's too dark to make out anything. "I-I think so."

"Here! There is something here!" Eliyah exclaims. "Yes, these are coordinates!" Raphaël and Eliyah check the map where we have to go next, and I notice I can make out a little more around me. The sun is rising.

It's light when we arrive at the last spot. My stomach growls and I haven't stopped shivering, but I'm happy we have finally found it. Thalassa sits on a tree stump with a bored expression on her face and her sleeping bag drawn over her shoulders to keep out the worst of the cold.

"Good, I have been found," she says without a smile and she points down the road where others are already standing. "You can go there to report you have found me."

"Are we last?" I ask.

"No, there are just three more groups who are still out there."

We trudge down the dirt road. Mud covers our uniforms and small sticks cling to them. A meager applause welcomes us. And Corporal Baël smiles at us as he sees us approach. It sends a shiver down my spine. He looks better than all of us put together, and I wonder if he had time for a nap after sending us away.

"Welcome, welcome. You completed your quest in 3 hours and 16 minutes. Congratulations, you have failed. Your buddy has been assassinated and chopped up into little pieces. If only you had found her faster. Because you are distraught at your loss, you won't be hungry for breakfast." He looks straight at me and winks. My hunger vanishes. Raphaël moans and sits down in the middle of the road.

The remaining groups show up. One Private has a shallow gash on her cheek and another's clothes imply she has been swimming. She shivers from head to toe and is close to tears. Corporal Baël smiles delightedly and throws her a clean uniform. The girl wants to go into the forest to change.

"Private Wells, the forest is full of enemies that killed your friend. You can't go in there, we might lose you too."

My heart drops and everyone watches her. *He wouldn't.*

Private Wells nods and she weighs her options. She glances at the clean and dry uniform and then looks at the team timidly. With blue, trembling hands, she unbuttons her uniform and my heart bleeds for her, yet my fear of Corporal Baël is too intense to help. In my mind, I curse at him, while berating myself for my own silence. He keeps his stare on her as she undresses. No one speaks out. I can't look at anything else other than my shoes. *I need to get out of here.*

Corporal Baël stays with us for the rest of the morning. His eyes burn on me as we march through the forest and as we tiger through the undergrowth, and as we sit down for lunch. "You are responsible for your own food. I have been gracious enough to bring ingredients with me, but you shall have to build your own fire. In this case, you can find a set of fire stones. It's up to you to make the fire to cook it," Baël says.

Raphaël and Thalassa rise and stand in line for the ingredients and fire stones, while Eliyah and I are assigned to gather some firewood. Leo digs a hole in the ground for the fire to go. The fallen branches in the forest are covered in moss and the ground is damp. Around us, others are also unsuccessful. Sheena complains out loud that she can't find anything. Another Private walks around with a handful of fallen branches that are going to give off more smoke than heat. We go deeper and deeper into the forest while we inspect the floor for something useful. I stare into what I think is West, but I don't dare make a break for it with Baël breathing down my neck. Eventually, I return with just a few wet branches. I didn't want to come back empty-handed. Eliyah has brought many more, they will all be useless. *Even for lunch, we won't be able to eat anything.*

Leo has dug a hole with his hands and has put rocks around the hole to keep all the fire in the center. Raphaël and Thalassa have already unpacked our box of ingredients with big slabs of meat.

"This is going to be no use, we'll only get smoke with these wet twigs." I complain.

Thalassa twiddles her fingers. "Elara, you remember what we can do right?"

"We can't," I say and my eyes shoot to Corporal Baël. "We're not allowed."

"Oh c-come on, we need a proper meal!"

"Fine, but I'm not doing anything." I sit down on the floor with my arms crossed. Raphaël's and Thalassa's eyes meet.

"Oh! Show me what you can do!" Leo pipes.

Raphaël draws up his sleeves dramatically. "Watch this." With more hand movement than is strictly necessary, he saps the water from the branches and Leo's eyes grow big as saucers. Eliyah and Sheena exchange a glance, but Raphaël doesn't notice and lets the water droplets hover for a moment for dramatic effect. Leo lets out a small 'wow', but my eyes are on Baël and I hiss at Raphaël to stop.

Fire catches easily after that and we are the first who have a fire burning while around us, a lot of filthy smoke rises into the air. This is something Baël is also quick to realize.

"That's a decent fire," he comments as he walks up to our little group. "You have done better than all the other recruits."

"Thanks, sir!" Raphaël says as he misses the dangerous undercurrent in the Corporal's voice, but the Dog leaves it alone. As he walks off, I let out the breath I had been holding. We make a little lunch of beef and some vegetables- after such a long time eating scraps, this food is the best thing I ever tasted. I lick the juices of the still half raw meat from my fingers and the vegetables. My body needs nutrients.

"Alright Privates, let's go and get busy after this meal! With your group, you are going to move a wounded soldier on a stretcher. This is the wounded soldier." Baël lifts a sack of 50kg grain as if it were a pillow. "Make a stretcher from the rope I give you and anything else you can find on the forest floor. First, I will show you how to tie a proper knot. Everyone, get a piece of rope and grab two sticks. Or a partner. Private Waywater, if you please,"

I clench my teeth and come closer to him. He stands so close to me I can smell him and my whole body tells me to run.

Baël ties my hands together while he explains how it works.

"Everyone gather round. Make sure everyone can see. Private Waywater, can you cross your arms at the wrist, hmmm? Yes like that, good girl. Today you will learn how to perform a square lashing. Observe!"

The rope bites into my skin, but I keep my mouth shut. I try to focus on my breath. In the end, he ties the last knot, causing my wrists to be tied together and my hands to grow numb.

"Come on Private, show them if you can get out of this one."

I try to free my arms but I am left to his mercy. I swallow hard. *He is making a point with this.* He laughs as he sees me struggle and my heart races in panic. "You can't easily undo these knots, as Private Waywater demonstrates." He grabs a short knife from his pocket. "Sometimes you need to cut it, with something sharp." He stares into my eyes. His hand holds me in an iron grip as he wiggles the blade between my wrists. He cuts the rope in one movement.

"Now scurry off," he whispers.

Raphaël walks up to us to get a big bag of grain and his eyes follow me as I flee toward my little group. It's a 20-kilometer walk and we are beat as we come back to camp. *If they keep beating us down like this, I won't have the energy to escape.*

As the rest of us get some sleep, Raphaël is assigned to patrol the perimeter. The rest of us sleep huddled up together. This time we get to sleep through the night.

Chapter 22

I am hungry, sleep-deprived, dirty, and cold. I need to get out of here now. Sergeant Aric has relieved Baël, which in itself is a relief. She tells us to wash up and go to sleep before we march back to the base in the morning. *This is the time. I need to leave before dawn. Momo, my baby, please forgive me. But even if Mrs. Applegarth would abandon you, Raphaël will take care of you.*

Night falls like a heavy blanket as we walk to the river. I have expertly separated myself from the others. The coordination trial has taught me the bearings of the land. *They handed me everything to get out.*

As everyone washes, I say, "I think dinner disagreed with me. I'll be back." No one pays me any special attention and in my mind, I say my goodbyes to Raphaël, Thalassa, and even Leo, who I've grown fond of in the last days. *Bye Momo.*

I turn around and walk up the hill I ran down on my very first day. After a couple of sessions with maps and coordinates, I developed a pretty good feel for the forest. If I head West for a while, I will find a cluster of farms. There I can get out of this damn uniform and get some proper clothes. Perhaps a farmer will take me in for a meal and after… I will head for the mountain range. It will take me approximately three days of walking before I reach the base of the mountains, but I need to get over them before winter starts. There is no room to question if I can get food somewhere and if I will be lucky enough to get some clothes. Before I can second-guess myself, I walk away from the group. If I keep going straight, I will find a small town. *What if I can't find food anywhere?*

No one appears to be following me. *Good!* I break into a run. The faster I leave this place behind me, the better. Running fills me with adrenaline and butterflies fill my belly. I try not to think about Raphaël or Leo, discovering that I vanished. *How long will it take before they get worried?*

The forest is filled with shadows and I run, dodging branches and holes in the ground. Sleep deprivation has made me less sharp and a branch whips my face painfully. Bushes scratch at my uniform.

This part of the forest is strange to me and the undergrowth is denser here. In the distance, moonlight shines through the canopy. It must be a road I saw on the map. It leads straight to the farms. Panting, I wrestle through a last bush onto the darkening road. *I'm not out of the woods yet, literally.* I keep up the pace as I walk down the wide road. It's a welcome change from all the moss and bushes. My ears search for any sounds of trucks or other things that might blow my cover. There is a bend around a little way up, but there is nothing except for the chirping of birds. This freedom seems to give me wings and with a smile, I trot along the road. Hours fly by and within the shortest of times, the forest ends. I do a little happy dance. *I finally made it out!*

Fields stretch out in front of me, cattle graze lazily, and the moon bathes the world in its light. A sound of bells comes from a herd of sheep while a sheepherder guides them to a shed with his dog. I chase after him. "Excuse me, Sir!"

He turns around and stares at my uniform for a moment. "How can I help you, ma'am?"

"I-, I seem to have lost my squad and I-, the light is fading. I'm looking for a place to sleep, maybe even something to eat… Before I make the way back to the base, of course."

"Aha, I see. Well, I'll need to ask the Mrs. Why don't you join me? You have a name, girl?" He doesn't believe me, but I'm not sure if it matters.

He called me girl instead of Private, that must mean he cares.

"Darya… Darya Ballard, Sir."

"Nice to meet you, Miss Ballard. Let me close up shop and we'll see what I can do for you."

I wait for him to close the fence. His little black and white friend follows us to a cozy farmhouse. The aroma of something grilling on the fire makes my mouth water. He opens the door and yells inside. "Jo, honey, I've got someone here in need of a warm meal and a haystack."

"Do they eat pork?"

He looks at me.

"I'll eat just about anything."

"She says she's fine with it."

"Then it's fine with me!"

The man kicks off his boots and walks inside the house. I take some time to unleash the heavy army boots, and when I get in, I see them standing over a pot. He has his arm around her. She has braided her gray hair and is wearing a simple dress.

"Just a minute. Dinner will be done in a minute. Now you get out of them dirty clothes. You stink like sheep!"

The man chuckles and slaps her rear. For a moment, the Swallows go through my mind and my mouth gets dry. He leaves and in the house there's opening and closing of doors.

"Well, don't just stand there! Make yourself useful and set the table. You'll need to set for four, dear."

I scurry over and collect cutlery and plates from the cupboard. I space the white plates over the round table and put the cutlery next to it. Next, I find a coaster and put it in the middle of the table.

"Dear, could you put the pan on the table? My back…"

"Of course ma'am." With three big strides, I'm in front of the stove and with two worn potholders, I lift the big pan. It's heavy, but my lean body makes it to the table with ease. The stew smells amazing and my stomach rumbles.

"Ah! It sounds like you are ready to eat. What do I call you?"

"Darya Ballard, Ma'am."

"Well, go sit down, Darya. We're waiting for the others. Do you want some milk? No? Some ale then?"

I accept the latter only because I fear coming across as rude. Jo places full mugs on the table and I try to make conversation.

"A nice place you got here."

"Oh honey, you think that now. To tell you the truth, it's one good storm away from falling over. Last winter we had a leak so bad it was pouring more inside than outside. Never you mind. You need to get a belly full of warm food, he? Warm yourself by the fire for now."

I stand in front of the fireplace with my hands stretched out. The warm glow is such a welcome change from all the cold and dampness. Jo fusses around and gives a nervous impression. For the second time, I feel guilty about putting this couple in such peril. "You know what. I should just go."

"Nonsense deary, we're not sending you away without a meal."

Straight after dinner then. More doors bang and the sheepherder walks back into the room. For a moment I'm confused- he's still wearing the same clothes. A figure appears from behind him. He's not in his uniform, so it takes me a second to realize how much trouble I am in. His tall stature makes my heart freeze. He wears a cream-colored coat that looks out of place here on the farm.

"Good evening, Private," he says gently, but his eyes spew fire.

"Good evening, Second Lieutenant Winchester."

He spared the life of the shepherd and his wife. Probably because they ratted me out. I'm too scared to be angry, though. Jo kept to her word and didn't let me leave until all four of us had a meal. The stew that had smelled so good before has lost its flavor. I play with a lump of potato while I wonder how he will do it. *Will he shoot me outside the door? Or hang me on the base grounds to make an example?*

I don't pay attention as they chat about the upcoming winter. Winchester even takes seconds. I decline, but take some ale for my dry throat. *Guns or Gallows. Huh, both start with a G.*

Apparently, Winchester has been close friends with this couple for years. Just my luck, he lives a short bit away. He thanks them as we leave the house and money exchanges hands. *I hope your house is worth it.*

He places his hand firmly on my shoulder as we walk into the night. Near us, I hear the soft cling of bells from the sheep.

"You cause us a lot of trouble, Private."

"I can explain,-"

"How did you think this was going to go? The first random farmer would welcome you with open arms, give you a new outfit and you would skip your way up and over the mountain range?"

Yes. "It's not-,"

"Private Waywater, I know you hold no respect for us, but are you that thick to lie to me? To *me!*?"

I'm armed, what if-? But before I finish the thought, the metallic click of his gun makes me jump.

"I would say, don't even think about it, but you did. Don't cause us any more trouble, Private."

Who's us? A feeling creeps inside my chest that he's not talking about the military. I gaze up at the stars. They shine brightly. "Are you going to kill me?" *Could Qautahna find me here?*

"I could, and possibly I should. If it was anyone else, they would, without giving it a second thought, but you are an elementalist and there are not a lot of you out there. Though this is not going to go away by cleaning some toilets, either." He takes my gun out of my holster and pockets it. Then, with one hand, he steers me into his automobile and locks the door. He sits down in the driver's seat and sighs before he starts the car. The engine roars to life and we drive away from the little farm. *Are you listening?*

"What do you want me to say? I told you I wouldn't listen in if I didn't need to. You have put me in a corner here and now I have to do something I really don't want to do." He doesn't bring me back to Sergeant Aric. Instead, we go directly to the base. *What are you going to do with me?*

Winchester opens my door and with a hand on my shoulder, steers me through the entrance. The nauseating smell of pine hits me. We enter a wing I haven't been to before and he keeps pushing me further and further into the base. There is no one in the halls, and I wonder if everyone is at dinner. He knocks on a white door. When he hears nothing, he uses a key to open it and walks me inside. It's not what I expected. There is a gigantic bed, a set of leather chairs, a rug, and some bookcases. The entire atmosphere of the room is comfortable. *Is he going to rape me?*

He retracts his hand from me quickly. "What!? No! Gods no! I can't believe you- ah. Stay here." He exits the room and I hear the lock turn.

I walk to a chair, but it feels wrong to sit down. *If it was Baël I wouldn't be so sure.* There is a portrait on the floor with its picture turned towards me. The brown cardboard looks unimpressive. I wipe my hands on my uniform. The only sounds in the room are the beating of my heart and the buzzing of electricity. My eyes shoot across the room. *I can't fight him off. Can I crawl under the bed?* I realize it won't do me any good. Too quickly, I hear footsteps again. The soft ring of keys and the click of the lock fill the space. The door opens again and two uniforms step in.

"Are you *completely* out of your mind!? You brought her to my room? Why didn't you throw her in the brig?" The fury in this voice is palpable. It sounds so different from the time he asked for some cinnamon rolls.

Winchester replies, "Because others will ask questions."

Others? What others?

"Do you know what would happen if they found her in my room!?"

They walk towards the leather seats. I could have been air for all the further acknowledgment they give me. Winchester continues, "we need to have a plan before we do anything."

"Yes, but my room! What about an empty office somewhere? Or throw her in her own room?" Hawkeye sits down and stands up again.

"Your room was the closest, and no one has seen us."

"Gods dammit! Alright, I need a drink." Hawkeye stands up and pours brown liquid into three wide glasses. He empties a first and then hands Winchester the second. Winchester takes a sip and then pinches the bridge of his nose.

My heart thumps erratically when Hawkeye gives me the glass without meeting my eyes. I'm too afraid to decline or draw attention to myself in any other way. The drink smells like oak and caramel. Because I'm not sure how long my life will last, I opt to try it. It's disgusting. I stifle a cough. *What are you two so afraid of?*

"What if we-" He turns to Winchester.

"No."

"We could-"

"Also no. It will hurt your relationship with her." Winchester swirls the drink around in his glass. It's like I'm a fly on the wall. Invisible. *Is it a 'them' or is it a 'her'? It can't be Little, maybe Aric?*

"The Privates will talk."

"Still no."

"Alright, so what-" Hawkeye folds his hands below his chin. He looks at his glass as if it will give him an answer.

"That's your plan?" The silence grows and I am still nailed to the floor.

"No one will dare ask."

He paces up and down the room. I watch him move as if he's the light of an anglerfish. "True, but it will raise suspicion."

Silence fills the room before Hawkeye asks, "do you see another way out?" He stands up and curses loudly. He's so angry, I'm afraid he'll take a swing at me. I take another sip of the drink and it burns my throat.

"And you think I can?" Hawkeye pours himself another drink and finishes it in one swallow. Winchester rubs his temples. Meanwhile, the few sips I have taken are already making my legs feel heavy.

"Can I say something?"

"NO!" they say in unison and I move as if they struck me. Hawkeye sits back down. Silence stretches out over us. The buzz of the electricity fills the room.

"I'm going to report to Aric that she's here. What do I tell her?" They're silent again. Every instinct tells me to keep quiet, but the strong alcohol has made me relax a bit.

"Tell her I had menstrual pains, and you found me during a stroll. You thought something was seriously wrong with me and took me to a doctor."

They both look at me in surprise. "Why would he have done that?"

"A girl complaining about pain, vomiting, and her pants are bloody. What would your first course of action be?" I peer into the drink. *It's like liquid courage.*

"No, it won't make sense. You would have to keep the room near freezing all the time, and you don't have that type of control yet. Besides, if you'd had that bad of a… cycle, your roommate would have noticed it by now."

Dumbfounded, I stand in the room. *How could I forget that?*

"You have two options. Brig or discipline. What will it be?"

"What is discipline?"

Hawkeye pinches the bridge of his nose. "I would take the brig if I were you."

I nod. There are little ice crystals in my glass now.

Winchester leaves the room. I'm left standing forlorn. Hawkeye rises and pours some more bourbon into my glass. "You have just royally screwed up… a lot. Let's pray one of us makes it out alive. In unity and reverence."

He clinks his glass to mine and throws the contents back.

Chapter 23

It's the smell that's the worst -after just a few hours, this has made me nauseous. The entire base smells like pine, but the brig, has a dark brown undertone to it. White tiles cover the floor, walls, and ceiling. Two room contains two things; a bed and a toilet. The mattress is old, and the springs hurt my skin when I lie on it. That is the reason I've been lying on the floor for a few hours now. *Mary had a little lamb, little lamb... Why did she just own one lamb? It followed her to school one day. It was against the rules. Oh, I wonder how Monster is doing. Monster was my lamb.*

59 tiles cover the ceiling. There is one missing where they put the light bulb. No natural light enters this space, so I assume they turn it on during the day. It hums when it's turned on. *Would discipline have been the better choice?*

The room is not a perfect square. But only just, if I hadn't spent hours staring at the walls, I would have missed it. *Brig does sound better than solitary confinement...*

They have stripped me of my powers. I suspect its something in the food. It started right after they gave me the first lunch. *Did it?* Or it might be in the air. Also, I'm seeing things. I'm not sure what is causing it. *Could I be high on the detergent? Or it might be in the food.* The tiles shift uncomfortably and I feel like I'm drunk. I giggle.

"Have people gone mad from isolation?" I ask Monster. He watches me from the bed. His enormous eyes are shiny. It's nice of Monster to keep me company. "Who is 'they'? Who is 'she'?" I ask for the thousands time. But Monster doesn't know either. Food appears 'on the flap from the door. Monster doesn't even have to jump off the bed to sniff it. He turns away from it and lies back on the bed. *It's probably the food.*

I eat it anyway. It's the only thing that gives this place some flavor. It's like Chef's cooking has gotten even better since I've been here. With the tray on my lap, I sit against the door.

"Are you sure you don't want any?" Monster shakes his head. I take as long as I can with the food. *Perhaps I should be a cow and regurgitate everything I eat. Focus!*

"They're afraid of something. Someone. That surely means they are doing something… What's the word.. Illegal? I wish Gran would come here and tell me what to do… What do you think is keeping her?"

Monster stays silent.

"How will I get out of here?"

I wait for him to respond. When I look up, he's vanished.

"That's easy for you to say."

Monster wines a few seconds before the lights go out.

Someone sits on the bed and peers down at me. It's Baël.

"No, no, no, no, no, no." I repeat as I hide myself in a corner.

"Good morning, sunshine. We're going to have a little fun today. You're going to tell me why you ran."

My heart thumps in my throat. Tears form in my eyes when he takes a blade out of his pocket.

"Just be a good girl and tell me everything."

He shifts closer to me and I'm repelled by his musk, but there is nowhere to go. The blade glints menacingly in the lamplight.

"I wanted to get out. I never wanted to be here."

"It's not about what *you* want, hmmm?"

"No one knew. It was only me."

He uses the blade to clean his nails. "And?"

"My parents- my parents' letters are in my bag. But I have no idea what they mean."

"I know about your silly little letters. Now tell me something juicy. Who are 'they'!?"

"I don't know! I don't know anything!"

He inches closer and the blade fades from my vision. I shut my eyes and wait for the sharp pain. For a touch. For the cold. Nothing happens. When I open my eyes, Baël is gone.

There are 65 tiles on the wall. "65 bottles of beer on the wall. 65 bottles of beer.. Take one down, smash it around, 64 bottles of beer on the wall... 64 bottles of beer on the wall, 64 bottles of beer, take one down, smash it around, 63 bottles of beer on the wall."

Food appeared on the flap. I wait for someone to join me, but it stays silent. Gran still hasn't come by. *Is she punishing me?*

Gran is preparing dinner in the kitchen. The scent of fried fish fills my head. My homework lies open in front of me on the counter. Letters keep on dancing on the pages and I can't make out the words.

"I'm happy you are making friends, dear!" Gran says.

"Gran, I'm not sure they're my friends. I don't know what they want from me." The bakery looks wrong. Tiles cover the floor and I stare at them while I wonder when I have seen them before.

"These are two Dogs you want to keep close," Gran walks out of the kitchen with two plates of food. With her free hand, she holds my cheek. "You need to learn how to keep your thoughts to yourself."

"I said nothing!" I protest. Somewhere I hear Monster sigh in his sleep.

"I didn't say you said anything." Gran holds a stone in her hand and shows it to me. The colors inside are moving. They shift from blue to green to red.

"What is this?"

"Private? Waywater!"

I blink at Gran.

"Private!" Winchester stands in the door frame. I close my eyes, trying to go back to the dream with Gran.

"Private, get up."

"Why?"

"You have served your punishment. You are free to go."

"Who are *they*?" I ask and stare at the tiles of the ceiling. Winchester doesn't respond, and I check if he's still there. "Did Baël really come in here?"

"*Corporal* Baël didn't set foot in this room as far as I know."

I let my head drop on the tiled floor in relief. "How do I know you're real?"

He sighs and rubs his temples. "You can stay here another five days. Would you want to risk it?"

I hurry to my room. It's a challenge as the texture of the walls move and it worsens when I run. I can't be sure that no one was listening in. Thalassa is not in the room and my bags are untouched. I sigh a sigh of relief.

The letters are still in my bag. I glance over my shoulder and listen carefully for any sign of footsteps. The halls are quiet. I sit alone, on the floor, with the letters in my hand. I have read the words so many times I can recite them word for word. They hold no news for me, only danger. I can't throw them in the bin. Anyone could find them there. *Should I eat them?*

My past self would have laughed herself silly if she knew what I had contemplated. But as much as I long for those times, my past self is not me anymore. I'm afraid to leave the room with my letters. Afraid that anyone might ask me to show what I have in my pockets.

I don't even care if these are the letters that link to my parents. But these are the letters that link me to Gran. Her teardrops stain the last letter my father ever wrote her. With a heavy heart, I walk to the sink. *I'll soak them, rip them apart and then let them disappear down the drain.*

With a heavy heart, I run the tap and put the plug in the sink. *Would the paper clog the pipes?* I don't know.

The first letter is of my mother. My hands flutter the moment I put the letter in the cold water. Her beautiful handwriting smudges. I swallow hard. With my eyes shut, I tear the wet paper into bits. First two, then four, and I keep tearing until a dozen pieces of paper float aimlessly around the sink before I watch the bits of paper disappear. A few pieces stick to the metal, refusing to go down. With hot water, I fill the sink the second time.

The second is a letter from my father. He mentions his new location and I'm disappointed I never figured out where it was, what Gran was right about, RR or who C. was. The paper feels brittle in my hands as I dunk it down into the water. *Forgive me, Gran.*

A tear rolls down my cheek. But then lines form across the parchment. "What."

The lines form as if someone is drawing them into place in front of me. Lines form a fist. *The fist... the sign of the resistance.*

My heart races and a million questions spring into my mind. My hands freeze in place, unwilling to rip this message from my father. I turn it over carefully, praying for more information, but nothing appears. For a wild moment I think of saving the letter, but what would they do to me if they find it. With trembling fingers, I rip it apart. I have to catch my breath after this one.

There is just one more letter and when I put it in the water, I gasp. It's as if someone is writing over the paper, more words appear.

I hope you catch on to this and all is not lost. Claude has helped us hide after the base got attacked. Send the next requests to him. We need to tread carefully.

Take Elara and run. I will find you.

Eros.

Still under the influence of whatever they gave me, I stare at the wall. I ponder the enigmatic words that have etched themselves into the inside of my eyelids. *Is he alive? He can't be, otherwise he would have found us. Wouldn't he? And what are Winchester and Hawkeye doing? Who are they? Who is this woman they are scared of?*

"By Quatahna- we thought you were… We were worried sick about you!" I jump when I hear Thalassa's voice. She looks awful. Her face is pale, there are bags under her eyes and there is a bruise on her cheek. She sits down and gives me a great big hug, tears prick in my eyes. The scent of dirt, sweat, and moss fills my nose. Something cracks in my back as she hugs me tight.

When it gets dark, speakers emit a shrill uncomfortable siren. In a knee-jerk reaction, I fly to a seated position and slam my head against Thalassa's bed.

"Is that the call for dinner?" I ask Thalassa as I rub my sore head. We follow the stream of Dogs into the dinner hall. Roast, salt, and fat decorate the canteen with their smells. White walls and ceilings make me feel unwelcome. White unfriendly lights hanging from the ceiling, it gives everyone a sickly pale color.

Dinner takes the form of a buffet, and we can choose between a big variety of things. After standing in line for some time, some things are already finished. There is a sign 'Fish cakes' in front of an empty bowl. Afraid to miss out on anything, I stack my plate with two pancakes, a sausage, a pie with unidentified meat, and cooked greens. *Gran would want me to eat healthily.* The two of us sit down together at an empty table. My eyes scan the canteen. Officers are seated at a table near the wall. A small distance away from all the recruits. Winchester has his old demeanor back and jokes around while Hawkeye laughs easily. It reminds me of how they used to be with us as well. *It's not gone, it's hidden under all this... Was is ever real, though?*

I now smell of lavender and citrus. Raphaël finds us and sits down next to me with a full tray.

Raphaël's welcome is different. "Look who has made a m-m-miraculous return!" He stuffs a too-big piece of pancake into his mouth. A few tables behind him, Hawkeye watches me. His eyes narrow in warning.

"Yeah… Tada," I say awkwardly while waving my hands as if I did a magic trick. Raphaël and Thalassa, who are now rested, question me about what happened. Raphaël loses interest as soon as I mention my female distress.

Thalassa is harder to fool, but she doesn't question it too much. "I'm happy you're okay and Winchester found you before… before someone else did."

The rest of our team joins us a bit later. Leo, Eliyah, and even Sheena accompany us. Sheena's eyes narrow as she sees me, but she stays silent. Thalassa is the only odd one out. She looks around and asks if she should sit with her team, too.

"Sit here with us!" Raphaël says with a warm smile.

Sheena looks at Raphaël and throws her beautiful blond hair back in protest, but stays quiet.

***

One of my more lasting punishments is working as a secretary for the Mountain. After breakfast, he leads me to his office. Someone freshly mopped the hall and the stinging odor of pines wafts through the hall. There is a small desk in front of it and he tells me to sit down. There is no class today- I'm forced to sit here the entire day. But I have an idea, and just the thought of it makes my heart do somersaults.

"Can I do something for you?" I try to keep my voice steady, but it shivers like a scared mouse.

"No, sit here, look busy, and don't disturb me." He walks through his office door before he slams the door shut. I take a deep breath and ask; "Could I go to the library to catch up on my training?"

Officer Klippa turns the idea over in his mind, sees nothing wrong with my request, and nods. "But you are to read right here," he says. His blue eyes stare through me before he slams the door shut.

My heart races and I take a deep breath to calm my nerves. I hadn't expected it to be this easy. With a straight back I march the maze of halls to find the Military library, which is hard because sometimes the colors of objects still change- the last effects of the mystery drug.

The library smells like old parchment and wood, a welcome change of the ever present pine. Wooden shelves hold books piled two stories high, while dust swirls in the rays of sunlight streaming into the room. A few people I don't know sit in the back, reading in comfortable looking chairs.

"Can I help you, dear?" a woman with short black hair asks me.

"Hi, I'm looking for books about… mental abilities," I say. The woman eyes me with suspicious eyes. Her hands stroke the light blue skirt of her dress, as if she's trying to wipe away some dirt. "It's for First Lieutenant Klippa," I add hurriedly.

"Tell him he still has to return the book on Crystals. He's at least 9 days overdue," she says.

"Yes, of course!" My voice disturbs the peaceful silence of the library.

"Do you know why he wanted to read up on Cognisight? No? Do you recon' he wanted to read up on Psychotranmissions or Psygnosis?" She asks while she leads me up to the next floor of the library, while these new terms dizzy me and I hold on to the hand railing. Or it might still be the drug.

"I'm not sure. Could I just get everything?"

She laughs. "Dear, everything would be at least 30 books."

I get nervous. *If I ask for books that are below his level of understanding, she might get suspicious.*

"Ah, the fool gave you nothing to go on, hea?" She looks at my panicked face. "Don't worry, I won't send you back empty-handed." She wrings her hands as she looks at the bookcase in front of us. The dark covers with golden letters look impressive. She takes out three books, one thick and two smaller ones. The thick book pages are gold-plated. "Take these, and if he needs others, you come back to me, alright?" She smiles at me.

I nod frantically. "Would you also have a book on advanced herbology? That one's for me." She spins around and walks us back down. She closes the stairs off with a rope that I didn't notice before. "Frantic to get ahead, are you? That's what I like to see in a recruit!" The book she picks off the shelf this time has a deep blue cover with white letters. *Advanced Herbology: The key to successful healing.* "Will this do?"

I nod and give her my thanks. After signing my name in her book, I walk back and smile to myself.

The happy feeling fades as I sit at my desk and leaf through the first book: Cognisight Codex: Exploring the Frontiers of Thought, by Leonardus Balm. The book is at least a hundred years old and written by hand by someone who must have had the worst handwriting of the century. Some words are completely illegible. With the aroma of cigarettes wafting out of it, I wonder if the man himself was a heavy smoker or if Winchester borrowed this before me.

The other two; The Psygnosis Enigma: Bridging Science and Psychic Phenomena, by Alphonse Black, and Unlocking Psychotransmission: The Power of Shared Thought, by a Proff. Binns, are printed books and a much easier read.

I read one that I place on my lap, while the Advanced Herbology lies open in front of me as a beard. Sometimes I just stare at the crack on the wall or at the picture of the Leader Suprema. Her short hair is white as snow, even at a young age. Her face faces the camera. She wears the same uniform as I do, where my rims are stitched with red, hers are stitched with yellow. Or maybe it's gold. Her uniform changes color. Now it's red. I shake my head to clear my head. The fact that I'm defying her and her precious military fills me with a fiery determination. I drum my fingers against the wooden desk as I read.

A soldier walks into the hall and the sound of his boots squeak on the clean floor. He doesn't look up and reads the documents he is holding. With trembling fingers, I place The Psygnosis Enigma in a drawer. He walks right past me and is about to knock on Klippa's door.

"No!" I try to whisper and shout at the same time. The man turns towards me. "He is not to be disturbed," I whisper. *I probably appear drunk.*

"Who are you?"

"Private Waywater, Sir!" I jump up and salute him.

"He finally accepted a secretary? Okay, fine. I have no time for this. Tell Klippa to take a gander at these documents. He knows what to do."

I take the stack of paper and nod. "Yes, Sir."

He stalks off, and I put the stack of papers on my desk. The top sheet reads 'Potential personnel'. It takes a lot of self-restraint to not go through the files. The thought of being caught prevents me. The man leaves and I get out the heavy book yet again. By now I'm used to the handwriting and wrestle my way through sentences like '*the theta wave's subtle cadence harmonizes with the delta's whispered narrative, and the gamma's electric crescendo interlaces with the alpha's contemplative discourse.'*

For a moment, I'm transported back to my old classroom. Doodling on a paper with my classmates while the teacher tries to interest us in the layers of the skin or the names of the different arteries and nerves. The scratch of pens to paper and the teacher's voice somewhere in the background. I smile. *Home.*

My heart aches and a tear falls upon the paper. With my sleeve, I wipe away the moisture from my face.

A new Dog enters through the door on my left and his footsteps echo through the hall. He carries a big canvas sack, which he puts down next to the desk.

"Ah, I see Klippa caved and got a secretary. Good for him. Could you give him these?" Without waiting for an answer, he stalks off again.

I glance inside the big bag and it's filled with envelopes. I grab the one on the top and realize these are all personal letters. *What does he do with these? What should I do with these?*

To give my eyes a rest, I take a break from reading and order the letters into piles. First, I separate the men from the women. A letter for Raphaël pokes out, and I tuck it away in my drawer for safekeeping. I do the same for the letters which are addressed to Thalassa. My hands pause when I find a letter addressed to me. It's in Darya's handwriting. My fingers trace the ink she has used to write my name. With great care, I put it next to the other letters. A swarm of jellyfish tentacles dance in my stomach, each zap of nerves stinging a little.

At 12:05, the door handle behind me comes alive and the door opens. I'm so occupied with the book that I jump in surprise.

"Private, what are you doing?" First Lieutenant Klippa's bloodshot eyes scan over the desk.

"I thought I would separate the letters, so it's easier to hand them out… Sir." I sense I've done something wrong. Then I remember to salute and he walks to go through the letters that are piled on my desk.

"They left all of them at my desk again? Ugh. You separated them wrong. After lunch, I'll give you a list of how to separate them. Put them back in the bag now. I'll put them in my office. Let's go get lunch." He locks the door. Stretches and yawns. After lunch, I am forced to pile up the letters and get little time for my books.

My first task is to separate the letters, due to rank instead of gender or where they sleep. Letters from lower ranks, everything from Corporal to Private go back into the bag. Everything from Second Lieutenant to Sergeant goes on one pile and a few letters are even above that. The letter written by Darya burns in my hand as if it's about to go off. *Does she hold a grudge because I didn't believe she didn't tell on me?*

The higher the rank is the scarcer the letters are. There is one letter to Winchester, which is written in such clunky handwriting I surmise it must come from his daughter. If the handwriting didn't make it clear, then the little sun and expertly drawn red bike surely do. *Could there be clues in here?*

I hold the letter up to the light, but it reveals no secret. If I open it, I will be caught. At the end of the day, my thoughts about the contents of Darya's letters have spiraled. *Maybe the bakery burnt down, or the Dogs hurt her family.* For a while, I stare at the wall. White paint seems more and more yellowish until I close my eyes. *Don't think about that!*

Chapter 24

A few days later, we receive the letters. There is a gash in the envelopes and a faint smell of cigarette smoke lingers on them. Thalassa reads her letters, puts them away, and tells me she is going to hang out with her friend at the sick bay. I stare at the two envelopes that lie beside me. Too afraid to face potential hardships, I left them there. A book lies open on my lap and I read: Research shows that the neural integrity can be tarnished by the prism. I'm pondering that as Raphaël walks in with a letter in his hand. "Mind if I join you?"

I glance at him and put my book away. "Yeah, of course. Is everything alright?"

He sits down next to me. "I miss home." He sighs as he brushes his hair out of his eyes.

"Me too."

"Did you and Z-Zale become an item after Solemnitatum?"

Caught off guard, I look at him and laugh. "What!? No. The evening was… awkward. We weren't a good fit. What about you? You went with Miriam, right?" Solemnitatum seems as if it belongs to a different era. A life where I could worry about dresses, homework, and the bakery. It hurts in a bittersweet way to talk about it.

"It- it didn't work f-for us either. She instantly started talking about how she would take over Dad's bar and what we should name our k-kids." He shudders.

"It sounds like Zale and Miriam should have gone together."

He laughs.

"Did your mother write you?" I ask while I eye the letter in his hand.

"Yes, b-but I'm too afraid to open it. Silly, right?" I turn my eyes to the unopened letters near the sink and shake my head. "Want to open them t-t-together?" I nod and stand up from the bed to get the two letters I got. It saddens me that I got two letters and Raphaël got one. "You start," he says.

"Can you read it? I can't…"

Raphaël takes the letter from Mrs. Applegarth and smiles at me. He's got gray eyes, I never noticed before. He opens the letter and bites his lip.

"Dear Elara, that's you," he jokes and gives me a wink. "I hope this letter finds you well. Monster and I have been having a great time getting to know each other. He is as fit as a puppy and he loves his new home. I treated his paw to the best of my ability, but I'm afraid he will always possess a slight limp."

I breathe in deeply and swallow.

Raphaël waits a second before he continues. "Give it a few more days for him to get settled before you come to visit. I want him to embrace his new home. My husband has taken to calling him Tyke. I have attached a photo of him in front of our house with my husband. Kind regards, Mrs. Applegarth."

He hands me a picture of Monster. The big ball of fur smiles at the camera. A strange man is kneeling next to him. The man has his arm slung over Monster's shoulders. He is smiling too. *So, this is your home now.*

My eyes fill with tears. On the one hand, Monster seems to be getting on so well in his new home. On the other hand, it hurts that my friend has forgotten me so easily. Raphaël puts the letter beside me and hugs me awkwardly. I hold on to him tightly. He rubs my back. As we pull back, there is something in his eyes I have never seen there before. There is a light tension in the room.

"Your turn." He hands me his letter from his mother. I carefully open the white envelope and take out the letter. It is about three times as long as Mrs. Applegarths.

"My sweetest Raphaël," I read. "That's you."

He smiles at me.

"I hope this letter finds you in good health and high spirits. It's like months have passed since I last saw you, and my heart aches for your presence. Days without you have been challenging. I am doing my best to manage the bar and keep things running smoothly in your absence.

I must admit, the bar is empty without you. The customers often ask about you, and I see the longing in their eyes as they reminisce about the times you spent behind the counter, serving drinks, and sharing stories.

Running the bar alone has its share of difficulties, but I draw strength from the memories we shared and the unwavering support of our community. They have rallied behind me, offering help and encouragement during this challenging time. Bonds we have built over the years are a testament to the sense of family that exists within our establishment.

My dear son, I want you to know I am immensely proud of you for answering the call of duty and serving our nation. Your bravery and selflessness inspire me each day.

Please take care of yourself, both physically and emotionally. Your well-being is paramount to me, and I long for the day when you return home safely. Remember to lean on your comrades, and say hi to Elara and Thalassa for me. They, too, carry the weight of duty and understand the challenges you face.

In the meantime, I will continue to hold down the fort here at the bar, eagerly awaiting the day when I can see your face, embrace you tightly, and hear your stories firsthand. You are always in my thoughts and prayers, and I eagerly await news of your well-being and the progress you are making.

Remember, you are not alone on this journey. We are all here, supporting you from afar, and eagerly counting the days until we can welcome you back with open arms.

With all my love and unwavering support,

Mom."

Raphaël gently wipes tears away from my face, that I didn't know I shed. His eyes are misty, too. *Would Gran have sent me something like this if she was still alive?*

"I'm sorry." I avoid his gaze. The tension has grown between us, and I don't know if I want it to fade.

"Don't be," he says, his voice cracks and I meet his eyes. He moves towards me. His breath is on my skin and I glance at his full lips. His gray eyes pierce into mine and then I close mine. I breathe in the scent of him. It's sweet. It smells like home. His lips brush mine softly. He allows me to back away.

Should I? For a moment, I catch my breath and sit back. He opens his eyes again. *I should.* I move towards him and this time it's not soft. It's hungry. His full lips kiss mine and his hands hold my face. I climb onto his lap and keep kissing him. He pushes his tongue gently into my mouth. It's so good I let out a moan. Deep inside me, an itch grows. His hands travel down and he opens my uniform. With my hands, I undo his buttons. Not willing for the kiss to break, I do it blindly. I have to let go as he removes my uniform to reveal a skin-tight shirt underneath. We are both breathing heavily. His eyes drink me in and all I want to do is surrender. His nails scratch my back just hard enough and something underneath me grows. It makes me halt. "Have you... before?" I can't say the words. I swallow hard. *Will this be it for me?*

He chuckles. "Yeah, of course. Wait- you haven't?"

I breathe in. "No, I- I wanted to wait until marriage."

"Do you still want to wait until marriage?" He removes his hands from my back and my skin screams for him to put them back on me. His gray eyes gaze into mine. *He tastes like home.*

"No." I kiss him fiercely and his hands come back to me. It's like my skin has been starving for his touch without me ever realizing it. I pull off his uniform and he strips his shirt off himself. My fingers trace over his abs and the beautiful pecs he has developed. With one smooth movement, he moves me to lie on the mattress. His experience is evident. I tear off my shirt. Raphaël places his hands on my brassier and softly squeezes. Another moan escapes me and my hips move on their own. He sits up and looks down at me with hungry eyes. I get up to find his mouth again and his fingers undo the last piece of clothing I have there. He throws the brassier across the room and his hands cup my breasts. Now he groans, and he shifts so he can kiss in between them. When his tongue finds my nipple, I push my hips up towards him. He takes this as a sign and he undoes my pants. The itch between my legs is the only thing I can think of. He takes off my pants and sees my underwear.

"Is this the famous pair?" He asks, and I giggle. He gets off the bed and gently pushes me to a seated position, and I'm confused. *Shouldn't we be lying down for this?*

"Don't worry, you'll like it, I promise," he says with a devious smile.

He peels my underwear from my hips and down my legs. My mouth's dry. I have never been so exposed. My heart beets in my throat. He puts his hands on my knees and slowly pushes them apart. My first instinct is to hide it and I tense up. *Am I really ready for this?*

"Too fast? Ok, I'll take it slow. Sit back and relax." He kisses my feet and an electric current races between my legs. My skin has been deprived of human touch for so long that I feel like I'm already about to explode. I take a deep breath to steady my nerves. He strokes my calves and kisses the inside of my knees. Again, I moan. My hands grab the bed sheets as I try to control myself. He goes up and up. My heart beats fast in my chest and my eyes open wide. *This is fantastic!*

He kisses my groin and goes up to my navel. My hands find his long hair and tug on it softly. My mind screams to not let a man down there, my body needs him more.

He buries his head in between my legs, and his tongue explores me. I gasp. A thousand butterflies fill my body and my mind. My eyes close in order to only focus on this sensation. It leaves no room for worry or fear. His hands stroke my legs and my belly as he continues. One hand goes down and he enters me. *This is what Darya always talked about.* There is no way to describe it. My legs shake like they have a mind of their own. I want to push him away. *This feels too good.*

His moan only makes my itch worse. My hips buckle and if I was standing, I would have fallen to my knees. My brain is filled with this tingling. It's like waves are crashing down on me. The next is even stronger than the first. Suddenly he stops.

"El, you need to be quiet. They're gonna hear you," he says with a grin. I cover my mouth with my hand in shock. The butterflies calm down instantly. Raphaël stands up and slowly gets out of his pants. My heart thumps in my chest. There is something in his boxers that wants to get out. He nonchalantly takes them off. This is the first time I have ever seen a naked man. And I can't stop looking at it. *Is that going to go... there?*

"I'll be slow. Tell me if it hurts." He walks towards me and kisses me, and this time he lays me on my back. He leans on his arms, and something presses downstairs. His lips kiss mine, soft this time. Expectantly. He looks at me intently as he very softly pushes in. I gasp.

"Does it hurt?" I shake my head and put my hands on his hips. It hurts a little, but my need for him is greater. My muscles relax. I put my hand on my belly as if I could feel him there. Moving. He slowly grinds his hips and I groan again. He covers my mouth with his hand. "Shhhh," and he smiles at me. He picks up the pace and I wrap my legs around him. My hands grab his hair as if it's the last rudder at sea. I want him deeper still. The metal bed squeaks. I don't care. Raphaël kisses me and grunts into my mouth. Butterflies fly through my mind and make it impossible to think. He pushes and grinds and does it fast. We both pant. His weight on me makes me feel safe. Butterflies take over my mind. Sweat forms on his forehead and an intense expression comes over his face. He goes faster and faster and I cover my mouth to not groan too loud. It's like I'm on the edge of a cliff and if I relax, I'm going to fall. In one second, grows, and he slams into me. His face contorts in an expression of pure ecstasy. He groans deep and I bury my nails in his back. He slows down until he stops and lets out a shuddering breath. He strokes a hair out of my face. "Are-, are you ok?"

All I can manage is a nod as I breathe in. He lets his weight lean on me and I hug him tightly.

"How do you feel?"

I ponder it for a moment. All the stories I heard from Darya. Warnings I always got from Gran to be decent. It somehow feels bigger, better, and insignificant, all at the same time. I don't feel like a different person. At the same time, I'll never be the same. My whole body glows as if the butterflies have landed and are resting.

"Strange... It felt like I was standing at the edge of a cliff and I wanted to fall off. Is this what it's always like?"

He closes his eyes. "Next time, we'll make you jump off that cliff. It changes from time to time and from person to person. The first time is always the most intense, though." *Person to...*

"How many girls have you done this with?"

He grins and kisses my forehead. "A gentleman doesn't tell."

"Thalassa?"

He laughs with that melodious voice of his. "Are you serious? Elara… Thalassa is gay. She would rather do you than do me." He keeps on laughing as he traces his finger over my belly. I'm not sure what Gran would have thought of that. Raphaël lets out a big yawn. It takes me a while to wrap my head around it. When I am ready to ask another question, he has fallen asleep.

The angry voice of Lance Corporal Little calls for an inspection. Our room door is still closed. It won't take long before she barges in. It's forbidden to have men sleep in our dorm, for obvious reasons, and there happens to be one in my bed. My eyes grow wide as I fly out of bed. *Oh no!*

Raphaël lets out a yawn and stretches as he wakes up. "Good morning."

"What!? Raphaël! We are in trouble!" I hiss at him. In the bed above me, Thalassa sits up. "Good morning love birdies. Had fun last night?" She winks at me, and I don't understand how they're so calm. "Elara, relax! Of course, you will get in trouble, but we can't do anything about it now, anyway."

"You-, you could hide under the bed!"

"And be reported missing? Even worse. Calm down! We'll receive a scolding, say we're sorry, and -"

I can already see Captain Hawkeye's amused smile and I groan. Raphaël steps out of bed and he's not wearing anything.

"Damn, those are some fine buns!" Thalassa cat calls before she gets out of bed herself. I shoot her a look.

She shrugs. "What?"

Before all three of us are dressed, the door opens. I hide behind

Raphaël, fooling no one.

Little blinks twice before her face has all but turned purple. "What is this? *Unacceptable*! This is an outrage of the highest degree. I *demand* an explanation!"

My face is red and I dread what comes next. Raphaël finishes buttoning up his uniform and walks out for everyone to see. My heart pounds in my chest. Thalassa exits the room next, her head held high.

I can't believe within a month, I'm already the harlot of the base. Lance Corporal Little stares at me as if she knows I'm the guilty one. My red face probably gives me away. Raphaël stands next to the door, looking pretty proud of himself. I wish there was at least some form of shame in him. *Is this all a joke?*

"Who dares to claim responsibility for this individual's actions?" Lance Corporal Little's voice is cold as ice and I salute her. "It was me, Lance Corporal Little. But it's not-"

She stalks into our room. "Not what I think it is? You can tell Captain Hawkeye what you think this looks like. Private Sosa, report to your superior immediately. Private Waywater, your bunk better be impeccable."

Raphaël has been so nice to make the bed and everything is tidy. *At least he hasn't left me hanging. I think...*

"Private Waywater." Lance Corporal's voice comes from our room. "Report yourself to the Disciplinary Committee!"

* * *

I am back in front of the door, I dread more than any other in this building. The white walls have become too familiar for my liking and the wooden door already promises trouble. This time, there are four of us instead of two. Raphaël's superior has joined us and stands to attention outside the door. Raphaël looks quite presentable, not like he is wearing yesterday's uniform at all. Lance Corporal Little stares at me like she is about to punch me in the face. I dread what is waiting for me in this room. Raphaël will go first and tell his side of the story and after that, it will be me. My heart thumps in my chest and my mouth is dry. It's hard to not think about what Hawkeye must think of me now.

The same blond Dog ushers Raphaël into the room. Her blonde bun is immaculate and her golden necklace still hangs around her neck. Raphaël winks at me as he walks into the room. I glance at Little and hope she hasn't seen, but she is too busy staring daggers at me to notice.

The door closes with a soft click and I hear voices inside the room. I can hear Raphaël's voice as he calls out his name and rank.

Will he rat me out in front of Hawkeye?

I try to make out what they are saying, but I can't make out the words. Lance Corporal Little stalks the hall, up and down like a nervous shark. My eyes follow her walk left and right, and I find it is quite soothing for my nerves.

All too soon and Raphaël comes out again. He looks a little uncertain about himself this time around. He is immediately escorted off by his superior and he doesn't catch my eye.

It's my turn. I halt when I see it's Winchester who is here to collect me. I take a deep breath and follow him inside the all too familiar room. Behind the desk are the Mountain, him, and Captain Hawkeye. I salute them for good measure. My heart races in my throat.

Winchester starts by noting down who is present for this hearing. I meet Hawkeye's gaze, his Onyx Eyes search me, guarded. There is no emotion behind his eyes this time. I state my name and my rank. My scalp begins to tingle. My eyes lock on Winchester. I'm not alone in my mind and I hate him for it.

"Private Waywater. You have been accused of disrespectful behavior. Lance Corporal Little has reported you were found in bed with Private Sosa. Do you have anything to say in your defense?" I try to reach him, try to find the warmth that has once been there for me.

"With all due respect. Lance Corporal Little has not found me in bed with Private Sosa." This, of course, is technically true. My head grows warmer and my voice trembles. "Private Sosa fell asleep in my room after we were up late... playing cards." *Have I always been such a bad liar?*

Hawkeye frowns at me and says something for the first time. "Private Waywater. It is in violation of our code to have people from the other sex in our rooms. We condone it during the day. At night, this is a severe breach of our code."

I swallow and cast my eyes down.

"Luckily, Raphaël's story is the same as yours. It doesn't mean you will not be punished. Please leave the room while we deliberate."

I am left outside the room. When the door opens, I turn around. Both Lieutenants walk out.

"The Captain will see you now," the Mountain says as they walk away. My eyes shoot toward Little. For the first time since I met her, she seems unsure about the protocol. I walk through the door and close it in front of Little's nose. I stride to the middle of the room and salute Hawkeye, who sits behind his desk.

He frowns at me and I stare back at him. It's a battle of wills.

"Why did you do it?" he asks, and I'm caught off guard.

"Wh-why did I do what?"

"This is the third time you have gotten an infraction on your record. Why?" He stands up and puts his hands flat on the desk. His eyes shoot fire.

He sees me wrestle with words. "Speak plainly, Private."

I shake my head. I cannot be held responsible for what will come out of my mouth. He walks around his desk and up to me. He is at least half a head taller, and it forces me to tilt my head up. His eyes soften. "Elara, talk to me."

The sound of my name on his lips brings tears to my eyes. It reminds me of simpler times, but I can't get close to him again. "I-, I don't know Captain."

"Now, I think that is a lie. I will ask you one more time. Why do you insist on being trouble?"

Because I have a problem with authority. Because I miss home. Because all I want to do is get out. Because I want to bring the Military down to its knees. I just stare at the ground and shake my head. He sighs and walks back to his chair.

"If you were convicted for this, we would need to have you court-martialed. What will I do with you now…" *Please kick me out of the military.*

"One more wrong move. ONE. And I will have no choice but to discipline you. Dismissed!"

Back in my room, I close the door carefully. On my hands and knees, I search for my duffle bag and my few personal possessions. My eye falls on an unread letter that has fallen behind the bed. Craving a familiar note, I reach out for the envelope and read it.

The First One's blade shines as it catches the light of the light bulb and I lie down on the bed. Raphaël's scent is still on my pillow. I close my eyes as I twirl the blade around. Darya's letter was confronting, but wonderful- life has gone on for her as if nothing has changed. Alphonse finally asked for her hand and she's asked me to come back for the wedding. Her enthusiasm exploded from the page. It hurts me that I'm not there to take her out to celebrate- even if it's Alphonse. She tells me she's 'taking care of things' and I wonder if that's only the wedding or if she would be able to take me into hiding.

The ornamental blade is dull, and if I believe Captain Hawkeye on his word, it's nothing more than a piece of metal. I remember the expression on Darya's face when we found it. She was elated, as if there was nothing better in the world. The gems shine in the sunlight that enters my room. Their colors sparkle on the walls. Maybe it's because it's a piece of home. Memories of Darya and I finding it on one of our adventures attached to it. The blade must have traveled far before it landed on the shores of Eden. In my mind, I conjure up the sound of waves and seagulls. One of the gems catches the light and the white stone bursts with the colors of the rainbow, the colors of a prism. *Of colors of a prism!* Excitedly, I examine the white stone. *Is it a Diamond? Is it an Opal?*

Thalassa and Raphaël accompany me to class. We navigate the maze-like sterile halls until we arrive a few minutes late to class. The classroom greets us with disciplined pupils standing next to their desks, their backs stiff at attention and they stare at the teacher with their arms behind their backs.

The lesson is not given by Mrs. Applegarth but by a stern-looking man with glasses perched on his nose as if ready to take flight. He writes 'Corporal Poole' on the board as he introduces himself as our new Aquakinesis teacher. At first glance, I thought Poole was bald because his hair is cut so short, but his eyebrows make up for the lack of hair and fill his forehead like furry caterpillars. Corporal Poole pushes his glasses back up his nose.

"You three are six minutes late. It means the entire class will do 18 burpees as a punishment. Go!"

The man next to me shoots me an angry glance and I turn red. We are the last three to finish the burpees, and I'm panting when I let myself fall into my chair. I take a second to register everybody is standing next to their desk again and I jump up. I refuse to let the entire class be punished for a mistake of mine. Again.

We sit down only when Corporal Poole tells us to, and he starts his lesson. The lesson is a quick recap of things Mrs. Applegarth has taught us before and I am glad to learn we are not far behind. I can't help but be distracted. Counting the absurd number of times Corporal Poole pushes up his glasses in just a few hours. It seems never-ending, losing count around 164 times.

"Today, our focus is on theory," Mr. Poole announces and I deflate in disappointment.

***

There is an extensive outside gym behind the base, a track the size of Main Road is laid out in front of us. On either side are contraptions to help us get stronger. Their cold metal reflects in the sunlight. Behind it all is a high fence made of solid metal, with barbed wire all over the top. Above it, treetops reach for the sky, a beacon of hope behind all this metal. There is a door at the end, barely visible, locked, most likely. Sergeant Aric stands at attention. I would have loved to forget her after what she has put us through. Her black bushy hair acts like a twisted halo around her head. The three of us are nowhere near the level of the other recruits, but I'm glad we don't start from the beginning.

After class, I return to my desk in front of Officer Klippa's office. He walks out just as I sit down. "Could I also get a book from the library to read? I would like to read up on the use of Crystals."

"I have a book about Crystals in my office, you can have it. Do you need it for class?" Officer Klippa asks and I confirm.

The inside of his office smells of incense, the spine has been repeatedly bent, and there are countless of earmarked pages in it. My finger scans through the table of contents. Nothing jumps out at me. I feel like a detective as I flick through all the pages Winchester has earmarked. The pages are thin and fragile, and I have to be careful not to rip them.

The first one is a Jasper.

Chapter XXI: The Jasper Quartz - A Stone of Mental Protection and Empowerment

Power: 7/10

Stability: 8/10

Durability: 6/10

Cautionary note: Handle the Jasper Quartz with utmost reverence and responsibility, as its rareness and potency hold great power. The purer the Jasper Quartz is, the higher the durability.

The Jasper Quartz, a smooth crystal of great enchantment, is renowned as the "Supreme Nurturer". It possesses extraordinary qualities that safeguard against negative energies and absorb their harmful vibrations.

This crystal promotes courage, quick thinking, and confidence, empowering its bearer in the face of challenges.

The Jasper Quartz has the remarkable ability to remove neurotoxins from the mind, enhancing mental clarity.

Its traits make it particularly valuable for tackling important issues and tasks that require fortitude and clarity of thought.

What do you need with a Jasper Quartz? My fingers leaf to the next marked page.

Chapter IX: The Ruby - A Stone of Vitality, Passion, and Enlightenment

Power: 8/10

Stability: 4/10

Durability: 7/10

Cautionary note: The Ruby's allure and potency demand careful handling, as its intense nature requires balance and respect. It is a gemstone of profound significance, holding the potential for both great enlightenment and passionate intensity.

The Ruby, a captivating and vivid red stone, is renowned for the remarkable properties and simple use. This striking gemstone possesses the power to restore vitality and replenish energy levels, invigorating the spirit and infusing its bearer with renewed life force. Ruby is known to kindle the fires of passion and desire, promoting heightened sensuality and a deeper connection to ones sexuality.

In the realm of intellect, the Ruby serves as a supportive companion, enhancing mental capabilities and fostering a thirst for knowledge and wisdom. This radiant stone also catalyzes self-awareness, guiding its bearer to a profound understanding of their true self and aiding in the recognition of truth in all aspects of life. *Problems in the bedroom?*

I glance over at the door. The last two pages that are earmarked are a Tiger's eye (Strengthens your willpower and confidence and supports your physical vitality & wellness) and Tourmaline (green) a stone that also boosts physical vitality. Leaf through the book, I can't seem to find what I'm searching for. I go back to the index. There it is:

Chapter II: The Aurora Quartz - A Stone of Mental Fortitude and Psychic Shielding. Page 35.

However, someone tore out page 35. However, I now know what I need to keep my thoughts private and start actively searching for the resistance. *How do I get my hands on it?*

Chapter 26

Sergeant Aric waits for the class next to a pile of bags. I groan when I realize what that means.

"Privates, I assume you had a nutritious lunch because you are going to need the fuel. We are going for a run. Get your backpacks!"

We move towards the backpacks and sling them over our shoulders. My eyes focus on the door at the end of the field.

In a straight line, we march towards the back door of the base. I can't believe my luck, and a smile appears on my face. Sergeant Aric opens it with a key around her neck and we walk through it. The heavy metal door is thicker than the length of my hand, and S. Aric uses three separate keys to open it. All keys are attached to the same piece of rope that she hangs around her neck. My mind works out potential ruses I could use to get those keys from her, the one just as unlikely to be successful as the next.

Behind the door, bushes and shrubs cover the ground. This feels more like home than anything I have seen in the past few weeks. The path in front of us isn't paved, and I smile. My shoulders relax for the first time since Eden. I inhale the sweet scent of nature and tears well up in my eyes. *I want to go home.*

The Sergeant tells us to start and we speed up to a trot. She runs along with us. Boots hit the ground in a strict rhythm. She is wearing a tiny backpack and I wonder what is in it. We run until the base is out of sight and sweat is forming on my forehead. Raphaël's moving feet keep me in pace and I stare at them as if I'm hypnotized as sweat forms on my forehead. I pretend I am alone, running over the hills with Monster by my side.

Soon, the chafing of the straps on my shoulders forces me back to the here and now. I shake my head and focus on my breathing. Three steps, I breathe in, and three steps, I breathe out.

A heavy thump behind me doesn't register immediately and only when a high-pitched wail pierces through the air do I turn around. Thalassa lies on the ground, holding her right leg. Her face is pale and etched with pain.

"Privates! Halt!" Sergeant Aric orders and rushes to Thalassa, who has begun to sob. I take a step forward to help her, but the Sergeant orders me to stay put. Thalassa's face is white as a sheet and she groans. For a second I would have sworn she was wearing a violet dress and my mouth goes dry.

"That looks like a luxated patella," the Sergeant says to no one in particular. My breath speeds up squeamish to the pain that Thalassa is enduring.

"I can heal her," Raphaël says from behind me.

The Sergeant lifts her eyebrows. "You can relocate her kneecap with your Aquakinesis, Private?"

Raphaël shakes his head and averts his eyes. Relocating limbs is not something we are taught. I don't even know if we could without causing serious damage to the surrounding nerves.

"If you want to help, run back and get a stretcher. Leave your backpack here." Raphaël lets his bag fall and runs for the base. "Stop! Private Sosa! You need the keys." He jogs back. "You will give these back as soon as possible."

Then he runs, his heavy footfalls fade away, and I watch his back disappear into the forest before my eyes turn on Thalassa. Her kneecap sticks out sharply at an odd angle and my eyes go wide. A fly buzzes past and lands on her other leg. It sucks up the sweat there. *Don't freak out.* I lick my dry lips.

"Private Brooks, Private Walker, hold her down." The two women move forward and press on Thalassa's shoulders. "Private Waywater, have you relocated a joint before?" I stare at her blankly and I feel a slight nausea come up. Brooks makes soothing sounds to Thalassa, who is hyperventilating.

"Private Waywater, come here."

In reflex, I take a step back.

"Private, you are going to be a field nurse and you need to be able to react accordingly!" Her loud voice drags me back and sets me to work. "Now sit here opposite me." I sit down opposite her, leaning on my knees. "I am going to extend the knee. When I say go, you will guide the patella right back to where it belongs. Ready?"

No!? I place my hand on Thalassa's kneecap and she whimpers. Reflexively, I withdraw my hand before I put it on her knee again. Her skin feels hot and my fingertips flutter because of the swelling that has set in. I take a deep breath to steady myself. The Sergeant looks me dead in the eyes. "Here we go." She extends the knee slowly and Thalassa screams in agony. "Now!" I softly tug on the kneecap, but it won't budge. Saliva fills my mouth like I'm going to be sick as I hear Thalassa's screams. The sergeant flexes the knee back in its starting position. Thalassa cries in pain.

"Again!"

This time I tug harder and the kneecap shoots back in its place. The movement of the kneecap makes another wave of nausea hit me. Thalassa pants loudly, and after a second, I realize I am, too. Tears stream down the side of her face. "I'm so sorry, Thalassa," I say and I hold her hand. It's moist and cold, but she holds on tightly. With careful movements I steer the water that has collected in her knee back towards her thigh.

Raphaël comes running back with the stretcher and we carefully lift her onto it. As soon as her knee moves, Thalassa groans loudly.

The moment we get back, Thalassa is brought to the Base's sickbay. Raphaël joins me as I go to my room. We sit there for a bit as tension builds, which wasn't there before. It makes me uneasy. He strokes my arm and I know if I meet his eyes, we'll do everything again. Even if it's just to take our minds off things. He smells like cedar wood and home. "Did you t-take your tea?"

"I don't want any, thanks," I say absentmindedly.

"No, I mean, did you take it?"

I look at him with a blank stare. *What's all this about tea?*

"You didn't take anything?"

"Raphaël, I don't know what you're talking about."

"Did you do anything to m-make sure we don't have living, breathing p-proof of our night?"

Good grief. "No…" The tension in the room turns into a different type, the panic type. "I never thought about it. What kind of tea do I need?"

He smiles at me. "I'll get you some tonight. D-Don't worry about it."

In the evening, I lie on my bed and stare at the bottom of Thalassa's bed. It's just a few minutes till 'lights out'. An empty mug of tea stands on the floor next to my bed. The acrid taste still fills my mouth, but I welcome it. *I hope this is foolproof.*

In the hall, I hear a pair of heavy boots echo through the desolate hall Thalassa appears in the door frame.

"Thalassa! How are you?" I say joyfully.

Thalassa walks in and her face is all smiles. "Good! Seetha, the first-aid lady, fixed me up in no time. We got chatting and… lost track of time, honestly."

"I'm glad you're back. I was worried about it taking so long." I sit up from my bed. "Did your knee heal completely?"

Thalassa shakes her frizzy hair. "Not completely. It's still tender when I make a wrong move."

A gasp from the bed below wakes me up.

"You alright?"

"Fuck no! Could you get me some water?" Thalassa moans and I peek my head just over the edge and see that Thalassa has found her bag and takes a white pill from it.

I climb out of bed, and I am aware every nudge of the bed hurts her knee. An empty glass stands on the sink and I fill it with water. Thalassa pushes herself to a seated position and takes the glass. There is a little sunlight creeping through our window. It will be no use going back to sleep now, so I get dressed.

"Do you think you will come to class today?" I ask Thalassa, and she nods.

We leave early, because Thalassa can only move gingerly and navigate the blank halls together. This time we find the room easily. Poole gives us a lecture about the different kinds of wounds we can expect on the field paired with graphic pictures that still make me uncomfortable. Funnily enough, he also covers dislocations in this lesson.

After lunch, I guide Thalassa to our room. The painkillers are wearing out and she turns pale. She lies down, and I put my pillow under her knee to make her a bit more comfortable. Her knee has become swollen and I grimace at the purple bruise on it. To be sure we're not caught, I close the door and with soft movements I take away the worst of her pain. The purple bruise fades to a green, yellowish stain and the knee takes on its normal form again.

"Just don't tell anyone," I say. Thalassa motions that she locks her lips and throws the imaginary key in the rubbish bin. "Do you want me to stay?" Thalassa shakes her head. I fill a glass of water for her as I leave her alone and go to the shooting range.

When it's time for dinner, I wander back to my room and find Thalassa still on the bed, reading my book. My heart stops. *My book.* The letter from my father lies on the mattress next to Thalassa's pillow. "Did- did you read that?" My mouth goes dry. A fly ticks against the window, trying to find a way out.

Thalassa tries to sit up. "El-"

"Did you read it!?" I snatch the letters from the mattress. It has been folded open.

"Listen El, I'm sorry-"

"You can't go around reading people's letters!" My heart pounds in my chest. "You can't do-" I gulp for air but it's like someone has taken all the oxygen out of the room. *They'll hang me for having such a connection to the resistance.*

The shut window is not allowing any fresh air to enter. The fly ticks against the window in a feeble attempt to find a way out.

"El, relax, I won't-"

My chest squeezes and I gasp like a fish on dry land. I stumble to the window, desperate for fresh air. *I can't breathe.*

"You-" but I can't talk anymore. My breathing has become erratic. *I'm having a heart attack.* I sink to the floor, gasping for breath. The pain in my chest increases. Thalassa shouts something, but her voice is muted. My heartbeat thumps viciously in my ears. It's like my heart is mocking me. With every heartbeat, I hear *d-die, d-die, d-die.*

Thalassa flings her legs over the bed and moves towards me. "Elara! Snap out of it!" She sits down next to me. Her cold hands grab my face and I struggle to get away from her. "Elara, cut it out!"

I gasp for air. My eyes don't focus and all I hear is the *d-die, d-die, d-die.*

"I'm sorry for this." She slaps me in the face. Hard. The shock is so intense that it reminds me of suddenly been plunged into ice. My fingers caress the place where her hand print burns.

"You, you hit me!" I say, more surprised than angry.

Thalassa shrugs. "You needed to be hit."

"Thank you?"

"I won't pry, but you need to be able to manage them without someone slapping you in the face," she says.

My eyes follow a fly that walks across the window and I rub my cheek. "How did you know that would work?"

"The body responds to immediate danger... and I took a lucky guess." She sits against the wall next to me. "I'm sorry I read your letter, but trust me, I won't tell anyone." She makes a circle around her heart. It's a sweet gesture, but worthless. I can't confide in her without risking potential discipline.

I gaze into her eyes and take a leap of faith. "I know one way you can make it up to me. You need to help me find an Aurora Quartz."

Thalassa regards me for a second. Her green eyes and freckles stand out on her pale skin. "I'll do that, but you need to explain this to me one day, El."

"You're right. This is... I know.. But Winchester can- just trust me. Winchester has some bad mojo that prevents me from telling you anything."

Thalassa withdraws from me.

Telling her about Winchester was a dangerous move. "It's not that he's a bad person, but trust me when I say there are more than us elementalists out there. I need this stone in order to tell you anything else. Because it will protect me."

"Does anyone else know?" Her voice trails off.

"I haven't told a soul. Gran... It might give us a way to get out!" I flash her a broad smile, and the air hangs still as Thalassa takes a moment to absorb the revelation. The fly ticks against the window, trying to find a weak spot.

"Get us- Elara, don't you get it. I don't want to get out."

My mouth hangs open as I look at her. Of all the things I expected, this wasn't one of them.

"I wanted to come here, Elara. It's been a difficult journey, but the military will give me freedom from all the things I struggled with back home. There is no *need* anymore to marry a man to keep my parents happy. I can follow my own heart and be free. You have been so self-involved you didn't even see I'm happy here."

The room grows cold as I let this sink in. "You... You wanted to be in the army?"

"There are not a lot of options for me, Elara. This way, I have my education paid for, my future secured, and I can be myself. It's really not that bad. I wish you could see that."

"But you have to do whatever your commanders tell you to..."

"Has Second Lieutenant Winchester or Captain Hawkeye done anything, *anything* other than take good care of us?"

"Well- no, for now. But they have not sent us to war yet. Within the year, they will send us to the front lines. And what if the military decides you can be persecuted for being an elementalist again? Or believing a different thing? Or being gay? They will turn on us, Thalassa!"

"No. No, I refuse to believe that. I will keep your secret, Elara, but don't expect me to go out of my way to get you out of here."

After she leaves, I destroy the letter from my father.

* * *

Lunch is in the canteen and I try to rub the embarrassment off my face. The tiled walls amplify the sounds of utensils scratching on plates and human interaction. Despite feeling exhausted, my mind remains fixated on getting out of here.

"What d-did you ask Poole?" Raphaël asks with his mouth full of something that used to resemble a cheese sandwich. *Dammit, nothing goes by him.*

"I wanted to get his permission to go to a Quartz shop," I answer truthfully and take a bite of my sandwich. Stale bread with vegetables and some sauce that is called humus, despite the disappointing bread, it's quite tasty.

"You can get new Quartz at the First Aid," Thalassa offers unhelpfully, her apple pie cheeks smile at me. *She's a better friend than I deserve.*

"Yeah, he told me. I'm just looking for something specific," I say, covering my mouth with my hand to keep my lunch from spraying everywhere.

"There is a Quartz store in the city. Let's go after training." Thalassa says, and I look up in surprise.

"I can't." *Not without explicit approval or an escort.* My high fades as I look at the officer's table. Winchester is noticeably absent, but Hawkeye is munching away on his pie while talking to the Mountain.

"Oh, right. Raphaël, will you join me?"

The rest of our team; Sheena, Eliyah and Leo sit down with us and the conversation drifts to the new version of the State newspaper. Apparently, there will be a big event soon, but I feel disconnected from their conversation. Raphaël wants to go out exploring after training, and Thalassa talks excitedly about wanting to visit some boutiques.

"I've been entrusted with the task of getting monthly flowers for Second Lieutenant Winchester," Sheena says, as if that's something to be proud of. My emotions go from dark to light in a fraction of a second, and I could sing for joy.

"He gets them every month for his wife. Isn't that adorable?" She asks Raphaël.

I excuse myself to dive into my advanced herbology book. Because I should not put all my eggs in one basket. I search for anything brain-related and quickly, I am sifting through remedies for headaches and migraines. None of the herbs speak of shielding the mind.

Before lights out, Thalassa comes in as I lie on my bed, rereading the advanced herbology book for anything I might have missed. A jolt of excitement goes through me, and I raise my head expectantly. She shakes her head. It makes her frizzy hair dance around her face.

"I'm sorry El, the store didn't carry Aurora Quartz."

I let out a disappointed sigh. "Of course..."

"I will not look for it again, now- before you say anything. You should have seen the faces of the salesmen. It was like I asked for their firstborn. I think the stuff you're looking for is very illegal." Thalassa looks hurt.

I've betrayed her trust yet again. "I didn't know. Sorry." A wave of guilt comes over me, but push it aside. *I didn't know, but I could have guessed.*

* * *

Dies Veneris

Going to the hospital turns into one of my favorite outings. My abilities feel like a part of me now, more than ever before.

Then we arrive at a man with a considerable piece of wood sticking out of his shoulder. It moves quickly up and down as the man breathes. The piece of wood looks like it's lodged between his clavicle and shoulder blade. A sheen of water sits on the man's face and his skin is as pale as a sheet. Red blood trickles out of the wound in a steady stream. It has collected under him in a puddle. Corporal Poole is calm and collected. The opposite of how I feel inside.

"Private Waywater, what do you think we should do first?"

"Hi, Sir. I am Elara. Err... Sir?" The man doesn't acknowledge my presence and I glance at Corporal Poole, who pushes his glasses up with his finger. "Class, please note Private Waywater has tried to pleasantly converse with someone in Class Four shock. Private Waywater, try again. What do we do first?"

I contemplate the poor man. *Painkillers? Morphine? A tourniquet?* "A tourniquet?" I opt.

"Wrong."

I examine the man as the blood continues to trickle down. His eyes are dull. "We... We are supposed to put his legs higher than his waist... But-, but he will bleed out faster because of, of gravity. We need to stop the bleeding, Sir."

"Very good. Now, how will we do that?"

I stare at the trickling wound. *Will the man bleed out on my watch?* "Heal the wound around the wood?"

"No, we will yank out the wood and then close the wound. I need two Privates to assist. One will pull out the wood while the other ensures the man doesn't topple over."

My mouth fills with water. *I'm not ready for this.* Private Tanner and Private Iris position themselves next to me. Iris will hold the man, as Tanner will try to pull the wood out of him. People seated around the unfortunate soul have begun to retreat from our direct area. I make a water glove. My whole body tells me to run, but I can't.

"On my mark. NOW!" Tanner pulls the wood. Iris pulls the man. With a sickening sucking sound, the wood lets go bit by bit. Blood flows faster. Instead of a trickle, there's a steady flow. Blood pulses out too fast. The wood ends at a sharp point, but with the plug removed, blood spurts out. Tanner's blue uniform is sprayed in dark spots which stain black on his uniform. Iris yelps as she gets a mouthful. Corporal Poole nudges me forward. I put my hands on the horrific opening. I squeeze my eyes shut. My hands don't tingle this time. They burn. There is too much black behind my eyes. I can't heal the ripped arteries. The blood flow tears through the tender walls I build. Adrenaline races through my body. I clench my hands into fists to control the blood flow. There is a sound in my ears. As if I'm in a storm. Wind beats against my eardrums. With one fist clenched, I control the blood flow. With my other hand, I heal the wound. Arteries first. And the bleeding slows. But his torn muscles cannot recover. Swift movements help me build a thin layer of skin over the wound. The flow of blood stops completely. For the first time since we started, I draw breath.

The man's facial expression has changed. His mouth forms a perfect circle and his eyes are wide open. Iris still holds him upright. A thin, shiny layer of new skin sits over the wound. A considerable crater sits between the clavicle and the scapula. It's red and almost translucent. There is blood everywhere. Tanner's uniform is soaked. Iris looks like she is covered in red paint. The man's eyes turn forward in a glazed stare. Iris lets go off the man. With an anticlimactic thump, he keels over. I grimace as I hear his nose break.

"Nice teamwork, Privates. I think you all learned from this."

On the way back, we are all silent. Soaked and silent. Poole explained that this man was already dead before we started on him. He would have never recovered, 'You can't save everyone'. The tremor in my hands shows I'm not ready to believe him. *I should have done better.*

Chapter 27

Dies Martis

The iron gates loom over me as I walk towards them. They cast a dark shadow on the ground.

If I play my cards right, I can find the Aurora Quartz today and find the resistance.

My hands are clammy as I approach a bored young woman. I salute her and she absentmindedly waves it away. She doesn't seem to care that I'm not in my uniform. Her eyes go over my dress, but her expression doesn't change. *Good.* Despite the nippy weather, I have left the black military coat inside too.

"I'm not your superior. Relax." She asks what my purpose for visiting the city is. For a split second, I wonder if she's on to me. With all the conviction I can muster, I tell her that my name is Sheena Sinclair and that I need to get flowers for Second Lieutenant Winchester. *I'll give Sheena a proper reason to hate me.*

The young girl peers at me over her glasses and says, "So, business," and scribbles something down. She glances at her watch and adds the time. "What time will you be back?"

My heart thumps in my chest, and I look at the other side of the iron gates. They look very far away. "I don't know?"

"I can't write down 'I don't know'. How long will you be gone?" She asks irritably.

"What happens if I come back later?"

"We go looking for you," she says and studies my face and I can't tell if she's serious.

I can't cause more trouble. They won't save me again. "What happens if I come back sooner?"

She raises her eyebrows and sighs, trying to see if I'm messing with her. "You will be allowed to enter, but your leisure time will be cut short."

"Really?"

"Absolutely not. Sheesh. Where on earth did they find the likes of you?" she says and lets out an exasperated sigh. With her right hand, she jabs something down and says, "Just be back before 20:30." She stands up and walks to the gates and opens a small door Mrs. Applegarth left through weeks ago.

The door closes behind me with a metal screech and I hear her locking the door behind me. "Thanks!" I yell, but she has already disappeared inside her booth. I wet my dry lips and scan the square.

Balconies line the square like crown molding, all with the same flower design in the iron fences. Steps lead to every decorated front door. Mosaic red flowers decorate the square floor. I imagine every flower to represent a pool of blood. More than a dozen lampposts fill the square with a bed of white flowers underneath them. Their sweet scent intermingled with the stench of old trauma. My heart races as I walk upon the square and I walk to the place the Leader Suprema would have stood. There is no stage anymore. I am a meter or so lower than she was when she spoke to the crowd, but I see what she would have seen. *Were there people looking from the balcony that day?*

I try to swallow, but my mouth is dry. I make my way forward, my footsteps loud on the Mosaic tiles. *Where I was standing with my father?*

As I pinpoint the place I stand there, first I study the base and the gates, then the balconies and lampposts. I don't remember the lampposts. A couple walks into the square and passes me without a second glance. They are teenagers. They probably don't even know what happened here. Their white clothes flutter in the wind as they walk by.

From here we walked, and I scan the area to get a sense of direction. There is an opening between the houses where the couple walked through, but there are more exits. One in every corner and one along the straight lines of houses. I walk along the houses, all the white curtains are drawn.

The white flower beds are fragrant and the smell prickles in my nose. I make for the first exit and I peer through it. Mosaic turns into the white stone slabs with houses towering on either side of the street. There are four steps into these front doors, but the iron bars are elaborate. Should I follow this road or familiarize myself with all exits before I make a choice? But all the exits are alike. The same tall houses, the same elaborate bars, and the same purple, strong scented flowers. More people are walking around the square by the time I have investigated every one of the exits. Some of them are wearing uniforms. Others wear the same white clothes. Most people ignore me as they pass me by. But a few shoot curious glances. *How will I find the resistance between all these people?*

As if some kind of signal has gone off, the square fills up with people. Amidst the bustling crowd, a mesmerizing dance unfolds, and I marvel at the seamless choreography that prevents the people from bumping into each other. A blur of men and women walk past me by- I'm trapped. My heart rate flies up and my breathing becomes fast and shallow. I need to get out of here and I fly into the closest exit. The street is full of people wearing white or muted colors, and I keep my head down. My eyes search for a place where I can regain my senses.

Not used to this dance, I clumsily bump into people. But I keep walking. To my left, an empty alleyway appears and I hurry into it. My back leans against the solid bricks and I let my legs buckle under me. The ground catches me. *One, two, three, breathe, five, six, seven, breathe.*

After a while, the ringing in my ears fades and my breath slows down. I scan the surrounding environment. On my left and right there are big metal trash cans. Smells of rotten food penetrate my nose. On the opposite wall, there's an enormous poster with the text "March Towards a Brighter Future, Enlist in the Military!" Drawn on the poster is a young boy with a dirty face, his eyes hopeful. Next to it is another one. "From Hardship to Honor!" It reads in big letters. On the bottom in small writing, it says "Enlist in the Military and Build a Life Worth Fighting For!" In the middle, there is a picture of a rising sun. Much like the one represented on the Leader Suprema's flags. Both have been vandalized. On both posters, there is a fat black cross. 'Vanguard Unite!' Is written over them in child-like handwriting. A fist rises in charcoal. I rise and touch the symbol. This is the same drawing that my father's letter had. Charcoal sticks to my fingers. *So this must be the resistance.*

My heart bobs as if caught in a stormy sea. I look up and down the alley as if I expect someone handing out fliers. *Please find me.*

People on the street continue their normal business, meaning nobody pays any mind to me. With newfound confidence, I walk out of the alleyway, but I don't remember if it's left or right to the square.

For a few seconds, I stand there while I watch the people and the houses, fidgeting with the hem of my dress. Too late, I realize they're smudging charcoal on the dress. A scruffy-looking man catches my eye. His clothes are not quite the right shade of white, and his face is hidden behind his upturned collar. I decide to follow him. *He looks like a man trying to hide something. resistance maybe?*

The man walks along the white paved road and takes a left. This road is dirtier, and the pavement is cracked in some places. People seem to be in more of a hurry on this street. They scurry to their destination. One or two questioning looks get shot my way, but I ignore them. The high-collared-man walks purposefully, and leads me into increasingly shabbier streets. Elaborate iron window protectors turn into barred windows. People dress more in gray hues now than white and the man stands out like a sore thumb. He stops at a big house with a pretty girl outside, her red hair flaming in the sun. She greets him amicably. *Is this the headquarters of the resistance? Or is she his wife?*

The pretty lady opens the door for him. It doesn't seem like a residential house. It's bigger than the houses on either side. She considers me for a moment and then nonchalantly lights a cigarette. The sign above the door says 'Madame Antionette's'. *Could this be it? Could the resistance be hidden away in a tea room?*

She watches me with narrowed eyes. "Can Ah help ye?" she asks with an accent I have never heard before.

"I, uh, was wondering if I could come inside?"

"Ach, ye've got a good e'e, we dinnae see mony blues aroond here. And there's nae mony lassies amang them." She looks me up and down while I try to decipher what she said. "Dae ye want tae come in?"

I understand her invitation after she takes my hand and I let myself be led inside. My heart races with glee as she takes me in like a friend. But my glee turns to horror as I understand where I am. Inside there are a lot of men sitting in chairs and women in skimpy clothes, walking around serving drinks. One young woman straddles a man's lap suggestively. My cheeks burn as a few men turn toward me. *I have made a huge mistake.*

"Mind yer manners, dinnae stare!" The girl barks at the men and they go back to their own business.

"I-, I'm s-sorry, I-, I think I'm in the wrong place," I stammer while I step back, stumbling over the door frame. "Are ye gettin' cauld feet? Dinnae fash yersel', we hae richt braw laddies, or lassies if that's whit yer intae." She winks at me. Suddenly, she is not so pretty anymore. Disgust fills me as she laughs, and I wipe my hand, which she was holding, on my dress as if she is covered in soot.

"No, no, I'm sorry." I practically run out the door and back up the street. With red cheeks and a heavy breath. A left turn takes me to a dead end. I double back and take another left. This time there is a street filled with little markets and people selling their wares. The colors of their clothes are darker and I don't stand out much. I catch my breath. *Stupid, stupid, stupid!*

The smell of ripe fruit meets me and near me is a stall with a woman selling them. She catches me staring and I buy an apple from her to avoid any suspicion. She looks slyly at me while she tells me the price. It's twice as much as in Eden, but I'm glad to be doing something normal. When I bite into it, I am surprised at how juicy it is and I thank her. There is a fish stall, but the fish stinks, and I guess it's at least a day old. A fat man haggles over the price.

"Ya are crazy-e if ya think I will pay tha much!" He shouts and waves his hands dramatically.

"Chef?" I ask, relieved to see a friendly face.

He turns around and, surely, it's him. His big purple nose and his immense belly are a welcome sight.

"Elara! What are ya doing here?" he asks.

I tell him I got lost, but leave out my surprise visit to the brothel.

"Ya have no permizzion to be here. It is ze last circle before ze outzide!" He tells the salesman to keep his stinky fish and throws his arm around me. "Letz get ya back to tha base quickly," he mutters while he glances over his shoulder.

We take a few streets I'm certain I didn't take here, but we get back to streets with white roads. With a fat finger, he points in the direction I have to go. "Don't tell people where ya were, ya will get in trouble-" He raises a finger to his lips. "And letz hope no one saw ya."

We get to the square and we take a sharp right into a big shopping street. My eyes shoot left and right. *There must be some place where they sell Aurora Quartz.*

Chef talks about the fish he wants to make tomorrow for the recruits, and I smile at the idea. It fills me with joy that this man can worry about simple things like the quality of fish.

We pass a shop that has 'Boutiques les Fleurs' painted on above the door with golden letters. For the first time, I realize how cold I am. "One more thing. Do you know where I can buy Crystals?"

"Dependz on what ya need?" Chef asks.

"I'm looking for an Aurora Quartz."

Chef's eyes don't betray anything, but I feel he knows what it's for. "No, I don't know where to get tha," he lies. I don't dare press him.

It is a small walk back to the square, but it feels long because of Chef's uncharacteristic silence. When we walk into the square, he tells me he has things to do. We say goodbye. His big figure disappears into a street. With disappointment and a clenched jaw, I peer at the streets leading away from the square. *Just because something is illegal doesn't mean I won't be able to find it... but searching will take too long and I can't have them looking for me.*

In the span of a few weeks, I have to begrudgingly agree with Thalassa that we have grown wiser, and our powers have grown with it. Healing Class has been the number one reason why. With so much on my plate, I keep out of any sort of trouble.

Corporal Poole is bent over his desk reading something. There is a deep frown on his forehead. I stand next to my desk with my arms behind my back. He doesn't appear to notice the class has entered the room and writes something down on a piece of paper.

He looks over the edge of whatever he is reading and snaps, "Privates, yesterday we delved into theory; today, we shall assess your progress in practice. Fall in line and collect your bowls with discipline and order."

The water in the bowl sloshes lightly as I put it down on the table. Sound of scraping chairs fills the room. My fingers are tingling to begin. Row by row, he orders us to show him how far we've come. Raphaël conjures his waterspout, which gets him one raised eyebrow and a nod. Thalassa pours the water over her hand and forms a water glove. This only gets her a blink of Corporal Poole's eyes.

When he starts on my row, a Dog forming a water glove and directly next to me, a boy with blond scruffy hair makes his water slosh in the bowl. This last one only receives a sigh.

Corporal Poole walks to my table. From up close, I see he has brown eyes. Nervously, I put my hand above the bowl and I'm glad when I feel the familiar flutter of its heartbeat. My hand goes up and the water follows it like a rope. The fluttering feeling turns into pins and needles and travels up to my elbow. Surprised by the new feeling, I flick my hand and the water slaps Raphaël on his back before it falls to the floor in a splash.

Corporal Poole points at a mop next to the blackboard. "Private Waywater, get a mop and clean up this mess!"

I swallow, chant 'yes, sir' and hurry to fetch it. The whole class is turned to me and my cheeks burn. Poole orders me to stay after class is dismissed. The class leaves me alone with the stern Dog. As the door closes, he turns away from me and walks to his desk.

"Private Waywater, how long have you been able to do this?" he says, with a low timbre in his voice. I stare at him, afraid of being reported.

"The water whip, Private!"

"I don't know, Sir… I just.. did it."

"You are forbidden from using this movement again." He snaps and pushes his glasses up to the bridge of his nose. He has his lips pursed so tightly together they have gone white.

Please don't report me.

"Let me make one thing crystal clear: water is a healing element, not meant for offensive actions. If I ever catch you attempting something like that again, be prepared to face the consequences. Consider this a stern warning."

I salute him. "Understood sir!"

"Now. Get. Out."

I scurry out, afraid he might start screaming. Apparently, I have done something terrible, but I don't know how I did it.

The air of the canteen is heavy with the smells of fried meat and rice combined with the uncomfortable heat of electricity and it's suffocating. The contrast from how Poole's reaction couldn't have been greater than how Thalassa and Raphaël receive me for lunch. They all but applaud and Raphaël shows me the bruise on his back pride. Eliyah's eyes narrow at the mark and he turns slightly red, but he keeps silent and continues his lunch. *Uh, oh.*

Raphaël doesn't want to hear my apology and we poke fun at the strict Corporal Poole. Leo looks as though he might burst with excitement and stutters nearly as bad as Raphaël does.

"That was amazing!" He exclaims with joy. His cheeks are flushed and for the first time I notice that there is some extra meat on him. He looks more like the soldier he wants to be. I glance around for a second to check if no one has heard him, but the people at the other tables ignore us and the sound of cutlery against porcelain drowns out our conversation. Thalassa is bouncing around on her chair, begging me to show her how I did it.

No one has been this delighted by anything I did since I got the letter that I was accepted in Nursing school and Gran and Darya took me out to dinner (her acceptance letter came later). Raphaël celebrates by getting me a full plate of lunch. I am too polite not to eat it all. They keep on asking me how I did it, but I don't know.

The canteen fills up and Hawkeye and Aric walk among the officers. My skin still tingles as if they're watching me, which in fairness, they probably are. It reminds me I'm one step away from the bullet. My food isn't appetizing anymore and I wish I stayed in bed. The mind reader is not there and I let out a breath I didn't realize I had been holding. *Is Aric the woman you are so worried about? What are you up to?*

Leo repeats himself twice and has to wave his fork in front of my eyes before I notice he's talking to me. "Are you going to go to the opera?" Leo asks me for the third time.

I put a piece of food in my mouth. "The what?"

Leo looks thrilled and uses his fork to conduct an imaginary orchestra. "The Opera where all the military is invited to. Are you going? I thought we could go as a squad!"

"Hmpf, Operas are boring, but it's a good place to network and get in the good graces of the officers. I'm in," Eliyah says.

"I don't know. I have a lot of stuff to do." I say with my eyes on Sheena. She's still very interested in cutting her food. By now a three-year-old could have eaten it.

"Oh, come on! We'll have a blast!" Leo pleads. His enthusiasm is infectious and I promise him I'll come.

Dies Lovis

Winter started today. Snow falls in clumps out of the gray sky.

Today we have a lesson 'in the field'. Two ambulances take a group of maybe 10 elementalists to the local hospital. Of course, I am excited to put our theory to good use, but this is also a perfect opportunity to talk to a lot of people without drawing attention to myself. Raphaël, Thalassa, and I are in one ambulance with two Privates who have introduced themselves as Arroyo and Brennan. Arroyo has olive skin with a black short beard and black hair, while Brennan's skin is almost translucent and he sports a red beard. They've been at the base for a few months more than we have and have gone to the hospital regularly to help.

Private Arroyo tells us this is so much better than practicing on dummies, while Private Brennan stays silent and gazes out of the window. We stop in front of a shabby hospital. The word hospital is stretching it, even by my standards. It's outdated and the paint of the building is cracked and peeling.

"This is the community hospital where the... less fortunate people go. Rich people have their own private hospital. We never go there," Brennan says as he reads my expression.

Corporal Poole leads us to the shabby building. There are two women in gray dresses with their hair covered in something of the same fabric. They welcome us to the hospital, their faces hard and unforgiving. Private Brannon and Private Arroyo give them a little bow before they say goodbye to us and walk into a corridor behind the nurses.

The nurses study the left overs who glance around nervously. The eldest opens her mouth, "This is not a playground. We have a lot of ailing people here who need our help. So make sure you don't waste our time. Alright, follow me."

We follow them into another corridor. Corporal Poole walks behind the crew to make sure none of us fall behind. For the occasion, he wears his specialist's uniform. The same cut as the standard one, but instead of gray seams, they are red, to show his healer status.

A wall of noise reaches us long before we walk into a room filled with people. It feels claustrophobic, and the room is not small by any means, but there are not enough seats or room to accommodate all the people. Children cry, old women groan, mothers fuss and men talk loudly. It smells sour and sweet and it makes my stomach turn.

"This is the waiting room. There are not enough rooms to treat these people in. So you will do your business here. Corporal Poole will help with your triage. Under his supervision, you are permitted to heal wounds, burns, and rashes. Anything major you will send for us immediately. The Corporal knows how it works. You will help us for four hours today. After that, we will discover where your talents lie and where we assign you."

Poole holds a tissue in front of his nose to filter out the air and it fogs up his glasses.

"Alright Privates, listen up. Stay close to me. There will be no healing without my explicit permission. Now, follow." He leads us to a row of chairs. A young man sits there with a cloth over his eye. There is a woman with him, probably his mother. She has her hand on his shoulder. She squints at our little company as we get closer. Poole introduces himself and us as the 'helpers'. We haven't yet earned a proper introduction. The woman nods and tells us her name is Lisa and this young man is Harry. Harry has been in a fight and has gotten the worst of it. I hold my Crystal tightly, prepared to mend his busted eye, but Corporal Poole steps in. He has brought crystal infused water with him and shows us the steps to heal this, but leaves no space for any of us to have a private conversation with the patient. Nevertheless, I am itching to get started.

Next is a man with streaks of gray in his beard. He has put his foot on another chair to keep it elevated. The bandage around his foot has turned red. The man is oddly calm about all this. Poole breathes from behind his white tissue and lets us work on him.

The man says, "I was chopping wood when little Jimmy distracted me. I missed the wood and hit my foot."

Thalassa takes off the blood-stained bandages. The ax has left quite some carnage. Expecting a clear cut, I'm surprised that it looks like the man has struck himself in the foot at least three times. *How can you do this kind of harm to yourself?*

Poole guides Thalassa through the process. "Close your eyes and try to feel the flutter in your fingers. Imagine the color of the wound is black and your hand erases that color with light blue. Stay in one place until all the black has disappeared before you move."

I would swear the water illuminates light blue when it touches the wound. Behind his tissue, Poole gives Thalassa a rare smile while the patient thanks her and leaves without so much as a limp. "Privates. Did we see anything peculiar?"

Uncertainly, I raise my hand.

"Yes! Private, err, Waywater." Poole says and his glasses fog up.

I shift from one foot to another, overthinking my answer before I give it. "I expected there to be one cut, yet it were several, Sir"

Poole nods and the glint on his bald head glides over his head. "Correct. What do you think happened?"

I blink a few times, all the answers in my head sound silly. "He, err... chopped his foot multiple times?" I can't help but phrase this as a question.

"Unlikely, it would be very hard for a man to land an ax on his foot multiple times. Whatever the reason for the cuts. The man lied to us. This is what you all have to learn. People are either dumb or they lie. With the first young man, it wasn't as clear, so I'll forgive you all for missing it. However, this one was staring us right in the face. Why does it matter if they lie?" He looks around the group. Raphaël is the first one to raise his hand this time. "If you don't know what's wrong, you m-might treat them for the wrong thing."

Corporal Poole looks at Raphaël over his glasses. "Correct. Private Sosa, you have an eye for this. Do you know what the first one was lying about?"

Raphaël responds as if this thought had been right on his lips. "The man wasn't lying. The lady was. He didn't get in a fight. She hit him." *How did Raphaël notice that? Did the man remind him of himself with his father?*

Poole nods before he ushers us to the next patient. We treat patients with a chopped-off finger (reattached by Corporal Poole), and a grazed knee that Raphaël fixes up without breaking a sweat. He keeps a close watch on everything we do and I see the chances of talking to someone in private slip away.

I get to heal a mild burn on a lady's forearm. Her clothes, which are stained and thin for this type of weather, stand out. It accentuates her fallen in cheeks and I worry about her general health. With my water glove, I hold my hand just a hair away from the burn. My other hand grasps the Clear Quartz. Scorched skin radiates pins and needles into my hand and the pain travels all the way up to my shoulder. My other hand grips the Quartz with all my might in order to channel the feeling away.

"Close your eyes," Poole says and I focus on the burn. Slowly, the pins and needles fade away from my shoulder, then it fades out of my arm and hand. I open my eyes, and before me her skin is perfectly healthy, though maybe with just a tinge of red. The woman thanks me and without a coat, she makes her way back into the icy winds outside.

"Too slow, Private Waywater. You need to work on your speed. All of you, follow me."

Well... Gran would be proud.

Every week we go back to the run-down hospital. We go from

scratches and burns to more serious injuries. The Sisters keep a close eye on us while we work with Corporal Poole.

Chapter 28

Dies Veneris

It's the end of the moon and with our pocket money burning in our pockets, our squad goes for a drink outside the base. The light is fading when we walk up to the little booth next to the gate. The evening air is frosty. It bites at my face and I huddle into my big black coat.

A heavy-set man sits behind the book. He wishes us a great evening as we head out of the gate. My eyes fall on the blood-red flowers depicted on the ground. A shiver runs through me.

Eliyah, as a local, leads us toward one of his favorite bars. We walk past the square and walk for a bit. The wind claws its way through my coat and latches on to me as if it has barbs. Eliyah tells me how terrible winter was last year in the Capitol.

"We had a blizzard that lasted for days! It was excruciating. The entire city shut down and at some point the electricity went out. I don't think I have ever been that cold." Eliyah shivers.

"Yeah, we had the same thing in Arabachi. It was a real problem. Everything just shut down." Sheena says with less excitement in her voice. "We were lucky mother had a big pantry. The city didn't get new produce in days."

"This isn't a blizzard?" I ask, distracted as Sheena locks arms with Raphaël.

Leo and Eliyah laugh as if I made a joke. Sheena puts her head on Raphaël's shoulder and I swallow hard. Leo sees my face, misinterprets my expression, and explains.

"No, it will be a lot colder and the wind a lot stronger in a blizzard. Snow falls from the sky and you can see, like, up to that house over there. But not further."

"I think we had one when we passed over the mountains." I think out loud, trying to ignore Sheena and Raphaël.

We pass a wall and suddenly the Leader Suprema's palace materializes and I stop dead in my tracks. Lights of the grounds flood the street we walk on. The flags snap and wave in the wind. The fountain has been turned off. Two guards stand outside the entrance and two in front of the fence. You can easily mistake them for statues. I quicken my step to keep up with the group. Leo and Eliyah are now comparing what they ate during the last blizzard.

"When the bread ran out, we feasted on the cheese and nuts. Mother even let us have some mulled wine." Eliyah reminisces with a smile.

"When our bread ran out... We ate snow." Leo says quietly. Eliyah looks at the young boy and then drops his head. *Their worlds would have never crossed if we weren't in the army,*

"Ah, we're here!" Eliyah says, and pulls me out of my thoughts. The bar is full of people in uniform. "Isn't there another place we could go? Maybe somewhere quieter?" I ask. *There is no way there would be anyone from the resistance in a bar like this.*

"What? Why?" Leo asks incredulously. Without waiting for a response, he walks into the bar, followed by the group. Reluctantly, I head in. We sit in a booth with a big painting of a General above it and Sheena cleverly maneuvers herself next to Raphaël. The General's eyes follow our movements as we order our drinks from the young bartender. Raphaël perks up and talks to Sheena about different kinds of cocktails and she looks at him with too much enthusiasm.

I order a soda, while the others order cocktails and beers. Leo might be too young to be allowed alcohol, but his uniform makes him appear older and the bartender doesn't ask questions.

"Here's to surviving the first two moons!" Raphaël raises his glass, a smile playing on his lips. We all clink our glasses and Sheena shoots me a dark look but keeps silent. I drink deeply from my glass and ignore her. She turns to Raphaël.

"When did you find out you could control water?" Her question carries a hint of genuine interest, but her eyes are cautious. The group has turned their focus toward him now. Eliyah sits back and crosses his arms defiantly.

Raphaël chuckles awkwardly. "I-i-it's nothing, really. I felt the water's f-flutter for a l-long time. But I n-n-never knew Aquakinesis was a real thing until recently." He admits. Zophiel's words creep into my mind, 'some say it gets triggered by trauma'. *No wonder he is reluctant to talk about it.* "N-now I learn how to use it for a g-good cause. It f-feels natural," He says and stares into his drink. Sheena puts her hand on his arm and gives him a dazzling smile. I resist the urge to roll my eyes. Instead, I take a long sip from my glass to conceal my irritation.

"I think it makes you an extraordinary person," she says.

"Yeah, just don't use any of that on me," Eliyah says, and laughs uneasily.

"Why does it make you so uncomfortable?" I ask, annoyed. "It's a healing ability that we never asked for. It's no reason to treat us like lepers."

"It's… Nothing. I'm getting another drink." He stands up and leaves his half-full glass on the table.

"You can't ask that!" Sheena hisses at me, all her poise and dazzle forgotten.

"Why not? We can heal people. There's no reason to get weird around us."

Leo holds his eyes on his drink and Raphaël is suddenly very interested in the portrait on the wall.

"A *rube* like you wouldn't understand such complex city matters."

"Excuse me?" I feel my face grow hot.

"I said. A rube like you won't understand the delicacy of these matters."

"Well, this RUBE is outta here. Get bent." Fuming, I stalk out of the bar. The cold air greets me with its biting chill. *That was a lousy move.* I stand with my back against the wall and let the back of my head rest on it. Above me, a few brave stars shine. *Now what? Maybe I can look for a place that-* But I'm in uniform. A Dog on her own will never get intel when she goes poking around. The icy wind tugs on my jacket. The city looms over me unfriendly from where I'm standing. *I'll go back to the base.*

Raphaël opens the door, his face flushed. "You know, y-you two don't have to be friends. B-b-but keep it civilized."

I cover my face with my hands. "I know! It was immature, but she drives me up the wall. I'm sorry."

"Did you- Are y-you jealous of her?" Raphaël raises his eyebrows.

I shrug. *I don't know. Am I?* "I'm gonna go."

The icy wind lashes at my face as I trudge back to the base, a harsh reminder that I won't survive the week out here alone. *I need to find a place where I can buy some wool for a scarf.* My hands seek warmth in the depths of my pockets. Up ahead, the imposing silhouette of the Leader Suprema's palace looms against a black sky. The guards in front of the gate are gone and despite the cold, I stand still for a moment. *Is the Leader Suprema elsewhere tonight?*

A solitary figure closes the door of the palace and moves towards the gate alone. The figure's shoulders are hunched against the cold and their boots are loud on the gravel. I step back, plunging myself into the shadows. A black car rides up on my right and I take a step further into the cover of night.

The gates open, seemingly with no assistance. A tall man in uniform steps out of the black car and walks towards the gate. *Huh, I can identify Winchester by the way he moves. What is he doing here?* He leans against the car and rolls a cigarette as the other form comes closer.

The other figure is clad in a magenta scarf and white gloves. Winchester hands him a cigarette. When the man tilts his head back to let out the smoke, I recognize it's Hawkeye. He sways on his feet, and Winchester places a hand on his shoulder that is both gentle and protective. They talk, but the wind distorts their voices. It hits me like a tone of bricks, so heavy it makes me sway on my feet. *Her, it's Her they were talking about. The Leader Suprema is the mystery woman, but it doesn't make any sense.*

Hawkeye's shoulders tremble, and the electric light reflects the tears rolling down his cheeks. Winchester opens the passenger door and Hawkeye climbs inside. He walks around the car and gets in. The engine awakens with a deep rumble and they drive away. *Is she torturing him?*

Dies Saturni

I wake up in my bed to the shrill sound of the wake-up signal. No nightmares have come to haunt me. I get into my costume and stand at the door. Lance Corporal Little seems smug today, with her chin raised and a grin on her face. It's easier to go along with this charade now that I'm working on an escape.

Today is another shift at the hospital. Despite myself, I'm excited to hear which floor they will assign us to. I have applied for palliative care and look forward to it.

We sit in the ambulance with Arroyo and Brennan. Brennan's red skin is flushed as he tells us about his upcoming promotion. Arroyo is equally excited. I'm separated from myself as we congratulate them. As if I'm already gone.

We walk inside the hospital and Arroyo and Brennan head for their usual spots, while we wait for the sisters to tell us where we'll be assigned. They walk in a short while later.

"Private Hydris, you will assist me in dermatology today. Private Sosa, you will assist in surgery with Sister Daisy, and… Private Waywater, you will be in the emergency room." Everybody starts to walk in a different direction.

"Wait! I asked to be put in Palliative care."

A Sister glances at me. "I don't question the placement, honey, I just read the list."

A little piqued, I walk towards the emergency room. *Was I just not good enough to get assigned?* I thought I made great progress in the past months.

I walk towards the room filled with detergents and lemon, which will disappear soon enough. The emergency room is quiet. A Sister tends to a small girl and an older lady, the Mother is tending to a sprained ankle.

These quiet moments are always few and far between. The day goes by with little bustle. Until the doors swing open and three people rush in.

"Help!" a woman with short gray hair calls. My head snaps up.

Behind her are two strong men holding two unconscious children in their arms. Their hair drips with water. So I rush towards the smallest child first. Her lips are blue and my heart sinks. *Oh, hell-.* "What happened?"

"The sewers came up again, they got trapped," a big burly man says. Water drips on the floor. *They must be freezing.* But that isn't what's important now.

"What?" I ask, confused, but without waiting for an answer, we walk to the back of the small room. "Put them down on the bed over there." I point them to two beds by the door. "What happened?"

The man looks at me incredulously, but the woman who came in first steps in front of him.

"They nearly drowned. They're full of water!" She screams. Her frail stature shivers and I think she's in shock. A couple more people pour into the room and I usher them to the back as the Sister hurries to accommodate them. Panicked shouts fill the room. There is an odd odour in the air. I can't quite put my finger on it. With care, the men put the children down on the plank that makes do as a bed. It wobbles as the weight of the child is placed on it. Her skin is pale. A few blue bruises stand out on her skinny arms.

I hold my ear above the chest of the smallest. The stench is stronger here. There is no movement.

"She's not breathing! I have to expel the water. Call Raphaël, I can't do this alone." I tell the Mother. She barks orders at the Sister, but I don't pay attention.

Without waiting for her permission, I put my hands over her lungs and close my eyes. My hands flutter and in my mind's eye I see blue has filled up her little lungs. *One by one, bit by bit.* I move my hand up to see where the water has piled up.

"Help me put her on her side!" The man helps me and moves her like she's a rag doll. Doors crash open behind me as more people run in. In no time, the emergency room fills up. Panic has a sour smell, and it fills the hospital. My heart beats fast. *Focus!*

If I expel all the water at once, I will collapse her lungs. With great care, I guide out a little water. Then I open my eyes and see brown, vile water running out of her mouth. It splashes onto the tiled floor and covers my boots. *Thank the Gods they're leather.* It is revolting -a mixture of rot and feces. I hold my hand over my nose to filter it out. At that moment, Raphaël runs into the room.

"Raphaël, here!" My voice cracks as I point at the other unconscious child. Her hair is stuck to her head and covered in the same brown water. "Their lungs are full of water!"

That is all he needs to know. He instantly goes to work. Noise builds up behind me, but I block it out as I scoop another two handfuls out of the small lungs. The man still holds her on her side. His hands shake with the cold and his breathing is shallow. *Hypothermia, we need to get him dry.* My eyes scan for a pile of blankets, but they are already gone. *Darn it!*

"Hit her hard, right here." I point at a point on her upper back, a little left from her spine. His scared eyes contemplate me before he slaps her on her back clumsily. I tell him to hit her harder. He does so and in one burst, the child expels the water and gasps for air. Another wave of the revolting odour hits me. She's not conscious yet, but at least she's breathing. Afraid to turn around, I conjure the water from their clothes and off their skin.

"This will have to do," I mutter to myself. "Mother! Two for the wards. They're stable, but need to be warmed up."

The Mother directs three Sisters to take them. They walk through the next swing doors. I take a steadying breath.

I turn around and there are more. Shouts bounce off the tiled walls. People with bleeding wounds cry out in pain. An old man passes me. His wispy hair above his ears hangs down. His skin is red and his steps heavy. A dislocated shoulder shows even through his clothes. *Did he get here on his own?* There is no one fussing over him. He searches with panicked eyes. With a general swoop, I remove the water from his woolen coat. My heart breaks for the lost old man.

"Do you know Claude? Or Eros?" I whisper, but no luck. I point him deeper into the little hospital. *The Sisters will find him.* He shuffles to the doors when Private Arroyo walks in. He takes the man under his wing. My abilities can't relocate joints and the others need more attention. Arroyo walks up to me and offers me a cup of warm liquid. I take a sip without tasting it. My fingers tingle and energy flows back into my body. We walk through the rows while we triage. Some we send to specialist's departments, and others we leave for now. Amid the chaos I ask about Claude or my father, but I just get blank stares.

There is no fuss when we pass over people. Everyone seems to know there are people in dire need of help. The focus is on saving as many lives as we can. A little boy holds the hand of a man who sits, passed out on his chair. His eyes are too big for his head. With sunken in cheeks- like Leo when he just joined us. Skin is red from the cold and his teeth chatter.

With a quick scan, the gash on the dad's back is the most dangerous. There is no room to lay him down, so I bend him forward as Arroyo prevents him from tumbling over.

"I- I don't understand," I say as I heal the gash on the man's back. It burns my hand, but the strange tea has helped me get some energy back. Despite all the people in the room, it has gotten cold. *We are all leaching energy from any place we can...*

"It's the sewers. They flood a few times a year, but it's early... Normally it happens in spring."

"What?" I ask while I see Thalassa run through the door. Her hair is all over the place like it's static.

"We live in there." He leaves me at that while I still have a thousand questions. But we are needed. *How can the Military leave these poor souls to their fate?*

Even with my eyes open, the blue stain of water on the nearest people is obvious. Although less life-threatening, the wounds they have can cause serious infections. They are my next patients when a woman my age taps on my shoulder. She has a baby in her arms. A bright red arm hangs limply out of its bundle of soaked rags. Dark blue eyes stare at the ceiling, unseeing. Something inside me snaps.

"Please, please help him."

I put a trembling hand on his chest. There is water there. *Something feels wrong.* A sensation of something I haven't felt before - or perhaps the absence of it. I instinctively know that the baby is beyond saving. *I have to try.*

Gingerly, I take the baby out of its mother's arms. It is heavier than expected. My arms tremble as they hold the bundle, and I blink tears out of my eyes. My breath accelerates. People scream and some cry. Big blue eyes stare at nothing. *Should I be helping someone I can actually help?* My body freezes. As if I'm waiting for some sign, some deity who will tell me what to do. I blink. The mother pleads with red, shiny eyes.

Behind her, Raphaël runs to the next patient. He moves slowly as if he walks through the sludge this young man has died in. A woman vomits brown water over the floor. A man holds her up. His eyes plead for help. But there are just not enough of us to help all of them. There is a large piece of something sticking out of his wife's abdomen. I inhale the oxygen that would have helped the baby. *The one, or the many?* The sour stench of fear overwhelms me. Now it's not only theirs. It's also mine. I blink again. Warm water runs over my face. My hand hovers over the tiny chest. Bile rises in my throat. *No.* I give the baby back. The air is suddenly frosty. Goosebumps form over my entire body.

"I'm so sorry."

The mother collapses with her baby in her arms. Her shrieks will haunt my nightmares. But I have to help the many.

Raphaël walks into my view. He says something I can't understand. His hands hold my face and his gray eyes penetrate mine.

"You can't zone out now, Elara! Keep moving!"

But I don't want to. I want to curl up next to the devastated woman and cry for her baby. He hits me in the face. My head spins. The burn of his hand print wakes me up.

"Yes. Thank you." And I move on.

A boy lies on a few chairs. He shivers violently and coughs spasm through his body. On the floor, there is a brown pool of water mixed with blood. *At least he got it out by himself.* His parents see me walk over and stand up. The poor man holds a ragged hat in his hands.

"Please help my boy. Claude said you would!"

There is no time to process this. I turn to the boy, who has given no indication he has seen me. In my mind's eye, blue shows in his lungs. But it's just a little. With a practiced hand motion, I cast it out. The blood doesn't come from the lungs. He swallowed something that has torn the lining of his stomach.

"I need your hands. Put them on top of mine." I say and with a slight hesitation, the father puts his hands on mine. It is easy to tap into his energy and carefully I heal the boy from the inside out. He will need to vomit the foreign object out, but others can deal with that.

"Claude- is Eros with him?" I ask, my voice trembling.

The parents shake their heads. "No, no, I don't think so," the father answers, glancing at his wife.

A jolt goes through me. "Where can I find Claude?"

The parents are already moving away from me like I'm a rabid dog. "Please, tell me. Where can I find Claude? I need to find him." I have to refrain myself from shouting and scaring them even more.

It's the Mother that whispers, "We can't help you, but go to Mabel's boutique, she knows."

I drag my hands over the clothes to dry them. The same dirty water that is being retched up leaves the boy's clothes. Water drops to the floor. There is no better place to put it now. After the boy is dry and his condition stable, a Sister takes him to a ward to look after him.

It's past midnight. A Sister mops the floor. In the end, all the elementalists were called down. Our uniforms are filthy. Brown water has seeped into them. But the stench doesn't bother me anymore. My eyes have dried up. The temperature inside is close to freezing. Even though the door is closed.

They have taken the dead downstairs. It took all we had to separate the mother from her baby. I have lost count of how many we couldn't save. Poole is pale as he whispers to a Mother. She holds a tray with steaming mugs. He takes one and then she hands them out to us. I'm so tired I can barely hold my cup upright.

"Drink up, it'll help," she says.

The liquid's fruity smell is in stark contrast with the rest of my surroundings. I take a sip. It tastes extremely sweet and burns down my throat. There is a hint of apple, but also something sharp in it which burns my mouth and throat. My head becomes less fuzzy. But the mother's screams still fill the empty room. I take another sip. There is also an earthy undertone in it. The beverage has already cooled down. I look at the cup as I realize, *It's us that are making it so cold in here.*

"You okay?" Thalassa whispers from beside me.

"Better now. You?"

"Same. But I could sleep for a week." She yawns.

We clink our mugs. The sensation of a Guardian Spirit who is watching over me calms me, and I smile. *Claude can help me get home.* Giddy, I empty the mug. In an instant Gran's presence is so vivid, it is like she just walked through the door. In my mind I hear her voice, 'The resistance has been corrupted. Elara, it's...'. Thalassa's coughing snaps me back into reality, and I push the memory away.

After the first flood, the atmosphere in the city changes and there are extra guards present when we work. Protests are common and are put down violently, resulting in long hours in the emergency room.

Chapter 29

Dies Luane

The familiar shrill sound wakes me. Light creeps into the room through the dirty window. A spider has optimistically woven a web just outside it and it wobbles in the breeze outside. For the millionth time, I wish we could open the window and get some fresh air in here.

Like well-trained Dogs we get dressed and make our beds. The metal bed squeaks as we get out of it. Rustle of clothes and the buzzing of the single light bulb fill the room.

I fell asleep trying to figure out what Hawkeye and Winchester are up to, and who they would trust enough to share their plans with. The mornings have become such a routine I can let my mind wander while I go through the motions. I change my focus to my father, something I haven't gotten any further with either. *Are you still out there somewhere? Would this Claude know?*

Happy Thalassa can't read my mind. We stand at attention next to the door of our room. All the privates stand in a sleepy silence. Opposite me, Sheena avoids my gaze. Her eyes are dull and she stifles a yawn. Since the first flood she, Leo and Eliyah have been tasked to patrol more frequently and it's taking a toll on them. My heart sinks when I hear the familiar voice.

"Yes, very good, my little Privates. You have all learned a lot… Let's walk into this room, hmm?"

At the last syllable, my hair stands on end. In my head, I run through the checklist one more time. *Did I really get everything right?* I can handle another run-in with Lance Corporal Little, but an altercation with Baël I want to avoid at all costs. He pauses when he arrives at our room and I keep my eyes trained on the white piece of wall just behind Sheena's right ear.

Blue dead eyes take in every inch of me, as if his fingers probe every spot. When Baël can't find anything to critique, he wanders into our room. *Please don't touch my stuff, please don't touch my stuff.* My jaw clenches. The sounds of his footsteps echo through the hall like menacing thunder. He takes his time and walks around twice. My mind retraces every step. The sheet is pulled back, the pillow fluffed, we put all the little things in the cupboard next to the sink. I stifle a gasp at the sound of the cupboard being opened. He is looking for something. The sound of things being picked up and put down makes my palms sweaty. In my mind, I see him leaf through the books. After an eternity, he comes out.

"Very well done, all of you," he sounds disappointed. "Show-ARMS! Good, good, good. At ease. Go get your breakfast."

Relieved, I join Thalassa in the canteen.

The air outside is crisp as we walk out in our shorts and shirts. Fog has settled down on the base grounds. Smells of wet grass fill the air and the birds' songs sound vibrant. Instead of Winchester, Baël waits for us. A flutter of panic goes through my heart as I see his blond hair. *Where did Winchester go?*

Baël is ready for us and orders us for a run to get warm. He runs parallel with us over the frosty course. Birds chirp in the forest outside the base. When we are done with the run we are panting. My skin is still cold though. I've seldom seen Baël so happy, and it doesn't bode well. "Atten-TION! Today, we will be going over some basic tactics to see if we remember everything. Begin with a spar. The person to not get touched on the shoulders wins."

I team up with Eliyah. He is bigger than me, but I hope I have more speed. My hands come up to protect my body. Eliyah hops from one foot to the other. I lunge forward. He blocks my attempt lazily. And his eyes narrow. *I'm prey.* He takes a step to the left. Twice. Then he moves his left hand. I rush to block, but still his right hand hits me on the right shoulder. Hard. *Breathe.* "Stop, you're hurting me!"

Baël interjects, "There will be no stopping. Your enemy won't think twice to get you down."

This time Eliyah moves right. Then left. He moves his right hand. This time I'm ready and block it. But he simultaneously lunges with his other hand and he hits me on the right shoulder. On the same spot. I'm sure the skin underneath my shirt is turning purple.

"Come on, princess!" He teases.

I copy his moves. Step left. Step left again. Distract. Punch! But he blocks my attempt and a sharp pain shoots up to my elbow. He paces forward. Once. Twice. And I try to keep a distance between us. Suddenly, he crouches low. And his foot comes out of nowhere and he knocks me over. The ground scrapes my skin and forces the air out of my lungs. He taps softly on my sore shoulder. "You need to do better than that. I've been practicing for years."

Baël's cold voice cuts through the air. "Don't stop now, Private Eliyah."

Eliyah looks from me to Baël a few times before he speaks. "But I defeated her, Sir."

Glee flushes Baël's face. "Do you think you will get to stop when your enemy falls over and surrenders? *Continue!*"

There is a hint of panic behind Eliyah's eyes. He half-heartedly aims for my left shoulder and I block him. I try to reach Eliyah's shoulders, but he moves easily out of my reach.

"Is this what they taught you, Private? Hmmm? Now hit her like you mean it or I'll show you how it's done."

I'm aching all over, but the only thing worse than getting my ass kicked by Eliyah is Baël wrestling me to the ground. In my periphery, a few people have stopped to stare at us. Before I know what's happening, Eliyah lunges forward and hits my already aching shoulder. I turn away from him, but there is no avoiding his fists now. Three punches land on the back of my right shoulder and he wrestles me to the ground. The intense perfume of grass fills my nose. I turn on my back, covering my face. With all my might, I try to crawl away. But Eliyah is much faster than me.

"Please! Please, stop!" I yell.

"*Make* him stop!" Baël's voice sings.

If I don't counter, he will go on until I'm unconscious. I clench my hands together in one fist underneath me. Just when Eliyah pauses in between hits, I turn over. With my hands as a sledgehammer, I aim for his face. He is surprised and flinches. But doesn't move far enough. My swing catches him on the side of his face. I don't see the impact. But my bones tremble when we make contact. He falls off of me into the wet grass. We both pant. My shoulders hurt. So does my hand. The knuckles of my left hand are bruised and begin to swell. A sharp pain goes through my hand as I shake it off. *Broken.*

Eliyah is led away to be healed. And I'm pretty sure I left him with a broken nose. Maybe worse. *But he deserved it.* Baël just stares at me, unmoved. With a sickening jolt, I realize he knows what my weak spots are now.

There is a small 'Healers Room' in the headquarters. A room with a few beds and an office behind glass. The smell of chlorine and citrus is a surprising change from the permanent pine in the base. It's empty today, except for Eliyah- who has tissues poking out of his nostrils. He winks at me. "You got me good, Princess."

You had it coming, asshole. A Dog walks up to me with a round face and beautiful doe eyes. She wears a blue uniform lined with red. "Ah, the second victim. Let's have a gander."

I hold out my hand for her to examine. Her hands are pleasantly cold against my skin. She tugs and presses on multiple points until I wince.

"I can't tell you if it's broken or seriously bruised. Nevertheless, I can heal you." She gets out a chunk of Clear Quartz, the edges shine.

"What's that?"

"We gilded the Clear Quartz to keep it pure for a longer time and to enhance the abilities. It's quite a nifty invention, if you ask me." She beams at me as if it were her idea and conjures the water glove to hold it over my hand. The water flutters and a painful itch goes through my hand as it heals. I watch her work and I think of my father. "There we go. The bones will be brittle for a few days, so refrain from punching anything." A mischievous smile plays on her lips.

"I will."

The Dog walks away and I understand why Thalassa is so taken with her.

* * *

In the evening, the three of us sit in our room. We're playing cards and Thalassa is in the lead. I try to figure out how she got such a good hand.

"I've been thinking," Raphaël starts. "Do you remember that water whip thing from class?"

"You mean the time where I harassed you? No, haven't got the faintest." I smile cheekily at him.

"I'm serious! You should teach us that!" Thalassa looks up from her cards.

"You guys have manipulated water before. Better than me. Why-?" I hold my cards close to my chest.

"We can extract it. Sure, Raphaël can make a miniature-sized water spout-"

"It's a d-decent-sized water spout!"

"Whatever. There's never enough power behind it to actually form a bruise. And one time you made the water boil!"

I study them. *Are they pulling my leg?*

"Come on, Cookie, show us!"

"I-, I have no idea how I did it… Neither time was it something I did on purpose." Thoughtfully, I walk to the tap and pour water in a mug. "The time I made it boil was… I was so pumped with adrenaline…" I hold the mug in one hand and try to imagine the feeling I had when I made it boil last time. With one finger in the glass, I sit down on the bed. I take a deep breath and concentrate on the dread I had felt. My heartbeat quickens. Baël's face swims into my vision, and I don't sense the water heat up until it burns my hand. A yelp of pain escapes my lips and I drop the mug over the bed. Hot water spills over Thalassa's foot and she curses.

Raphaël waves his hand, extracts the water from the bed, and throws it back in the sink.

"What in carnation!? Elara! Watch where you throw that!" Thalassa says as she blows cool air on her foot.

"Can you heal yourself?" Raphaël asks.

"No," Thalassa says. "I tried once with my knee and I almost fainted. It doesn't work somehow."

"I had the same. I healed my broken lip and a wave of nausea hit me."

Raphaël stays quiet but gets some water to relieve the pain from Thalassa's foot. We sit in silence for a bit.

"So, any idea how you got it so warm?"

"I think it has something to do with negative emotions… Or a surplus of energy? I don't know…"

"Let me try it." Raphaël gets the mug and refills it. "If it's negative emotions, perhaps I can trigger it." Raphaël breathes and closes his eyes. He puts a finger in the water just like I did. Thalassa and I stare at the glass. At first, nothing happens. Then little pieces of white float around the glass. I move closer to the mug to see what's happening. Small drops of water begin to form on the outside of the glass. *The water is not boiling…*

"Raph?" I whisper, and he opens his eyes. There is a bright shine to them. Little ice crystals have formed around his finger. "What did you think about?"

"About my mother… About how we felt when my dad got home drunk." He takes a sip of the water. "It's nice and refreshing, though, and we would never need ice cubes!"

It's Thalassa who has figured it out. "Elara thought of something that gave her adrenaline and it made the water boil. You think of something that mentally drains you and the water freezes. It's… depressing, really. Alright, we know this now. Now El, show us how to throw some punches with the water."

Raphaël laughs and I'm grateful for the light tone Thalassa brings. I'm too tired to have thought of it. I yawn while I fill two glasses with water. Two pairs of eyes focus on my movement as I try to recreate the forbidden water whip. The water stretches out of the cup easy enough and then I flick my hand as if I'm trying to scare away a fly. It loses its form and falls onto my bed. Raphaël conjures it out and refills my glass. Thalassa copies my movements. First, my hand guides the water up. Both my mug and hers hold a vertical stream of water. This time, I extend my arm while I flick my hand. Water rains down on Thalassa.

"Heyy! Stop that!" With one fluid movement, she whips my hand with the water. Hard.

"Ai!"

Thalassa's eyes grow wide. "Did I do it? I did it!"

"Yes. You. Did. Hmmm?"

Thalassa's excited smile drops. Three pairs of eyes shoot to the door, where Baël leans against the door frame. *Shit! Shit! Shit!* We don't move.

"I believe the punishment for assaulting a fellow Private equals one night in solitary. Tut tut tut, Private, I thought better of you."

His smile makes my heart beat erratically in my chest. I avert my eyes and shame builds in my stomach. *Just like when the girl had to undress herself. Why can't I speak up against him?*

"It, it was an accident, Sir." Her voice is soft.

Baël puts a finger against his lips in mock contemplation. "No. No, that looked intentional."

"It's t-t-true! She d-d-didn't mean any h-harm, we s-swear!"

"You swear now, do you? And what will the Sergeant believe? Three privates who swear nothing happened, with one already on her naughty list. Or her Corporal? Hmmm?"

There is no way out. And he knows it. Thalassa's weight shifts off the bed as I keep my eyes on the floor. Raphaël makes a move to stand up, but he doesn't follow through.

"Good lad, you just stay there. But not too long. We don't want to catch you trespassing after dark *again*, now do we?"

Thalassa's boots walk towards the door, their size almost childlike next to Baëls.

"Atten-TION!" Raphaël and I jump up as if an electric current starts us up. "Present - ARMS!" We salute the Dog. Thalassa's face is blotchy and her eyes shine. He steers her out of the room and he throws the door shut with a loud BANG.

The sound makes me jump. It takes a minute before I sit back down. Raphaël sits down next to me. "Th-there is nothing we can d-d-do."

I sense he tells himself this as much as he tells me. "No- No, I won't accept it." I walk out the door, run through the hallway and take a right to the back of the building. People are on their way towards the bed chambers and I stumble in the opposite direction. At a fork in the road, I look around. My instinct tells me to go right and after a few steps, I recognize the hall. But all the doors look the same and I curse myself for not paying more attention last time.

Out of breath, I choose a door and pray I'm right. I knock thrice. Already at attention and in my salute, a second goes by. Then another one. All I hear is the sound of my own breath.

The door opens slowly and I thank Qautahna she has led me here.

"What do *you* want? By the Gods! Come in." Hawkeye hisses and pulls me into his room. It smells like tobacco. *Winchester has been here not long before.* "Well!?"

"Baël's got Thalassa. Please, please can you make sure he doesn't..." I can't finish this sentence.

"What happened?" Hawkeye's face grows grave.

"We were trying out something new with water. Thalassa tried to do this thing... She slapped me with the water. Baël saw it and took her into solitary."

"Are you ok?"

For the first time, I look into his eyes. They're not dismissive or angry. A glimmer of compassion sits in them.

"Yes, I'm fine- that's not... Please, I'm afraid of what he'll do to her..."

"Fine. I'll handle it. You- you go back before the lights go out."

I stand completely still. "And I want- you're going to get me an

Aurora Quarts."

He blinks and a muscle in his jaw twitches. "No." He walks to his desk and fills himself with a glass of brown liquid.

My heart races in my chest. "Yes, yes you will. Otherwise I'll tell them. And her."

"You're bluffing." Hawkeye shoots his half smile at me, but has gone a little pale. *I've got him right where I want him.*

"Would you risk it?" I ask with only a minor tremor in my voice.

Hawkeye takes a swallow of his drink and studies my face, that has turned a brighter shade of red. "Consider it done."

"Thank you."

He takes another sip of his drink. "Leave."

On the last part of my way back, I run in darkness. They have already dimmed the lights and there is no one in the halls. My footsteps echo right back at me. They have never sounded so loud. I get to my empty room without being seen and I pant with my back against the door. *Please, Quatahna, make sure she's safe.*

I toss and turn. The empty room feels haunted without Thalassa. Well into the night, I fall into an uneasy sleep.

Pine trees float by on either side of the truck. Gran sits on the bench opposite me. Her eyes are closed. She must have dosed off just now because we were talking about... about something. Suddenly, the truck screeches to a halt. I turn at Gran, unsure of what to do. Gran, on the other hand, has gotten up and walks towards the canvas curtains. Outside are those pine trees.

I follow Gran closer to the opening of the truck. We gaze outside. Bodies of both civilians and soldiers lie left and right along the road. Old men and children lie among them. I gasp at the nightmarish sight before me. I hear the thousands of flies buzz. Near the tire of the truck, Thalassa lies on the ground with her eyes half-open. She is wearing a violet dress on top of her military boots. Her bushy hair crowns her face.

Underneath her is a pool of blood with so many flies on it that it's more black than red. My heart beats in my ears. To my left, Baël's propped up against a tree. He moves his face towards me and smiles.

"You should have done something," Gran says.

"I did." With my knife, I hit him right between the eyes.

Dies Lovis

I walk into the canteen early the next morning. Thalassa hasn't come back to our dorm and snakes writhe in my stomach. I greet Chef and sit down at an empty table. Raphaël accompanies me soon after. We sit in silence while I play with my scrambled eggs. My eyes flit from my plate to the door. *Please let her be ok.*

A group of people walk through the door. Winchester's long stature walks through it and I scan around for Hawkeye. I spot him striding to the other end of the room to grab some food. With a jolt, I realize that behind him Winchester is talking to Baël. *Please give me a hint, something, anything!*

Winchester ignores me while he gets his breakfast, seemingly relaxed. Stacking a plate full and greeting Cheff. Baël oozes down the canteen with a smile that tells me he is pretty pleased with himself. *Baël is way too happy.* Hawkeye walks towards the Officer's table and sits down with his face away from me. Baël sits down opposite him and says something to Sergeant Aric, who laughs. The Second Lieutenant avoids my eyes like a pro while he walks back to the table. An unsettling feeling fills my gut. But then my scalp tingles. Winchester sits down in the empty chair next to Hawkeye, facing me.

WINCHESTER! His eyes flicker towards me. *Oh, eh sorry. Do you know how Thalassa is doing?*

He blinks at me and looks away. *Does that mean she's alright?*

He gets his knife and fork and gives me a minuscule nod.

Thank you. Can you please tell him for me?

Winchester nods at his breakfast and takes a bite.

However, Thalassa doesn't join us for breakfast. *Why isn't Thalassa here? Winchester said she was alright... What if he's lying?*

"D-Do you think Thalassa is alright?" Raphaël asks.

"She's fine."

He frowns at me. "How do you know?"

"Because she has to be."

Thalassa misses her shift at the hospital and at lunch, she's another no-show. A tray filled with food sits untouched before me. Officers walk into the canteen and sit at their usual table. Both Winchester and Hawkeye sit with their face away from me. I will my scalp to tingle and to get a connection with Winchester. But nothing happens. Below the table, Raphaël puts a hand on my leg and smiles at me.

"She's fine."

While the others get up to go to firearms training, I hang back. I want to speak to Hawkeye. The canteen empties and we're playing a game of chicken. Raphaël leaves me after I urge him to go. Winchester leaves Hawkeye and there are only a handful of people left. *Dare I go to him now?* I stare at the back of his head. My heart thumps at the idea. I get up and leave my untouched plate of food on the cleaning racks. Hawkeye still hasn't moved.

I walk up to him and wet my lips. When I'm just a few steps away, I hear his voice. "She's alright, Private."

"Where is she, Sir?" I ask in a small voice.

He turns around and there is the same compassion I saw yesterday. "She did have to answer for her actions. So Winchester gave her the same option as we did you. She chose the brig. She'll be out after dinner."

"Thank you... Cas." My heart thumps audibly as I say his first name.

He's surprised at first and raises his eyebrows. His eyes are a little sad. As if no one has called him by his first name in a long while.

"You care a lot about your friends, Elara. Good quality for a leader."

"They would do the same for me."

"I don't doubt it." He stands up and his chair scrapes over the tiled floor. And we stand face to face. The memory of his lips burning on my hand flashes through my mind. I don't want to break this connection and I hold my breath. His Onyx Eyes burn in mine. For a second, or maybe two, before he turns away from me and I exhale. "Better get to your lessons, Private."

Thalassa finds Raphaël and me waiting in our room. She's pale and her hair has lost a bit of its bounce, but she smiles when she sees us. I hug her as soon as she sets foot in the room. "I'm so sorry!"

She relaxes in my embrace. Thalassa tells us Baël was leading her out of the base. She shivers at the thought. But then Winchester came out of nowhere and told Baël he would take care of her. Baël didn't like it, only because Winchester outranks him. He gave in. "I don't know how Second Lieutenant Winchester found me. But he saved me."

"El, d-did you have something to do with it?"

I smile and put my fingers against my lips. For the first time since I entered the base, I'm in control.

Chapter 30

Dies Solaris

The shrill sound of the morning alarm wakes me from a dream about my father and a young boy named Claude. Today I am in a good mood. Even the blue-gray uniform doesn't feel as heavy as it normally does. Lance Corporal Little is on duty again to check on us and we pass. With Thalassa, we make our way to the canteen. It is busy with a lot of recruits and the chatter echoes against the walls. Raphaël has beaten us to the breakfast table and is wolfing down his bacon and eggs while reading a book that is lying to his right.

The three of us make it to class right on time. We stand next to our desks until Poole lets us sit down. Behind him is a sketched picture of the organs. On all our desks there is a torso of a dummy, with a plastic head attached to it. Its blue eyes stare at the ceiling.

"Today we will not be diving deeper into Aquakinesis. You will do only what I tell you to. If I catch you fooling around, there will be severe punishments. Ahem, ok, we will go through the movements dry before you do anything. Now, to start, place your hands over the patient's chest and try to sense the liquid inside. Move your hands from chin to navel like so." He places his hands on top of each other, and keeping a fist distance, he moves his hands from chin to navel. We copy his movements and my fingertips already perceive the flutter.

"You need excellent anatomical knowledge to steer something out of a body. Luckily for you, you can use my drawing today to help you along. Now, all of you close your eyes and try to envision the water in the torso." With my hands on top of each other, I try to sense where the water is. Just above the left side of the navel, the flutter is strongest, and I glance up at the picture on the board. The water is located in the Colon Descendants. *How would I ever be able to steer this back out?* I steer the water along the Transversus carefully and then down the Ascendense, but steering it through the small intestine seems impossible. *Would you need to steer it out through the lower end?* Around me, Raphaël is making slight movements with his fingers, trying to steer the water to the mouth. Thalassa's face is flushed, and she seems to have a hard time finding the water at all.

"Privates, who has felt the water in the dummy?"

All of our hands go up, but Thalassa averts her eyes, embarrassed.

"Good, good. Who could see the water in their mind's eye?"

Two hands go up this time. It's a lanky, olive-skinned boy with short hair who I think is called Tanner and Iris, the bushy-haired girl.

"Good work, you two. Who is steering their water towards the mouth?"

This time around five hands shoot up into the sky.

"Congratulations, you just successfully killed your patients. If you don't know why, go over your physiology and anatomy again before you come back to my class." Raphaël, who had stuck up his hand, deflates.

"Private Tanner, Private Iris, come to me for a new assignment. The rest of you continue with this practice."

After class and physical training, I report to Lieutenant Klippa's office. He sits me down at my desk and gives me a file.

"These people are going to get a promotion. Could you write their addresses on the envelopes? After that, you can put the letters in." Winchester hurries across the hall and we salute. The First Lieutenant lets Winchester walk into his office first. He follows suit and shuts the door. With my pen at the ready, I scribble down the addresses on the envelopes. Most names I don't know, but some I recognize. Amber Little's name is on here and her address is not the base, I note. Wade Boyle will finally be a Lance Corporal just like his brother. I wish I could climb inside the envelope and join it to Eden.

Just as I try to imagine the scent of the sea and the sound of the waves, the door of the hall opens. It shocks me out of my daydream, and I turn my attention back to my list. I sigh. Eliyah Hartman is on the list. Footsteps are hurrying towards me. I jump to my feet and salute when I see who it is.

"At ease, Private Waywater. How is your friend doing?" Hawkeye asks as he walks up to me.

"She's fine, thank you." *Thanks to you.* I smile at him and he smiles back at me. It reaches his eyes, and he gives me a once-over. There is alcohol on his breath.

"Don't mention it. It's my job to protect my team." He keeps his eyes locked on mine. He's too close, and it feels like…

"Is there anything I can help you with?" I blurt out.

"No, Blue Angel. You just keep your nose out of trouble." He walks past me and knocks once on the door before he opens it. "Good, you're here." He says before the door closes.

I don't hear voices come out of the room even when I press my ear to it. *Nothing.* I sigh. With my luck, they're talking telepathically. I sit back down again and continue my work. To my disgust, Baël is also on the list. *How can they?*

Arroyo and Brennan are also getting promoted. Probably because they have been working in the hospital on a weekly basis. My pen hovers above the last name on the list. Castiël Hawkeye. *Is that why you're drinking?* I eye at the door.

I get up to go to the bathroom. It's a small distance away from the office and the female ones are seldom used. After only a few, I walk back to my desk. I sit down to fold the letters. But my eyes fall on a little white box where I left my pen. Attached to it is a gray piece of paper. The hall is empty and I unfold the note.

It was a pleasure doing business with you, Blue Angel. Do you like it?

Excitement bubbles up in me like champagne under pressure. I jump up so quickly my chair falls to the floor. It clatters on the tiles like thunder and echoes through the hall. I hold my breath. My heart beats in my chest. Afraid that in a moment, Dogs will swarm in and arrest me. One second goes by. Two. Four. Ten. Nothing happens. The doors of the hall don't open. There is no sound of people. Behind me, the door stays shut. Still, no voices come from the room. I put the box in my pocket and put the chair back where it belongs. My footsteps echo through the hall as I hurry back to the ladies' room. The click of the lock shuts out the world and I take a few steadying breaths. In my mind I hear Gran's voice, 'not all of them… Align with our values, Elara. And one as green as yourself might not see the difference between what is good and what is right'. Her presence is tangible. *But I'm not green anymore.* I shake my head.

I take out the white box. It's made of whitened leather and, with a closer inspection, golden letters are printed on it.

'Luminous, Crystals & Co.'

It even smells of luxurious leather. In front of the mirror, I open the little white box. A perfume of sweet flowers comes out as soon as I lift the lid. In the box lie two stud earrings. They sparkle in the bathroom light. At first glance, I think they're diamond studs. The stones, set in silver, are as big as the nail of my little finger. Too flashy for my liking. With trembling fingers, I take one out. I put the earring in the palm of my hand and inspect it from all angles. A giggle escapes my lips and I hold my hand in front of my mouth to keep myself from laughing hysterically. I read the text again and mumble, "I like it."

A short while later, I'm back at my desk. Wearing a beautiful pair of earrings. I sing softly as I fold all the letters and put them in the envelopes one by one. In my mind, I already hear the ocean and the laughing of the gulls. *Maybe I'll buy a bikini on my way back.* I fantasize about the hot sand under my feet and the smell of salt. *I can go back to the bakery and make those beautiful lemon loaves.* But there is another voice in my head that is unsure. *Go home to what? So they can find us again? What about making them pay for what they did? And what about Monster?* The hall door opens and footsteps echo while my focus is on stamping on the envelopes. I don't register the blue-gray uniform until he stands in front of my desk.

"Excuse me, Private," a soft voice asks. "Is Winchester available?"

I jump up to salute the uniform. Letters fall to the floor in my haste. In front of me stands a short man with streaks of gray in his hair. In a flash, I see an unfamiliar badge. "Sir! He's here, but he's meeting with Captain Hawkeye. I could-"

At that moment, the door opens and Hawkeye walks out. When he sees the man, he salutes him.

"Major General, Sir!"

The old man salutes him with no enthusiasm. "Congratulations on your well-deserved promotion, Major. Your tireless efforts and exceptional achievements have not gone unnoticed." The man smiles, but the smile doesn't reach his eyes. "The Leader Suprema herself expresses profound satisfaction in your ability to identify and mobilize the elementalists hidden away throughout the borderlands."

My eyes dart toward Hawkeye. He doesn't seem fazed. A small part of me wishes he would at least have the decency to look ashamed. With intent, I study the crack on the opposite wall. I do not know how well the earrings work. Or *how* they work. *Won't Winchester notice he can't read my thoughts anymore?*

"Under your command, these elementalists shall serve as a formidable asset, fortifying our ranks and enhancing our capabilities in this challenging time. I knew you were destined for great things, Hawkeye."

"Thank you, Major General. It's all thanks to your support and guidance that I've made it this far." But his tone doesn't convey gratitude at all.

"In unity and reverence!" The General Mayor says and Hawkeye echoes it back before he excuses himself as he goes into Winchester's office. The door closes.

"You lied to me. You weren't looking for refugees when you infiltrated Eden." There is a pit in my stomach. The high I got from the earrings has evaporated.

"It wasn't my information to tell, Private. Your question was out of line."

Dies Martis

One frosty afternoon, the three of us notify the gatekeeper of our plans and she tells us to stick to the upper-class areas. With that warning in mind Raphaël, Thalassa and I step outside. Sun rays fall down and the flowers in the flowerbeds sparkle with ice. When the door closes, I take a deep breath. *This square will always equal death.* And today, that is the last omen I want to see. My eyes flit over the square for any sign of blood. But it's pristine. I feel uncomfortable in my pressed uniform as it restricts my throat. With a finger, I try to give myself some extra room, but to no avail.

Thalassa confidently walks towards an exit on our left and Raphaël and I fall in line behind her. My eyes scan for any sign of a charcoal cross or a drawn fist. Disappointed, I have to conclude the resistance hasn't left its mark here yet. *Drawing that in front of the base would be suicide. Or maybe someone has cleaned it away?* There are many people heading for the same exit we are going to. With all the surrounding fuss, I have to refrain from grabbing Raphaël's hand for support. It's too busy.

The street we enter is wide and the white tiles shine bright in the sun. Snow has been cleared away from the streets. Even in this cold, people wear light-colored clothing -white coats and cream scarves. White shoes and hats in pastel colors. Everything is so white it hurts my eyes.

On the side of the street, there are a lot of fragrant flowers, but there are no birds in sight. The first buildings we pass are residential houses, but soon I recognize 'Boutique les Fleurs'. Exotic smells come from the flowers stalled outside. Thalassa bumps into a lady with a white parasol when she turns to gaze through the window of a boutique called Edgar's Haberdashery. The woman excuses herself and Thalassa stares at the lady as she walks off. *Does Thalassa find her attractive?* We walk towards the big shop window.

"These costumes are so pretty," Thalassa gushes. There are two mannequins in the shop window dressed in expensive pantaloons and decorated dress shirts. "What do you think they will cost?"

"Probably a m-month's wage," Raphaël says and moves forward to have a better look. "Do you want to buy one for the Opera?"

As they discuss colors and styles, I take in my surroundings. I have done some research and Mabel's is close to the main street, but I don't want to bring anyone with me. I tug at a loose thread on my coat.

Everyone is dressed to the nines. Men wear their hats, some walk with decorated canes, and a lot of women are walking around with parasols. The parasols are made of lace or other expensive materials.

How do they keep all their white clothing so clean? A man walks by and I smell his flowery perfume. It's all wrong. *It's all fake.*

I wander to a boutique close by with the sign 'Sophia's Apparel Emporium' covered in delicate flowers. Beautiful white dresses with very light embroidered flowers, butterflies, and birds flaunt in the store's window. I try to imagine myself in such a dress, but it's impossible. I'll spill something over it in the first two minutes. In the window's reflection, I watch ladies walk with such grace that they appear to float down the street. None of them have something simple in their hair, like a ponytail, but have complex braids or intricate buns on their heads. An older woman walks by, wearing a hat that seems elevated at least three inches above her head to not touch her hair. She smiles at me, her smile in-genuine. For a fleeting moment, I think that she's on to me, but she continues to walk and I exhale.

"Thalassa, uh, the dresses are over here."

She wanders over and investigates at the dresses. "Wow, how much time do you think it costs to embroider a dress like this?"

I shrug. "Can't we just wear our uniforms to the Opera?"

"And miss an opportunity to dress up? No way!"

"I don't imagine we can buy these from our salaries…" I say.

"Hey, guys!" Raphaël calls from down the street, resulting in some disapproving looks from the crowd. "There is a b-bakery here!"

We walk towards him and, sure enough, the scent of fresh bread comes our way. I breathe in and let it tug on my heartstrings. A wooden board tells us this is Lisa's Bakery. Inside the bakery, mosaic covers the floor. In between the birds and flowers, I can make out pies and loaves of bread. Big slabs of stone make up the counter and the walls are tiled. In the back of the shop, a tiny bell goes off when we walk through the door. A plump woman with rosy cheeks welcomes us. My mouth is dry and I just nod at her. My heart beats fast in my throat and I stay standing in the door frame. Thalassa wants to buy three small cherry pies, but after hearing what they cost, she gets one, 'to share'. When we walk back outside and when Thalassa offers me a bit of her pie, but I decline. It feels like cheating. What if it's better than anything we ever made? Raphaël tells me, with a mouth full of pie, Gran's pies were better and I decide to believe it.

We cross over to another street. This street is not as high fashion as the one we came from, but still safe. People wear simpler clothes here and there are fewer people wearing hats. Thalassa sees the mechanical shop she was talking about earlier. I have never seen her so excited about anything. She literally drags us to the shop window and we peek inside. To me, they are just tools, shiny tools, but tools. Thalassa's face flushed with excitement. She presses her hands and nose to the glass, trying to get a closer look. She talks to us about the things she sees, but she might as well be talking Dolphin because I have no clue what she is saying. She walks in to get herself something called a titanium wrench. Raphaël goes in with her and I stand outside, looking at the surroundings. Big posters are plastered on some walls, all made by the military. One reads "Empower Yourself, Serve Your Nation!" in big bold letters on a blue-gray background, the sun of the Leader Suprema shines in the middle. Another one says, 'Defend, Protect, Excel–Join the Military!' on it two Dogs gaze importantly into the distance. Both of the posters have a brief text at the bottom Hawkeye used in his welcoming speech, "In unity and reverence". *Why would they have posters to recruit people if they could just take whoever they want?* I inspect the posters more closely, but there is no sign of anything else on them.

Thalassa walks out a short time later with a defeated look on her face. "It costs 100 M's!"

After our disappointing trip, I say goodbye to Thalassa and Raphaël with the excuse that I need a new coat. Thalassa eyes me skeptically and half-heartedly offers to join me. Raphaël is thankful to be done shopping and after telling me to be careful he whisks her away.

Alone and with a pounding heart, I walk along the shops and try to find Mabel's. It's not on the high-end street, so I wander to the more affordable shopping streets. I'm better at ease as soon as the white streets become a bit more gray. Prices are now shown in the store windows. A violet coat catches my eye as I walk past a boutique and above it a sign written in curly letters.

Maybel's

A bell pings somewhere in the back as I enter the empty store.

"Be right there!" a sweet voice calls from somewhere in the back.

The temperature is pleasant here and I open my coat. The heavy black thing is probably bulletproof, but not very user-friendly. However, the violet coat, on the other hand, feels light.

"What can I do for -" The woman notices the soldier in the middle of her store and halts. Everything about her reminds me of a plush toy, from her soothing voice, to her plump body, to her white fur vest.

"I was interested in your violet coat," I say as I point to it. My heart is racing and I hide it as best I can. *I am so close!*

"Of course Ma'am." Her eyes stay on the floor as she walks past me to the mannequin. *She's probably terrified of my uniform.*

"A nice place you've got here."

"Thank you, Ma'am." She hands me the violet coat.

I take off my heavy black monstrosity and put on the violet coat. It fits like a glove, although it clashes with the blue uniform underneath. The woman points me to a mirror.

The moment I glance in the mirror, my eyes grow wide in shock. *I look like the dead girl.* In my head, I can hear the buzz of countless flies.

"No, No. It's not for me, thank you." I hurry to take it off and to my distress, the coat catches behind one of my uniform buttons.

The woman stands motionless behind me as I wrestle to not break anything. My fingers fumble at the thread and sweat forms all over my body.

"I'm, I'm sorry. I just -sorry. So Sorry." I give it back to the woman. I'm not even sure what I'm apologizing for. She still hasn't lifted her eyes. Her intricately braided hair frames her round face beautifully. "I'm actually here to see Claude," I say. For the first time, she meets my eyes.

"Who?" She hoots in a small voice, but there is recognition in her eyes.

"Claude? And- Eros? I need to speak with them." It's a wonder I haven't physically taken off yet, with the amount of adrenaline I have in my system. *Is there a password? Something I should say?* The silence grows between us, and the hope that she will open up diminishes. "Mabel -it's Mabel, right? Mabel, it's better you tell me now, than if I have to come back with my superior. Then you will be in deep trouble." I have to refrain from saying 'please'.

For a long time we only stand there looking at each other, sizing each other up, but at last Mabel gives the slightest of nods.

"You can't contact Claude. Claude contacts you," she says. "I don't even know how to contact him. He comes and goes as he pleases, but I can tell him to contact you if he comes by."

"He can't. I live at the base."

She gives me a small smile and repeats herself, "I can tell him to contact you. What is your name?"

I swallow. *To give my real name could prove disastrous. What if she turns me in instead? But I can't walk away now.*

"Tell him that the daughter of Eros and Hera is looking for him," I say. *It's a gamble, but what other choice do I have?* The woman's eyes show no sign of recognition and I deflate a little. *They might still be dead, even if they weren't at the time that father wrote those letters.*

"Does he know who you are?" Mabel asks with a soft voice.

"I don't know," I say, truthfully. I wet my dry lips and I want to ask so many questions, but the tension in the store is unbearable. I escape and flee into the winter air. The wind is a welcome refreshment. Not wanting everyone to stare at me, I flee into an alleyway next to the store.

Get a grip! You can't fall apart like that! This time, a full-blown panic attack stays out. *Gran, I miss you.* A combination of grief and relief swallows me and forgotten to the world. I allow myself to weep for Gran, for Monster, and for Darya who is so far away. Tears fall for the bakery I long to return to and for the loneliness I feel inside. I cry for all the times I have gotten into trouble. The coldness Hawkeye and Winchester have towards me, the scrutinizing looks I get from Thalassa. I mourn the girl in the violet dress and the people in the hospital I can't save.

Chapter 31

Dies Luane

After my shift, I walk straight to Raphaël's dorm. Nervous butterflies fill my stomach. It's as if I'm already halfway home. I get a few stares from the Dogs, but I don't care. Raphaël isn't in his room, but when I turn around, Leo is there. With a big smile, I realize he has been gaining weight. He looks healthy aside from a shadow of a bruise on his cheekbone. *Did he get that from patrol?* I ask him where Raphaël is, and he takes me to his room where Raphaël is playing cards with Eliyah and the Privates from the hospital. He throws a card on a pile when he sees me. It's probably the expression on my face that makes him jump up.

"Sorry, guys, I've gotta go!"

Loud protest erupts from the group, but he walks out undisturbed.

"Come on," he says and we walk to his room. He does something with the door before he shuts it. But I don't see what and I don't care. The moment the door clicks shut, I turn around and press him against the door. "Wow, wow, wow, El, what's this?"

"Just don't speak."

I crave his body. I want to celebrate, because my time here is limited. I need to know someone in this hellhole is on my side. I need to not think. I need to not feel.

393

He obliges when I press my mouth against his. My hand travels under his shirt and his abs are smooth under my fingers. He wraps his arms around me. His arms have grown in size and there is nothing left of the bartender many moons ago. I press up to him and I kiss his jawline, down to the nape of his neck. He groans. This makes me feel powerful, and I undo the buttons on his uniform. I smile at him.

"Damn, you're hot." He pulls me close again.

He undoes my buttons and kisses down to my collarbone. *Yes.* I yank off my uniform. *It won't be a part of me for long.* I take off my shirt and Raphaël turns me around. I press myself unto him. He cups my breasts and groans.

This time it's different. This time I'm not nervous and he's not careful. We're like two animals which have been deprived of touch. My nails scratch his skin and he bites my shoulder. With clumsy fingers, he undoes my pants while I rub up on him. His hand disappears and an amazing sensation gets hold of me. I gasp and grab his hair. He keeps on going until my knees buckle.

"Let's see if we can get you over the edge." He whispers in my ear. I want him to not just nudge, but launch me over that edge.

Dies Lovis

The next day, while the others get to sleep in, I walk towards the desk in front of First Lieutenant Klippa's office. I smile at myself. My protective earrings and the fact I finally got over the edge last night give me a superhuman feeling. The door is closed, but this time I hear loud voices behind it. At least two men. Sounds are so muffled I can't make out distinct words. I'm so surprised by the commotion I don't spot the little girl sitting on my chair until I look her dead in the eyes. It's a little girl, about five years old with red ribbons in her hair.

"Oh! Hi! Who are you?"

"My name is Terra." The little girl says, but doesn't turn to me.

Terra... I've heard that name before... She draws on a sheet of paper with an orange crayon. Beside her, there's a big fluffy unicorn. *What do I do now?*

"Do you know who is in there?"

She nods again. "Mommy and Daddy."

Ok, now what?

"Your words sound funny."

"I'm sorry, what?"

"Your internal words sound funny."

I try to hide my surprise. *This kid can already read minds? Must be Winchester's kid.* "What do my internal words sound like?"

She ponders this for a moment. "Like Mommy when she wears her necklace. Like your radio station is mixed up."

"Do you know what they are talking about in there?"

"I'm not allowed to listen right now." She draws a circle. "But we're going to live somewhere else now," she says matter-of-factly.

"What? Why?"

"Because the bad men have found us and now we have to play hide and seek."

The bad men. The 'They'. It's what Winchester was worried about when he caught me trying to escape.

"But you're safe here at the base. The bad men can't hurt you."

"Daddy says the bad men are everywhere, so we should go soon." she says as she fills the circle with an array of colors.

Is he afraid of the resistance? Or is something going on in the military? I watch the closed door as Terra continues to draw. "Do you know why they are after Daddy?"

Terra shrugs and continues to draw. I struggle with what I want to ask her to make any of this make sense.

"Do you want to see if we can find some hot cocoa for you?"

Her enormous eyes look up at me again. "Daddy says I'm not

allowed to go away with strangers." Pitty fills me for the small girl, as I see her sitting here in this sterile hall.

"I'm not a stranger. My name is Elara, I'm Daddy's secretary."

"Then why do you hide your thoughts?"

My mouth hangs open, but no words come out. *Are all 5-year-olds this perceptive?*

"You know what? I'll just get you some hot cocoa myself."

She doesn't answer me and I'm glad I can leave her behind. *How did a child her age learn how to read minds? Is that what they're after?*

I return with a big jug of hot cocoa and Terra is still in my chair. The multicolored circle is now surrounded by something that must be clouds. The voices in the office have died down.

"Here you go!" I put down the hot cocoa next to her.

"I'm not allowed to drink anything I get from strangers."

I sigh. "So you don't want the cocoa?"

"I didn't say that."

"What do I need to do so you can drink the cocoa?"

"Daddy needs to say it's ok."

I hesitate.

"Why are you afraid of Daddy?" She gets a green crayon and continues to draw.

"I'm not."

"Liar, liar, pants on fire!"

At that moment, I'm saved by the door and I sigh a sigh of relief. A woman walks out. She looks just like her daughter.

"Mommy!" Terra jumps off her chair and flings herself at her mother. "Mommy, this woman wanted me to drink cocoa. Is that ok?"

I notice the smallest of glances at Winchester as he walks out of the door. *They are afraid of something inside the military. Is Hawkeye in danger too?*

"Of course, you can have cocoa, honey," Winchester says with a bright smile.

Mrs. Winchester gives her husband a kiss on the cheek and thanks me for my effort with Terra.

"No problem," I say awkwardly.

She walks away.

"You have a wonderful daughter, Sir. Is there anything I can do for you?"

He gazes into my eyes and then glances at my earrings. "No Private." He turns around and walks into his office.

"Permission to speak, Sir? What… people are after you?" I walk after him.

"Close the door."

For a second I stand in the doorway, uncertain which side he wants me on. I close the door behind me and stay in the room. The room is a lot like Hawkeye's room. With an enormous bookcase on one side, two big leather chairs, and a desk. He sits behind his desk, creating space between us. Behind him hangs a picture of the Leader Suprema.

Winchester places his fingertips together and stares at me intently. "Do you want to help?"

I nod.

"I'm going away for, ah, business. Could you take care of Cas in my absence?"

My face flushes. "Do you think *I* can protect him?"

"He needs friends in my absence."

Chapter 32

Dies Donars

The day of the Promotion starts. As we get ready for the day, Lance Corporal Little is extremely pleased with herself. With her chin up and chest puffed out, she reminds me of a puffer fish. *If only I could kick her little behind.* Because of the hostile environment outside, we will hold the Ceremony inside. Since the sewer overflowed people are protesting, and I hear it gets ugly.

The canteen staff have already prepped it for the ceremony, so we have to eat in our own rooms. The Officers are absent this morning and I can just imagine Hawkeye sitting on his comfy leather chair - which doesn't improve my mood. Before the promotion, the showers are packed. Two women, slightly older than me, sit on a bench, gossiping. Usually, I would steer clear of them, but now there is no place to avoid them. Our hair needs to be in a specific bun and I wrestle to get it right. It's a mystery why a normal bun or even a ponytail isn't allowed. *It's all part of the charade.*

"So the kid turns to me and says, 'But ma'am, I swear I'm not a rat.'" The woman's hair is so short her scalp shows. They both laugh.

"So you threw her in prison?" says the other while she buttons up her uniform. They high five and I feel nauseous.

After a few tries, I yank the ribbon out of my hair in frustration.

"Do you need some help?" The lady with the visible scalp asks me.

"No, I'm fine. Thanks." I hold the brush in my hair again to brush it all back.

"C'm on, I'll help you." She takes the brush from my hands and I endure her doing my hair. Her fingers are deft in making the bun.

"I used to hate these buns. That's when I shaved my head. It's unfair the men don't have this kind of problem."

I grunt.

Like copies of each other, we march into the hall. We do this to show the higher-ups how compliant we have become. The hall, which is loud during our meals, is now silent. Rows upon rows of chairs are waiting for us in the hall. There are more people here than I have ever seen. *Do all these people live at the base?* I doubt it. All of us have donned a fresh uniform and have to look our best. We are seated first by rank, then alphabetically by last name. The to-be promoted Officers have not yet arrived and their seats sit empty against a wall close to me.

In front, there is a little stage draped in the Nation's colors. The golden sun hangs behind the stage with a flag draped next to it.

The Dog on my left is so excited I believe he might wet himself. To my left is a Dog who sits as though someone has shoved a broom up her...

Music starts with the thump of the national anthem and I stand at attention just like every other Dog. For the first time, I notice a small band next to the stage. On this beat, they walk in. This time by rank rather than alphabetical order. Hawkeye walks fourth in line. Little walks behind a few men that resemble bulls and the rear is brought up by Hawkeye, Arroyo and Brennan. They fill two rows of seats and Lance Corporal Little looks around with a puffed out chest. She glances a few times at Hawkeye, who sits seated close to her. It takes everything I have to not roll my eyes. But then my gaze catches

Hawkeye. He doesn't beam or puff out his chest. His face tells me this is serious business. *Relax, you're practically already promoted.* The man next to him ignores the crowd and keeps his eyes trained on the stage.

A man walks in with so many medals and patches he resembles a walking earring. And next to him… My heart jolts. I should have expected it, but the sight of her makes me sweat. She exudes sophistication, and her uniform is laced with gold. Her short white hair makes her skin appear darker than it is. If I would run through the crowd, I could reach her within seconds. I could… I could… But I won't be able to do anything. There are rows of lethal Dogs between me and her.

The man steps up the stage, and applause greets him. Noise that echoes from the walls and makes it sound like thousands of hands clapping. His belly is almost as big as Chef's and even from a distance, I can see his mustache is neatly combed. The Leader Suprema stands next to the stage. Her chin jutted forward and her eyebrows raised. The microphone lets out a shrill noise as the Lieutenant General moves close to it. The applause dies down.

"Distinguished guests, and fellow soldiers! Today, it is my great privilege to stand before you. We gather here to witness and celebrate the remarkable promotions bestowed upon our exceptional soldiers by the highest authority—the revered Leader Suprema herself." There is another wave of applause. "In the presence of our esteemed leader, we honor these distinguished individuals who have risen above the ranks through their unwavering commitment, exceptional skills, and unwavering loyalty to our great nation. To the deserving recipients of these promotions, I extend my heartfelt congratulations. Under the watchful eye of the Leader Suprema, you have demonstrated exemplary leadership and unwavering resolve in the face of adversity." My eyes drift to the candidates. Lance Corporal Little is hanging on this Dog's every word. Hawkeye, on the other hand, has plastered on a smile as he gazes through the crowd. It doesn't reach his eyes. Eyes linger at what I assume is Winchester's general direction. As though he feels my gaze, his eyes catch mine. And it's as if a physical connection that takes hold of us. If I look away, it'll break, and I don't want it to. *What do you want from me?*

For a moment we're back at the beach at sunset. The applause is the wave crashing on the sand. I swallow. Hawkeye is the one who breaks the moment, leaving me with a pit in my stomach.

"For Unity and Reverence!" the crowd chants.

Now the Leader Suprema walks up the stage to the microphone. White eyebrows match her white hair. My fingers ache -I want to hurt her.

"Attention, soldiers!" the Leader Suprema says in a voice that's both strong and lower pitched than I expected. "Today, I address you with a resolute spirit, for this is a gathering to acknowledge those who have risen to higher echelons within our esteemed military. Your unwavering dedication to our cause has not gone unnoticed, as has your burning ambition for triumph." It's easy to imagine how a younger version of her would incite action. Her gaze goes over us as the beam of a lighthouse. "But with this promotion comes a greater flame to bear, a burning responsibility which shall need your very soul. No longer are you mere soldiers; you are now commanders." Her focus has shifted to the candidates. *Is it me, or is she speaking specifically to Hawkeye?*

"The charge bestowed upon you demands unquestioning loyalty and unwavering obedience. In the pursuit of victory, we shall make sacrifices. The path to glory is paved with the ashes of the fallen, and it is your duty to traverse that path with unwavering conviction. You shall strike fear into the very core of our enemies. Unleash the inferno within you. Let its scorching fury consume all who dare to defy our righteous cause." *Wait, what righteous cause?* "In Unity and Reverence!"

Everywhere, people jump up and clap. Hawkeye is also on his feet. His focus is on the stage. One by one, the Dogs are called up and each of them gets a little speech from the Leader Suprema. The first candidate gets commended for his tactical work at the front, and so is the second. Little is called forward, and she walks towards the stage like a bride towards her groom. She praises her for her essential work with the recruits and other nonsense. Carpathia hands her a little piece of cloth -her new insignia and she salutes her. Corporal Little walks back to her chair to the sound of our chant with tears brimming in her eyes. My ears prick as Hawkeye gets called up. He strides to the stage.

"Captain Hawkeye, for your excellent work in the field and the fiery passion for our mission. I bestow upon you the rank of Major." They share a glance. It's just a fraction of a second, but it's there. My heart stops. It's the same look Raphaël started giving me after…

He's sleeping with her. He's sleeping *with her. He's* sleeping *with* her.

My mouth falls open as I realize it. He walks back as he receives his applause. His gaze betrays nothing. But his eyes shift to me and in a split second, and we both know it.

At night I stare at the slatted base above my head. My thoughts go around in circles. *He sleeps with the Leader Suprema. Why was he crying that night? He flirted with me… while he was searching for elementalists. He sleeps with her. She's old. Why was he crying that night? Is he doing it against his will? Why would he?* And around again. In the dark, I can see his eyes. I turn to face the wall. *Why do I care?* I pray to Claude to get me out of here.

Chapter 33

Six of us are crammed in an indigo-blue car. We inch towards our destination in a file of the same indigo cars. The entire squad is crammed into the metal container. Multiple smells clash with each other. Sheena and Eliyah emit expensive perfume, while I am pretty sure Leo forgot to put on deodorant.

Someone high up the food chain has decided it would fit the image better than the trucks they used to get us to the Capitol. My stomach flutters with nervous butterflies. *Tonight, I'll meet them.* The roads are smooth, but the ride is unpleasant. I find myself squeezed between Eliyah and Raphaël, with Leo pressed against the window. Raphaël smells like he always does, like fresh air and sea salt. Sheena sits comfortably in the front with the driver. They are talking excitedly if the Leader Suprema will make an appearance.

For the occasion, we're dressed in something they call a ceremonial uniform. The fabric is lighter than our usual outfit and has subtle patterns in the blue cloth. Stitched on it are silver flowers and suns. Complementing the expensive uniform is my secret weapon. My crystal earrings glint as we pass a streetlight.

Thalassa almost wet herself with excitement when she saw the uniforms. Instead of trousers, it has a skirt. It's odd to wear something so feminine. Apart from the skirt, the women get a bit more waist in these models. But, it makes me sweat faster than usual. Or maybe it's just the car.

We stop in front of a large building. A woman in a white dress opens the door for Leo, causing him to nearly fall out of the car.

"Good evening. Welcome to the Opera House." She greets us one by one as we try to maintain a bit of dignity while we clamber out of the car. As soon as we are out of the car, it makes a U-turn. My eyes study the people that have collected in front of the building. *How will I recognize them?*

The building is impressive. It's as high as the base, but all lit up by invisible lights. "Come on, you guys never saw an opera before?" Eliyah teases as he takes Sheena's arm. I'm happy I'm surrounded by Leo and Raphaël. Raphaël looks like a fish out of the water, while Leo... Leo looks like he wants to run away. I squeeze his shoulder.

"Let's go watch some people sing."

An enormous crystal chandelier is suspended from the ceiling. *It probably costs more than our entire street back in Eden.* It reflects the light beautifully and I catch myself staring at it.

Winchester, Hawkeye, the Mountain, and the blond woman from the Disciplinary Committee sit at the bar. Winchester sees me for a moment and a faint tingle on my scalp makes me walk in another direction. *Let's steer clear of those.* I glance around nervously for the iconic short white hair, but she's not there.

The squad has been seated together on a balcony way on the side. The seats are covered in red velvet and the cushions are softer than our beds. Thick red curtains hang from the ceiling. Sheena and Eliyah have sat down in the front and the rest of us sit behind. I wobble on my chair, enjoying the soft cushions. My eyes dart around the building. *Where are you?* The lights dim. On the other side, Thalassa's frizzy hair pokes out over the railing. The officers walk towards the front, as they have the best seats in the place.

An invisible band plays. It starts so softly that at first, I think I'm imagining the sound. But it swells just like a wave. An invisible system pulls the curtains away, and a stage comes into view. A fat woman stands in the middle of the stage. She wears fantastical clothes that shimmer and sparkle in the light. *How many poor people could you feed from that dress alone?* Her voice is pure and sings over the waves of the music.

The woman sings in a language I don't understand, but her emotions flood the entire space. She sings about longing and despair. Just when I can't take it anymore, a man walks out of the curtains and joins her. His voice is loud and passionate. Sheena has clasped her hands together in utter devotion. A tear falls down her cheek. *What a facade.* I sink back into my comfortable chair and scan through the crowd.

After what feels like ages, my eyelids almost drop. I believe the woman is tired too because she has walked off the stage. Now other people are singing.

I mumble to Raphaël I'm going to use the bathroom. He furrows his brow sleepily and strokes his hand through his hair.

"Yeah, sure. You d-don't need me for that, do you?"

Leo is already fast asleep. A small snore escapes him before his head lolls to the other side. *Claude... where are you?*

The door closes behind me, and sweet silence fills the halls. Everyone is listening to the drama playing on stage. I don't really have to go to the bathroom. *Now what?*

I stroll around and buy a drink at the deserted bar. How am I supposed to meet people who could look like anyone? For a second, I study the bartender. *Him?* But he shows no sign of recognition.

The polished bar is smooth and cool to the touch. The fresh zing of lime wakes me up a little, but my melancholy remains. A breeze moves the chandelier and I hear the tingle of crystal. From the bar, the enormous doors shut us off from the rest of the world. *Should I just have an alcoholic drink to take the edge off?*

"Not a fan of the opera?" A familiar voice asks behind me. I start, but my eyes stay fixed on the colorful bottles behind the bar.

"No."

The chair screeches as it moves back and Hawkeye takes a seat next to me. He signals for a drink. We sit in silence. *You?* The tension builds again. It frustrates me, and I keep my eyes away from him. The bartender cleans his glasses and lets us be.

Hawkeye sighs.

"What?"

"I would have helped you anyway, you know, you didn't have to lower yourself to blackmail," he says. Turning my gaze towards Hawkeye, I reluctantly meet his eyes. The weight of our secrets hangs heavily between us.

"I apologize, Major," I say, my voice tinged with frustration. "But I'm not sure if I believe you…"

Hawkeye's expression hardens slightly, but he nods understand-ingly.

The bartender places a drink in front of Hawkeye, who takes a slow sip before speaking again. "But remember, Private, dwelling on the past won't change a thing and there is a future to focus on."

Is that something a member of the resistance would say? I take a deep breath. The tension in the air dissipates as I raise my glass to join Hawkeye in a silent toast.

"Can I ask you just one more question? And this time you have to tell me the truth.

"Are we still doing that? Alright, ask it." He takes another sip of his drink and watches the bartender walk away to clean a table.

I play with the napkin on the bar, tearing it into small pieces. "Why?"

"Why what?" He says, his eyes bore into mine, forcing me to say it out loud. A breeze makes the chandelier behind us clink softly, and the bartender's shoes squeak on the polished floor.

I swallow hard. "Why... her?"

"Truthfully? I think you already know."

"In unity and reverence," I say.

Hawkeye raises an eyebrow, a hint of a smile playing at the corners of his lips. "In unity and reverence," he echoes, clinking his glass against mine.

We sit there, side by side, with the weight of the past and the uncertainty of the future.

The bartender glances over our shoulders and we hear multiple doors open at the same time -the recess begins. The crowd thickens and I make my way back towards our private balcony.

I'm unsure what comes first, the sound, or the sensation of the universe moving. The floor trembles under my feet and for a fraction of a second, I wonder if I'm drunk.

My hands find the wall as I try to keep upright. It all happens so fast, I don't have the ability to be scared yet.

The sound is overwhelming. A tsunami will sound just the same. A roaring sound. Bricks crack and wood breaks. Confused, I cover my ears. Then, a high-pitched ring. In a reflex, I shut my eyes tightly. A wave of heat finds me and flings me off my feet. Into the bar. I gasp when I land on my knees painfully. Terror fills my chest. *What's happening?* The pretty uniform is useless. Small things pelt against my back. Some of them slice through my skin. Others burn through the fabric. A heavy sound, like the beginning of thunder, crashes overhead. I blink. *Is this how I die?*

A force lunges into me and throws me a couple of steps from where I was. An animal-like scream erupts from my chest. The glass chandelier crashes to the ground right where I was standing. The ground trembles under its weight. My brain refuses to catch up with what happens around me. Someone shields me. Shards of crystal fly through the air. My eyes find my savior. *Onyx Eyes.*

"What…?"

The stench of metal reaches me. For a wild second, I think it's me. But the red liquid flows from *his* shoulder, staining his blue uniform black. My eyes and brain focus. Glass flies everywhere. He protects me as a human shield. The ring in my ears continues. I'm exposed as he stands up. Every instinct is telling me to stay down. My heart pounds in my throat. Hawkeye presses down on the wound on his shoulder and looks around. A dozen cuts and bruises on my back begin to sting. My eyes water from the pain.

Hawkeye stands up, his posture full in command; "All eyes on me! Healers, put your training to use! The rest, evacuate the building!" Thankful for not having to make any decisions, I follow his.

My hand grabs the Quartz in my pocket. I flinch. More surprised than hurt. There is a shard of glass sticking out of the palm of a hand. My hand. No blood has left the skin. Yet. It will be only a matter of seconds. My surroundings blur as I remove the glass. It's painless. *That's the adrenaline.* As soon as the glass leaves my skin, I bleed.

The bar has been pulverized, and the bartender is nowhere in sight. Panicked people flee by it. Water spurts from a broken pipe. Shards of glass glisten on the floor like the streets outside did over two decades ago. Uniforms run towards the doors. It smells of burning wood. *Just like a fireplace.* The ring in my ears has moved to the background. People shout and a girl who passes me cries. The cacophony drowns out her sobs. With unsteady feet, I walk to the bar. I guide the water towards me and make the water glove. My eyes scan for potential healers.

My hand is red with my own blood. *I don't want to.* In the chaos, there is no one to help me. I mend my hand. Instantly, the urge to throw up fills my chest. But I keep it down. Bits and pieces fall from the cracking ceiling. Hawkeye has disappeared in the flurry of people.

He wouldn't do such a thing. My heart beats in terror. I'm an island in the panicked crowd.

Breathe.

The people part for me as I make my way outside. *That's funny, I should look into that.* The night air is icy and hurts my nose when I breathe in. My eyes spot Leo cradling himself on the stairs.

"Where does it hurt?" I sound calmer than I feel. As if I'm in control. I swallow away the nausea and will my heart to calm down.

Leo has panic in his eyes. His hand moves away from his chest. He looks at his blood-stained forearm.

I close my eyes. It's only a superficial wound. Without a second thought, I heal it. The wound burns my hand. I prevent myself from fully healing Leo. *There will be more.*

"Go, go to the hospital. The Sisters will take care of you there."

My hand moves him towards the cars where people climb in. *Has anyone checked the cars for bombs?* I recognize Arroyo and Brennan at the bottom of the stairs. Arroyo is pale underneath his olive complexion. We stand together but alone and heal everyone who needs direct attention. Others are brought to the car. I don't know where they go after that. But it's not my concern. Residents have formed a crowd, watching us clamber and panic. Shock is apparent on every face. One tall figure stands out. He exudes calm and his long face is devoid of emotion, but I don't recognize him.

A crash alerts us. Windows shatter from the heat and smoke billows out of them. More glass litters the floor and people run away screaming. An acrid smell tingles through my nose. Through the crowd which flows by me like water, two people walk deliberately to me. Both are injured, but one supports the other. Just like me, this girl has glass that has broken through her skin. Their hands are slick with blood. She's in shock as her friend leads her to me. She doesn't talk and her eye swivels around wildly. The other eye is bloody and a piece of glass sticks out of it. I clench my jaw. *I can't recover that eye.*

But there is no one around me who can. The girl tries to pick the glass from her face. *Shock.* Her friend forces her hand back down.

"Poole! I need Corporal Poole!" I shout, but no one listens. *What was the name of the base healer?* But nothing comes to mind. "Hold her hands to her side," I tell the friend. She's pale and tears fall down her face. I try to stall removing the piece in her eye for as long as I can. But no one shows up to help me. After the other wounds are healed, I am left with no choice. *I'm so sorry.*

With a trembling hand, I pull out the bit of glass. Nausea swells up in my stomach. The glass shard falls to the floor and the girl screams. I push my hand over her eye and feel the burn. My heart pounds in my chest. *I wish I had the gold-laced Quartz.*

A few more people come over for help and my energy drains. In a moment of rest, I regard the healers. Arroyo is the farthest away from me. His slow movements tell me he is losing energy fast. Brennan seems better. He's on his knees looking over someone's face. He is definitely the most charged of the two. Then there are a few from my class. Tanner puts his hands on a man's shoulder and our eyes cross. He smiles grimly. Close to me is Thalassa. She points a few people to a car. It will probably head to the hospital. *Is Leo on his way there? Where is Raphaël?* Terror grips my heart.

An officer with short blond hair stumbles towards me.

"My. Back." She says through gritted teeth.

She turns around and I grimace. Her skin is merged with the molten uniform. Patches of it have turned black. Around it, the skin is an angry red. Blisters are already forming. *This is going to hurt me almost as much as it does her.* The black skin is dead. I can't do anything about that here. Hesitantly, I start with the angry red skin and the blisters. My hand becomes so hot my sight flashes white. A burst of air leaves my lips. *I sound like a wounded animal.* The woman groans as I move along her back. Just like the young girl, this is going to leave permanent marks. And with burns this bad, she is not out of the woods yet.

There are a multitude of wounds, some made by glass, others by blunt trauma. People shout that the ceiling is going to come down. People pass me with the same wild expression in their eyes.

Eliyah finds me. He looks confused. "Sheena, she, she won't move. I- I can't move her."

The one, or the many... But I still can't find Raphaël. And what about the ceiling?

"Show me."

I leave my self-appointed post and run back inside. Inside, the air has become cloudy. The acrid smell is stronger here. Hakweye supports an older man outside. He glances up and sees me. But before he can say anything, I follow Eliyah. Who takes a left. I cough. *It's not cloudy, it's smoke.* My eyes sting. I catch a glimpse of a shadowy figure watching from afar. *Claude?*

We make our way up the stairs. I'm pressed against the walls as a few people pass us. One has a limp. His pant leg is black with blood. We run back to our balcony. There is barely a soul left up here. Smoke is thicker and I cough again. It makes the pain in my back flair up. My fingers bend and flex to feel the comforting feeling of the water's flutter. Eliyah pushes open the door. My heart drops. A big piece of the ceiling has dropped on where we were sitting not 30 minutes ago. Sheena did not get up in time to evade it. Her eyes are still half open as her eyes stare at the wall. A heavy beam has fallen on her chest. I don't know if she was alive after it fell. But the heavy beam crushed her ribs and she may have suffocated. *Don't think about that.*

Next to her is Raphaël. His hand is stretched towards her. The beam has fallen on top of his lower abdomen. His chest rises and falls erratically. There is no other movement on the balcony. I walk towards him.

"No! We have to help Sheena first!" Eliyah cries out.

I look into his eyes. They show too much white.

"Eliyah, I'm sorry. I can't help her. She's gone." My voice is higher than I'm used to. "I have to help Raphaël."

He walks up to me. His face has turned red. "No! No, you can do magic. That's what they said. You can- you can heal people, you can move things, you- you-" He falters as his hands move helplessly around him.

"I can't bring people back from the dead, Eliyah."

His hand grabs the shirt on my chest and twists it. "You haven't even tried! You're petty! You never liked her! TRY!"

The words spit in my face and his eyes are even bigger than before. I want to move away from him, but he is stronger. My heart beats in my throat.

"Eliyah, let me go!"

He lifts me by my uniform. My hands grab at him. Terrified. My feet lift off the floor. For a second, I fear he's going to throw me off the balcony.

"Private, put her down. Your Officer demands it! Go help the troops outside." There is a recognition in the back of Eliyah's eyes. He puts me down mechanically, unable to ignore a direct order from the Major. My feet land on the floor and I gasp. In his eyes, the struggle is evident. His breath is fast. His grip lasts a second too long. But his grip loosens. It hurts him physically to let me go. *Good Dog.* Our gaze holds before he turns on his heel and stalks off. The gasp has let in too much smoke in my lungs and I cough. It sounds like the barks of a seal. My ribs ache and the wounds on my back tighten. I double over. But that just stretches my wounds and I yelp. Hawkeye walks up to me.

"Help," I wheeze and I point at Raphaël.

"What do you need?"

"Free. Him." I manage between excruciating coughs.

"Private Sinclair?" He asks as he stares at Sheena.

I shake my head. Hairs on the back of my neck stand up and I have the feeling we're being watched, but there is no one there.

Hawkeye is stronger than he appears. But the beam is heavy. My muscles scream in protest as we pull it off Raphaël's body. I have to take a few seconds to breathe before I can start.

"I need your help. I can't do this alone."

Hawkeye understands what I mean and sits down on his knees on Raphaël's other side. My heart thumps in my chest and my hands tremble. I've only ever been the helper. I've never used someone's energy before. *Let us pray it's as easy as it looks.*

Cas's eyes are determined, and he nods. A jolt of electricity zings to my stomach. *You can do more than meets the eye.* But it's not important now.

My eyes close, and I focus on Raphaël. In my mind's eye, I see an array of colors. Most of them mean nothing to me. I scan him. Apart from a mild concussion that paints this area with a mix of red and blue, his head is fine. *Let's heal this first.* Without Hawkeye's energy, this would have drained me far more than it does. With more confidence, I scan the inside of his throat and lungs. They are remarkably clean -*thank the gods*- his intestines have taken some damage, but nothing too severe. I move deeper. There is a faint color, a stain I haven't seen before, and it fills me with dread.

"We need to move him to his belly."

Carefully, Hawkeye turns him over. His face shows exertion he wouldn't have moments ago. For a non-healer, he knows his way around the wounded extremely well. A few people run down the hallway. *The building is nearly empty.*

"Major! We got the live ones out!" one says.

"Good! Now get out of here. Report to First Lieutenant Klippa." He barks as he holds out his hands for me.

The same zing goes through me as he puts his hands over mine. This time, though, it's less powerful. From this angle, the stain is clearer. It's just at the lower end of his spine. *His nerves are damaged.*

"Breathe," Hawkeye tells me. I look into his eyes and he gives me an encouraging smile.

As I repair the damage, my hands start to tingle. As if dozens of tiny little fish are nibbling at my hands. The stain shrinks, but only a little.

"Come on!" I urge myself.

The fish make way for pins and needles. Again the stain shrinks. It's halved in size. I hear Hawkeye pant. *Just a little more.*

The pins and needles climb through my elbow, up to my shoulder. I grind my teeth to manage the pain. The stain has become the size of my nail.

"Private, stop."

Just a little more, we're nearly there. The pins have made way for shards of glass. A tear rolls down my face.

Hawkeye growls, his voice strained, "Elara! Stop!"

I open my eyes. "But we're so close."

"I can help." A strange man leans against the doorway as if he is watching a mildly interesting play. He has a long aquiline nose and looks down at us. His long black robe makes him resemble a bird.

"No." Hawkeye makes for his gun, but there is little energy left in him. The man walks up to him and in a flash maneuvers the gun out of his hand.

"Let's not do anything rash, Castiël." He takes the gun in his own hands.

"No! Leave him alone!" I yell.

"You must be Elara. I'm so sorry it took me so long to introduce myself face to face."

"Elara, don't listen to him. He's bad news."

"Oh, and let me guess. All has been sunshine and rainbows since she met you?" His voice grows fierce. "Now, you killed one of mine." He nods towards Sheena. *Sheena was a mole?* "I'll free one of yours. Elara, would you be so kind?"

My eyes flit from him to Hawkeye, who shakes his head in warning.

"But- but Raphaël."

"I am afraid you have done all you could for him without killing yourself my dear. He will be alright." He turns to Hawkeye, who is struggling to get up. "Now, where is your pet? I would hate to miss the mind reader in all this chaos."

Hawkeye leans against the wall and gives a defiant smile. "You won't find him here."

Claude shrugs. "We will come back for him one day."

I stand up. *This will be my only chance. I have to go. But then why does it feel like I'm doing the wrong thing?* My mind races, torn between the desire for freedom and the nagging guilt of leaving Hawkeye and Raphaël behind. My mind is cloudy. This is everything I wanted. Hawkeye will be fine… I glance over at him again. Gran's voice screams in my head, 'The resistance has been corrupted'. I shake my head to get rid of the voice. *She doesn't know.*

"I'm sorry."

"Let us go. Elara, this place is not safe." He holds his arms out invitingly.

"My father, my mother- are they alive?" I ask as I take a step towards him.

"Elara, is this really the time and place? The building is quite literally falling into pieces around us."

I walk towards Claude and smell cinnamon and oranges.

"Raphaël needs to be brought to safety-"

"I understand your worry about your friend," Claude says testily. "but this is not the moment to be giving orders. What would your father say of this behavior?"

This last sentence shocks my senses, and I take another step toward him.

"Private! I order you to stay!" Hawkeye's voice is unsteady, his hand trembles as he reaches out, his eyes filled with a mixture of worry and desperation. *You're sleeping with the Leader Suprema for your petty promotions. You brought me here. You ruined my life.* I look down at him, Raphaël's body limp at his side.

"She is not your property, Castiël. She is a grown woman and can make her own decisions."

"Can you- can you help me?" *Find my parents, get me home... What do I want?* Claude's brown eyes smile. "I will do that and so much more if it's within my power. Now, let us go."

Claude wraps an arm around me. With one more glance at Hawkeye and Raphaël, I allow Claude to lead me out.